The Third Wife of FARADAY HOUSE

Also by B. R. Myers

Adult Novels
A Dreadful Splendor

Young Adult Novels
Rogue Princess
Butterflies Don't Lie
Girl on the Run

The Nefertari Hughes Mystery Series
Asp of Ascension
Diadem of Death
Medallion of Murder

The Night Shift Series
Night Shift
Black Friday
Final Sale

The Third Wife of FARADAY HOUSE

a novel

B. R. MYERS

wm

WILLIAM MORROW
An Imprint of HarperCollins*Publishers*

THE THIRD WIFE OF FARADAY HOUSE. Copyright © 2024 by B.R. Myers. All rights reserved. Printed in the United States of America. No part of this book may be used or reproduced in any manner whatsoever without written permission except in the case of brief quotations embodied in critical articles and reviews. For information, address HarperCollins Publishers, 195 Broadway, New York, NY 10007. In Canada, address HarperCollins Publishers Ltd, Bay Adelaide Centre, East Tower, 22 Adelaide Street West, 41st floor, Toronto, Ontario, M5H 4E3, Canada.

HarperCollins books may be purchased for educational, business, or sales promotional use. For information, please email the Special Markets Department in the U.S. at SPsales@harpercollins.com or in Canada at HCOrder@harpercollins.com.

FIRST U.S. AND CANADIAN EDITIONS

Designed by Diahann Sturge-Campbell

Library of Congress Cataloging-in-Publication Data has been applied for.

Library and Archives Canada Cataloguing in Publication information is available upon request.

ISBN 978-0-06-320987-9
ISBN 978-1-4434-6638-7 (Canada)

24 25 26 27 28 LBC 5 4 3 2 1

To Ken
My best decision ever

The Third Wife of

FARADAY HOUSE

CHAPTER ONE

October 25, 1816
Lieutenant Frederick Fletcher, British Royal Navy
Halifax, Nova Scotia

My dearest Frederick,

It has been over a month since we saw each other and yet it feels like a century. Memories of our last time together give me solace, but also remind me how much I yearn for your attention. I know you are much too busy with your duties to return my correspondence, but a simple line or two will ease my suffering heart.

Mrs. Shackleton watches me with her ever-critical eye, and I worry she suspects our plans. When Judge Shackleton arrived home, they spoke in his study for nearly an hour, which is quite possibly the longest they've been in the same room since I've lived here. I fear she has passed on her suspicions to him. I cannot predict what his actions might be, but if we act quickly, disaster will be avoided.

Forgive me for the grim warning, darling. Let me end this note on a prettier vision. Do you remember the last thing you whispered in my ear? I do. In fact, I go to sleep every night reliving that wonderful moment over

and over. How eager I am to see if you speak the truth.
You told me my hair will outshine the Bermuda sun.

Yours adoringly,
Emeline

◇

November 1, 1816
Lieutenant Frederick Fletcher, British Royal Navy
Halifax, Nova Scotia

My dearest Frederick,

Another week has gone by without word from you.
I want to be strong, but my spirit is crumbling.
The rain on the window matches my silent weeping.
I am counting the days until I can announce our
engagement. The heat rises to my cheeks even as I write
this, recalling our stolen moments.
But being apart aches my soul. Please send word,
even a short note will do. My fretting is noticeable, and
I fear Mrs. Shackleton will send me to the sanatorium.
The house is large, but I feel her disapproving
gaze no matter where I hide. I do not exaggerate
her vindictiveness. How cruel and unbelievably
heartbreaking it would be if I was taken away only to
have you arrive the moment after, unable to rescue me.

Yours forever,
Emeline

November 8, 1816
Lieutenant Frederick Fletcher, British Royal Navy
Halifax, Nova Scotia

My dearest Frederick,

I am delirious with anticipation as I will most certainly see you at the admiral's ball tonight. I scarcely believe I will be able to keep from wrapping my arms around you. However, I know we must keep our interactions appropriately respectable, so as to not alert Mrs. Shackleton. But I believe too much distance may be just as suspicious, so I expect you to dance with me at least once.

Frederick, she plans to marry me off to the highest bidder among a handpicked selection of the wealthiest bachelors. I heard her speaking with the judge of it last night. They even talked of some arthritic old cousin with a title in England. My skin crawls at the thought of any man but you touching me.

Let me assure you, my desire to be your wife has nothing to do with the pull of Bermuda or even leaving this house. It is you. Only you. As I write this letter, I keep looking up to stare out the window with such intensity I'm surprised I haven't conjured you before my eyes, walking down the street outside.

I can picture your smart navy-blue uniform, how your bronze hair feels through my fingers, your smile, your lips, your fingers untying the ribbons of my dress.

Forgive my shaking hand as even the memory of our time together stirs every fiber of my being.

Until tonight, my darling.
Emeline

Hooves clopped on the cobblestones, echoing through the fog, growing louder as they neared the house. My heart began to race. The afternoon post! I turned toward the long bedroom window, nearly rising off the vanity seat. "Ouch!" My scalp smarted with the sudden tug of hair. I eased back down, facing forward again into the mirror. My face frowned back at me from inside its oval mahogany frame, the wood carved into intricate rosebuds. Beneath it on the vanity table sat a porcelain dish of hairpins, a crystal perfume bottle, and a cup of tea that had long grown cold. The only item here I could claim as my own was the small frame of Mother's portrait.

Ada twisted another of my blond curls and fastened it with a pin. "Sorry, Miss Emeline," she mumbled, the words polite, but her tone tired and impatient. Ada had been my maid since I was ten, and I had the feeling she still viewed me as that little girl.

Her tongue worked the corner of her mouth while she added a pink ribbon to my curls. Mrs. Shackleton had insisted upon the style: parted down the middle, the top brushed flat, with the sides curled in tight ringlets and pinned close to my ear. In the back, a long braid was to be wound into a high bun.

Ada had been working on it for nearly an hour. Her round cheeks flushed brighter as I squirmed on the embroidered cushion of the vanity. My entire head throbbed from all the pulling and pinning.

The chance of a letter from Frederick gave me hope. I could bear the tediousness of preparing for the ball if I knew it would be one of the last times I would have to endure Mrs. Shackleton's orders. Since breakfast, I had been stuck in my bedroom, made to wait in my dressing gown. Mrs. Shackleton believed my complexion suffered from unnecessary activities such as moving about the house and idle conversation. Reading was also forbidden, for the strain would cause my eyes to redden and squint. Arriving at the dance with a tired expression and a weary smile, she said, would be a tremendous failure.

A brand-new dress, dyed a soft pink and trimmed with lace, hung at the front of the wardrobe, freshly pressed by Ada. The short, puffed sleeves and low bodice were a shiny satin, while the skirt was covered in a silk gauze accented with a dozen ribbon rosettes. It also came with a pair of matching wool shoes and long evening gloves in the same sheer gauze. I would be a picture, just as Mrs. Shackleton wanted. I wouldn't be stepping into that frock until the last moment. I was surprised Mrs. Shackleton didn't insist I stand for the entire ride to prevent a wrinkle. She mentioned several times that the lace had been ordered especially from England.

"Wouldn't it be more fun if we could put on our hair like a bonnet?" I said to Ada, wanting to make amends for raising my voice. "None of this fussing about, wasting time sitting and staring at the mirror."

A limp brown strand of hair fell across Ada's face. She blew it off her forehead impatiently. "I wouldn't mind an hour of sitting," she replied.

Heat bloomed across my cheeks. She would never utter that kind of reply in front of Mrs. Shackleton. How was I ever going to run a household for Frederick if I couldn't keep my own maid in line? The familiar tremor started in my stomach.

Outside the window, I watched the post carriage come to a stop. After a few moments, a knock sounded at the front entrance downstairs. I closed my eyes and wished for the one thing that would make my troubles disappear. I waited for one of the maids to come with a letter.

Silence ticked by, and each passing second pressed tighter against my chest. I could barely breathe.

There was a muffled cry of elation from the foyer, and at first my heart swelled, but then I steadied myself. The letter I was hoping for would not have elicited such a reaction from Mrs. Shackleton. Ada and I exchanged curious glances in the mirror.

Frederick was known to my guardians, but only as Lieutenant Fletcher, a regular guest who accompanied the admiral—certainly not my secret lover. Two years ago, before the war ended, the harbor was cluttered with ships, and naval officers were regular visitors to the house. They spoke fondly of their port in Bermuda. Brightly colored birds serenaded them with lush, throaty songs, like the most gregarious opera singers. And the hot sunlight radiated off long stretches of beaches, making the powdery soft sand feel like burning coals. But shade could always be found under the long stretching leaves of the palm trees, their coconuts split open for a refreshing drink. The turquoise waters were always warm and welcoming. It was the perfect opposite to Halifax's foggy waterfront, which was lined with taverns that carried the odor of stale draft beer and urine.

Mrs. Shackleton's shoes sounded like an unrelenting hammer on the staircase, growing louder as she ascended to the second floor and gaining momentum as she came down the hall. My bedroom door nearly came off its hinges when she burst in.

I shrank in my seat, ignoring the familiar splinter of irritation at her continuous disregard for my privacy. The one time I asked Mrs. Shackleton to not barge into my room without knocking, she pinned me with a cold stare and said, "Your room? Nothing in this house is yours. You'd do best to remember that an ounce of gratitude will go a long way."

I had learned that gratitude, like respect, didn't require sincerity to elicit the desired outcome. As such, I curled my lips into a well-practiced smile as she entered without knocking.

"Tremendous news!" Mrs. Shackleton's eyes were wide and sparkling. The elation looked out of place on her pinched face. She held up a letter, then began to fan herself with the paper, trying to catch her breath. I was unsure if she was hot from the quick climb of the stairs or the obvious excitement. When she saw my hair, though, her usual judgmental expression pulled down the corners of her mouth, her uncharacteristic grin erased.

"No, no, no," she said to Ada. "There's too much height in the back." Her tone was harsh and scandalized, as if Ada had brought in a wharf rat and plopped it on my head.

"I prefer this style," I said.

Mrs. Shackleton ignored me. "Take it all down and restart," she ordered. Ada stiffened behind me, chewing her lip. Her eyes started to fill. I sat still and forced myself to remain indifferent. I was encouraged to be beautiful and silent, much like everything else in this house.

"What was your news?" I asked brightly, hoping to deflect attention from Ada, who was clearly trying not to cry.

Mrs. Shackleton's expression lifted. She held up the letter. "Another suitor has been found!"

The breath left my lungs. This was the first time she had mentioned her marriage scheme to me directly. I had discovered that she was making inquiries nearly six months ago, hence my determination to marry Frederick, but having her confirm my fear so frankly was chilling. She had no consideration for my feelings; even my very awareness of the matter was irrelevant to her. "How many will it take?" I tried to tease to disguise my anger. "Surely one is enough."

With a patronizing air, she said, "This offer will give us more leverage against the other interested parties."

Nothing is more romantic than leverage. I bit my tongue to hold back from saying this out loud. She dominated every choice in my life, but I would not let her pick my husband. And the only way to accomplish that was to marry Frederick and leave as soon as possible.

"You're nearly twenty-one, Emeline," she explained impatiently. "Your beauty is renowned, but it's not eternal. With the navy relocating to Bermuda in the coming months, the local merchants' income will most certainly suffer. It's only a matter of time before they leave as well. If we wait any longer, the only eligible bachelors in Halifax will be pirates, rum runners, or farmers." She gave me a satisfied smile. "My cousin on the South Shore confirms Captain Graves is presently looking for a new wife. He's a retired shipping merchant who found his fortune in trading and now owns several sawmills." She squinted at the letter, then added, "And the general store as well."

"*New* wife?" I questioned.

Mrs. Shackleton ignored my question and continued to read. "He has an estate with a staff large enough to take care of a home three times the size of the governor general's. He's worth a considerable amount and has influence with the magistrate." Looking up at me, she concluded, "He'll certainly be the head figure of a very powerful family for generations."

I didn't need Captain Graves or his large estate and several businesses. I had the love of Lieutenant Fletcher, which was worth all the wealth in the world. But as she continued to stare at me, waiting for an utterance of gratitude, I realized my future with Frederick was not secured . . . not yet. Not officially. And if Mrs. Shackleton knew what I was planning, she'd lock me in this room until my wedding day to the old buffoon of her choice.

Pushing that miserable image away, I concentrated instead on how it would feel to finally be in Frederick's arms again, and how liberating it would be to board a ship bound for Bermuda with him, leaving behind this wretched city and all its horrible memories. "He sounds promising" was all I said to Mrs. Shackleton. My hands clenched together in my lap, my thumbnail pressing into the crook of my pointer finger, hard enough to leave a half-moon on the soft flesh.

Ada scrunched up her nose. "Why send word to Halifax, though? Are there no suitable prospects closer to his home? If he's such a catch and all?"

I silently cheered Ada for her thoughtful question, which I hadn't even considered asking. I wasn't clever enough to think of these things myself.

Mrs. Shackleton's brows came together. Her eyes clouded over, a warning before the storm. As much as I envied Ada's gumption, she was not as sensitive to Mrs. Shackleton's moods, and I was often left to take the brunt of the blow.

"As a man of wealth, he has the luxury of being selective." Then she added, in a matter-of-fact tone, "He's had two previous wives. Both died in childbirth. Such tragedy to befall a good man." She turned to me. "You're very lucky. Any young woman would be dying for the chance to marry Captain Graves."

Two already have, I thought.

"Hurry now and finish that," she ordered Ada, pointing to my hair. "We're leaving for the admiral's within the hour."

I frowned. "You're coming with me? But I already told Jane I would pick her up in our carriage."

Mrs. Shackleton made an exasperated sound at the back of her throat. "Jane Finney? I won't have you arriving with the likes of her. I have it on good authority her father has ties to the Acadians, blood related even. You know those French Catholics would sooner see the entire British Navy sink to the bottom of the Atlantic than defend our shores against the Americans."

Her reasoning sounded far-fetched; Jane wasn't Catholic, and I couldn't think of any way the Acadians had ever done Mrs. Shackleton wrong. But I knew little of politics, and perhaps Frederick would agree with her. Still, I replied, "Jane is my friend."

She gave a sigh of bored indifference. "All girls are competition. They may pretend to be your friends, but they are sly and cunning. And you . . . ?" She shook her head at me with a look of pity. "You're not clever enough to know when they're using you." She put the letter on the vanity and pushed Ada to the side, taking her place behind me. Then she leaned down so our faces were side by side.

We regarded each other in the mirror.

"Your father wasn't suited to business. He invested more than he could afford, even gave loans to those he knew would not be able to pay him back," she said. "When he died, he left you and your mother penniless." She tutted, then paused, letting my mind fill the silence with everything I already knew. She repeated the horrible story I'd heard a thousand times: "Nothing and no one could bring her out of her misery. She died of a broken heart." Sighing, she placed a hand on my hair. "It's a shame she never saw how lovely you turned out."

She spoke as if my beauty could have saved my mother. I remained quiet. I knew what had truly killed her.

Then she smiled. "But it was God's providence, as it allowed you to come to me, so I could groom you for better things."

The knot in my stomach tightened. I looked at our faces in the mirror, side by side. Her long nose had a point at the end that reminded me of a crow. Even when she was amused, her thin lips had a way of naturally turning down, as if fighting the smile. Though gray had begun to streak her flat curls, purposely ironed close to her face, Mrs. Shackleton hadn't changed much from the very first time I saw her, when I was brought to her house ten years ago. "I'll take care of her like she was my own," she had told Mother. Even then, at the age of ten, I could feel her critical stare push down on me.

"Hmm?" she prompted, bringing me back to the present.

"Yes," I agreed. "I am grateful."

She rose to her full height and left the room, abruptly closing the door behind her. The letter remained on the vanity, a silent prop reminding me that time was running out.

I had to secure my marriage to Frederick. Tonight.

Ada's shoulders relaxed as soon as Mrs. Shackleton left. She attended to my hair and wove the strands into a more traditional style. Then she went to fetch the dress hanging on the door of the wardrobe, quickly skimming her eyes over the pleats to check for any possible flaws.

I went to my desk and penned a note to Jane, apologizing for the removal of the offer of the judge's carriage. When I handed it to Ada to take for the houseboy for delivery, her face was pale, not at all like her usual rosy complexion. She chewed her lower lip.

"What is it, Ada?"

She scrunched her nose. "That man, Captain Graves," she began. "Pardon me for saying so, Miss Emeline, but doesn't it seem odd that both his wives died in the same way?"

I turned to the dress, pretending to examine the puffed sleeves. "In childbirth? It is unfortunately far too common. Surely those misfortunes had nothing to do with him."

I meant that; it did not seem all that odd, though indeed very sad. I knew nothing of Captain Graves. He might be a good man or bad man, though he was certainly a wealthy man. None of this mattered to me. I would thwart Mrs. Shackleton's plans before I ever gained an audience with him.

But even as I thought all this, a shiver ran down my spine.

Mother always said that meant someone had walked over your grave.

CHAPTER TWO

The evening brought a continuous drizzle that lacquered the city in a cold, wet sheen as the pasty gray sky slowly churned to black, like a bruise setting in. I sat in the carriage across from the judge and Mrs. Shackleton, wishing my thin pink cloak were a fur wrap. Before we left, Ada had offered to fetch blankets for my knees, but Mrs. Shackleton shooed away the notion immediately, reasoning the extra weight would surely crush the silk gauze of my skirt.

I tried to conjure a sunlit beach with a chaise longue under a palm tree.

As we bumped over the uneven cobblestones, the fetid fish odor of the waterfront seeped into the carriage. It lingered even after we passed the taverns and managed to entwine itself with the heavy scent of Mrs. Shackleton's rosewater perfume, creating an aroma that was somehow both floral and dead and reminded me distinctly of funerals.

A desperate wanting grew inside my chest, expanding with every turn of the wheel as we neared our destination. I took small breaths through pursed lips, keeping my gaze on my lap, unable to trust my own expression. I was certain Mrs. Shackleton would be able to detect my scheme; every wish and every prayer I had been repeating in my mind all day would be written across my face.

At last, we turned off the main street and eased onto the pebbled circular driveway of the admiral's manor. The three-story stone mansion stood before us, its elegant British style proudly on display. The sloped roof was topped with a balustrade, and wide steps rose to the front entrance, flanked by four columns. Candlelight glowed from within, including from the dormers on the third floor, making the house seem alive, joyful.

My heart was jumping a terrific beat inside my chest. I would see Frederick soon and everything I'd been praying for would materialize. We could finalize our plans in person and set a wedding date.

Judge Shackleton took a sip from his flask and tucked it back into his jacket pocket as our carriage drew closer. His silk top hat sat on a mop of gray curls. He'd barely mumbled a word the entire ride, and I had the distinct notion he was sore at missing an evening at the gaming house. Judge Shackleton was a powerful man with many people under his employment, but when he arrived home, Mrs. Shackleton was the one in charge.

Our ride came to a stop. The judge offered an arm to escort Mrs. Shackleton. I followed behind them. She hissed over her shoulder to me, "Lift your dress! The puddles will ruin the hem."

As we stepped inside to wait for our cloaks to be taken by the footmen, I slipped my hood back, looking up at the foyer's large chandelier. Mrs. Shackleton nudged the judge as she pointed admiringly toward the vibrant yellow flowers hand-painted on the wallpaper. I surreptitiously brushed my fingertips against them as we were ushered forward in line, hoping I would see those vibrant hues in real life soon enough.

Mrs. Shackleton exchanged greetings with the elderly couple in front of us. I lowered my hand and stood in place, staying quiet until they'd finished speaking. Then Judge Shackleton waved a hand in my direction. "And, of course, you remember Miss Fitzpatrick," he said. Then he paused two beats—like he always did when he had to explain my relationship to them—and added, "My wife's ward of eight years."

"Ten," Mrs. Shackleton corrected.

My smile appeared automatically. I curtsied and thanked them when they complimented my hairstyle. Mrs. Shackleton declared it was her particular inspiration.

After our cloaks were taken, we were ushered toward the ballroom. The hallway carried the muffled conversation of partygoers and the lilt of violins. The dancing was already underway. My pulse quickened, eager and restless, as I imagined waltzing with Frederick.

The doorway to the ballroom was flanked by columns carved with images of cherubs holding wreaths of flowers. The judge took a glass of wine from a waiting servant and promptly meandered away to greet various acquaintances.

My legs shook as I stood beside Mrs. Shackleton at the threshold of the candlelight-bathed room. A group of musicians, no fewer than twenty in number, sat on the balcony, playing a lively tune that spun around us as if luring us closer to the dance floor. Their bows moved across the strings in quick, darting fashion, the festive tempo of the song competing with the boisterous conversation of the party below.

The perimeter of the dance floor was lined with eager young women, each hoping to catch the eye of a future partner. They giggled and spoke to one another from behind their gloved hands. I snuck a few glances their way as I dutifully followed Mrs. Shackleton to a cluster of gray-haired women resting on a settee beside the grand fireplace. I curtsied and smiled to each one while Mrs. Shackleton provided them with laborious details about my dress. They all congratulated her on such a fine purchase, then slipped into their usual gossip. Unlike their younger counterparts across the way, they did not speak in hushed tones or behind gloved hands. They also didn't laugh.

But neither did I. Sadly, I fit in with the older ladies more than I wanted to acknowledge. I rallied against my gloom by picturing Mrs. Shackleton at the next party, having to tell them all I had eloped to Bermuda. I would only be sad to miss hearing their gasps of shock.

Swaths of silk dresses blurred past us as dancers spun in time with the music. The deep blue jackets of the Royal Navy officers punctuated the scene. But where was *my* officer? I put a hand to my curls, hoping the ribbon Ada had braided in was still in place. Mrs. Shackleton stood like a sentry at my side, taking all the air. She and her spiteful ensemble of judgmental cohorts were given a wide berth by most of the partygoers, with no one stopping longer than to give a polite nod or curtsy. Ever so slightly, I craned my neck, surveying the crowd, hoping to catch the familiar wave of copper hair, standing head and shoulders above all others.

Two painfully long songs later, panic had set in. My palms were sweating as the air became thick with the warmth of the crowd. Doubts trickled like raindrops down a windowpane, continuous and unrelenting, as I imagined the various reasons for Frederick's absence. What if he had never even received my letters? What if he was sent away on a secret mission for the admiral? What if his ship became lost at sea or destroyed in a storm or hit an iceberg? What if he was captured by privateers and thrown overboard? What if I never saw him again?

Mrs. Shackleton eyed me suspiciously. "Smile," she said.

The order was so ingrained, my lips turned upward without thought, like I was her living doll. I continued to search every small swatch of blue uniform, hoping the face I had been dreaming about for weeks would appear. My imagination started to mold my worries into visions of doom.

I'd seen those large, hulking ships on the waterfront. I knew far better than anyone that accidents happened. Deadly accidents. The pulse rose to my throat as I pictured a grave with my love's name etched into the granite.

Finally, I recognized a face—one that sparked a keen sense of guilt. Jane Finney stood by herself at the room's entrance. Her profile was so much like that of her brother, Joseph. He had a relaxed smile and kind eyes, but he could never hold my gaze for longer than a second—even when he proposed last year. I wondered if he still stuttered. I wondered, secretly, if he still thought of me.

Last year, when I told Mrs. Shackleton of his proposal, she burst out laughing. "Joseph Finney! If you want to end up with scurvy and eight babies pulling on your skirt, then go ahead, but don't expect the judge and me to keep you in this lifestyle."

I told her that I'd politely turned him down, but she sensed my uncertainty, my wondering. "I don't love him," I declared.

"Love?" She scoffed, waving her lace handkerchief in the air. "Money is the only thing that can assure you a comfortable life. Amiable companionship is much easier developed if your stomach is full and your bed is warm."

The music ended, sending a new rush of dancers to the floor. A server paused in front of us with a silver tray of oysters. I silently declined; my stomach was so knotted it felt impossible to consider eating anything. I had skipped lunch earlier, hoping my nerves would be settled by now. Mrs. Shackleton slurped two with astounding speed, but then made a face after the last one and finished it off with a generous sip of wine. "Mind the oysters," she said. "I believe they might be a touch warm."

I noticed Jane making her way closer. Then I froze, for her

companion had joined her. Mrs. Shackleton uttered a poorly disguised sound of dislike as the couple stopped in front of us.

"Evening, Mrs. Shackleton." Joseph Finney stood beside his sister, doing his best to stand taller than his ordinary stature would allow. I appreciated his bravery in making sure to address her first. "I h-h-hope your health is well?"

She frowned. "God willing."

Jane and I merely curtsied to each other. I hoped she understood the decision about the carriage had nothing to do with me. A horrible awkwardness followed, and my face warmed.

Joseph cleared his throat. His kind eyes pinned me in place. "May I have the p-p-pleasure of the next dance, Miss Fitzpatrick?"

Mrs. Shackleton's fingers clasped painfully around my elbow like a claw.

I wondered if I could subtly shoo him away before Mrs. Shackleton swatted him like a fly. I had already done enough to break his heart; the least I could do now was shield him from her barbed comments. "Thank you, but—" My sentence was cut short as I watched Frederick enter the room.

One by one, heads turned as walked past the guests lining the dance floor. His pace was relaxed and at ease; he was comfortable in this crowd. The men shook his hand or slapped him on the back, yet I could tell they envied his effortless charm. When he neared the group of young girls, they nudged one another, their faces glowing with matching blushes. He smiled graciously, absorbing their admiration as if each guest had come tonight just for him—as I had.

Everyone else blurred as I took in his broad shoulders and straight posture. A wave of copper hair complemented his fair complexion, but the steadiness of his eyes was a testament to the strength and courage that gave his uniform a more pronounced respect. Even without looking at the insignia on his epaulets, any-one could tell he was a man of high rank.

A calmness enveloped my soul. He was here. He was safe. Everything would fall into place. All my problems would be erased.

I stared at Frederick, ignoring everything else but him, willing his attention to turn to me. Then finally, miraculously, he angled his face and our eyes locked. Heat grew in my chest as he continued to hold my gaze. The intensity in his expression nearly took my breath away. Any moment he would stride across the dance floor and reach for me. My hands flexed inside the delicate gauze gloves, anticipating his touch. An eternity passed, but he remained in place, watching me from a distance. Then something softened in his expression, almost aloof. A sudden coolness straightened the hair on my arms. The air crackled around me; I nearly screamed his name. The waiting was torturous. The only thing keeping my wool shoes planted on the floor was the fear of Mrs. Shackleton's reaction if I raced across the dance floor to meet him.

Why did he refuse to come closer? Surely there was no etiquette that would prevent him from approaching Mrs. Shackleton, as he had dined at the judge's house several times and was always regarded with delight on her part.

Anger grew under the thin lacquer of trust. I could not imagine treating him the same way, ignoring his pleas or dismissing his suffering so easily. My fragile relief hardened into a sharp sting of betrayal.

Then, with the slightest of movements, his attention switched to the man standing with me.

Joseph still waited patiently for my reply, his eyebrows raised hopefully. The next selection of music was a livelier tune. "Yes," I said, giving him my standard smile. He replied with an expression of delighted surprise.

Mrs. Shackleton did nothing to soften her sound of dissent at my answer.

The tempo of the dance gave us little time to converse, which was a blessing as Mr. Finney stuttered more when he was also trying to concentrate on steps. Mrs. Shackleton was in deep conversation with one of her acquaintances. Their noses nearly touched as they leaned toward each other, no doubt exchanging bits of whatever scandalous gossip provided entertainment for them. My attention was purely fixed on watching Frederick watching my dance partner and me, but every time I caught his eye, he turned away.

I started to shake. My limbs became heavy, and I nearly tripped into another dancer. My emotions coupled with the lack of food had made me unsteady. The song seemed to stretch on forever, depleting all my hope and energy with every note.

At last, the music ended.

"Are you enjoying y-y-yourself?" Joseph held out his arm to escort me back to Mrs. Shackleton. Her face was an interesting shade of red. I imagined she hated me spending time with a match so unworthy. A few whispers broke through my daze as my name was repeated on various lips.

Joseph regarded me with a growing expression of concern. Spots appeared before my eyes. The floor tilted sickeningly as blackness took over my vision. My knees unhinged. I fell backward . . . and into a pair of strong arms.

I blinked up at Frederick's face. His blue eyes glinted as if he was enjoying a private joke.

A rush of concerned voices filled the air around us, but Frederick ignored them as he stood me back up. He put an arm around my waist and maneuvered us through the gawking dancers to a set of double doors. A fellow officer ran ahead and opened them, leading us to the back stone patio. The cooler air was welcoming and helped clear away some of the overwhelming dizziness. A million questions were on the tip of my tongue. My gaze lowered to his boots, suddenly overwhelmed and oddly shy.

We reached a corner of the patio where tall shrubs provided some privacy. I was gently sat down on a bench flanked with lanterns. Frederick spoke with authority to the other officer. "Please fetch a glass of water for Miss Fitzpatrick."

"Aye, sir." The young officer nodded.

I considered asking for a glass of punch paired with several cheese servings. My appetite had returned.

Then Frederick added, "And let Mrs. Shackleton know I'll arrange for an early carriage ride home for Miss Fitzpatrick—but get the glass of water first."

The young officer nodded again and turned on his heel, eager to accommodate his superior's orders.

Frederick sat beside me and tucked a finger under my chin, raising my face to his. "Are you all right, my love?" His voice was a chorus of angels, soothing my nerves.

Tears welled. My emotions seeped out, unburdened, now that we were in privacy. "I thought you were dead," I whispered.

He kissed my forehead. "Silly girl."

I sniffed. "But you didn't answer my letters, and tonight you made no motion to stop me from dancing with Mr. Finney."

He laughed quietly, then pulled me closer. "I couldn't reply to your letters because Mrs. Shackleton would have become immediately suspicious and opened them."

Of course. It was so logical. I frowned at my own shortcomings, for failing to come up with such an obvious explanation.

"Hmm?" He leaned in, leaving a kiss on my cheek.

"You're right," I said quietly.

Then his lips moved to my neck, kissing the skin there. "My

silly girl," he repeated. "Think of my poor soul. Imagine how torturous it was for me to not be able to reply to you."

I wanted to tell him how I had worried, how the agony of the last seven weeks still stretched my nerves taut, unbearably so. Seeing him tonight was doubly worrisome because he hadn't come to me. I wanted to remind him I'd had to faint to get his attention. I wanted to let him know there was another, more serious matter for us to discuss.

"We must set a date," I told him. "Mrs. Shackleton is already lining up potential husbands and—"

His mouth found mine, stealing the words from my very lips. There was a rushed urgency in his kiss. His fingers moved to my hair, working to undo Ada's style. I let myself slip into the moment, remembering the thrilling shivers I felt the first time we embraced like this. Frederick was my hero; I had to trust him. I kissed him back, making sure to match his enthusiasm, but I had to be certain he knew he was the only person who could save me.

My palm pressed against his chest, feeling the polished buttons of his uniform, cold and hard. "Frederick," I said, breaking off the kiss. "When are we going to marry?"

He answered quickly. "In a few months, when I return. Now let's not waste this time together." His lips found mine again.

I must have heard him incorrectly. I pulled away. "Don't you remember our last night together? You proposed and I accepted. You said you would take me to Bermuda. You promised."

"And I will, but not this time." As he regarded me, his eyes clouded with uncertainty. Then his shoulders dropped. "The ship will be leaving in a few days, but that's all I can relay. I cannot tell you the details of the mission," he whispered. "It's secret."

"Secret mission?" Just as I feared. Images of Frederick drowning or being shot by the enemy replayed in horrible vividness. He might never return. An invisible hand gripped my throat. I tried to gulp for the cool air. "No." I shook my head. "We cannot wait. We must marry soon."

"My love." Frederick cupped my face with both of his hands. "I am doing this for us. I'll most certainly earn a higher rank. Don't you want to marry a decorated officer? Don't you want to have a wedding the entire city will celebrate? I promise it will only be a few months."

His words made sense but had little effect on my heart, or my situation. I said, "A few months will be too late. I may be married to someone else by the time you come back." A tinge of venom slipped into my words.

Frederick's expression darkened. He crossed his arms in front of his chest. "Do not tease me with such cruel threats, Emeline."

"I speak the truth!" My pleas tumbled out as thoughts of Mrs. Shackleton's ambitions filled my mind. "We must marry before you go, tomorrow even. I don't need a big wedding. I only want you."

He remained rigid, sporting a stern pout.

What was the problem? Why was he being so obtuse? I took his face in my hands, searching for at least a flicker of the lover I knew. Desperate to coax him into the same urgency as before, I leaned in and brushed my lips against his. I begged, "Don't you want me?"

He groaned, kissing me back. "Of course I want you. One time will never be enough."

Glass shattered behind us. We jumped apart.

Over his shoulder, a silhouette emerged from the ballroom. Two heeled shoes stepped over the shattered remains of the crystal goblet that had been dropped. All the blood in my body turned to ice. Mrs. Shackleton glared at us with her mouth in a grim line.

Then, one by one the wrinkled faces of her friends peeked around her, their eyes widening as they took in the improper scene.

BY THE NEXT morning, the rumors were rampant. It seemed there had already been talk of my affair with Frederick circulating, and our being found in each other's arms last night solidified the speculation. I did my best not to panic. Frederick would come and explain to Judge Shackleton we were engaged. Surely that would give the situation credit.

So why hadn't he shown? My pacing wore a path on the bedroom rug as I fought tragic scenes of Frederick being accosted on his way to the house.

Then the post brought letters of condolence from all of Mrs. Shackleton's gossiping crones. Her voice reverberated throughout the house. Not only was I the ruin of their good reputation, but now the previous suitors would soon hear of the scandal and withdraw their offers of marriage.

The yellow walls of my bedroom mocked me as I listened at my locked door, crouched with my ear to the keyhole.

"And how can I ever show my face on Barrington Street?" Mrs. Shackleton shrieked.

Judge Shackleton pounded his cane on the floor, finally commanding her to be quiet. "There's only one solution," he said. "The convent in the north."

"Not the French nuns!" Mrs. Shackleton gasped as if he'd ordered me to be hung on the waterfront like a pirate.

My jaw dropped. Even in my most disastrous daydreams I hadn't considered that hopeless reality. There would be even less autonomy than in this house.

The judge said, "It's secluded. No one will know her true story or her connection to us." There was a weight to his proclamation that defied any rebuttal. "She can leave at night so no one will line the streets to gawk." The door to his study slammed shut.

An eerie quietness descended over the house. Ada soon arrived with my lunch tray. I begged her to take a letter to Frederick.

She gave me such a look of pity. "'Tis no use, Miss Emeline. It's already the talk of the city." Putting a gentle hand on my shoulder, she added, "You can't be a little girl using your imagination to make things better. It's time to grow up and accept the consequences of what you did."

I flinched as if she'd slapped me. Ada had always been my champion, taking care of me when I was sick, and never without a kind word to rally my spirits. If she thought the convent was a justified option, I was doomed.

She closed the door behind her, clicking the lock back in place. I stood there stunned, picturing my bleak future. The irony of it was not lost on me: Frederick had been my only hope of escaping Mrs. Shackleton, but the actions I had taken to solidify his commitment had led to the very thing I thought I was fleeing. Instead of being whisked away to the tropics to run my own house, I would be shunned and hidden within the stone walls of a convent. Forever.

Even though there was a small amount of relief that I wouldn't have to earn my keep by smiling, I knew the nuns would make me give up something dearer.

I shook my head. No, I could not be sent to the convent.

Ada thought I needed to grow up, but what she didn't realize was that I hadn't been a little girl since I was ten. I went to my bedroom window and regarded the distance to the cobblestone street below. I had nothing to fashion a rope for an escape, and if I made one small misstep, the drop to the ground would most likely break my leg or my neck. I wished I was capable of imagining a viable solution.

Sighing, I pressed my palm against the cool glass remembering all those nights I'd sat at this very window, wishing for my parents to rescue me.

A sting of tears welled up. Wishes had never served me any good. I sniffed, knowing my parents were never coming for me—neither was Frederick.

I went to the vanity and looked at the framed portrait of Mother, hoping some long-lost memory of advice would surface. Instead, my eyes fell on the letter left by Mrs. Shackleton the previous day. The one about Captain Graves, the twice-widowed sea merchant looking for a new wife.

My pulse picked up as I remembered he lived in the southern part of the province, far away from Halifax. Far away from the latest gossip.

As I read the letter, it was clear Mrs. Shackleton had not revealed out loud all the details of Captain Graves. He was a successful trader, and indeed owned several sawmills, and the general store of his small rural community. But the most important fact was that he lived on a private island—a private island that Frederick's ship could easily access.

I began to devise a plan. The convent would be avoided, and there might be a way to still convince Frederick to take me as his wife to Bermuda. Once he knew I was betrothed to another, he would not hesitate to rescue me. Furthermore, I could not imagine a situation where I would have to marry Captain Graves immediately. Frederick could be there within a few days!

But for my plan to work, I had to act with no further delay.

Mrs. Shackleton was surprised when I went to her with my

choice, but she and the judge were easily convinced I was sincere in offering my hand to Captain Graves. A letter was dispatched via Pony Express to my new fiancé's home before news of my scandal could reach the South Shore. Ada was ordered to start packing my trunks.

Dearest Frederick,

Even though I dream of returning to your embrace, the situation has compelled me to make a drastic choice. By the time you read this I will be halfway to the southern part of the province. I am to be engaged to Captain Graves. He is a very successful trading merchant, and I'm certain the location of his seaside estate is known to you. A man of such wealth will most likely have ample docking options, even for a large schooner bound for Bermuda.

Picture me by the shore, waiting for you.

Only you have the power to set this right and rescue me.

Devotedly,
Emeline

CHAPTER THREE

Before dawn, my trunk was packed and loaded onto the carriage by the hired driver. I stood on the steps of the judge's house, shivering in the mist. Ada handed me a basket of provisions for the journey; she was the only one who had risen to see me off.

I waved goodbye from the carriage as the driver pulled away. The moon reflected in the puddles with cruel poetic satire. All I had wanted was freedom under the hot sun.

My bones seemed hollow. The farther the carriage took me from Frederick, the more painful the pull behind my ribs. I remembered our hushed promises, imagining our life in Bermuda, where I would finally be away from Mrs. Shackleton's constant critical gaze. At least in the carriage I could relax my expression and let the stone smile slip away. I had to have faith he would receive my letter.

Shoreham was nearly a full day's journey. The sun rose, revealing that the stone houses and shops had been replaced by trees and thick forest growth. It was a never-ending journey of ruts and bumps. I had never been outside the city, and to see the world stretch on with no buildings or other persons in sight was jarring. The unfamiliarity of it made me feel like a kite that suddenly lost its string and was at the mercy of the breeze.

After we changed horses, I ate a pork pie and a wedge of cheese. All that remained in the basket was an apple. I picked the last few crumbs of Ada's pastry from my skirt as I willed an image of

Frederick leaving the harbor, setting a course for Captain Graves's island with my letter folded inside his jacket pocket, close to his heart. The salt spray beading his copper hair as he stood at the bow, eager to rescue me.

I was brought out of my daydream when the carriage came to a stop. I pulled back the curtain. The late-afternoon light had dulled as the evening closed in.

I took in a tidy rural street with pleasant-looking buildings. The driver jumped from his seat and sauntered into the post office. Through the window I could see him speaking with a thin man. He touched his spectacles, nodded, then handed the driver several packages.

Without a word to me, the driver took the mail and added it to a satchel slung across his chest. Before we pulled away, the postmaster came to the doorway. Mrs. Shackleton's order sounded as a ghostly echo. I smiled and gave him a wave. He didn't return the greeting. Instead, he dropped his eyes, shaking his head at the ground.

I leaned out of sight, pressing into the seat. My cheeks warmed with embarrassment and confusion.

The land sloped downward, affording me a view of the shore ahead, and beyond it, a vast slate-gray ocean. In the distance, an island studded with trees jutted out of the mist. The carriage veered closer to the beach, allowing me to make out a winding road of stones that emerged from the ocean floor itself. There was a *thump* as the carriage settled onto this precarious path.

Jostling back and forth, I gripped the seat to keep myself steady. The view from either window afforded the same scene: nothing but water. I hazarded a peek at the wheels and saw the carriage barely fit the width of the trail. All that separated me from being swallowed up by the North Atlantic was a few feet of rock.

Gulls cried overhead, sounding like a screaming warning of death. The fog claimed its victory, eating up anything that resembled land.

Once the carriage made it to the island, the ride became smoother. I let go of the seat and wrapped my cloak around myself more tightly. I survived the trip across, but what exactly would be waiting for me? Who was Captain Graves, really?

Another thought slipped through, one I had been pushing away since stepping into the carriage. How long did I have before the wedding? And how was I supposed to introduce myself? I practiced it out loud a few times. "Hello, Captain Graves," I said, trying to calm my voice. "I'm Emeline Fitzpatrick, your new wife." A shiver rippled over my skin as if someone had walked over my grave.

New wife.

How odd both wives had died the same way. But it was an unfortunate reality of womanhood, one I found difficult to shake: the joy of a new life can so often turn to death instead.

We took a sharp incline. The trees reached out, nearly touching the carriage, blocking the remaining light. Night was opening her mouth ready to swallow me whole.

The carriage lunged then tipped dangerously. It seemed to hang in midair before slamming down with a crash, tilting to the side. The horse snorted ferociously as the driver hollered a few expletives. My own scream got swallowed up in the chaos as I fell with a *thud* to the floor. My dress pooled around me. The door wrenched open. The driver was breathing hard with his cap askew.

"Are you all right, miss?" He offered me his hand.

I stepped out of the carriage with his help. "I think so," I said, testing my legs. My elbow throbbed.

The back wheel had broken its axle. The driver lifted his cap and scratched his head as he looked up the lane, measuring some invisible solution to our problem. He sniffed, then unhitched the horse. "I'll head up the rest of the way to the house," he said, reins already in his hands. "I don't have a saddle for you, and I'll make better time if I ride by myself."

I thought this was rather selfish of him but stayed quiet.

"You'll be safe here," he said, nodding to the tilted carriage. "It's warmer to wait inside."

I refused to agree. He was leaving me all alone in a strange place.

He mounted the poor horse, still a bit wobbly himself after that crash. "I'll return with the steward to bring you and your things up to the estate. It won't be but a quarter of the hour."

"That long?" I rubbed my sore elbow. The trees of the forest seemed to lean in as if listening. How large was the island?

He turned away. "Faraday House is only on the other side of the hill."

Faraday House. I repeated it a few times to myself, surprised at how pretty it sounded, almost regal.

As he rode away, I watched until I could no longer see the back of him. Then I strained my ears until the thumping of the hooves disappeared as well. Then all was silent.

Too silent.

I had never been inside such an absolute void of sound. It was unnerving. The city was always humming with life: the clip-clop of hooves on the cobblestones, the jovial jokes from the butcher's boy who delivered to the house every week, the canons going off from Citadel Hill when the navy ships entered the harbor.

But the only sound on this island was my breathing. It was as if I was the only thing alive here. The gloominess seemed to deepen as dusk claimed the sky. The cold penetrated through my petticoats and long stockings. There wasn't enough wool to keep out the dampness of the ocean air. Shivering, I climbed back into the carriage.

My stomach growled. I found Ada's basket tipped over in the corner. The apple was underneath, bruised, but I finished it with gratitude. I wondered how far "on the other side of the hill" was. And what if the driver had an accident on the way to the house and never got there? What if I was left here all night?

The driver would return in the morning to find me frozen to death, lips blue and perfect curls stiff with ice.

Mrs. Shackleton would never forgive me if I didn't take steps to die in an attractive position. After adjusting my bonnet, I leaned back in the seat, eyes closed, hands crossed over my chest. I could almost hear the mourners say the same thing as they paraded by my coffin: *She's the most beautiful corpse we've ever seen.*

I allowed myself the morbid satisfaction of Frederick crumbling, knowing he was responsible for my early demise. He'd never marry, but instead would grow into a bitter old man, crippled with secret guilt. Only when he was on his deathbed would he finally admit our engagement.

The faint echo of heavy hooves got my attention. The driver was quick! I pulled my thoughts to a more reasonable matter, hoping there was a lovely fireplace and steaming supper waiting for me.

The horse came closer, but then it growled. My insides twisted with fright. The bruised apple threatened to come up. The creature outside my carriage was no horse. A bear? I held my breath and crouched to the floor, covering myself with my cloak.

Claws scratched at the door.

"Go away, go away," I whispered. "Please, almighty Lord, make it go away."

The door handle sounded noisily, frantically twisting and turning. The beast had hands like a man! I quaked uncontrollably, certain it could smell my terror.

So much for an open casket. Mrs. Shackleton would be livid.

The door was flung open. I pushed myself to the farthest side of the carriage, clutching the cloak under my chin. White fangs dripping with saliva lunged toward me. The head was huge with deep-set eyes, and a sloppy wet nose.

"Moses," a man's voice called out. "Get down!"

The beast backed up and sat on its haunches, a long pink tongue lolling to one side.

"Come," the man commanded. The animal clamored back outside.

I peeked around the door to see a humongous dog trotting toward a man sitting atop a horse. A shaking breath left my tortured chest. The man gracefully swung himself off the saddle, then patted the dog's head. He wore a long black cloak that swirled around his tall legs. A wide-brimmed hat hid his face. He approached me with the confidence of someone who had never had to depend on another to rescue them.

"I'm so glad you've come by," I said, voice shaking. "I was worried I would be stuck here the whole night."

He kept his chin down, only allowing me a glimpse of his sculpted cheekbones, covered with the dark shadow of a day's worth of beard.

Ignoring me, he put all his attention on the broken wheel. "Are you all right?" he finally asked. I wasn't sure if he was addressing me or the carriage.

I said, "I'm on my way to Faraday House, but as you can see . . ." Words left my brain as he turned to me. I had not been expecting someone so young—or handsome. I was held in place by his large brown eyes. And unlike most men, whose gazes drifted down my figure and back up again, his eyes stayed focused on my own, never wavering. There was a quiet strength in his stance, and I was certain he'd never cowered under a blanket but faced every fear. There was no question—he was a man of importance, and of course there was only one reason why he'd be on this island. I had met my fiancé.

"Captain Graves?" I couldn't finish the statement I'd prepared as the whole situation became too real in that moment. I had promised myself to another man, a stranger, because it was the only way I could force Frederick to honor his proposal.

He stood tall, then answered in a slow and deliberate tone. "No, I'm not."

There was a slight accent to his words. I stayed quiet, entirely at a loss.

He nodded up the lane. "I visit weekly to give a private sermon." Then he said, "I'm Reverend Pellerine."

Pellerine? French name. That explained the accent. A coolness rolled over me. Although we'd been at war with the Americans, the French were never allies of the British either.

His serious expression matched the bleak wilderness of the island. Any small scrap of energy left in my body disappeared. "Such a coincidence," I said wearily. "I was just praying for a rescue." I may have intended for the remark to showcase my wit, but it fell flat.

He frowned at the lopsided carriage again. "And is that your trunk?"

I nodded, desperate for one small thing to make sense. "I was on my way to Faraday House," I started to explain again.

"Yes, you've already mentioned." He gave me a sideways glance.

I paused momentarily, silenced into shock by his rudeness. "The driver had to go ahead and get the steward for help." Then I added with emphasis, "He left me all alone."

He didn't comment on my situation. It was quite possible all countrymen—French reverends included—expected women to fend for themselves. A pit sank in my stomach. I had not the stamina nor the skill to be alone. I wished the winds to blow Frederick's rescue ship to me quickly.

The reverend walked to his horse and picked up the reins. "Come," he said. "We'll ride together."

I took in the sweaty and dusty horse. Mrs. Shackleton's voice spoke for me. "In this dress? The embroidery took nearly a month to complete."

He sighed, then pushed up the front brim of his hat. A fringe of black waves escaped. "If you want to wait for the steward, you'll have to do so by yourself." There was no smile in his suggestion. "I must reach the house before nightfall." The accent was coming out stronger now, adding an extra dimension to his words . . . and his impatience.

"Why?" My head swiveled, trying to peer into the forest behind us, thinking there was something lurking in the dark woods, waiting for the sun to set. I was only familiar with crows and the odd mouse that scuttled into the kitchen.

He gave me a curious look. "It will be dark, and I don't desire riding into a tree."

"Of course," I said. I had the sense he was holding back information. His insistence on reaching the house without delay struck me as curious. "Reverend? Not Father Pellerine? I thought all the French were Catholic?" I asked.

His answer came out crisp and precise. "Evidently not."

I continued to hesitate.

He said, "But the horse is Protestant, if that makes a difference to you."

Heat moved to my ears, and I was glad my bonnet was in place. "I was only curious," I tried to explain. "I accept your offer of a ride, thank you." I managed to mount the horse and ride sidesaddle without too much disaster. He took his place behind me, making sure to leave space between us.

Soon we were making our way up the narrow road with the large shaggy dog following. On either side, the closely bunched trees gave little hint to what lay beyond. The air lost the salty scent of the ocean and grew more earthy, heady with decay.

I turned my head, giving him a view of my lovely profile. "Does your beast turn during the full moon?"

"Moses? He's only a dog."

I scoffed at that. "He's huge. What does he eat, smaller dogs?"

He chose not to reply.

The road flattened out as we reached the top of the hill. He urged the horse to quicken its pace. Another path split from our trail and deviated to the right, disappearing into the trees.

"What's that way?" I asked, as we stayed on the main road.

"A pasture, a small pond, and a few old bunkhouses where workers used to stay during harvest seasons. Although it's been years since this land has been farmed. The only living people on the island are all in Faraday House."

I found it odd he said "living people," instead of just "people."

The path curved sharply to the left, limiting our visibility. Twilight covered everything with a shadowy dimness. Then, slowly, the path straightened out and up ahead Faraday House stood in all its fierceness like a lone fortress. Any romantic ideas I had derived from its name vanished.

Built with stone blocks that seemed to be chiseled from the very island it rested upon, the manor boasted an unusual roughness. Even the tall fir trees seemed spindly and fragile in comparison. The house was two stories high with dormers along the top floor, and the windows were all dark, not even a hint of a candle glowing inside. No sign of life at all.

The manor was grim with its hard edges and unyielding stance. A prison. The only unique detail was a large round window on the second floor. It was situated above the front door and gave the impression of a giant eye. I expected it to blink.

The road circled in front of the entrance with another path leading to a carriage house, partially hidden through the trees. Although much smaller, the building had a style similar to the manor's, with its granite façade and black-painted doors and window frames.

Reverend Pellerine dismounted and motioned for me to do the same, holding out a hand. "We'll walk the rest of the way."

I was too surprised to question the request, and frankly, too tired. I landed on both feet without breaking a leg, miraculously.

Small stones crunched under our feet. "What brings you to Faraday House?" Reverend Pellerine asked, pulling the reins as we continued. The horse resisted at first, seemingly reluctant to come with us. "From the size of the trunk, your stay will be a long one."

A burning rose in my throat. "Captain Graves is an acquaintance of my guardian's. And I'm . . ." I hated to say the words out loud, but there was no use in pretending. He was the reverend; he'd know soon enough. "I'm to be his new wife."

He stopped walking and turned to me. A flash of fear swept across his brown eyes, but it was so fast, it may have been the reflection of the clouds moving across the evening sky. He finally replied, "I see."

For a moment I was convinced he could see into my soul, and that my shame was visible. Could reverends see the secrets of sinners? Was he able to know what I had done and what I was hiding?

But a new threat came to me as panic gripped my heart. "Are you to marry us tonight? Is that why you must hurry to the house? So soon? I don't even have my wedding dress," I said, desperate to prolong the event. I must stay unwed for Frederick to take me back.

He studied me intently until I dropped my gaze. "No," he said. There was a hollowness to his voice. "That is, I won't be marrying you tonight."

I nearly fainted with relief.

We continued to the house, and by now I could make out stone figures on the top corners of the roof. At first, I thought they were gargoyles, but instead, they were mortars. I wondered why anyone would have need to fire cannons from the roof of their house. But then another thought occurred to me. I asked him, "Why are you coming so close to the evening, then? Is it a special sermon?"

"I'm giving last rites." There was a heaviness to this statement.

"I'm sorry to hear that," I said. A faint glimmer of hope sparked deep inside as I made a private wish. Perhaps my fiancé was not long for this world. It would certainly explain the odd looks from the postmaster and the reverend. "Is it Captain Graves?" I asked, trying to keep the hope from my voice.

"No," he replied, still looking at me intently like he was unsure whether I was sincere. "It's Mrs. Graves."

"His mother?" I hadn't even considered the added burden of a mother-in-law. So many horrible possibilities to fret over. Of course, if she was on her deathbed, I wouldn't have to worry about her for long.

Reverend Pellerine held my gaze as the forest quietened around us. "No," he said again. "Not his mother. His wife."

CHAPTER FOUR

Shock reached down my throat and stole my voice. Not only was I arriving to a home where I knew no one and was destined to be the third wife of a stranger, but the second wife was still alive.

I stared at the reverend, certain I'd misheard him. The horse snorted and dug in its hooves, scattering the loose stones.

"Steady, now," Reverend Pellerine ordered. He led the spooked animal in the opposite direction, away from the manor. Up ahead, I saw the driver who had abandoned me wave from the carriage house.

Reverend Pellerine took the satchel off the horse, then slapped its rear. It hardly needed the encouragement to go to the carriage house, where the driver met it halfway, easily taking the reins and walking it into the enclosure, and, I noted, farther away from the house itself.

Without a backward glance, the reverend strode toward the front door, clearly not wanting to waste any more time. Lifting my skirts, I ran to catch up, nearly tripping when the toe of my boot caught on the pebbles. I was out of breath, and my shift clung to the sweaty skin of my back. I couldn't have arrived more inauspiciously if I'd tried.

With the large black door looming closer, I had a momentary spark of hope that maybe there had been a mistake and instead of a wife, Captain Graves had requested a nurse for Mrs. Graves—

and her baby. Mrs. Shackleton must have been wrong. My heart lightened at the thought. The threat of a quick marriage was removed. I could easily wait for Frederick to come while I stayed here and tended to Mrs. Graves. I wasn't qualified as a nurse, but what did that matter? A cool cloth to the head, a fresh nightgown, feasibly a story and a tonic. What's to learn?

I envisioned myself in a nurse's uniform—flowing white fabric—and a smile full of compassion as I sat by her bed, holding her hand. And Frederick would be so impressed with this useful side of me, he wouldn't hesitate to marry me on the spot and whisk me away to Bermuda.

"Your guardians arranged this?" Reverend Pellerine looked at me questioningly. "The marriage, I mean?"

I blinked back at him, needing to reorient myself. I was still walking beside him. My daydreams were apparently powerful enough to keep my mind busy while my body carried on unaware. "Yes." I nodded. Then I added, "We were told he was widowed, that his wife had died in childbirth." I left out the first wife from that tragic equation.

Reverend Pellerine's somber expression did nothing to alleviate my apprehension. "No," he replied. "There is no baby."

We neared the front steps. The door knocker was an iron ring gripped in the jaws of a lion's head. I could practically hear it growl at us. "Maybe there's been a mistake," I said, unable to keep my voice from shaking.

Reverend Pellerine lowered his voice even though there was no one around. Moses was a few feet behind us, sitting in place with his head lifted as if gazing at the top of the manor.

"He probably reasoned she'd be gone by the time you arrived." He spoke with an underlying harshness. I imagined his sermons likely spoke of nothing but the devil and hell. And when he spoke of angels, they were the vengeful kind who punished sinners. He probably filled the pews every Sunday with his fiery passion. That, coupled with his pleasing appearance, must have made him a favorite in the village. I snuck a glance at his left hand, but there was no wedding ring.

Moses whimpered from behind us. He'd stayed back, choosing to not follow his master to the house. For the first time I saw a glimmer of something close to a smile from the reverend.

"Go on, then," he said to the dog. Without hesitating, Moses ambled away, cutting a route halfway between the manor and the carriage house.

Reverend Pellerine lifted a shoulder in a casual shrug. "He prefers the beach."

I watched as he disappeared between the trees. "All by himself?" I asked. "How are you certain he won't get hurt? Or lost?" I envisioned sharks and rogue waves sweeping him out to sea. Without trying, I began to picture such disaster for myself as well.

"He knows the places to avoid," he replied. Then he ascended the stone steps and lifted the door knocker. A resounding echo seemed to go on forever on the other side of the door.

I adjusted my bonnet and smoothed out my cloak. First impressions are important, Mrs. Shackleton always said, regardless of the situation.

Hurried footsteps sounded from the other side. There was a grunt, then the door was heaved open. A robust woman wearing a white cap and an apron splashed with the remnants of sauces and jams stood at the entrance. A deep frown and heavy brows gave her a stern appearance. Her sleeves were rolled to the elbows, her arms dusty with flour, and her cheeks were flushed. I had assumed the captain would have a full staff, but it seemed this woman performed kitchen duties *and* those of a butler. She stepped back, ushering us inside. "Thank goodness you're here, Reverend," she said. "Poor thing is barely holding on."

"Thank you, Mrs. Clayton," he said, taking off his wide-brimmed hat and handing it to her.

She tucked a wiry tuft of hair under her cap, suddenly looking nervous. "I'll take your coat too," she said to him.

I stepped over the threshold and took in the expansive foyer. Above us a massive wrought iron chandelier hung from a black chain. All the walls were a washed dark gray, as if trying to imitate the fog outside. Even though all the sconces were lit, the bleakness seemed to smother their very flames. Long wooden beams crossed the ceiling. I took a small step forward, hearing my boots scuff on the flagstone floor. Everything looked like it had been plucked from a shipwreck.

On either side of the foyer was a set of double doors. Neither was open, giving the air a concentrated feeling. I tucked a finger into my collar and gave it a slight tug, hoping to relieve some of the stuffiness. A wide ebony staircase dominated the area. It led upward to a small landing, where a grandfather clock stood like a sentry. The stairs then diverged left and right, going to opposite sides of the second floor.

The design of the house invited a feeling of being very small to anyone who entered. I felt like a mouse. I thought of the judge's home, which was much smaller but somehow managed to be full of light even on the foggiest of days.

The echoing clunk of a door closing in the silence made us all turn. "Reverend Pellerine!" A young woman came running. She regarded him with bright eyes, her back straight and chest out, her confident energy out of place in this gloomy house. She wore an apron similar to Mrs. Clayton's, but her dress had more style than I would expect of a maid. "I hope my note wasn't too difficult to read; my script was shaky due to the terrible turn of events." Under her cap, she wore her bangs straight across, with pigtails of long curls tied just below her ears.

I stood invisible, as if I were his shadow.

"The note was satisfactorily legible."

Her smile never wavered, but in fact grew—until she turned to me.

Noticing her gaze, Reverend Pellerine began, "She's with—"

"I know who she is," Mrs. Clayton interrupted. Her voice was sharp. "The carriage driver already explained. Mr. Clayton is getting our horse ready to bring up the luggage and help fix the wheel." She said all of this to Reverend Pellerine, pointedly not making eye contact with me.

I wanted to say thank you, but I was worried my words would come out as a pathetic squeak. The floor creaked under my weight as I stepped back.

"Apologies for my frankness," Mrs. Clayton said, furtively glancing my way. "But I believe the present Mrs. Graves is the one who requires our attention now."

"I take it he's with her," Reverend Pellerine said, nodding to the staircase.

Disappointment pulled at Mrs. Clayton's features, elongating her already-sour expression. "No, he's, er . . . waiting for you."

The young woman pressed her lips into a thin line and snuck a peek at Mrs. Clayton.

"Then fetch him immediately." Reverend Pellerine let out an impatient sigh.

Mrs. Clayton nudged her. "Go, Hettie," she said.

With one last imploring look to Reverend Pellerine, Hettie touched the cross at her throat and ran back down the hallway and disappeared through an archway.

"I'll go to her room now." The reverend made his way to the staircase. I watched him quickly ascend to the first landing, then turn right and go up another set of steps. The space was quiet again.

Mrs. Clayton had his cloak and hat in her arms. "Come with me," she ordered over her shoulder at me. Although she was gruff, I was grateful she didn't leave me alone. The house, in all its dramatic darkness, seemed to push down on me.

I followed behind her stocky figure as she roughly muttered. I didn't want to appear rude in ignoring her comments, so I replied, "The manor is lovely, especially the walls." *Dead fish gray*, I thought. I worked hard to sound sincere. "Such a unique palette choice."

The hallway was dominated by a gallery of sailing ships. I walked by one framed painting of a schooner after another, nearly feeling seasick by the time I reached the last one. She opened a door and ushered me inside.

The dining room was narrow, but three large windows in a row gave a pretty view of the forest, and what I recognized as the corner of the carriage house. The walls were painted a dark green that reminded me of being on the bottom of the ocean. Everything was heavy and suffocating, like the stones of the house itself were pushing inward.

She nodded to one of the eight dining chairs. "You can wait here for now."

The cushions were embroidered with plain flowers. I tucked my dress under me as I sat down. I'd never had the patience for needlepoint and always abandoned every project. I ran a fingertip along the stitching of the chair beside me, marveling at the amount of time it would have taken to complete even one chair, let alone the entire set of eight.

The room became intensely quiet. Mrs. Clayton was watching

me. I quickly withdrew my hand and placed it on my lap. "The workmanship is lovely," I said.

"Hmm." She lit the candelabra. I wrinkled my nose at the amount of tarnish revealed by the light. The shadows seemed to grow on her face, accentuating her grim expression.

"This walnut table is exquisite," I said, patting it with the same amount of care I would a kitten. I smiled at her, hoping she couldn't see my quivering lips.

When she replied, her voice was like gravel. "She ain't dead yet, so don't be going on about all the fancy things you already seem to lay claim to."

My jaw dropped in shock at being spoken to with such frankness. The possibility that I could step into this life suddenly seemed ridiculous. My only asset was my beauty, and so far, that was useless at Faraday. There was no point in being pretty if everyone looked at you with poison in their heart. Nevertheless, all I had to do was survive until Frederick came.

The same firmness remained in her tone. "When they bring your trunk, I'll have Hettie show you to your room. It's in the east wing, so you won't be in the way of Mrs. Graves. Until then, make sure you stay put and don't go wandering around."

Tears threatened with alarming urgency. I sensed the worse thing I could do was cry in front of this woman. I pressed my thumbnail into the soft flesh of my finger and kept swallowing until the urge faded. "Thank you for allowing me to stay in such a lovely spot," I said. "I will be most comfortable here."

She left, and I hunched over, completely exhausted. I stared at the candle flames and tried to imagine something happy, a daydream to escape into, but the only images that came to me were of a poor soul somewhere in this house taking her last breaths.

CHAPTER FIVE

O utside the dining room windows, the world darkened, erasing the forest and the carriage house.

Mrs. Clayton returned with a tray of tea. I sat up straight as she placed the serving in front of me. The pattern was a light blue flower with gold trim. On the plate was a wedge of cheese, a generous serving of salted pork, and two biscuits already slathered with butter. My stomach growled. It seemed like an eternity since the bruised apple.

I should have said some word of thanks, but I was kept silent by my insecurities. I was conscious of her standing there, watching me, studying my every mannerism. I took a bite of the biscuit, letting it melt on my tongue.

She lingered at my side, then her expression softened. "It was a long journey," she remarked. "Especially since you were traveling alone. Your parents must have steady nerves."

Her voice lifted at the end, making it sound like a question. She was naturally curious, but I wasn't about to announce the real reason for my sudden appearance, nor the fact both my parents were dead. Still, I was encouraged by the change in her demeanor. "The tedious trip has made the food even more satisfying," I said, hoping I hadn't added so much praise as to sound disingenuous.

"Hettie is a good talent in the kitchen, but I'm the main cook." She said the last part with obvious pride. "We may not have the same menu you enjoyed in the city, but country cuisine is as satisfying if not more so." Then she gave me a sad sort of smile, but it was given in earnest, and to my aching soul it felt like a hundred warm embraces.

"Thank you," I finally said. "I'm away from my home for the first time, and I wasn't sure what to expect."

A faint blush colored her cheeks. She opened her mouth but then closed it as if changing her mind about how to reply.

I found this encouraging, and I badly needed a kind soul to give me some information. "And please let me assure you, I don't understand why Captain Graves invited me here if he already had a wife."

She grimaced. "Just his practical nature, miss."

Her answer was straightforward, but there was a hint of foreboding in her expression, a warning almost. And whatever the wife's diagnosis was, it must be mysterious and unpredictable. Was it some horrific contagious disease? Maybe I was already infected! Not knowing was worse than any tale of a gruesome death. Fear broke the dam that had been keeping my manners in check. "What is she dying from?"

Her mouth set in a firm line, and I realized I had unearned any kindness she might have bestowed upon me. "This is hardly proper conversation for the dining room. I would think someone of your upbringing would have better manners." She sniffed impatiently. "Mr. Clayton and the driver should be back shortly. I'm going to see if the reverend needs anything."

I finished the last bite of pork, unable to taste anything. I was brave earlier, thinking it would be easy to stay here until Frederick came, but now I doubted I could endure even one night in this house. I had picked up the teacup and brought it to my lips when the piano music started.

The notes were simple, but it was a pleasant and sweet melody. Rather the opposite of Faraday House. If someone here could create something so lovely, I needed to meet them. Taking the candelabra, I went to the door at the end of the room and listened.

With my ear pressed against the wood, I was certain someone was playing in the next room. I glanced over my shoulder at the doorway that led to the hallway. Mrs. Clayton had told me to stay, but moving into an adjoining parlor would surely be permissible.

I opened the door, hoping to catch a glimpse of the musician, but as soon as I peeked into the room the music stopped. I hesitated to make certain, but the only sound was my breathing. I pushed the door open all the way.

A soft illumination came from the standing candlestick placed beside a grand piano. The instrument sat in the middle of the room with the lid in the down position, hiding the strings. The player was nowhere to be seen, but one of the double doors to the main foyer was open. I frowned. Why would someone leave quickly?

I squinted through the dimness. Like the foyer, this room was decorated in the same bland shade of gray. Across the far wall were a set of bookshelves. Ignoring the texts, I went directly to the piano and placed the candelabra carefully on the ledge. A memory pulled at my heart as I sat on the bench. I had taken lessons when I was younger, but it was soon obvious my talents were limited to only the most pedestrian pieces. My teacher was kind, though.

"If you ever get lost in a piece," she'd told me, "just find middle C and you'll know what to do next."

I was more lost than ever, and I hadn't even gone to the second floor of Faraday House. I was overwhelmed at the thought of navigating the entire manor. I found middle C and gently pressed the ivory key. Nothing happened. I pressed it harder, and still, silence. I tried the next key with the same unsuccessful effect.

Uneasy, I took the candelabra and moved away from the instrument, wishing I had stayed in the dining room. The flickering candlelight illuminated the opposite wall. I gasped, startled by the lifelike appearance of the paintings on the wall. Two large portraits stared back at me. In each one was a young woman sitting in nearly identical poses in the same chair. The two wives.

The wife in the first painting wore a dress with a low neckline and puffed sleeves. She had alabaster skin and long black hair adorned with two pearl combs. Her red lips evoked a sense of contentment, but her green eyes glinted with mischief. The second wife—this was the woman who was currently waiting at death's door, I assumed—had a gentler expression. Her wedding dress had satin covered buttons up to the neck. A matching bonnet was tied under her chin, with brown curls reaching her shoulders.

The most obvious common element between the portraits was the man standing behind them with his hand on their shoulder. He was older in the second one. He was wearing the same outfit, though: a long black coat with polished buttons. There was a saber at his side, and a silver pistol poking out of a leather holster worn around his waist. I was certain I was looking at my fiancé.

There was nothing outstanding in Captain Graves's appearance: medium height with dark hair, and a build that suggested he was neither exceedingly strong nor a weakling. I suspected he wouldn't be noticed walking down Hollis Street.

A cold chill blew across the back of my neck as I noticed there was space on the wall for a third portrait.

"Miss Fitzpatrick." The voice was hesitant, mournful.

I let out a small squeak of surprise as I rushed to turn. He was standing in the doorway. I wondered how long he'd been watching me. His silhouette was outlined by the light from the foyer. In his portrait he was unassuming, but in real life, his stance was authoritative and sure. His coal-black hair was gray at the temples, but his posture was straight, with long arms hanging at his side. He wore a smart overcoat with gold buttons on the sleeves. His presence filled the entire room, nearly stealing the breath from my lungs. Dark, heavy eyebrows and sideburns framed his weathered face.

"Captain Graves," I said, giving him a curtsy, my actions automatic after so many lessons from Mrs. Shackleton.

The edges of his mouth lifted in a hesitant smile. He was cordial, but almost shy.

He cared not to linger on my blond curls or my embroidered dress. Instead, his focus went to the portraits of his former brides. He came into the room. The soft light from the candles highlighted his deep-set eyes, heavy with grief.

He said, "I'm sorry I didn't meet you when you arrived." There was a politeness overlaying his words, but I could hear the sorrow underneath.

I wanted to ask about his present wife, but now that I was in his commanding presence, any gumption I'd built up earlier had hidden in the shadows of the room. "Perfectly understandable," I replied. "Considering the circumstances." I concentrated on keeping the candelabra from shaking.

His brow furrowed, adding to the misery of his expression. When he spoke next, his voice was full of despair. "You must think I am horrid for bringing you here before Georgina has died." He took a step closer. "She hasn't been in her right mind for several months, a mere shell of the woman she used to be. I fear it weakens her by the hour."

Georgina. In her portrait she had curly brown hair. Her sweet smile was full of hope.

I had to remind myself I wasn't going to be marrying Captain

Graves. The wind rattled the windows as if tapping to be let in. Bermuda would not have cold, noisy winds.

"She may not last the night." He sounded depleted, hopeless. I wondered how long she'd been sick.

Questions stacked upon one another in my mind, but I dared not to utter them out loud. The silence grew awkward and painful. Mrs. Shackleton's mental quips nudged me into action. "Having Reverend Pellerine here must be a great comfort," I finally offered.

"Yes." He nodded and regarded me with a surprised look of admiration. Perhaps he thought someone as young as myself hadn't had the chance to be familiar with devastating sorrow. The edges of his mouth turned down as the haunted expression slipped back into place. Then he said, "And of course, he'll be able to marry us soon after, as well."

"Soon after?" It sounded like he wanted us to be united at her grave site. Mrs. Shackleton criticized my lack of decorum. My lips trembled as I fought to smile.

"You'll understand why when the times comes." His tone was dull and tired. "You've had a long journey. I hope you will find your room comfortable."

"Thank you," I said, but it came out like a tiny whisper.

He started to leave, but then stopped at the doorway as an afterthought. His voice became demanding as if he was issuing an order on his ship. "Stay here until someone takes you to your chamber. Death will be visiting this house tonight, and I'll not have you disturbing Georgina's final hours."

I nodded. My tongue seemed large and useless. Interesting how he could talk of marrying me and burying his wife in the same breath.

He disappeared into the shadows of the foyer.

Even though I came here with the idea of accepting Captain Graves's proposal, I had not anticipated the marriage would take place so quickly. My chest tightened painfully as my heart raced. Georgina may die tonight! "What have I done?" I whispered.

Hurry, Frederick, I thought. *Hurry before it's too late.*

CHAPTER SIX

"You shared a horse ride with Reverend Pellerine?" Hettie's question had a soft high quality, but there was the hint of an accusation. If only she knew the breadth of my actual scandals. She walked a few steps ahead, leading me to the second floor. I held on to the railing as we ascended the staircase. My trunk had arrived and was waiting for me in my room.

My room.

The bleak reality was sinking in each second, weighing me down.

"Yes," I replied tiredly.

She snuck a peek at me over her shoulder. "And did you converse?" Again, her tone was polite, but there was a needling quality. I could hardly think why it was any interest to her.

"We spoke very little," I said. "His main concern was reaching the house quickly."

I followed her up the stairs. Each one creaked a different note. The sounds echoed in the quiet. I had only been in Faraday House for the better part of an hour, and already I had a sense of it being big and stagnant, like a lazy giant. There were nice things, but most of them were covered in dust or tired-looking. There was an undeniable lack of energy. Of life.

We reached the halfway landing where the grandfather clock stood on guard, its pendulum swinging back and forth, marking the time. *How long before Frederick's ship leaves Halifax?* I wondered.

Turning left, Hettie led me up the rest of the stairs to the other side of the manor. The railing curved sharply all the way to the top. From the second floor, I could see part of the foyer below. The flagstones blurred, and I became light-headed. I stepped back, imagining how easy it would be to fall.

The two ends of the second story were connected by a walkway that edged the stairs and met in front of the large round window. In the daytime, the sunlight must spill into the house, but at night, the glass acted as a mirror, reflecting the chamber candle that Hettie carried.

Across the opening, I could see the hallway of the opposite end of the house. In the gloom, a small bit of light came from one of the doors. Mrs. Graves's room, I assumed. There didn't seem to be much activity.

Hettie had grown quiet and was looking in the same direction. Her pouty grimace was disheartening.

I met her gaze and whispered, "Is she . . . ?" I couldn't even say the word out loud for fear it would make it reality. Captain Graves had made it obvious our wedding would follow soon after. It was all I could do not to run out of the house and into the night. But even if I managed to make it to the mainland, I had no money to get back to Halifax.

"Not yet." She spoke quietly. "Come, let's get you to your room for the night."

Numb with trepidation, I followed her down the dark hall. Her single candle afforded only a small preview of my surroundings. The walls were deep red. Bloodred. If Faraday House was a giant, this was its throat.

"It's a queer place to be sure," she continued. "Some doors you expect to find a room and it's only a closet. When I first came, Mrs. Clayton told me to be careful as the house had a few secret rooms and sometimes the doors stick. Her husband, Mr. Clayton, went missing for nearly a whole day before they found him in one." She scrunched up her face. "I'm not sure if she was teasing me or not, though."

"Secret rooms?"

She looked at me like I was speaking a different language. "For hiding from the American privateers when they'd raid the village, of course. You saw the cannons on top of the house, yes?"

I nodded, having thought they were gargoyles at first.

"When Faraday was first built, they were used to fire at enemy ships in the harbor." Her eyes reflected the candlelight like two fireflies in a summer garden at midnight. "Many a man lost their life not far off the coast. Think of all those skeletons among the seaweed."

"I care not to, thank you." I was still distracted by the thought of getting locked inside a secret room with no way to escape. "When did Captain Graves build the house?" I asked, thinking Hettie had her facts wrong.

"He didn't," she said. "It's over sixty years old."

My room was at the end of the hallway. Hettie wrestled with the stiff doorknob then pushed the door open with her shoulder. The hinges cried out in protest. I stood at the threshold with a finger under my nose as a waft of stale air washed over us.

She lit several candelabras around the room. I saw my trunk, and the familiarity of it in this bleak setting seemed wrong. A chill washed over my skin.

Hettie began to unpack my things, moving quietly and efficiently. I was going to tell her she needn't bother, that I would be leaving Faraday in a few days, but then I held my tongue. I didn't have the sense that Hettie would be an ally, much less able to keep my secret.

The room was appropriately furnished with a matching armoire and vanity, but the painted walls were dull and faded. A crack ran up one of the corners and continued halfway across the ceiling. The air reeked of neglect and sadness. It seemed like the rest of the estate—tired and aged, yearning for its younger, vibrant self.

I went directly to the window and pulled back the curtain, releasing a plume of mustiness. The sliver of moon hung over the outline of spruce trees that bordered the cliff. Even from the second story, I did not have a good view of the ocean. I stared at the small speck of water I could see, almost convincing myself the white sails of Frederick's ship were appearing on the horizon.

The bed had a substantial frame, plain and unimaginative, with several layers of quilts already in place. I noticed more folded on top of a blanket box at the foot of the bed. I wondered why the need for such warmth. As if in answer, the wind whistled under the eaves, and I realized the room didn't have its own fireplace.

The only element of some interest was a tapestry hanging on the wall. It was a view of Faraday House, but the tapestry version of the estate had a tower rising from the corner with a long, arched window.

Hettie followed my gaze. "The sunroom is through there," she said, nodding to the tapestry.

I pulled aside the tapestry to reveal a low archway. The room beyond it was hidden in shadow. Cold air rushed forward, carrying the same staleness. I turned away, letting the tapestry settle back in place.

She continued, "It's yours to use whenever you like. Although it's not much use at night—morning's the best. The doorway to the widow's walk is there too."

"Widow's walk?"

"It's the highest part of Faraday House." She pointed to the tower room on the tapestry. "The long window that looks out over the ocean is for the wife to keep watch for her husband's ship to return. If the ship's black flag was flying, she'd know her husband had died at sea."

Except in this house it's the wives who keep dying.

Hettie held up the pink dress I'd worn the to the admiral's ball. "How very grand," she said.

My throat tightened as I recalled how Mrs. Shackleton had discovered Frederick and me. His words about the secret mission replayed. No matter. He'd told me we would be married. I clung to the promise desperately like a drowning sailor holding a piece of wood from a rotten lifeboat.

"It's a shame no one visits," Hettie said, placing the dress carefully in the armoire. "I fancy you won't be able to do much more than drink tea and write letters."

I couldn't even visualize myself staying the night in this room, and Hettie already had me married and writing letters in my fine dresses. I applauded her sense of hope. "Penmanship is not one of my talents," I said. I could make up a million stories in my head, but putting them on paper was tedious and I grew bored before I ever reached the happily ever after. However, she had given me an idea. I said, "I need to send correspondence right away. If you could supply me with writing supplies, I'd be most grateful." Then I added, "It's rather urgent."

She nodded, regarding me with an open expression, intrigued and curious. "I wasn't expecting someone close to my own age," she said. "Reverend Pellerine said you'll need a lot of support. He knows I'm helpful like that. He admires kindness and honesty.

Says those traits are more appealing than someone who is naturally good-looking."

Hettie was honing her sharp tongue at my expense. I had no energy to match her barbs, but she was in a talkative mood, and since Mrs. Clayton was unforthcoming, I wanted to see if she would be more informative about Georgina. If she was as sick as Captain Graves implied, then I must ensure Frederick knows, and if there was anything that was within my power to help her survive, I would do it. The longer she lived, the more time Frederick had to come for me.

I made certain to choose my words carefully. "Reverend Pellerine told me a little bit about the other wives. I saw their portraits in the room with the piano."

Her gaze pinned me in place. "Yes, the music room."

"And the first wife died in childbirth?" I pried, knowing that wasn't the case with the present wife, but I hoped Hettie would be eager to correct me.

"Is that what he told you?" She tilted her head.

I grew anxious, certain she was going to call my bluff, but she swiftly moved to the door, closed it completely, and pressed her back against it. "I only arrived at Faraday after Miss Georgina became its mistress, but I'd heard enough rumors on the mainland about the first Mrs. Graves to know it wasn't childbirth that killed her. Mrs. Clayton says she doesn't like to speak ill of the dead, but according to my cousin, Miss Esther got some kind of fever. It acted quickly, before the doctors could rightly figure out how to treat her."

Esther. I recalled her wedding portrait downstairs with a much younger Captain Graves. She had a worldly sense of style and confidence. The pearl hair combs made her look like a princess. Captain Graves hadn't spoken about her, but I remembered the look of devotion in his eyes when he gazed at her portrait. He seemed to have aged much since then. I wondered how long they'd been married for. Hettie watched me carefully. I nodded encouragingly. "And Georgina, the present Mrs. Graves?" I prompted.

This time she lifted her chin with a touch of defiance. There was a loyal connection to her mistress. "Mrs. Clayton wouldn't be pleased to know we were talking about such matters, as it's only your first night." She twisted her mouth to the side as if wrestling with the decision to tell me the rest.

I suspected she was dragging this out on purpose. She knew I was a rapt audience. How often was Hettie the center of attention at Faraday? Were there other servants here? I'd only seen her and Mrs. Clayton. It must get lonely not having a companion your own age.

I clasped my hands and tucked them under my chin. "Please, Hettie," I begged. "It's not for want of gossip. In order to be a comforting wife, I need to fully understand all the grief the captain has gone through."

She finally conceded. "Since you were already talking to Reverend Pellerine about it, I suppose the truth should be shared."

I agreed with a solemn nod.

She said, "Captain Graves had been a widower for nearly ten years, and most thought he'd remain that way, but then he met Miss Georgina. Unfortunately, they had only been at Faraday a short time when her symptoms started. A queer weakness that came with delusions. Nurse Gibson says she was born with a weak heart and that's why she can't recover. She's been worsening for months." She gave a slow shake of her head. "Sadly, nothing can be done."

"I haven't met Nurse Gibson," I said, taking some comfort that

Captain Graves was a caring enough husband to not spare the expense of hiring a private nurse for his dying wife.

"And you won't." She scoffed. "She left last month and isn't coming back." Hettie dropped her voice. "She wasn't useful, anyway. Mrs. Clayton says too many people on the mainland are prejudiced about Faraday."

"I see," I replied, even though I didn't. All I had learned was that both wives died young.

I thought of Georgina, the second wife, in the west wing. "And she only married Captain Graves last year?" I asked.

Hettie nodded. "Esther didn't last long either. Two years at the most, I think."

All the candle flames flickered in unison.

I thought of something Reverend Pellerine had alluded to but hadn't confirmed. "So the captain has no children?" I asked. "Not even with his present wife?"

Hettie looked me up and down. "No wonder he hopes that won't be the case for long."

Her meaning was clear. My stomach flipped. "I envy your romantic nature," I said, but my attempt at wit was not appreciated. I suspected she thought I was making a joke at her expense.

Putting her hands on her hips, Hettie said, "Now you know." She turned briskly and continued to unpack my trunk.

An unexpected trepidation started to race through my veins. I planned to keep to myself and not get in the way, but it wasn't comforting to know the one person I needed to stay alive was without proper medical care. "If Nurse Gibson isn't returning," I asked, "who does most of Mrs. Graves's care?"

Hettie puffed out her chest. "Mrs. Clayton and myself. Oh, don't look so surprised. My mother's a midwife. I've been helping her bring babies into the world since I was twelve. I've got a knack for healing too."

I regarded her with amazement. She spoke of it so easily, almost flippant. "I can't imagine doing such a scary thing," I told her. "There's so much potential for things to go badly."

The wind screamed under the eaves, making the glass panes rattle.

She gave me a triumphant stare. "Reverend Pellerine says some people are molded by their circumstances and others create their own fortune through fortitude."

"And which category do you fall into?" I asked primarily to keep her talking. There was something unsettling about this drafty house, and even though I sensed rivalry from Hettie, her company was less bothersome than being alone.

She snickered in reply. I was about to ask her the reason behind the nurse leaving, but decided against it. I'd heard enough unnerving gossip for one night.

Hettie finished the unpacking, and I was grateful to have some of my own things, even if it was only my hair ribbons, my perfume bottles, and my hairbrush, on the vanity. The familiarity was comforting. It was a welcome sight even though I was only staying a few more days.

With a yawn, Hettie made her way to the door. "Need anything else before you settle?" she asked wearily.

"No, but I will pray for Georgina tonight." *With all my might,* I added silently.

A quirk of surprise lifted her brows; there was a crack in her mask, it seemed. It felt like a small win to be underestimated, especially at the end of such a tumultuous day.

Feeling triumphant, I said, "You must be brave to work in a house where so many misfortunes happen."

She gave me a look full of pity. "I'm not sure about misfortunes, but I know a simple housemaid like me has nothing to fear," she said. "Besides, I can leave Faraday whenever I please."

Goose bumps pebbled up my arms. I'm sure my face was an open book.

Hettie smiled and gave me an unnecessary curtsy. "Night, miss."

Then she closed the door. Leaving me all alone.

CHAPTER SEVEN

I woke in the middle of the night to a tapping at my door. Despite the quilts being pulled up to my chin, I was freezing. The tapping came again, insistent and demanding. The grogginess lifted. There could only be one reason for someone to be waking me at this hour. Georgina must have died.

No!

An anxious fist gripped my heart as I lit the chamber candle on the side table. The person knocked on the door again with so much force the doorknob rattled.

Now that I was more awake, I realized the cause of my alarm did not make sense. Surely the news of her passing could have waited until I woke in the morning. I prayed the captain would not want to be married for another few weeks, or at least until Frederick arrived.

Frederick! Of course!

He must have landed! That's why the knocking was so insistent. He must have come straight to the house and woken Mrs. Clayton, unable to wait until the morning. Captain Graves would be understandably upset, but he only met me for a moment last night. . . . Any other girl would do as his next wife. And Frederick was so charming. And surely one seafaring man to another would make his sudden appearance more palatable.

I twirled to the door, trying to keep the laugher from escaping my lips at the joyous relief of it all. There was no time to do my hair, so I pinched my cheeks for color instead.

"Yes?" I opened the door, making sure to have a look of complete surprise.

Nothing greeted me but the dark, empty hallway.

A chill from nowhere brushed against the hem of my nightgown, but the flame of the chamber candle stayed upright, unaffected by the draft. "Hello?" I said, more softly this time. My heart sank as I settled into my own skin again, heavy and worrisome. The cold reached up through the floor, penetrating my woolen bed socks.

An image of Hettie's bright-eyed expression while she gossiped about shipwrecks and the bones of sailors surfaced. She would know all the shadows and hiding places at Faraday. If she had nothing better to do than creep around the house and play tricks, I pitied her. But what would be her motive for getting me out of bed?

Images of Frederick gallantly running up the grand staircase pulled cruelly on my heart. The unfairness of it all hit me with more force than I could handle. An unexpected anger burned in my chest.

Gritting my teeth, I pulled on my dressing gown and made my way toward the staircase. My small chamber candle was the tiniest illumination as I stomped down the hallway, hoping to catch a glimpse of Hettie.

A sound echoed thorough the stillness of Faraday House. A faint cough.

I stopped at the railing as I tentatively peered down at the foyer. I expected to see Hettie darting across the flagstones, suppressing a giggle, but the space was empty. There was no movement at all, not even a fleeting shadow.

Across the gap and halfway down the opposite hallway, a dim pool of light spilled out from an open door. The coughing came again, even more feeble, if possible. Perhaps it was the plea behind the sound, but instinctively I knew it was no prank by Hettie. It must be Georgina.

I waited, but there were no voices to go along with it as an answer. No soothing tones from Mrs. Clayton or prayers of comfort from Reverend Pellerine. My unease grew until I was no longer able to stand waiting for the next sound. I could not explain the lure, even though I knew I should turn around and return to my own room.

With one hand shielding the candle flame, I hesitantly took the passage in front of the round window, then around to the west wing of the house. Timidly, I padded along the wool runner, ears straining. The hallway was the same as my end of the house, except there was one strong difference: the odor. It was thick and sour, but with an underlying softness. Death.

Captain Graves made it clear I was to avoid this area. And yet something pulled me along, as if I needed to prove that Georgina was still alive. She was the only thing stalling my hasty marriage. A marriage I could not go through with if I ever wanted to have a future with Frederick.

I took care to not be seen, peeking around the door frame. There was a single candle burning on a small table in the middle of the room, illuminating a tray with various bottles and a basin with a cloth draped over the edge.

The rest of the chamber was barely visible, but I could make out pink walls with a gold floral design. Long white curtains covered the windows like shrouds. A dainty writing desk was positioned against the wall, but there were no quills or inkpots.

Her armoire was trimmed with an elaborate rope design. Both doors were shut. Unlike my wardrobe at home, there were no ribbons trailing over the pulls or lace cuffs poking out. I wondered when was the last time it had been opened. I supposed there wasn't much use for gowns anymore.

My attention went to the four-poster bed. It was kept partway in the shadows, with only the bottom edge showing. There was no sign of movement from the lumps under the pink quilt that must have been her feet. A warning hummed at the back of my mind.

There were only two possibilities: that she had died earlier and the coughing was only my imagination, or she had died seconds ago. How long would Captain Graves wait to marry me? How long would Frederick take to arrive?

"Help." The frail voice matched the cough.

My shoulders eased away from my ears at the relief she was still alive. And yet my feet would not take me any closer. I wondered if this was too risky an endeavor. I should go back to my room before anyone discovered me. Surely she wouldn't be alone for much longer.

"Please?" she pleaded.

Her voice was achingly fragile. I was ashamed for wanting to leave.

On shaking legs, I approached the bed. The glow of my candle revealed a scene that clutched my heart. She was turned away from me with one hand reaching for the bedside table. Half of her upper body was draped over the edge of the mattress. Her thin fingers shook, and I could see her intention. A glass of water.

I gasped and immediately went to her, placing my candle on the bedside table. She was not surprised to see a stranger, but instead collapsed into my arms. Her white nightdress had a lace collar with pearl buttons. She weighed no more than a bird as I eased her shoulders onto the pillow. Then I lifted the rim of the glass to her chapped lips.

She took a small sputtering sip as she put her hand over mine.

Her fingers were bony and pale like a skeleton's. Dry skin stretched over prominent cheekbones, and purple half-moons were under her eyes. She was a shadow of the beauty in the wedding portrait downstairs. Her dark hair was brittle and dull. It hung around her face like a moth-eaten curtain.

She whispered something as she pushed the glass away, but I couldn't understand.

"Do you want more?" I asked. Despite whispering, my own voice sounded loud and garish compared to her faint peeps.

She closed her eyes, but her fingers stayed linked with mine. "Don't leave," she murmured.

I used my other hand to place the glass back on the bedside table. Why had she been left alone? She seemed so helpless. I looked at our entwined fingers and wished I knew a proper prayer or a blessing to say. I would have to wait until she fell asleep and relaxed her grip.

I took in more details of her room. A vanity off to the side was used to house several folded washing cloths and a glass pitcher filled halfway with water. Then I noticed a porcelain doll wearing a painted smile and silk dress. She sat in a little pink chair that was just the right size. Seeing the toy made me imagine how Georgina would have played with this doll as a young girl. She must have pictured a bright and happy future—certainly not her current state. My heart broke for her; even the doll's painted smile seemed grim. It was the only unique object in the room that gave any hint to what kind of person Georgina was. I had only moved in today, but already the vanity in my room was topped with my brush, hair ribbons, and several perfume bottles.

Creaking footsteps sounded on the stairs. Someone was coming from the first floor. I could not be caught in this room. I started to pull away.

Her eyes opened as she clenched my hand tighter. Her sharp fingernails dug into my skin. "Don't leave," she gasped.

"Shh," I whispered, trying to gently pull her fingers from mine. For someone who was on the brink of death, her grip was surprisingly strong. The creaking grew louder, and I knew they had rounded the landing.

Between labored breaths, she said, "Don't leave without me." Her voice was raspy but rising in volume.

My heart was beating at a fierce pace. I stared at the darkened doorway, knowing Captain Graves would appear at any moment. The faint glow of a candle grew larger in the hallway. A shadow stretched tall and menacing, carrying something large.

I peeled her fingers from mine with more force than intended.

She gaped at me in a silent scream, her deep-set eyes completely black with enlarged pupils. She took in a sharp breath, then went completely limp. Her hand dropped to the side of the bed like deadweight.

I stifled a sob as I stepped away. I'd killed her! I kept walking backward until I knocked into the table that held the basin. Several small vials tipped over. A tall bottle engraved with a cross wobbled dangerously, but I managed to right it before it toppled to the floor. The candlelight was outside the door.

I raced to the armoire and stepped inside, parting several dresses out of the way to crouch down. Pinching the inside latch, I closed the door, leaving a crack to see through.

Mrs. Clayton strode into the room. "I'm back, Mrs. Graves," she said, her voice was flat, serious. She frowned at the vials lying on their sides. After she righted them, she picked up the bottle with the cross emblem and went to the bed, sprinkling its contents around Georgina's form.

I held my breath, waiting for her to discover the body.

When she was finished, she bent over Georgina, straightening the sheet. "Sorry for taking so long," she said, a bit softer. "The candles were not in their usual place."

There was a faint mumbling. Mrs. Clayton bent down closer. "What's that?"

The knot in my chest began to uncoil. I hadn't killed her after all.

"Fetch him." Georgina's order came out like a wheeze.

Mrs. Clayton reached into her front apron pocket and withdrew a small blue bottle. "The captain is resting." She placed the dropper close to Georgina's lips.

"No." Georgina turned away from the medicine. "Get the reverend. Death is close." She pushed with her elbows, trying to sit up in bed.

Mrs. Clayton paled. She crossed herself, still holding the dropper medicine. "Reverend Pellerine was here all evening. You prayed together."

Georgina shook her head. "I must speak to him. There's no one else." She became restless, her thin body moving under the covers.

My leg cramped painfully, but I dared not move for fear of making a noise.

Mrs. Clayton put a hand on her shoulder, keeping her in place. "Don't tax yourself, dear. Your memory is affected by the disease." She tried again with the dropper. "For the pain, Mrs. Graves. Please, there's no need to suffer."

Georgina took the medicine but scrunched up her face.

"That's good." Mrs. Clayton turned away and began to place the new candles on the bedside table.

Georgina watched her with hooded eyes. She pressed her lips together as if trying to gather the strength. "An angel came," she said, her words slightly slurred. "With golden hair."

Shame rolled over me in waves. *Don't leave without me.* She thought I was an angel coming to take her to heaven. Instead, I pushed her away and ran off. I was amazed at her ability to have such faith even in the face of certain death.

Mrs. Clayton's hand hovered close to my chamber candle. "Blond hair?" She turned and scanned the room. Her iron-hard gaze stilled on the wardrobe, then she narrowed her eyes, focusing on the small crack I was peeking through. I tried to shrink smaller, wishing I could turn invisible.

Any moment Mrs. Clayton was going to rush across and wrench open the armoire. I pictured her pulling me by the hair to Captain Graves, letting him know how horribly I had acted. And there was nothing I could say to defend myself; I had made a terrible mistake. I should have stayed at the bedside and calmly explained why I had entered the room.

But it was too late now.

Georgina soon quieted, no longer talking about the angel. Mrs. Clayton's expression softened as she put her attention back on her patient. Slipping into the chair by the bed, she started to read a passage out loud from the Bible.

My muscles began to relax. She must have only thought she saw me. I would have to wait until Mrs. Clayton left before returning to my room. I was safe, at least for now. My head rested on the back of the wardrobe as tiredness crept over me, heavy and irresistible. The last thing I heard was the rhythmic drone of Mrs. Clayton's voice as I fell asleep.

I WOKE WITH a start as a cold hand was pressed over my mouth. Mrs. Clayton's face leered at me with murder in her eyes. She motioned to the bed and Georgina's sleeping form. I nodded to her in understanding.

With a steel grip on my elbow, she escorted me out of the room.

Once we were in the hallway, a stream of apologies spilled from my lips. "She was reaching for the water and nearly fell out of bed. After I gave her a drink, I thought she'd stopped breathing. I was afraid you'd think I'd hurt her, so I hid." My explanation sounded pathetic. Even I had a difficult time believing it was the truth.

She held up a finger quieting me, then motioned to the door across the hallway. "You'll wake Captain Graves," she whispered. Handing over my chamber candle she took me as far as the round window. The faint moonlight highlighted her thin lips and sharp nose. For an instant, I thought I could see the skull beneath her skin. My knees shook under my dressing gown.

She thrust a small glass bottle into my palm. It was light green and had a rubber stopper. There was no label.

I looked at her questioningly.

"Keep that close to you at all times," she said. "And don't leave your bedroom after dark."

"Can you tell me why, exactly?" I was hoping she'd provide some information about Georgina's condition, anything that would explain what was going on.

She leaned closer, her piercing eyes holding me in place. "I've seen many diseases in my lifetime, and I know a perfectly healthy young woman doesn't fall victim to a mysterious illness for no reason. That's suspicious enough on its own, but when it happens to the second wife . . . ?" Her eyebrows rose so high they disappeared under her wispy hair. "Be careful and watch your step." Then she leaned closer, and the candle flame between us flickered with anticipation. "At Faraday House, the wives always die young."

CHAPTER EIGHT

The next morning, I jolted out of sleep, sitting up in bed with my heart racing. I gasped, trying to suck in mouthfuls of air. The pale sun poured through the window, even though I distinctly remembered closing the curtains the night before.

My forehead was slick with sweat despite the chill in the air. Tendrils of the dream slipped away.

Georgina and I were outside. She pulled me along, both of us in our nightgowns, toes freezing and hems mud-caked. She pointed to a hole in the ground. There was a headstone engraved with her name. A collection of stones were piled neatly along the edge.

She jumped into the grave, taking me with her. Mud rained down on us. She laughed as earth covered her hair in thick tangles. I tried to scream, but my mouth filled with grit.

Even now, fully awake, I thought I could taste dirt. Feeling foolish but still needing reassurance, I pulled back the quilts. My feet were perfectly clean.

It didn't take someone particularly clever to uncover the meaning of this dream.

The small green bottle sat on the vanity beside my perfumes. I removed the stopper and smelled the contents, but there was no medicinal scent to hint at what the liquid was. Mrs. Clayton had told me to use it to protect myself. But how?

After putting on my light blue dress and extra-thick stockings, I wrapped a shawl over my shoulders and went down for breakfast. I purposely avoided looking toward Georgina's room. I feared the nightmare had somehow predicted her death. If Captain Graves wanted to get married as quickly as possible, I needed to send word to Frederick without delay.

I gripped the railing with white knuckles as I made my way down the stairs. The heel of my shoe scuffed several times on the narrow steps. How had no one broken their neck yet?

In the daylight, I could see the paintings of schooners that lined the hallway differed only by the number of masts or the size of the waves. Captain Graves should at least have a pasture scene or a lovely flower arrangement—anything to break up the nautical theme. Anything to bring a bit of color or life to the house. The last painting caught my attention.

The ship wasn't unique, but the details were more intricate than the others. From wind billowing the sails to the expression on the figurehead, it was like looking out a window at the real ship anchored in the bay. I leaned forward and saw the initials *GG* painted in small delicate strokes in the corner. Was Georgina the artist?

The memories of the fragile woman and the one from my nightmare were impossible to reconcile.

The aroma of fresh baking pulled me along. I was about to enter the dining room when I paused at the doorway. Reverend Pellerine was already there, standing at the sideboard with his back to me. There was a silver flask in his hand, which he was filling from a water pitcher. I stepped to the side, trying to partially hide myself.

The floor creaked under my feet, giving me away. He quickly ended his task and tucked the flask into his jacket as he turned to me. "Good morning," he said, although his tone hardly matched the sentiment.

His French accent swirled around the words, making the pedestrian greeting sound exotic and intimate.

I entered the room and gave him a slight bow of my chin. "Morning," I replied; I had not the heart to add the "good." We regarded each other for a moment. His black hair was pulled back at the nape of his neck, making his jawline more noticeable. There was a definite ruggedness about him that hinted at strength and confidence, but the refined features of his face softened the overall image. I waited, expecting him to explain the flask. He remained silent on the matter, almost daring me to speak of it first. I decided to let him have that peculiarity—I had secrets of my own.

He was wearing a black suit with a white shirt and a cravat knotted at his throat. Although his attire appeared freshly pressed and he'd shaved, there was a fatigue about his eyes.

I put a hand to my mouth, knowing there could only be one reason he was so tired. "Is Georgina . . ." My voice refused to utter the word.

"Dead?" There was no hesitation on his part, but at least his tone was respectful. "No, she's still with us, amazingly." He studied me for a moment. "You're using her first name as if you're acquainted."

I froze, uncertain if Mrs. Clayton had told him about last night. Where were his loyalties? Was he trying to catch me in a lie so he could tell the captain? I tried to read his expression, but those dark brown eyes only stared back.

"Hettie," I finally said. "She speaks of her so affectionately I can feel how much everyone at Faraday House adores her. When I referred to her by her Christian name, I did so without pausing to think if it was appropriate or not. I meant no disrespect."

"None taken," he said. "It was only a simple observation." He motioned to the sideboard, already set with covered dishes and a large teapot. "Please, don't let me keep you from breakfast. I'm about to sit down myself. I hope you don't mind."

His expression was weary, but there was an underlying tension.

I stayed quiet, sensing he was not fond of conversation. And I was all too aware of how my unexpected appearance had added another bizarre layer to the precarious situation of Georgina's dying.

The sunlight should have brightened the dining room, but instead it highlighted the cracks in the wall and mounds of dust in the corners. There was no fire in the grate either.

I was soon sitting down to a steaming bowl of porridge and several slices of raisin bread toast and gooseberry jam. It seemed ages since I had eaten, but as soon as I took a bite of toast, my stomach protested threateningly. *It must be the lingering nightmare*, I told myself. I eyed the creamer, thinking it would be best to eat the porridge without it.

Directly across the table, Reverend Pellerine had his chin bowed in prayer, hands clasped over his plate of untouched food, whispering grace. I paused my chewing until I heard him finish.

"Amen," I added around a morsel of toast.

He sprinkled a pinch of salt over his hard-boiled egg and took a bite. I watched him gently use the butter knife. There was no haste in his mannerisms, only a careful properness, elegance even. I had fallen upon my toast in my hunger, crumbs dribbling onto the plate, and I felt clumsy by comparison.

We continued eating in silence, with only the clinking of the utensils to fill the silence of the room. I didn't mind; it was almost respectful of him not to insult me with idle chatter. We both knew my reason for being at Faraday. The silence gave it the dignity it didn't deserve. I pushed the oats around with the back of my spoon before taking the smallest taste.

I reminded myself I had survived the night, and so had Georgina. It was a ghoulish way to claim a small victory, but time was not an ally. A coldness rolled over me unexpectedly as I remembered Captain Graves's plans for a quick wedding. I dropped my knife, creating a racket as it clattered on the plate. "Is it only us eating this morning? Where's Captain Graves?" I asked.

"With Georgina," he answered matter-of-factly, but there was a note of irritation. He turned back to his plate, clearly disinviting me from conversing further.

Warmth crept up my neck, but it wasn't from embarrassment. I was hurt. I'd thought it was a sensible question.

No one at Faraday House was forthcoming with information. I still didn't have a clear explanation for how the first wife, Esther, had died. And Georgina's illness was a mystery as well.

No matter for me. I would be gone soon.

I glanced down the dining table, wondering when all the chairs had last been filled. A wispy cobweb hung from the ceiling in the corner. Reverend Pellerine finished his egg.

I said, "I haven't seen anyone else but Hettie and Mrs. Clayton. Are there more servants?"

"Servants?" He lifted an eyebrow. "Mr. Clayton is married to Mrs. Clayton, and he acts as the groundskeeper and takes care of the animals."

"That's all?"

His reply came out clipped. "Should I have included myself?"

I shrugged, unsure of the source of his irritation. "You are a servant of God." I had no inkling of why I said that out loud. Our first conversation had revolved around me being completely clueless, and I was eager to give a different impression. I took a sip of tea. "Actually, Hettie mentioned there used to be a nurse."

He brushed the napkin across his mouth. "Yes," he answered. I thought he was going to leave the subject untouched, then he added, "She was here a few weeks, but she had an unfortunate accident."

"Most accidents are unfortunate."

He blinked back at me, then he said, "She had a fall on the stairs."

That was hardly surprising considering the shallow steps; however, there was a hitch to his voice that made me stare at him a moment longer than typical. "And she wasn't replaced?" I asked.

He cleared his throat. "Mrs. Clayton thought it best she manage caring for Georgina." His tone hinted that he thought otherwise. "Captain Graves feels she's more than competent, and as she puts it, only someone who knows Faraday is fit to work here."

"I see," I said. Mrs. Clayton struck me as the kind of person I didn't need to be nosy and asking questions about. Her warning from last night was ominous. And what was in that little green bottle?

For the second time that morning, I apologized. "Forgive my blatant curiosity," I said. "Sometimes my questions come out before I even realize I'm talking. I can prattle on for a few minutes before I say anything logical." I twisted the napkin under the table, wishing he would at least smile. I'd never had to work so hard for a small bit of pleasantness from a man.

Reverend Pellerine took a long drink of his tea, but unlike earlier, this time the silence was obvious, like a third member at the table. I had to bite my tongue not to tell him I'd been in Georgina's room last night. Once again, I considered he could sense guilt and used silence as a means of coercing sinners to confess.

Georgina had wanted to speak to him last night. I remembered how she'd pleaded with Mrs. Clayton to get him.

Humming came from the hallway. Hettie appeared with a tray and a fresh teapot. "*Bon matin,*" she pronounced, going to the sideboard to drop off the empty tray. She looked at the reverend expectantly.

"*Bon matin*," he replied softly.

Beaming, she asked him a question in French, or at least what I assumed was a question from the way her voice rose at the end.

The lines between his eyebrows became pronounced. "*Oui*, fine. *Merci.*"

Hettie nodded, then looked my way. Her eyes went wide in a dramatic fashion. "*Je suis désolé*," she said. "I'm sorry you don't understand. There can't be many French in Halifax, considering it's a base for the British Navy and all."

Color filled Reverend Pellerine's cheeks.

I sat straighter. Her poorly veiled comment was supposed to vex me personally, but I took offense on Frederick's behalf. "The same British Navy that prevented the Americans from attacking Nova Scotia? Yes, that's correct. Something I'm sure Captain Graves would appreciate."

A smug grin played at the corner of her mouth. "He's only a captain because he owns his own ship. He's never fought in any war."

I thought of his wedding portrait with the saber and pistol. He certainly seemed outfitted for battle.

Hettie went to Reverend Pellerine's side and replenished his cup before placing the teapot on the table. "Oh no." She pointed to his vest. "The top button is loose. I can mend it for you."

He adjusted his posture, leaning away from her slightly.

I busied myself with taking another spoonful of porridge, watching them from under my eyelashes.

"Your attention to detail is admirable, Hettie," he said, carefully. "But I know you have enough chores on your list." He cleared his throat and focused on me. "This would be a good day for you to explore the isle," he suggested.

"Alone?"

"Yes." He motioned to the long windows. "Take advantage of

the clear weather. The peninsula is small enough to see by foot." He blew on his tea before taking a sip.

I pictured myself walking deep into the woods, never to find my way out. I remembered how the forest grew thick only a few feet from the road. Still, I should locate the beach so I could have the best view to watch for Frederick's ship. I may even have to make a hasty escape. "Is there a map?" I asked hopefully.

Hettie snorted and tried to disguise it into a cough.

Her continued jabs were quickly getting irksome. I was accustomed to constant critiques from Mrs. Shackleton, but not from someone my own age, and certainly not a servant. Even though Ada's tone and choice of words sometimes carried the weight of a reprimand, they always came from a place of concern. But Hettie's comments stung with the barb of bitterness. If I had plans to run Frederick's house in Bermuda, I must learn to exude authority.

I addressed her directly. "Is it possible to get that ink and paper you promised last night? I was hoping to mail a letter today." I tried to use a steady tone, but there was an underlying quiver to my words that betrayed my confidence as a ruse.

"You'll have to curb your enthusiasm, miss." Hettie's voice was overly sweet in a patronizing manner. "This isn't the city. We must wait for low tide first." She smiled at me like I was a child who couldn't understand the simplest of commands.

Her gaze stayed on me for a few seconds longer than was comfortable. I suspected she was daring me to make another request, giving her another opportunity to demonstrate her talent for subversive insults. Heat prickled my scalp as I imagined my entire face going blotchy. I was allergic to confrontation, it seemed.

There was a clatter as Reverend Pellerine dropped his cup, spilling the tea. "Blast," he said. Then he shrugged apologetically to me. "I'm clumsy this morning."

I frowned. Nothing in his manners suggested being clumsy; in fact, I found him exceedingly calm and methodical. Had he dropped it on purpose?

Hettie swooped in, taking a cloth from her apron to mop up the mess. "Did you burn yourself?" she asked breathlessly, attempting to dry off the sleeve of his jacket.

He took the cloth from her. "No harm, Hettie," he said. He covered the spill and moved his teacup to the side.

She stood there, staring at him, eyes brimming with concern. "Are you certain?" she probed, her voice soft and full of exaggerated remorse.

"Any chance Mrs. Clayton is making biscuits?" he asked.

Roses bloomed on her cheeks. "I'll check." She stopped at the doorway. "And you're sure you're not burnt? I have a salve that could help."

"Not needed," he replied, putting up his hand to show her it was unmarred. "But thank you for the concern."

"Bien sûr!" With a swish of her skirts, she left the dining room, taking all the energy she'd brought.

I sipped my tea, watching him over the rim. His posture eased as if letting out a breath. His discomfort with Hettie's flirtation was obvious. So why would he drop the cup intentionally with the purpose of getting her attention? There was an ulterior motive, but I couldn't fathom what his true intention might be.

Reverend Pellerine cleared his throat. "I don't believe there is a map of the island, but you could draw your own. You seem as if you'd be a lady who is proficient in drawing."

His assumption was off-putting and not at all insightful. "Why is that?" I asked.

He shrugged then listed off, "The size of your trunk, your expensive dresses, the efforts you take with your style . . . your hair.

That kind of refinement usually comes equipped with such abilities." There was an underlying sense of something I couldn't put my finger on, rather like playfulness but with a hint of malice.

I answered without checking my tone. "You are not as good at reading people as you think, Reverend. I cannot draw, at least in the ways that would suggest I have any such artistic flair." I put down my teacup. "I was a child who had neither the natural talent nor the tenacity to develop such a skill. I'm sure Moses could do a better job." I gave him my usual, automatic smile.

I was twelve when I overheard Mrs. Shackleton tell the judge I didn't need drawing lessons. I spied them through the crack in the door. "Beauty should be exceptional when there are no other attributes," she told him. "The art and music lessons you insist upon her taking are a waste of time. She needs to concentrate her efforts where her real assets are. If Emeline has to depend on intelligence to secure a husband, we will have to reconcile that she will live as an old maid."

"She's only a child," he replied, his pipe halfway to his mouth. "So much has been taken from her already. Why steal this bit of fun from her too?"

"Fun? You may be clever with the law, husband, but in these matters, you must allow me to do what is best. You'll thank me when the time comes."

"Men are simple creatures," he grumbled. "Emeline can handle simple."

Mrs. Shackleton hit him with a cold stare. "You of all people should know, Judge. Simple is the most dangerous. It's driven by primal means."

I blinked, coming back to the present. Across the table, Reverend Pellerine stared at me. I wondered how long I'd been quiet. He was studying me like a passage in the Bible, but he hadn't decided if it was about being good by being good or by avoiding evil—which I have learned were not entirely the same thing. Then his expression lifted. He said, "As long as you can always see the house, you won't get lost. Think of it as an anchor."

I saw a massive iron anchor, lying at the bottom of the ocean, covered in crustaceans and slimy silt. And me down there with it, my long hair forever ebbing and flowing with the tides.

CHAPTER NINE

My red cloak and bonnet were a stark contrast to the bland November landscape of the peninsula. The grass had yellowed, and the trees were bare of their leaves, leaving only finger-like branches clawing at the air. The only color was the dark green of the spruce trees. Wind blew off the ocean, carrying a salty chill.

I walked as far as the carriage house and stopped. The house was still in sight, of course, but there was an eerie feeling that if I hadn't checked, it wouldn't have been there. I shook off the shiver, embarrassed by my rather feeble attempt at exploring. Reverend Pellerine suggested I make a map. I rolled my eyes. I cared not for exploring the island; I only wanted to find the place that would afford me the best view of the water so I could be the first to see Frederick's ship.

I needed to find a way to the beach. He would be coming from the northeast, and presently the only thing I saw from my bedroom window was the tops of the spruce trees that bordered the cliff's edge.

The wind came through the forest carrying with it the sweet scent of pine and fir. It reminded me of Christmas and how there would be bowls of oranges and peppermints. The fire would be on, and Ada would bring in lemon punch and molasses cookies.

It wasn't always miserable in Halifax.

Pain squeezed my heart.

When Mother and I first arrived at the Shackletons' large home,

I was quickly occupied by exploring the expansive gardens. They even had a fountain with a statue of a lady holding a jug, the water pouring out of its opening in a continuous stream. A groomed lawn led to a private pebbled beach. The sun glistened off the quiet bay. It was so different from the harbor full of naval ships on the other side of the city. And a world away from our little apartment above Father's store.

After his death, Mother stopped talking. Then she was unable to get up. I remember going to her bedside with my brush. I had tried to do my own hair, but it was knotted from neglect. She looked at the brush as if she'd never seen it before and didn't know what it was. The house grew gray as the sun set. Then night came, and it turned so cold.

On the fourth day, Mrs. Shackleton arrived with a team of staff. Mother allowed herself to be enveloped into her embrace. Our belongings were packed up quickly. The only place I'd known as home grew distant as I looked out the back window. Mrs. Shackleton's carriage took us to her house.

Mother was led to a bedroom with pink roses on the walls and a large bed with layers of quilts and its own fireplace. I wasn't allowed to see her for a week. The maids fussed over me, and soon my hair was shiny and in colorful ribbons.

Judge Shackleton was a looming figure with a natural scowl and a robust belly. He was gruff and always slid off to his study whenever he saw me. Mrs. Shackleton explained he wasn't used to children. She patted her eyes with her lace handkerchief after she said this and would quickly usher me to the front parlor, saying we must leave him in peace.

But one morning we met each other in the front hallway, both of us struck dumb by the awkward circumstances. I pretended I was frozen, like the statue in his garden, staying absolutely still.

He stared down at me, hands in his trouser pockets. He shifted his weight back and forth, unsure.

Then he placed a coin in my hand. "Off you go, now," he said.

He looked pained as he sidestepped around my still-frozen figure. Only once I heard his carriage pull away from the house did I look at the shilling, marveling at how much I could buy with it. Then shame and worry rolled over me in waves. What if this was a test and I failed? My heart raced with panic, picturing Mother and me being sent away. She still wasn't well enough to leave her room.

I began to shake. I had to return it to him, but I had to do it without Mrs. Shackleton knowing. I needed to leave it in a place where he would find it and no one else. The door to his study was made of a dark wood. I'd never seen it open and imagined there was a whole other world inside. However, it was a place I had no desire to explore, for the risk of being caught was terrifying.

A maid was coming, and I didn't have an excuse for why I was lingering in the hallway—Mrs. Shackleton was not happy whenever I lingered too long in one place.

Making a split-second decision, I ran to the study and opened the door and slipped inside. It was a shadowy room with dark walls and thick green velvet drapes and shiny brass sconces. It smelled of shoe polish and tobacco. Shelves heavy with books lined three of the four walls with a ladder on rails that immediately tempted me to ride.

Ignoring the ladder, I went to the large desk. An oil lamp with a crystal base sat like a treasure on display. Then I saw his pipe and ashtray. With a shaking hand, I placed the coin perfectly over the pipe's opening and left as quickly as a mouse sneaking a crumb from the kitchen.

That evening, the coin appeared in my room with a note in bold script. *Delightful surprises are rare. Thank you. JS.*

I smiled wide, and my heart was light. The next day I hid the coin in his top hat. I put a hand over my mouth, trying not to giggle when he exclaimed in the front hall. Mrs. Shackleton came from the front parlor to see what all the commotion was about, but he calmly said it was only a joke he was remembering from the day before.

I leaned over the staircase in time to see him wink up at me.

The game continued as our secret. Me hiding the shilling for him to find. I would always put it in a place unique to him; inside his boot by the door, his glove . . . his favorite teacup. I even stumped him for several days when I slipped it between the pages of one of his books. However, with the unexpected joy of the game, there was also a guilt because the judge wasn't my father, and I shouldn't be happy while Mother was so sad. The game continued until the day she died—only a few weeks after we arrived.

A crow called out from a high branch. The woeful landscape of Faraday slipped into place around me, banishing my memory, dragging me back to reality. I continued on the footpath behind the carriage house, hoping it would lead to the shore. It grew darker under the canopy of the forest, and I began to worry I might lose my sense of direction and walk in circles for hours. There was a prickling sensation between my shoulder blades. I turned around, certain there would be someone watching me. I remembered how unnatural it was to hear the piano play without seeing the musician, and how I woke to urgent tapping last night only to open the door to an empty hallway.

Everything at Faraday was shrouded in an eerie cloud of gloom.

I began to hasten my steps. The scent of damp earth filled my nose and throat. The vegetation grew closer, eating up the pathway, making the actual trail indiscernible. I stopped and put my hand to the closest trunk, certain I had already passed this marker.

The ground started to swirl as panic built inside me. Was I going in circles? What if I never found my way out? I pictured Hettie as an old woman discovering my skeleton in a bush, my beautiful red cloak moldy and partially chewed away by critters.

I squinted through the trees, trying to find a bit of daylight. If I ever found the beach, I'd dive in and swim back to Halifax. Then something bright caught my attention. Unexpected colors poked through the ground.

I pushed aside branches, trying to get a closer look. There was a cluster of mushrooms growing in the middle of a clearing. Some were red with tiny white dots, and others were as yellow as an egg yolk. That small surprise of beauty pulled on my heart. It seemed almost magical. I hoped it was a sign to not give up, and that Frederick would soon be here.

I went nearer, wanting to pick one. Then a sudden crack sounded underneath me. I screamed as the forest growth gave way underfoot. I dropped. My chest slammed into the ground with my cloak bunched up around my waist, holding me in place as my feet dangled underneath in nothing but air.

CHAPTER TEN

Help," I screamed. My legs pedaled frantically, unable to find
purchase. There were rotted planks on either side of me,
digging into my armpits. I spread my reach and pushed down
desperate to leverage myself up, but the wood sagged dangerously
under my hands.

Twisting, I managed to grab a root, but it snapped as soon as I
tried to pull myself up. I screamed again, my voice garbled as tears
streamed down my cheeks. At least my cloak was thick enough to
prevent me from slipping through the hole any farther. But how
long would the rotten boards hold?

This was not like in the carriage, where I imagined Frederick
weeping at my grave. This was real, and I wanted to live.

"Help!"

Heavy breathing sounded from behind me. Footfalls grew
louder as branches snapped. I dared not move for fear of jostling
my precarious position. A man's voice I didn't recognize called
out, "I'm coming!"

Someone reached under my arms and pulled. I could do nothing but allow myself to be lifted out of the ground. Once my heels
hit solid earth, I managed to get my boots underneath me to take
my own weight.

We moved backward until we were clear of the danger. I'd
left an Emeline-shaped hole in the moss-covered boards perfectly
camouflaged against the forest floor. The bright mushrooms were

partially trampled. I covered my face and quietly wept into my gloves.

"Miss, I'm so sorry," the man said, out of breath. "Are you all right? Shall I fetch the horse to take you back to the house? Do you think you need a doctor?"

"No." I sniffed. "I'm fine, just a bit shaken and very grateful you found me." I dropped my hands and saw the kind, weathered face of my rescuer.

He took off his cap and wrung it in his hands. With a slight build, he wasn't much taller than myself; however, the cut of his jacket hinted at broad shoulders, and judging by how easily I'd been plucked from the earth, he must have been strong.

He put a hand to his chest. "I'm so sorry."

I smiled wearily. "You're my rescuer. Surely that"—I waved to the hole behind us—"is not your fault." My red cloak was soiled with mud. I brushed a few stray spruce needles off the front of my cloak and fixed my bonnet. "I'm Emeline—"

"Fitzpatrick," he finished. He put his cap back on and touched the brim. His sky-blue eyes crinkled at the corners in an earnest smile. "I'm Mr. Clayton. The missus told me you'd arrived. I regret this is our first meeting. Those blasted holes are all over the island. I thought I had them all marked off." He offered his arm. "Let's get you back to the house. The missus will take a look at you. She's as good as any doctor on the mainland."

I went cold at the thought. "I don't want to take her attention from Mrs. Graves. I don't even have a limp. See?" I let him lead me up the hill.

"All right," he conceded. "But a cup of tea wouldn't hurt matters once I get you back to the house."

I stayed quiet, knowing it would take more than a cup of tea to fix my problems. He had an easy charm, and I was grateful to be in his company. "I'm indebted to you, Mr. Clayton. You saved my life."

His cheeks colored as he nodded shyly. Then his expression clouded over. "Don't mind my boldness, miss, but it's not safe to wander the grounds without an escort."

"It was Reverend Pellerine's suggestion," I offered a bit accusingly, like a small child hoping to get a sibling in trouble.

"The reverend," he repeated under his breath. His mouth set in a stern line. "He's not familiar with the island. You come to me next time. I'll give you a proper tour." There was an obvious dislike for the man in his voice.

That won't be necessary, I thought. *I'll be leaving soon.*

He brought me to a clearing, and we paused atop a hillside. About halfway down, there was a large oak tree encircled by a wrought iron fence. Inside the enclosure were several gravestones. Even from this distance I could see a fresh hole had been dug. No mystery who it was for.

I wanted to give the area a wide berth, but my hand was on Mr. Clayton's arm and it would be disrespectful to pull away. We walked through the small opening in the fence and paused by the closest headstone. Above us, the bare branches of the oak tree spread over us like an umbrella of bones.

I hated graveyards.

The first time Mrs. Shackleton took me to my parents' grave at the cemetery, I couldn't cry. She squeezed my hand and nodded approvingly. "Proper thing to not waste your time," she'd said. "The dead can't see your tears." When we started back for the judge's house, she told me I would live with them until I married. Then she added, "I'll make sure you don't repeat your mother's mistake of marrying for love. It killed her in the end."

I knew Mrs. Shackleton was lying. My mother was deeply in love with Father, but her heart didn't stop from grief. Only the judge and I knew the truth.

Now I found myself at another cemetery and looking at the final resting place of the captain's first wife. Esther's burial site was well-kept. There was even a posy of dried flowers, a gesture that hinted at genuine affection and planning. Flowers in November were a scarcity. There was something tragically romantic about it.

Mr. Clayton crouched down and picked a small piece of brown grass away from the headstone. He sniffed. "Esther wasn't much older than you when I met her. Away from her family for the first time." He was talking to the headstone, not me. "She was so full of life. It's hard to imagine her lying below us, asleep."

Such an odd way for him to imagine her. Dead is dead, not asleep. "I saw her portrait in the music room," I told him.

"That's her piano. Captain Graves brought it here especially. No one has played it since she died."

That was a lie. I'd heard it myself last night. I began to appreciate the span of Hettie's abilities.

Beside Esther's grave was the freshly dug one I'd seen from the top of the hill. Obviously, that was the reason Mr. Clayton happened to be close enough to hear my calls for help. A curious guilt began to needle its way under my skin. "I'm sorry I disturbed you," I said, motioning to the preparation for Georgina's plot.

A shiver rippled through me. Her grave looked exactly like it had in my nightmare. Even the rocks were piled the exact same way.

How was that possible?

Mr. Clayton motioned to the pile of rocks. "The land is so rocky, we can't dig too deep."

I asked, "If the land is so rocky, how can there be deep holes all over the island?"

He put a finger to the side of his nose and winked at me. "Very astute, Miss Fitzpatrick."

Despite the circumstances, I stood taller. No one had called me "astute" before.

He chuckled nervously, a bit of energy left over from our adventure. "Those holes were here long before Captain Graves ever set foot on this island." Mr. Clayton readjusted his cap then nodded toward the only other tombstone. It was the biggest and directly under the oak tree. "There lies the man who built Faraday. He's the one responsible for all those holes."

His tone was factual—none of the personal connection like when he was talking about Esther. He said, "The missus tells it better than I. Apparently he built the house for his bride as a wedding present, but there was an accident . . ." The rest of his story was drowned out. I couldn't absorb any more tales of death. The wind wound through the branches of the oak tree, dropping my name in careless whispers.

I had a premonition of Mr. Clayton standing in front of my own burial plot, telling the next Mrs. Graves about me. *She was a beauty, but not much by way of intellect. She got lost one day and fell into her own grave. Split her head open right then and there. It was quite considerate, saved me the task of burying her.*

I stared at Georgina's plot. The ground seemed to rise as if beckoning me closer. There was a growing urge to tell Mr. Clayton he wouldn't have to dig one for me. I wasn't going to be in that graveyard; I was going to Bermuda.

"No one knows for certain, though," he said, getting my attention. Then he sighed and made a *tsk* noise at the back of his throat.

All I wanted to do in that moment was run away. Still, there was something about the scene that made me stare awhile longer, something out of place I couldn't put my finger on.

I moved out of the fenced area. "I believe I should start back," I told him.

He rushed to my side. "Let me escort you." He offered his arm. "I'll even make that pot of tea myself." His eyes were a vibrant blue and seemed out of place on his weathered face.

The gallant gesture warmed my heart, but I feared he would talk of more Faraday tragedy, and I craved silence. "Another time. Thank you, Mr. Clayton."

He deflated slightly, and I worried he may think I was going to say something to Captain Graves about the unmarked hole I nearly fell into. I was compelled to give him some assurance, especially since he was the one person here who seemed trustworthy. "I won't let on about my clumsiness. And may I say, you have the bluest eyes I have ever seen."

He blushed. "I was about to tell you the same thing. It's a rare color. The missus says my eyes make up for my ugly feet."

"Nothing a good pair of socks can't fix."

He chuckled and touched the tip of his cap. "Please, call me by my first name: Bagnall."

I studied him to make sure he wasn't teasing me. "A name uglier than your feet."

He enjoyed the joke. Despite my almost dying, my time with Mr. Clayton had been the most enjoyable at Faraday.

Pointing down the hill, he said, "The trail back to the house is at the bottom. Not more than a few minutes' walk from here."

Then he sauntered over to Georgina's grave and stepped in. He gingerly picked up a rock and tossed it to the pile I'd seen in my dream. I had to look away.

By the time I reached the bottom of the hill, my boots were

soaked and my muddy hem was heavy against my steps. Even though this pathway was much flatter than the one from the carriage house, each step took effort.

I wondered how far I was from the land bridge to the mainland. On the hill, Mr. Clayton continued to clear Georgina's plot.

Death was leering at me constantly. My mind filled with images of disastrous accidents. I had to leave this place and its long shadows and cold rooms and weird servants with their nighttime secrets and tricks.

But where would I go? Judge Shackleton would send me straight to the convent if I ever managed to get back to Halifax. I had neither money nor friends to assist me in escaping. Then I thought about Frederick. What if he arrived on his ship and I wasn't on the island? That thought helped me focus.

I had to stay here, but I would write him another letter. One detailing my dire situation. If he knew the truth, he wouldn't leave me here.

He wouldn't.

Hettie must have brought the writing supplies to my room by now, and I was certain Mr. Clayton would take a letter to the post for me. I began to feel a glimmer of hope.

The pathway eventually opened to the ocean side of Faraday House. I could hear the waves far below. I criticized myself for not asking Mr. Clayton for a direct path to the beach.

I stared at the house with a peculiar sense of familiarity. This angle matched the tapestry in my room. I assumed the artwork must have been done from this vantage point.

The stone façade was the same as the other side of the house, with the addition of a covered walkway instead of a front door. A tower rose from the corner of the roof, with its lone window.

The widow's walk.

My bedroom was below it and off to the side.

Thick ropes of ivy grew up the sides of the house, claiming some of the rocky surface. In the summer, the green leaves must make the house look like a living plant.

I walked closer, head tilted back, taking in the details. Even though I was firmly planted on the ground, a twinge of nauseating dizziness crept in as I regarded the tower. Then a wonderful idea dawned. From that vantage, I would be able to see Frederick's schooner. Of course! I'd see the ship at least an hour or two before it docked. Enough time to prepare myself and pack my trunk.

A breeze blew off the waves, sending a salty warning. The window in the tower room was made of multiple panes. I caught movement behind the glass. Hettie was there.

I waved with a smile, enjoying the small satisfaction that I had caught her. It was important to acknowledge I was wise to her poor attempt at a ruse. I still hadn't forgiven her for the bizarre prank of knocking on the door.

Instead of waving back, she stared at the ocean as if I wasn't even there.

CHAPTER ELEVEN

The foyer greeted me with the same coldness as yesterday, and I wondered if this house was ever warm, even in the summer. I was halfway to the stairs when raised voices caught my attention. The double doors opposite the music room were open slightly. Through the crack I could see Mrs. Clayton standing with her hands clasped in front of her. Her face was as rigid and unmoving as the grandfather clock on the landing.

Captain Graves was out of sight. His voice sounded surly and commanding. "You assured me you could do the job."

Mrs. Clayton tilted up her chin. "I've been doing everything I can, but only God knows when her time will come. Until then, I'll continue to keep her safe."

Safe? I thought back to the bottle with the emblem of a cross and how she'd sprinkled its contents around Georgina's bed. Was it holy water? And why would she think that was proper treatment for someone who was dying?

Captain Graves sounded bitter. "I'd hoped the reverend would bring her peace, but she's just as agitated, even more so."

"When grief is not addressed, it opens the door to unwanted attention, sir." She lowered her voice, but her confidence remained steady. "Your anguish over Esther has festered all these years, feeding the restless spirits here, and now Georgina is at risk. Something on this island is trying to claim her soul before she dies. How else do you explain when she's having one of her spells and her eyes go all black? You've experienced enough on the seas to know some occurrences cannot be explained."

A heavy silence lay over the room.

Taking care to walk on my tiptoes, I ventured closer. I could see a sliver of the captain's figure. He was standing behind a hulking desk, which looked more like the helm of a ship than a piece of furniture. His attire was more formal than last night, and his hair was combed back. In the daylight, his beard was almost entirely gray, and his wrinkles were more pronounced. He seemed to have aged another decade since our encounter in the music room.

His fist pounded on the desk. I jumped, but Mrs. Clayton stayed calm. I was amazed at her fortitude. He snarled, "I will not have my wife tied to her bed like a lunatic."

Tied to the bed? No wonder he was upset.

Mrs. Clayton replied, "She'll wander the house and hurt herself. I found her near the railing this morning. She would have gone over if I hadn't pulled her back in time."

I shuddered, imagining Georgina's brittle form violently hitting the flagstones.

"She deserves better," he replied, more docile. "Have the staff take turns watching her."

"What staff? Hettie has too many chores for one girl, Mr. Clayton faints at the sight of blood and is completely useless as a caregiver, and Reverend Pellerine cannot give us all his time. He has his parishioners to tend to. It is you who must sit with her, even if it burdens you with guilt."

"Have Miss Fitzpatrick take a turn." It came out like an order.

My stomach cramped in apprehension. She'll remember me and realize her vision of an angel was wrong.

"I want to only remember her as she was before." His voice cracked. "She painted such beautiful scenes. How can you say someone like that has evil in them?"

Evil? A new kind of trepidation crept over my skin.

Mrs. Clayton said, "You and I both know the nurse falling down those steps was no accident. I saw Mrs. Graves standing at the top with her eyes all dark."

I'd heard enough. I must write to Frederick at once. There was no way he would leave me in a house that had so many secrets— with so many untrustworthy people. I hurried up the stairs and had nearly reached the landing when I heard his voice.

"Miss Fitzpatrick?" Captain Graves called out. Turning, I saw him standing in the open doorway, regarding me with an expression of unfocused politeness.

Mrs. Clayton slipped out behind him. Her eyes were downcast, yet her posture hinted at a semblance of triumph. It was an interesting power dynamic. I couldn't imagine any of the staff speaking to Mrs. Shackleton in such a manner.

She nodded demurely as she brushed past me on the stairs. There was no indication of a bond resulting from our conversation last night. She warned me not to leave my room at night. But where or who was the danger? If she was warning me about Captain Graves, why had she not seemed troubled to be in his presence? And what was in the mysterious bottle to be used for my protection? More holy water? But if that was the case, who was I in danger from— Captain Graves or an evil sprit? Or perhaps Georgina?

I could not think of a logical reason for her erratic actions.

Captain Graves watched as I made my way down the stairs and across the foyer to him. My muddy boots had left a trail from the front door to where he now stood. I hoped he wouldn't notice.

I smiled on cue, and it was easily returned. I noted how much easier it was to please him than Reverend Pellerine. The image of the reverend filling the flask resurfaced. He had his own mysteries and was therefore not to be trusted either.

The captain's gaze lowered, lingering on my waist. I gave him a small curtsy to alter his view. He waved me into the room. It was a large space for a study, and the scant amount of furniture made it feel empty and devoid of purpose. His desk was placed in front of the window that gave the view of the main road. Off to the side, a settee and two wingback chairs were arranged in front of a fireplace. A meager fire glowed in the grate, emitting a feeble attempt at warmth. The lamp on his desk was the primary source of light and was precariously placed on top of a stack of papers.

The overall effect was one of loneliness and neglect.

At the back of the room, a long window allowed in a small patch of light. Specks of dust danced in the sunbeam as we walked closer to the glass. I crinkled my nose, fighting the urge to sneeze.

If Hettie was the housekeeper, she must be kept busy with other chores, as certainly dusting wasn't her top priority. I was re-minded of her face in the high window and wondered what trick-ery she'd been doing there. The theories went around in my head in an unsatisfying rotation. Nothing made sense in this drafty, forlorn place.

There were no bookshelves, which seemed odd for a study. Judge Shackleton's office had shelves that went straight to the ceil-ing and had their own ladder. Sometimes he would let me slide across, but only when Mrs. Shackleton was out—another secret we shared.

It was obvious Captain Graves didn't have nearly the same number of texts. Instead, there were several small tables placed around the sitting area. Each one was topped with random stacks of leather-bound volumes. There didn't seem to be any order, and it must have been a long time since anyone had picked one up to read. Even in the daylight, a tiresome gloominess hung in the air.

The only feature that prevented the room from being completely depressing was the mural on the long wall. Faraday House was on a hill, its image reflected in a small body of water. It was cheerful and alive; even the bullrushes along the water's edge seemed to move. I walked closer, wanting to reach out and touch the mural. The initials *GG* were in the corner, small and shy. Georgina Graves.

"She captured it perfectly." Captain Graves stood beside me. I could sense his shoulder nearly touching mine. I leaned a fraction of an inch away, trying to create space between us.

"She was very talented." Realizing my horrid mistake, I quickly blurted out, "Is! She *is* talented." I closed my eyes, embarrassed by my lack of tact. Mrs. Shackleton shrieked reprimands in my mind.

"No need to correct yourself," Captain Graves said. "You speak the truth. The poor creature upstairs is not the same woman who painted this." He put his back to the mural and gave me his full attention. I could feel the weight of his desperation.

Without altering his piercing stare, he said, "Nothing can prepare you for life's most devastating tragedies, but there is one thing I must ask you, Miss Fitzpatrick, and I need you to be completely truthful with me."

My heart moved to my throat, racing painfully. I was certain he'd discovered I'd visited Georgina's room. Or worse, he knew about Frederick.

Panic filled my mind with images of me sent adrift on a small boat with only Mrs. Clayton's tiny bottle of mysterious liquid as provisions. Frederick's schooner would race through the waves only to bypass my small craft, invisible from his deck, high above the ocean. I would scream his name as the ship grew smaller, leaving me.

But when Captain Graves spoke, his query was the last thing I expected. "Do you believe in ghosts?" His expression was completely serious.

The tension melted from my shoulders. That was a question I could answer truthfully. I thought of my parents' grave and the real reason Mrs. Shackleton became my guardian. It wasn't God's providence as she was so fond of claiming.

"No," I answered straightforwardly. I believed in bad luck and the finality of death, and I certainly didn't believe in ghosts or angels. He regarded me with raised eyebrows in a hopeful manner, clearly wanting more of an answer. I added, "I believe people who have passed on live in the memories of those they left behind."

He nodded. "Good. Sometimes young women have fanciful notions, and Faraday has been the target of misplaced folklore."

I wondered if he was referring to Mrs. Clayton's warning of restless spirits.

He walked past the fireplace to the window at the end of the room, hands clasped behind his back. There was a sense of defeat in his posture. I reminded myself he ran this house. It was important I stay in his favor.

I followed and took in the view of a pond below and, beyond that, the small bay that acted as a back harbor to the village. It seemed close from this height, as if I could easily swim to freedom. But the water was ice-cold this time of year, and the tide would carry me out to the Atlantic before I could utter one syllable of regret.

He said, "If I stay in this spot long enough, I can almost see her down by the pond with her sketch pad." His eyes crinkled at the edges, lost in a memory. "She told me she put a surprise in each picture. I should have asked her more about it, but I thought we had the rest of our lives together. I thought the walls of Faraday would be brightened with her paintings."

He seemed genuinely remorseful.

Would he give me truthful answers about his young wives' fatal illnesses?

At Faraday House, the wives always die young.

According to Mrs. Shackleton, a pretty smile set men at ease and made them feel important, and more likely to trust you. I gave Captain Graves a thoughtful smile and put my hand on his arm. "I'm sorry. It must hurt so much to see her suffer."

Still looking out the window, he said, "I have worked hard all these years hoping I would have something to pass down to my children. Even though this house, my shipping business, and the general store will remain after I die, the thing I fear the most is that no one will remember my name." He turned to me. "I have no legacy. No one to carry on my bloodline."

An unexpected emptiness took hold of me. The floor seemed to rise and fall like we were on the ocean.

He let out a tired sigh. "Everywhere I go in this house I'm reminded of what I've lost. Esther played the piano every day, but now it sits quiet. Georgina painted scenes around Faraday, bringing even the most mundane object to life. But now she's the still life, slowly fading, like one of her sketches left out in the rain. I'm living with ghosts, Miss Fitzpatrick. You see, Faraday House is not cursed—I am."

"In what way?" I prompted. The more truth I learned, the better the chances of keeping Georgina alive. I was weary of the tricks and vague threats of ghosts.

He let out a shuddering sigh. "It all started with Esther."

CHAPTER TWELVE

Energy buzzed in the air like a million invisible bees. I worked to keep my expression open and sympathetic. I wanted Captain Graves to see me as someone whom he could trust. I needed him to consider me as much an ally as a fiancée.

A darkness clouded his eyes as he spoke. "Trade is my business. Back when Esther and I were first married, the seas were complicated. If it wasn't the French trying to sink us, it was the American privateers looking to board and steal what they could. I would be away for long stretches, but each time I returned I had crates full of dresses, exotic foods, all the best wines. Then slowly, Esther began to change. She no longer wanted gifts and began to resent my absences, taking any opportunity to argue with me. Once she even had a violent fit and locked herself in her room." He rubbed his forehead with a shaking hand. "I left for another trip, and I'm ashamed to say I was relieved.

"That last shipping voyage was particularly brutal. It dragged on longer than the planned six months. There were storms and other complications. I returned home in time to shovel the dirt into her grave."

"What happened?" I asked breathlessly.

He spoke as if seeing the final scene replay on the wall. "I made them open the coffin so I could see her one more time." He touched a fist to his mouth and squeezed his eyes shut. "The wind breezed through her hair so naturally that for a moment I thought she was still alive. The fever had been quick, Mrs. Clayton said. It had ravaged her heart. There was nothing anyone could do."

He began to sob, but then caught himself. "I spent more time at sea, leaving the Claytons in charge. I was only going to take a year to heal my wounds, to try and deal with my grief, but the longer I stayed away, the more I pretended Faraday didn't exist. And if it didn't exist, then neither did Esther's grave."

I thought it was cowardly of him to pretend she didn't exist. Especially after he'd told me he wanted to be remembered. What about Esther's legacy?

"For the last ten years, I returned to land once or twice a year, staying a week or so at the most." A sad smile curled under his moustache. "Then I met Georgina. She was young and full of life. The exact thing I needed . . . and that Faraday House needed too. Or so I thought." He hung his head. "I should have known better than to bring her here, but I reasoned enough time had passed. I believed I had earned a second chance at happiness." The devotion on his part was authentic.

It occurred to me I could possibly alter Captain Graves's hasty plan for us to marry if he still considered Georgina curable.

"Curses only exist if you believe in them," I said with a confident vibrance. "Georgina may rally. Her body may still fight off the illness." I added the last bit hoping he would elaborate on her specific condition.

His eyes brightened slightly, and I could almost see how dashing he must have been as the man in the portrait with Esther, when they were both young and in love. "You have a sweet spirit," he said. "But Georgina is beyond being cured. I know the end is near."

His gaze dulled as he looked over my shoulder, focusing on the dead space of the sparse area. The haunted expression returned, aging him again. "This was supposed to be a ballroom, but no one has ever danced here." There was a tired pause. When he spoke again, his voice assumed the same weariness. "You can decorate any way you like. I have the means to order any material for curtains or upholstery. I have access to anything you want, even exotic trinkets half the world away."

Although his tone lacked any hint of enthusiasm, his words conjured an image of a comfortable life. One where I was taken care of and would have my own home. And wasn't that what I'd always wanted? The room began to take on a new look, one with musicians and garlands of flowers hung over the doorways, of crystal punch bowls and tables laden with sweets and cakes, and my own private suite of rooms with several armoires filled with . . .

". . . and our children."

His last sentence brought me down to Earth. The party images melted away to reveal the ballroom as the dusty tomb it was.

"Children?" I repeated. I pictured Frederick and his bright red hair and blue eyes, the opposite of Captain Graves's darker complexion. Faraday came at a price I was unable to pay.

My expression of panic must have been obvious, for Captain Graves sniffed and stepped back, putting space between us. "I want to assure you I'm a God-fearing man and I will not consider you my proper wife until we're married." It was a declaration of civility with no suggestion of anticipation. I admit, I felt slightly insulted.

He motioned to the door. Our conversation was over, apparently. I was disappointed. I wanted to ask him more about Georgina's illness. I certainly didn't concur with Mrs. Clayton's "restless spirits" theory.

For the time being, I would have to put that curiosity at the back of my mind. I had a more pressing matter. Even though

Hettie had given me no reason to hope I could get my letter to the post today, I suspected she was trying to impress the reverend. "Is it possible to have a letter delivered to the mainland later this afternoon?" I asked brightly, anticipating the captain would be able to grant my request. "Mrs. Shackleton will be wanting to know I've arrived safely."

"I already sent them word." He gave me a queer look that bordered on annoyance. "I'll take care of your every need."

Deflated, I walked through to the foyer. Hettie was on her knees, scrubbing my muddy footprints off the stone floor. The captain ignored her as he offered his arm and escorted me up the staircase. I was surprised he didn't acknowledge her. I stayed quiet, unsure if I should apologize for the extra work I had caused.

"What is on your cloak?" he asked. His query hinted at mild disappointment and a bit of an accusation. I suppose when you're the head of the household and used to overseeing several businesses and your own ship, most people you deal with work for you or are inferior to you.

I wasn't sure in which category I fit.

I remembered how apologetic Mr. Clayton had been. I didn't want to tell the truth and possibly get him in trouble for not marking all the holes. I decided it was best to make up a half-truth.

"I slipped during my walk today. My boots are not fit for this terrain, I'm afraid, sir."

"Call me Edgar."

Pressing my lips together, I nodded, feeling the heat spread up my neck, knowing Hettie was listening to every word.

When we reached the landing, he let go of my arm as we would continue to opposite ends of the house. I was grateful he hadn't asked me to sit with Georgina. It was possible talk of Esther had distracted him enough. Longing and remorse had etched themselves permanently on his face. I wondered when he'd last laughed.

Once I reached my room, I slipped off my cloak and laid it over the trunk. I crinkled my nose. There was a pungent scent, something tangy but not offensive. I'd brush it clean myself later; asking Hettie to complete the chore was too cruel.

Then I paused, remembering what was so odd about Mr. Clayton and the cemetery. He'd said he was close by because he'd been digging Georgina's grave. But his clothes were clean, even his hands. And there was no shovel.

What was he doing at the cemetery if he wasn't digging her grave?

Captain Graves said he was cursed, but it seemed his wives were the ones who'd suffered the ultimate consequence.

My head began to throb. I'd had enough of curses and graveyards for one day. I stood in front of the mirror and turned sideways, taking in my figure. Mrs. Shackleton's voice came through, correcting my posture. Even across the miles, she continued to lecture. She then told me I looked tired and should have eaten more breakfast.

At least here I had privacy. People knocked before entering a room—even if knocking was part of a prank.

I pushed aside the tapestry and entered the sunroom. The walls were a soft white with a pattern of faded pink flowers blooming on branches. Upon closer inspection I saw they had been hand-painted to cover the long cracks that grew from the floor to the ceiling. Despite the stonework façade, I had the notion a good wind could knock down Faraday House.

The sunroom was long enough to accommodate a chaise longue and a writing desk. Paper and a fresh pot of ink had been left on the desk with a nub of sealing wax. Guilt immediately set in as I pictured Hettie scouring the stone floor by hand.

I sat at the desk and opened the top drawer and was glad to find a quill in reasonably good condition.

Dearest Frederick,

I have only spent one night here, but the situation is much worse than I expected. Everything about Faraday House hints of tragedy and mysterious illnesses. No one can give me a straight answer about how the first wife died, and now the second is on her deathbed.

My own safety is at risk here. I am sure of it.

I will send this to the post on the mainland as soon as I can, but we are dependent on the tide. I will keep writing and sending you word. Captain Graves told me he has sent notice to Judge Shackleton that I arrived safely, but I do not believe him. In fact, I'm not sure I can trust anyone here.

Please, my darling, save me before it's too late.

Ever yours,
Emeline

I melted the nub of wax over a candle, sealing the letter, satisfied it would be enough to convince him to make haste. A heavy layer of fatigue set into my bones as I looked out the window to the grounds below. A dark, lumbering form stretched out on the grass. Moses.

A murmur echoed from the floor, sending a chill through my veins. I put a hand to my temple, trying to contain the throbbing pulse. I couldn't take any more unexplained noises. The murmurs continued, and I recognized the voices: it was Mr. and Mrs. Clayton.

Intrigued, I followed the sound until I discovered there was a grate in the floor behind the chaise longue.

I crouched with my ear close to the opening. Dishes clattered, followed by the sloshing of water. The sunroom must be directly over or at least close to the kitchen.

Mrs. Clayton swore as something thudded hollowly. "You better hope she stays quiet."

Mr. Clayton replied, soft and apologetic, "I'm sure she won't say a word. She wasn't hurt, more embarrassed than anything."

"Can you imagine how upset the captain would be if he found out you let her walk into one of those old death traps?"

"I'd tell him the only reason she went on the walk was because the reverend suggested it."

"Think that'd be enough to save your skin?" she huffed. Then Mrs. Clayton dropped her voice. "We know better than anyone how dangerous the captain's temper can be. If that silly girl had half a brain, she'd be gettin' off this island as fast as she could."

Silence.

After a moment came the sound of a heavy knife chopping, its blade thudding in a troubled tempo. Mrs. Clayton sobbed then caught herself. "Sometimes I wonder if we're better off leaving this cursed place before it claims us too." Her words were thick with tears, but there was an underlying challenge as well, almost a threat.

"We've got nowhere else to go," Mr. Clayton tried to soothe. "Remember how good it was when it was only the two of us? Captain Graves isn't a well man; you said so yourself. All we have to do is wait. I promise it will be worth it."

The tension in the room changed. I leaned closer with my ears trained for the next part.

"Story of my life, Bagnall," Mrs. Clayton scoffed. "Maybe I'm tired of waiting for your promises to come to fruition. Did you ever think of that? Maybe it's time I start taking control for a change."

"What are you saying?"

"Any fool who comes to this miserable rock gets what they deserve."

There was the sound of feet stomping away, then a heavy door slammed. The argument was over.

I returned to my bedroom, exhausted from all the secrets in this house. I was disappointed Mr. Clayton may not be the kind soul I thought he was. I lay on the bed, feeling the energy slip away from my bones. I could think of nothing but napping.

I took several quilts and covered up, grateful for the escape of sleep.

I made a list of tasks: find a way to the beach so I can regularly check for Frederick's ship, learn more about Georgina's illness so I can keep her alive, and last, determine what exactly was in the bottle Mrs. Clayton had given me.

I closed my eyes.

The last thing I heard was footsteps above me. Someone was pacing.

CHAPTER THIRTEEN

I knew I was dreaming, but the scene unfolded as if in real time. Georgina was lying in bed, sleeping. A strip of cloth had been tied around her wrist. The fabric trailed over the quilt, with the other end secured to the bedpost.

Mrs. Clayton was at the writing desk, cursing under her breath, trying to open the top drawer. She stopped abruptly and tucked a small knife into her apron pocket.

Reverend Pellerine entered and handed her a silver flask. He watched with a bored expression as she decanted its contents into the tall clear bottle with the cross emblem. When she returned his flask, he nodded and took the chair beside the bed. He opened the Bible and began to read to Georgina, but as soon as Mrs. Clayton left the room, he closed it. A look of anguished defeat darkened his features.

The scene blurred.

A gentle tapping started on my forehead. Each drop heavier than the last.

I was lying flat on the bed with the quilts kicked off. I took a few breaths, trying to understand where I was. The disorientation was unrelenting.

My room came into focus, dim and full of late-afternoon shadows. I must have slept for hours.

Another drip hit my forehead.

Above me, the ceiling had a monstrous rust-colored stain. The drip fell again. I screamed as I rolled out of bed, tumbling to the floor. The next drip splattered on the white pillow. I slowly backed away, then caught my reflection in the vanity mirror. My forehead was covered in the same dark liquid.

Whatever was dripping on me was coming from the room above. The tower. I gritted my teeth, remembering Hettie's face in the window. She must be up there now, playing at some kind of sick hoax.

I tugged the tapestry across and marched into the sunroom. I had been so keen on writing Frederick's letter I had forgotten to search for the door to the tower.

It took me a few moments to locate the entrance as it had been camouflaged. It was painted the same as the walls, even with pink flowers added to make it blend. If I hadn't known it was there, I wouldn't have seen it. A nameless dread settled over me. Why was it purposely hidden?

Barking came from outside. I went to the window over the desk and saw Moses looking up at me. He gave a few giant barks, then started pacing back and forth. It was as if he was trying to convey a message.

If he was up here, he'd be able to sniff out Hettie. With the fear subsiding, anger took its place. I'd had enough of her misplaced jealousy.

I went to the door and gripped the knob. It turned easily in my hand, but the door wouldn't budge. "Open up, Hettie!" I called out, slapping my palm on the wood. "I know you're up there. I'm wise to your tricks!"

Nothing. I kicked at the door. "Open up!" My voice rose, grating my throat, but I didn't care. I kicked the door again, painfully stubbing my toe. A curse flew from my lips.

"Miss Fitzpatrick?" Reverend Pellerine's voice came from the hallway.

I left the sunroom and opened my bedroom door. Lines of concern furrowed his brow. He asked, "Can I be of assistance?"

"Do you have a key to the widow's walk?" I lifted my sore foot, putting the weight on my heel.

"The what?"

Frustration made my words spill out quickly. "I need to access the tower room. Something is dripping down through the floor onto my bed, and it's horrible."

He looked alarmed, but his tone was calm. "Show me."

Relief poured through my veins. I took him into my room, explaining more of the details. Then I froze midstep. The ceiling was completely blank. No sign of the stain remained. "That's impossible," I whispered. I went to my bed, and the pillow was pristine as well; only a few of my blond hairs were there.

Hettie came to the doorway. "I heard my name," she said. "What's going on?" Her voice rang out sweetly soft, her face open, the perfect vision of innocence.

I frowned, trying to understand how she'd slipped out of the tower room. There must be another entrance. She'd even told me herself the house was queer and had many secret rooms.

I pointed a finger at her smug face. "I know what you're trying to do," I said. "You've been sneaking up to the tower room, trying to scare me."

Hettie's jaw dropped. She was a very good actress. I reasoned she was prepared for this accusation and had rehearsed her reaction. "That makes no sense, miss. Why would I do that?"

"Why indeed." I hit her with a pointed stare.

Hettie didn't back down, but instead kept her stance.

Reverend Pellerine cleared his throat. He motioned to the bed with the quilts messed up. "You stated you woke from a nap. Perhaps you were dreaming?" he offered. I chose to keep my bizarre dream about Mrs. Clayton and Georgina to myself. The fact his flask was part of it was slightly embarrassing. I couldn't have the reverend know I was dreaming about him.

"I felt the drips," I said. "I saw the stain." I pointed to my forehead. "See? It left dirt on my face." I said "dirt," but I was quite certain it was supposed to be blood.

Reverend Pellerine and Hettie exchanged uneasy glances. I went to the mirror and checked my reflection. My eyes widened in alarm. My face was perfectly clean. I wished for the floor to open and swallow me. Why had I called out? I must sound positively crazy. I had to rectify this mess. Captain Graves had already relayed his belief in being cursed with tragically dying wives. If he suspected I was mentally unstable, there would be no hesitation to send me packing. I'd be at the convent before sundown. But there was no denying what I'd seen was real. I had to prove I wasn't hallucinating.

I turned back to them. "Captain Graves said I should have access to the entire house if I'm to be its mistress. I would like the key to the tower, please, so I may inspect it for myself."

Both were quiet, then Reverend Pellerine turned to Hettie. "Can you please get the key for the tower room?"

Hettie glanced up at him from under her lashes. "I would be more than happy to accommodate Captain Graves's wishes, but you don't need a key to get to the widow's walk. There's no lock on the door."

Reverend Pellerine looked at me for an explanation, but I had none. The doorknob had turned easily in my hand, yet the door refused to budge.

"It's probably swollen shut from the weather," he offered.

Hettie chimed in. "Rusted hinges too, no doubt. No one's been up there for ages."

I tilted my head at her, surprised at her blatant lie. "I saw you in the window this morning when I was coming back from my walk."

A new level of worry crept into her expression. "It wasn't me," she replied. "I was helping Mrs. Clayton in the kitchen since breakfast, then I was in Mrs. Graves's room." She looked at Reverend Pellerine and said, "I passed you on the stairs as you were bringing the holy water, remember, Reverend?"

He crossed his arms and put a finger to his lower lip as he considered this. He said to me, "You slept through lunch. An empty stomach and staying in a strange house may have contributed to this . . . misunderstanding." There was a curious hitch to his voice. Almost like a warning.

My stance melted. "I would still like to have access to the room," I said, with less conviction.

"Mr. Clayton is most likely able to help with that." Hettie smiled. "Not that you're not strong enough, Reverend, but he'll have a set of tools that will do the job proper. Heaven knows a young woman like myself wouldn't be able to do it on my own."

It was a blatant attempt to showcase how illogical my argument was. If Mr. Clayton was needed to open the door, then how could Hettie have opened it herself that morning?

She stood in place, triumphant. I could feel her itching for Reverend Pellerine to walk down the hallway with her so they could discuss me and dissect all my faults. She must have been overjoyed.

Reverend Pellerine replied, "That's a sensible suggestion. Let him know at once. And afterward, please bring up a plate for Miss Fitzpatrick. Thank you, Hettie."

She smiled, but only with her lips; the rest of her face was hard as stone. Her footfalls stomped down the stairs.

Reverend Pellerine took a step closer and leaned down to my height. "Faraday House is not a place you want to have complete access to. Please trust me on this."

"And yet you sent me off on my own to explore the island to-day." I wondered what he would say if he knew I'd nearly fallen to my death.

Concern lined his face. "Did something happen?"

"No," I answered quickly, shy all of a sudden. I wondered if he shared Mrs. Clayton's view of restless spirits lurking the hallways. I remembered the dream I had with her decanting water from his flask. Hettie said it was holy water, but I had seen him pour it directly from the water pitcher at breakfast.

How could I trust him?

He then said, "Captain Graves told me you'll be sitting with Georgina."

My stomach dropped. He had only discussed it with Mrs. Clayton, not me. But how could I refuse? "If he wants me to sit with her, I'd be happy to."

He gave me a sideways glance. There was a curl at the corner of his mouth like he was fighting off a grin. "It's perfectly under-standable to not want to sit with her. It's difficult to watch some-one waste away, especially if that someone holds the position you will inherit. I'd lie if I were in your position as well."

"You're accusing me of lying?"

He shrugged. "This morning at breakfast, when you said it felt as if you already knew Georgina, even though you hadn't met her yet, your left eyebrow twitched."

"And?"

"And it moved again when you spoke of how you'd be happy to take a shift by her bedside."

"I have a twitchy eyebrow, that's all. You're giving a considerable amount of credit to your own opinion, aren't you? Are all men of God so convinced of their powers?" The insult flowed from my lips as if I'd been planning this confrontation for ages. I was eager for what comeback he'd compose.

He reached into his pocket. "When I sat with Georgina this afternoon, she spoke of an angel visiting her last night."

I concentrated on keeping my eyebrow perfectly still.

"She whispered to me that she had proof, then she gave me this." He opened his palm and my hair ribbon uncoiled from his hand, dangling from his finger like an accusing pendulum.

I swallowed.

"That could easily be Hettie's or even Georgina's own ribbon . . ." My voice faded as he went to the vanity and pointed to the matching ribbon.

"May I?" he asked.

I nodded, then looked down at my shoes, truly sorry. I could only imagine the penance he was considering bestowing upon a sinner like me. Ha! He had no idea.

"I'm not proficient in hair adornments, Miss Fitzpatrick, but I think you would agree these are a match." He held them together for a moment, the evidence I could not refute. Then he gently laid them back down. There was a curious fluttering in my stomach as I watched him touch my personal things. His hand paused when he saw the tiny green bottle.

I groaned inwardly; it was getting worse. "Before you accuse me of stealing as well," I started, "Mrs. Clayton gave me that bottle last night. You can ask her." With a regretful sigh, I explained how I'd only gone in to help Georgina with a glass of water, and that I was afraid Mrs. Clayton would tell Captain Graves I'd disturbed Georgina when he'd specifically forbidden it.

Reverend Pellerine stayed quiet the whole time, his eyes never leaving mine. There was a curious pull, and I found the words slipped out effortlessly. "I'm sorry she was deceived," I concluded. "That was not my intention."

He gave me half a smile. "Good intentions, for whatever reason, tend to elicit the opposite result of the desired outcome. But it gave her comfort, and it wasn't done in malice. There's nothing for you to regret."

A lightness eased my heartache. He hadn't given a formal forgiveness, for there was nothing to forgive; it was more the fact that he understood my reasons.

He pointed at the small green bottle on the vanity. "She gave you holy water," he said.

I remembered how fierce she was with her warning last night. Now, though, her reaction almost seemed laughable. "She told me to carry it with me at all times." I tried to keep my expression neutral. Was it the same suspect holy water I had seen him decant from the water pitcher?

He let out a tired sigh, and I sensed we shared an opinion about her. I was reminded of his similar reaction this morning, after Hettie had left us in the dining room. Except then, his sigh was one of relief. I wondered again why he'd dropped the cup on purpose. I replayed the scene; it had happened directly after her patronizing comment to me. My face had grown hot under her embarrassing ridicule. Was it possible Reverend Pellerine had done it to deflect Hettie's attention away from me? A quiet, gallant gesture that was so subtle and refined only he and I were aware of it?

Whether or not he was doling out fake holy water, I decided he might be someone who could help me. I told him what I'd overheard between Mrs. Clayton and the captain. "She believes Georgina is suffering from possession, and she is trying to convince Captain Graves of the same. I wonder if she's not doing everything she can medically for Georgina."

If Mrs. Clayton was using holy water as the only treatment, Georgina was going to be in her shallow grave before long and I'd be at the altar. *I must do all I can to keep her alive.*

Reverend Pellerine didn't reply.

I prompted, "Surely any opinion from you on the matter would set her straight." I paused. "Or do you also believe evil walks the hallways?"

He answered without hesitating. "I believe in the evil of man, not spirits."

I could not have been more surprised. Mrs. Shackleton regularly spouted that God was responsible for everything, good and bad. All controlling, as if God had time to spend on every single person.

I was intrigued by this unexpected insight he seemed to be offering. I asked, "Do you know what's killing her? They say her mind is affected, but no one says what kind of disease it is." I thought he would be the right person to ask, to help me finally learn the truth. We weren't exactly allies, but we weren't enemies either.

He steadily replied, "I believe her symptoms are more to do with an organic condition and not some spiritual interference. But I'm glad you'll be able to sit with her. Mrs. Clayton is no substitute for Nurse Gibson."

He went to the door, but stopped for one last comment. "If you happen to think you see something suspicious again and are uncertain, tell me."

It sounded like a reprimand. A disappointing weight pushed away the small amount of mutual understanding I thought we had managed to conjure. I glanced at the ceiling; it seemed to mock me. "One last thing, Reverend."

He turned to me.

"When I told you about the ceiling, did my eyebrow twitch?"

"No," he said, but there was no celebration in his tone. "I believe you're telling the truth. And that's most worrying."

"Why is that?"

"When Georgina first moved to Faraday, she stayed in these rooms, but only for a few weeks."

As I spoke, my voice quivered slightly. "Naturally, she switched to the larger bedroom, the one across from the captain."

He gave a quick shake of his head. "She asked to be moved. As far as I know, she never gave a reason, but soon after that, she started getting sick." His eyes latched onto mine for a lingering moment, then he nodded briskly and shut the door behind him, leaving me in the room with only the gloom and mystery keeping me company.

No longer was he speaking of residual dreams as an explanation for what I saw. He was warning me.

CHAPTER FOURTEEN

E ven though I was hesitant to visit Georgina for fear of her recognizing me from last night, I was in no position to refuse a request from Captain Graves, and I was invested in keeping her alive, so whatever I could learn about her mysterious illness was my priority. I was hardly a medical expert; however, I knew I could do more for Georgina than treating her with holy water and reading from the Bible.

There was also the matter of the strange dream and the vision of the stain on my ceiling. The warning from Mrs. Clayton and her belief in possession must have contributed to my "vision" as I slept. And perhaps, as Reverend Pellerine had suggested, I was still groggy from the nap.

I continued to tell myself these things as I made my way down the hallway, past the large round window, and then finally to outside Georgina's room.

With a shaking hand, I knocked gently on the partially opened door and stepped inside. The curtains were pulled back, but the weak afternoon light only marginally improved the mood of the room. The heavy sense of impending death hadn't dissipated.

Georgina was sitting up in bed, supported with a lofty pile of pillows. Her eyes were closed, with her hands folded on top of the covers.

A sense of ease released a small amount of tension between my shoulder blades. She was not restrained; at least that was different from my dream.

I snuck a peek at the medicine table. The tall bottle with the cross emblem and a tiny blue vial were lined up. Beside them was a serving tray with a green teapot.

Mrs. Clayton sat on a settee by the far window. A pile of laundry was folded beside her. She stood and came toward me. An expression of irritation flitted across her plump face before a hardness took its place. I could almost see the anger behind her thoughts. My insides tightened, preparing for battle.

"I know who sent you and why," she said. "I don't rightly agree, but he's the head of the household." She crossed her thick arms over her chest. "What kind of medical experience do you have?" she asked.

What a ridiculous question. I couldn't even take care of myself. "Only my stint as a surgeon during the war," I replied.

She was not amused.

I couldn't stand the feeling of meeting her gaze, so I stared at her chin instead. Mrs. Clayton seemed like the kind of beast that would strike when you're not paying attention. I knew how horrible my presence in Georgina's death chamber must appear.

"I'll make sure she's safe," I finally answered.

She scoffed then rolled down her sleeves, buttoning the cuffs. "I'm going for a quick bite of supper and a rest, but I'll return before the sun goes down. If you need anything, Hettie is one door down at the end of the hall." She grabbed the green teapot.

"Her bedroom is beside Captain Graves's?" That struck me as peculiar.

"She was hired as Mrs. Graves's personal maid; of course she'd sleep close by."

I nodded and stepped out of her way. My eyes slid to the tray of bottles.

That small gesture did not go unnoticed. Mrs. Clayton glared. "Don't give her any medicine either. Her dosing is strictly up to me." Then she plucked the tiny blue bottle from the table and slipped it into her apron pocket.

"Is she allowed water?" I asked. I couldn't help it. We both knew Mrs. Clayton had left her all alone last night.

She looked like she wanted to reply, but she kept her mouth rigid and disappeared into the hallway.

I had been ambitious earlier, but now I couldn't remember any of the bravery I'd displayed when I called Hettie's bluff—an act that didn't end up working in my favor, unfortunately.

Doubt slipped in.

What if Georgina woke and thought I was the angel again? What would I say to her? I should have an answer at the ready; I couldn't hide in the armoire again. Should I say I'm an angel and play along with her delusion? I didn't want to upset her, but I didn't want her to let go of her last grasp on life. I needed her to stay alive!

Panic squeezed my chest. My only hope was that she had already forgotten about last night. Just as she had forgotten she'd spoken to Reverend Pellerine. I remembered how insistent she was with Mrs. Clayton. What did she need to tell him that was so important? She was quite adamant.

I hadn't moved and was still standing in the doorway. It seemed painful to go any closer, but I knew I couldn't pretend to be a statue, waiting for Mrs. Clayton to return. I tentatively took a few steps toward the bed.

Fresh fear rose up within me.

Wound around the bedpost was the strip of fabric I'd seen in my dream that had been used to restrain Georgina.

My thoughts became frazzled, and I was overcome by the sensation of the floor moving beneath my feet. Worse than being found standing in the doorway would be for Mrs. Clayton to discover me having fainted on the pink carpet. I had to pull myself together. I pressed my thumbnail into the soft pad of my pointer finger as I took deep breaths.

I must have seen the fabric last night and didn't consciously remember.

I had almost convinced myself when I spied the small writing desk between the two windows. An eerie warning started to sound in my mind as I eyed the top drawer keyhole suspiciously.

My shaking hands gripped the pull handles and gave a yank, but the drawer stayed shut. It was locked. Whatever was in there, Mrs. Clayton was desperate to get, but more troublesome was the proof my dream may have been real.

Nothing made sense at Faraday House.

Evil walks the hallways. I shook off Mrs. Clayton's warning. All I had to do was last long enough for Frederick's ship to arrive.

I crept to the window closest to Georgina's bed, making sure to be extra quiet. I decided to let her sleep as my head began to throb.

On the bedside table there was a small teacup. I peeked inside and saw a few mouthfuls remained. I crinkled my nose at the earthy and pungent smell. No wonder it wasn't finished.

Outside, gray clouds moved across the sky, bloated with the threat of a cold rainfall.

Picture sunny and bright Bermuda, I kept telling myself. But my daydream was not strong enough to penetrate the dark clouds hanging over Faraday. Even my imagination wasn't allowing me to escape.

I stared at Georgina, counting her breaths, thankful for each one as she was the only thing preventing Captain Graves from putting a ring on my finger—in addition, I cared not to think about the reaction of the others if she were to die on my watch.

Georgina barely resembled the young woman in the portrait downstairs. What was killing her so quickly? Was there any way to stall its progress?

I thought of the beautiful mural she painted in the study. I looked around the room, but there wasn't any of her work on the walls. Curious for someone whom Captain Graves said was always creating art. Not even a sketch was in sight.

In fact, there was hardly anything to hint at who she was. What were her dreams, her ambitions? And what did she desperately need to tell Reverend Pellerine when she was convinced she was dying that very moment?

What do most people want to say to a reverend when they're close to dying? It suddenly came to me. A confession.

What secret guilt did she have? Was it related to her illness?

The gears in my mind started turning. I noticed the doll again, propped on its own chair. The dress was handmade, with expert stitching, but the fabric was faded and frayed at the hem. Her hair hung loose as all the curl had been brushed out years ago. A parasol rested over her shoulder with one hand tucked inside the looped handle to keep it in place. Both boots were missing, so her feet had been painted black instead.

I could tell the ill repairs were not the result of aloof disinterest but were instead proof of it being a much-loved toy. She must have had it since she was a young girl. Had she been hoping to pass it down to the child she never had? Had she been hoping for a legacy as well?

I picked up the doll. Behind me there was the rustling of sheets.

I jumped, losing my grip. The doll fell to the floor with a dainty *clack*. Panicked, I scooped it up, trying to smooth out its skirt. Its unblinking eyes stared back accusingly.

There was a soft sigh.

Silently cursing my own clumsiness, I turned to face Georgina. She regarded me from under hooded lids, sleepy but curious. I held my breath, waiting for her to identify me from last night.

She gave me a curious frown. "Who are you?" she asked.

A small trickle of relief unclenched my jaw. Her expression held none of the desperation from when she'd clung to me last night. There was no sign of recognition.

I finally found my voice. "I'm Emeline. Captain Graves is an acquaintance of my guardians," I said haltingly. "They arranged this visit."

Confusion clouded her pale features as if trying to arrange my words in her mind. Then her attention landed on the doll in my arms. A weak smile made her look almost childlike as she reached for it.

Feeling like the most villainous charlatan, I gave it to her. Then I bent down and picked up the parasol. My heart sank when I saw it was in two pieces. "I'm sorry," I told her. "I was admiring the doll, and this dropped from her grip." I tried to explain my mistake as something the doll had been responsible for. I never anticipated reaching new lows such as this.

"Martha is old," she said, her voice soft and weak. "I never wanted her out of my sight, so I made sure to do all the fixing myself."

That explained the painted feet.

And when I studied it closer, I saw the handle of the parasol was an old key. I managed to fluff open the canopy. "I'm sorry," I repeated, and handed it over as well. Georgina gently rested it back in place, over the doll's shoulder.

The silenced lingered. An uncomfortable heat rose up my neck. I was unsure how I could tactfully ask about her illness without sounding insincere. I needed to establish some kind of rapport. My gaze went to the teacup. "Would you like more tea?" I asked. I needed to be of some use—anything to give my presence in her room meaning.

"No, thank you." She lowered her voice even though it was already a whisper. "It's bitter, but Mrs. Clayton says it's what my body needs."

"I see." I wondered why a dying woman would be denied a bit of sugar to sweeten the steeped drink.

She cradled the doll in the crook of her arm. "I'm unsure of most things lately, but I know it makes me sleepy, so I suppose it works somewhat."

"I'm sorry it's unpalatable. Maybe I can get you something else? Porridge and cream? Raisin toast? A cup of cocoa?"

"I've never met anyone so apologetic." She chuckled, then winced, putting a hand to her stomach. "I haven't been able to tolerate solid food for . . . I'm not sure how long it's been." She smiled weakly. "Visitors are a nice distraction, though."

"What of your family?" I asked her. "Don't they visit?"

Her eyes become wistful. "My father died two years ago."

She was truly alone.

I had no reply. She was brave, and I was the coward using the pretense of a convalescent visit to covertly gain information that would benefit my own circumstances. I perched on the edge of the chair, my hands clasped tightly in my lap. The beat of my pulse was like a clock ticking down the time she had left before she died in this room. Coming here was a horrible idea. Mrs. Clayton was right. I shouldn't be here, it was all wrong for all sorts of reasons, not the least of which was that it was blatantly disrespectful.

Georgina looked at me expectantly. I thought madly for something to say.

"I . . . I've discovered you're an artist," I stammered, grasping for a conversational topic that would be appropriate to discuss with your fiancé's dying wife. "The schooner painting in the hallway. It's so lifelike I was almost seasick." I laughed shakily at the end.

I glanced at the door wondering how long it would be before Mrs. Clayton returned. The only thing worse would be for Hettie to be listening from the hall, rolling her eyes at my feeble attempt at conversation.

She squinted at me. "You look familiar."

The lie came out swiftly. "Impossible. We've never met." My words were sharp and not at all natural. I smiled to try and soften my answer, but it felt like I was showing too many teeth.

She continued to stare at me from her deathbed with those large eyes. I thought I saw a flash of accusation. The silence hung in the air between us, threatening to allow all the secrets to be heard.

I cleared my throat. "I also saw your mural. It's so realistic and beautiful. I especially appreciate the detail and how you have the house reflected in the pond."

"When did you arrive?" she prompted again.

"Very recently." I put on an exaggerated expression of curiosity. "Does the pond freeze over in the winter? I wonder how the fish survive. Have you skated on it? I can't skate. I never learned. Halifax Harbour is full of schooners, and Mrs. Shackleton thought that with my family's terrible bad luck it was wise to avoid any invitation to deadly disaster." I took a gasping breath and realized I had been rambling.

Her dainty eyebrows came together. "Who is Mrs. Shackleton? Your mother?"

"No," I answered. "She's my guardian."

"Oh." Her mouth stayed in a perfect O shape as her eyes reflected a sympathetic understanding. "And was it your family's terrible luck that took your dear parents from you?" She leaned forward, eyes sharper, but her focus wasn't one of suspicion, it was of thoughtful concern.

Her conclusion took me by surprise. She was the only person since I had arrived at Faraday House who had asked why I had guardians instead of parents. Even if the reason was obvious, no one, not even Reverend Pellerine, had asked me about them.

She continued to look at me expectantly, frail and cradling her small doll. I found it impossible to deny her simple request. Even though I had heard the details relayed many times, I hadn't told the story of my parents' deaths very often.

"Yes," I said. "The most tragic kind of terrible luck, in fact." I then told her of how Father died when a slab of ice slipped off the tavern roof and struck him on the head as he walked home.

Relaying this to Georgina had a relaxing effect. I hadn't a confidant; even my friend Jane was kept at arm's length by Mrs. Shackleton and her belief in competition. I'd never had a close friend. Ada was probably the only person who came near to meeting the description. I found myself taking no shortcuts, describing the whole awful time afterward when Mother was so depressed she could not get out of bed.

I continued, "Then Mother and I were taken in by her childhood friend, Mrs. Shackleton, and her husband, the judge. You see, my father owed a lot of bills." I put a finger to my chin. Mrs. Shackleton had always said that, but I'd never questioned it. "Then the following month Mother choked to death on a cup of tea."

Georgina put a thin hand to her chest. Her eyes were wide with shocked concern. "So quickly after the other."

"It's all the sadder because she never particularly liked tea, only the cookies that went with it." I had added that last line when I told Frederick. It made him laugh and prevented any further questions.

But Georgina tilted her head and watched me for a moment before replying. "Terrible luck indeed," she said. "Death arrives in many guises, doesn't it? Even teacups." There was an acceptance in her tone, and I sensed she was hinting at her own situation.

If I gained her trust, she might be willing to share what she knew about her own illness . . . and Faraday House itself. I had to tell her the complete story, the true version only the judge and I knew. My lower lip quivered, for I had never said this out loud to anyone. "She actually choked on what was inside the teacup. A shilling, which I had hidden there," I finally confessed. I paused as a fresh blanket of guilt engulfed me, pulling down my shoulders and filling my ears and mouth and nose, deadening all my senses. It was my action that had killed her, and I would always live with that burden. I often wondered how different my life would be if I had chosen another hiding place.

Then I explained about the secret game Judge Shackleton and I had created. "Only he and I know the truth . . . and now you." I held my breath, waiting for her reply. Although she was a stranger, I didn't want her to think ill of me. Selfishly, I wanted her pity.

Georgina reached out her hand and offered it, palm up. I took it in my own, noting how cold it was. "Thank you for sharing that with me." She gave my hand a small squeeze before releasing her grip. "I will keep your secret. We're both orphans, after all."

A comfortable silence settled between us, and with it an unexpected sense of camaraderie. She must have felt it too because she began to talk about painting. The topic put a little color in her sallow complexion. When she first arrived at Faraday, she wanted to paint the house from all different angles and in every season.

"Edgar encouraged it," she said. "He'd take all my supplies and set them up wherever I wanted to paint."

I easily imagined her sitting at an easel by the pond, her brown hair shining in the sun, dabbing her brush in a swirl of colors. I remembered how Captain Graves spoke of those early days and knew her bright paintings would have breathed a much-needed life into the house.

I motioned to her bare walls. "Where are your other paintings?"

Her forehead crinkled. "I don't know," she said with a lack of confidence. "I can't remember if I stored them away or destroyed them. I'm my own worst critic." Her mouth turned downward. "When I became sick, I couldn't go outside any longer. I mostly worked from the sunroom."

"Did you paint the pink flowers on the wall?" I asked.

Her breath stopped for a moment. She hit me with a pointed gaze; all gentleness had been swept to the side. Invisible spiders crawled up my arms.

"You've been in the front rooms?" she whispered.

"That's where I'm staying," I confirmed cautiously. Reverend Pellerine told me those used to be her rooms . . . before she requested to be moved. His warning echoed back to me.

If you happen to think you see something suspicious again and are uncertain, tell me.

I had the feeling we were playing a game, a bizarre dance neither of us wanted to acknowledge. I gripped the armrests of the chair and leaned forward; she was going to tell me the truth that everyone else deferred.

Her expression became pained. She looked down at the doll and pressed her lips together as if fighting whether to continue or not.

"The ceiling?" I prompted her.

Her gaze snapped to me as she grabbed my arm. "It's blood,"

she whispered harshly. "Her blood." Her strength surprised me, nearly yanking me out of the chair as she pulled.

I let out a startled cry.

"What's this, then, Mrs. Graves?" Hettie stood in the hallway, holding a serving tray with a teapot, taking in the scene. She came into the room, eyeing the piece of cloth tied to the bedpost.

Georgina let go of my arm and collapsed into her pillows. She murmured, "So much pain."

I was stunned at how quickly her mood had changed. I said to Hettie, "Get Mrs. Clayton. She has the medication."

"Not to worry, Mrs. Graves," Hettie said, calmly coming into the room, completely ignoring my request. She placed the tray at the foot of the bed and poured a fresh cup of tea from the same green teapot Mrs. Clayton had taken away.

Georgina tried to shrink away from her.

"Here." Hettie stood on the other side of the bed and brought the cup to Georgina's lips. "Mrs. Clayton put an extra dose in the pot. Take a quick sip, now. There, perfect. One more, then you can rest."

Hettie kept the cup in place until Georgina had swallowed several times. When she was finished, her face twisted into a grimace.

Hettie produced a clean cloth and dabbed Georgina's chin, then she reached for her wrist. Her eyes widened as she felt her pulse. "Gracious, Mrs. Graves," she said. "Your heart is racing." Hettie sent me a reprimanding glare across the bed. "Your visitors are supposed to bring you comfort. I'll make sure the captain is aware."

I winced, knowing full well I had brought this on.

Georgina coughed, making the cup fall off the bed and onto the floor. Hettie shot me another look, as if I were responsible for the mess. "Time for you to go," she said.

I stepped over the overturned cup and saw the leftover dark tea pooling on the floor. Dark liquid. Just like the ceiling.

The room went blurry as I pictured my mother with her hands at her throat. Her wide eyes silently pleading with me. A broken teacup on the floor between us.

I headed straight for my room, still shaking from Georgina's episode. The red walls of the hall were closing in, swallowing me up. I shut my bedroom door and leaned against it as I caught my breath.

It's blood. Her blood.

How was it possible Georgina and I had had the same vision of the ceiling? Did that mean her present condition was related to her hallucinations? And if so, did that mean I was to suffer the same fate?

At Faraday House, the wives always die young.

I saw myself taking her place in the very bed she was now lying in—another young woman with a mysterious illness. A coldness enveloped me as I envisioned Hettie forcing bitter tea down my throat while Mr. Clayton dug my grave.

CHAPTER FIFTEEN

I was out of sorts as I changed into an evening dress for supper. It was dark blue velvet with gold trim and long sleeves. I reached for my black lace shawl, hoping there would be a nice fire in the dining room. Captain Graves had all this wealth but remained stingy with the firewood.

If I ran Faraday, there would be a glowing fire in each room all the time. What was the point of having nice dresses if I had to cover them up with shawls?

A knock at my door was followed by Mrs. Clayton's voice. "Supper, miss."

I marveled at how she was able to sound tired and oppositional in the same breath. "I'm about to head down," I said, opening the door. The sentence died on my lips when I saw she was holding a tray. The covered dish and small pitcher of wine meant I would be eating in my room.

Mrs. Clayton cast an amused look at my attire, then she cleared her throat and waited until I stepped aside before she brought in the tray and placed it on the bedside table. "The captain has turned in early this evening. I didn't think you'd want to eat by yourself at that long table." That was all she offered as explanation. The dining room had closed for the day, apparently. She stood with her hands clasped in front of her apron. "And Mrs. Graves has requested you visit her again tomorrow. She'll be presentable after breakfast."

"Oh." Remembering how our visit had ended, I felt trepidation slip under my skin. However, there was a spark of eagerness because I needed to talk to her again. She had also seen the stain on the ceiling, and other parts of our conversation had been warm and a rare bright spot for me at Faraday. "Of course I'll see her. Thank you."

Mrs. Clayton nodded and departed without another word. I blew out a grateful breath when she closed the door behind her.

I lit the candelabra and had my meal in the sunroom at the writing desk as I didn't have a proper table and chair for dining. On the other side of the window, the blackness of the night hid any signs of life. I hoped Frederick's ship was out there with its compass pointed to this forsaken island. An icy gust howled outside. It curled around the corner of the house, gaining access through every nook and crevice.

The food was a welcome distraction. I couldn't remember the last time I dined alone, and I was surprised to enjoy the experience immensely. There was no forced conversation or concern if you had sauce at the corner of your mouth. Again, I was impressed with the food: roast pheasant, boiled potatoes with sage, and cornmeal bread. I used the last piece of cornmeal bread to sop up the gravy, ignoring Mrs. Shackleton's criticisms in my mind.

Now that my stomach was full and my mind more focused, I made a mental list for the next day. I needed to ask Georgina again about the stain on the ceiling. It was troubling that we both had experienced the same vision. And I needed to find a way to mail Frederick's letter and gain access to the widow's walk so I could watch for his ship.

I moved across the sunroom and tried the doorknob again. It moved easily, but just like earlier, the door was stuck fast.

A heavy rain began, lashing the glass panes. I lit another candle, but it only amplified the strange surroundings, confirming I was indeed stuck on this island. More and more, Faraday felt like a prison.

The floorboards creaked above me. Then once more, but in another spot. I tipped back my head, tracing the movement on the ceiling. Back and forth the footsteps creaked, clear and natural, as if Mr. Clayton himself were up there pacing in front of the widow's walk.

But I knew no one was up there. Coldness rolled over my head and down my back. "Hello?" I croaked out, barely a whisper.

The pacing stopped.

At once the doorknob started rattling on its own.

Panic surged through me. My legs propelled me out of the room before I had made the conscious decision to move. With the candelabra in my grip, I made my way to the stairs. I only paused at the railing to catch my breath. A quick backward glance showed no one was chasing after me.

Below, a panel of light spilled through the open door of the music room, stretching across the flagstones. I heard voices, one soft and feminine, the other deeper and less talkative. I thought it was the Claytons until I heard Hettie laugh. It was amplified with exaggeration, and I knew Reverend Pellerine must be with her. I've flirted enough to recognize the embellished reaction.

Although it might feel awkward to be in their presence, my legs were still wobbly from fear. I suppressed a shiver and went down the stairs to join them. I was desperate to not be alone for another second.

Pausing outside the music room, I stood in the doorway a few seconds before they noticed me. Hettie was seated in the middle of the settee with a bundle of mending on her lap and a sewing basket at her feet. Reverend Pellerine's chair was on an angle with his legs outstretched and crossed at the ankles. He was in only his white shirt, with both sleeves rolled up enough to show his muscular forearms. If another man was in such a casual position, it would strike me as entitled or lazy, but the reverend had the ability to always appear confident and at ease. Most men I knew gained their confidence with fighting or status. I realized I preferred the quieter version.

A large pot of tea and plate of cookies were between them, with several candles providing the warm light. It was a cozy picture—for them. The pain under my ribs was not a welcome feeling. I must have been missing Frederick and wishing it were he and I enjoying this charming domestic moment. I tried to conjure an image of him relaxing in the chair, looking completely content to be with me, but I only saw him in uniform. The image of him I'd fabricated gave me a flash of a smile then disappeared from the scene.

"Oh? Evening, miss." Hettie's startled expression greeted me. "Need something?" Her hair was curled a bit more than usual, and I noticed her dress was freshly pressed. Despite the chill of the evening, she had forgone the use of a shawl.

"Are you all right?" Reverend Pellerine straightened in his chair. "You look pale," he said.

I took a few tentative steps into the shared glow of their space. I had run down here convinced something otherworldly was sharing my rooms, but I wasn't going to divulge that. It was obvious I had interrupted their personal time. "It's the storm," I simply said. "I can't sleep, and I wondered if a bit of tea might help."

Hettie's shoulders slouched in a quiet sigh. I disliked being the cause of extra work for her, but I needed an excuse to explain why I was wandering the house and not tucked in my bed. "As soon as I finish this, I'll make a pot and send it up." Her tone was polite but guarded.

"Unless you'd like to join us." Reverend Pellerine stood, never taking his eyes off me. He motioned to his own chair. His tone left no room to doubt the sincerity of his offer. My chest grew warm as I returned his gaze. It was a new sensation to receive attention without flirting.

The only sound was the rain battering the windows. Despite the awkwardness of my sudden appearance, I couldn't bear to return to my room yet.

"Yes, thank you." I took his place, adding my own candelabra to the candles on the table. I helped myself to a cookie. Across the room, the wedding portraits sat in the shadows. I had the strange sensation they were staring at us, murmuring to one another from their gold frames.

Hettie's attention returned to her mending, and I noticed it was Reverend Pellerine's vest. From the corner of my eye, I watched as he eased onto the other end of the settee.

Neither spoke until I took a bite. "Lovely shortbread," I said, trying to catch the crumbs in my hand.

Hettie moved the needle expertly, piercing the fabric then giving the thread a quick tug, all while her thumb kept the button in place. Still looking down, she asked me, "How are you finding Faraday?"

"Consuming." I took another bite.

The needle disappeared into the fabric again. She worked so fast I wondered how she never pricked herself. I imagined a bead of blood breaking through the skin.

One of the candles burned to the nub and flickered wildly before going out. Our shadows extended along the wooden floor and up the ash-gray walls, stretching into unrecognizable inhuman shapes.

She tutted like a grandmother brooding over a child who had scraped their knee. "No small wonder you're a bit out of sorts. This place leaves its mark on everyone. It has from the very beginning."

"Hettie." Reverend Pellerine's tone was warning.

She laughed. "I will not have you try and dissuade me. The night is perfect for ghost stories." She nudged my leg with the toe of her shoe. "Don't you like to feel the shivers?"

I took another bite of cookie. "I prefer the warmth of the sun."

Reverend Pellerine gave a shake of his head. "Ghosts only exist to people who believe in them," he answered.

Just like fake holy water, I wanted to reply.

Chuckling, Hettie wound the thread around the button a few times, then knotted it off. She gave the button a gentle pull to test her work, then deemed it was sufficiently mended. "All done," she said, handing the vest to Reverend Pellerine. "Every time you button up your vest, you'll think of me." She dropped the needle and thread into the sewing basket and poured herself more tea.

"Thank you." He kept the garment folded on his lap. "You didn't have to bother, but it's appreciated."

"Nonsense. I understand the simple pleasure of taking care of something yourself." She raised her mug. "Even making a good pot of tea."

Reverend Pellerine took a quiet sip.

I had already admitted I couldn't do needlepoint, draw, sing, or play any kind of instrument. I could only smile and look pretty. I thought of Martha, giving Georgina comfort. I felt more useless than a doll.

"You're lucky to be so industrious," I finally replied to no one in particular, having a conversation with my cookie.

Hettie perked up. She said, "My parents were much older than most when they had me, but my mother knew to teach me all the basics of having a good and honest life. She said it's important to be useful wherever your feet happen to be."

At that moment my feet were at Faraday, but I couldn't envision anything good or honest about staying here. The weight of her stare made me squirm. She couldn't deny the reverend's invitation for me to join them, but she could attempt to persuade me to leave them.

A surprising fire of defiance lit inside me. I masked it with the reasoning that Hettie might give me some information that could help keep Georgina alive. I also found it peculiar Reverend Pellerine was trying to discourage her from talking about the house.

"And how did you come to work at Faraday?" I asked, suddenly interested in her gossip.

Her eyes lit up. "My dearest cousin was going to have a baby and requested I come and be with her. On a clear day you can see the lights of Faraday from her house up on the hill. I was enthralled with the stories and stared out the window every night."

She laughed and looked at Reverend Pellerine as if they were enjoying a secret joke. "Remember the first time I came to church?"

"Of course."

The candlelight danced in her eyes. The confident satisfaction in her smile gave her an elegance no imported lace could compete against.

"And your cousin?" I prompted. "Doesn't she need you now?"

Hettie laughed. "Little Francis is a wonder and so healthy. When the time came that she didn't need me around so much, I found I wasn't ready to leave Shoreham yet." She took a dainty sip of tea, purposely injecting silence to give her last statement more weight. "Then Reverend Pellerine told me about Captain Graves and his new bride returning to Faraday and that they might need additional staff."

Reverend Pellerine had been staring at the candles. He flicked his gaze to her and smiled. I'm not sure if Hettie noticed, but I knew a pretend smile when I saw one. I had perfected mine over the years.

"I see," I said.

Hettie dropped her voice and continued in a sultry tone. "It has a dark history, but I don't believe places absorb the horror of their past." Then she laughed. "That doesn't mean Faraday isn't rife with spirits. Think of all the shipwrecks. Many a schooner went beneath the waves not far from here."

"Yes." I nodded, feeling a queer sense of agreement with Hettie. Being around the British Navy meant realizing there was no one more superstitious than a sailor. Except maybe Mrs. Clayton.

"Hauntings don't bother me, though," she said. "Ghosts don't even know they're dead. They wander around completing their daily tasks same as when they were alive." She took another sip of tea. "Sometimes, late at night, I've heard the sound of crying come from the cemetery."

"That's a bit too much on the nose, Hettie," Reverend Pellerine rebuked.

"Are you calling me a liar?" she playfully teased. Then she turned to me. "Don't you want to know the full history of the house you'll be running?"

It seemed foolish to deny her offer as there might be something that could help me with Georgina. I was calmed by Hettie's explanation of spirits. The dead sometimes wander around, not knowing they're dead. Such as pacing in front of the widow's walk, for instance? How could that hurt me?

Reverend Pellerine let out a bored sigh and ran a hand through his hair. I wondered if he realized how attractive that gesture was.

Hettie leaned closer. "Faraday House was built by a privateer name Lionel Baker. He had a reputation for being cutthroat on the high seas, and most people suspected he'd used stolen gold to finance the building costs. Regardless, only a few months after it was finished, tragedy struck. His young wife drowned when her little dory got dragged out to sea. Every few weeks, a bit of clothing or a shoe would be found among the rocks on the beach, confirming she'd been claimed by the ocean."

Her voice adopted a melancholy tone, but there was fascination in her eyes. "Lionel went mad with grief. He refused to let anyone on the island for decades. Finally, the magistrate came over with some militia as they thought he might have been rum-running. Instead, they discovered what he'd really been doing—digging deep holes all over the island. My cousin says everyone thinks he'd buried the last of his stolen Spanish gold but forgot where it was. The militia found him at the bottom of one of his pits. He'd cracked his leg in half and bled to death." She blew on her tea and took a long sip. "The mainlanders say Faraday will remain cursed until the last of the stolen treasure is found."

I stayed quiet. Even though I still didn't have explanations for the strange events I'd experienced so far, it was a large leap to accept that Esther and Georgina's ailments were the result of a long-lost treasure. However, it made what Mrs. Clayton said even more interesting. I began to wonder if Mr. Clayton hadn't boarded up all the holes because he'd been digging them himself.

Hettie yawned into the back of her hand. "Gracious, I need to retire. My day starts early."

Reverend Pellerine stood and slipped on his vest, but he left the buttons undone. I couldn't help wondering if he'd done so on purpose.

I rose as well and took up my candelabra.

"I'll walk you back," he said, taking a chamber candle for himself. "Good night, Hettie."

We quietly made our way to the foyer and then up the staircase. I was very much aware of how our shadows seemed to dance with each other up the steps. The grandfather clock on the landing told me it was a few hours until midnight.

He said, "Hettie has a flair for the dramatic. I hope this evening's discussion wasn't upsetting for you."

"I don't mind Hettie's talk of ghosts," I said. In truth, she had a refreshingly playful attitude toward them as being merely an echo from the past. Nevertheless, an unsettling feeling had attached itself to the back of my mind, purposely staying hidden.

"I meant about Faraday's history," he corrected. "That kind of story can be off-putting for a home that will eventually be yours."

We reached the second floor and continued toward my room. I saw the cobwebs in the corners and how there was always a lingering staleness in the air. The music room felt different tonight, though. I considered a new idea: the house wasn't scary, it was neglected. I said, "Maybe houses dislike being alone as much as people do. Faraday needs someone to love it, that's all."

"You speak as if it's a living thing to be admired."

I sensed an energy, but I wasn't going to tell him that. Instead, I replied, "There's a difference between being admired and being loved."

"How can you tell?" he asked curiously.

"It feels different."

"How?" he asked. He was determined to keep me talking, to know my opinions. A rare feeling of happiness eclipsed any of my remaining anxiety about the spirit in the tower room.

I replied, "Admiration stems from a place of jealousy, and is in the moment, short-lived." I pictured Mrs. Shackleton warning my beauty wouldn't last.

"And love?" he nudged. I stared straight ahead but kept him in my periphery. I knew he was watching me keenly because I could feel it. My palms became clammy. I had to readjust my grip on the candelabra.

An image of my parents surfaced. "Love is not envious," I said. "It comes from a place of wanting to share, to make someone else as happy as they make you. It never fades but intensifies with time." I was glad the candlelight kept my face in partial shadows, for my blush was so intense my ears burned. I kept forgetting he was a reverend—and that I was another man's fiancée.

We continued walking the same pace, our steps matching, then he said, "It is a great testament to the person you are if you've felt both loved and admired."

"Me? No, I was speaking about Faraday." I chuckled nervously and dared a sideways glance. A smile pulled at the edges of his lips— a true smile. My neck was warm enough to make a few curls cling to my skin.

I reprimanded myself for being foolish. He was only making conversation. I changed the subject. "I hope I wasn't a dull addition to your gathering," I said. "It was kind of you and Hettie to allow me to join you."

"Not at all," he said quietly. "And it wasn't a planned gathering. I was simply looking for a book to read. Hettie arrived with an offer to fix my button, and before I knew it there were tea and cookies out."

No doubt. I could hardly blame her.

When we reached my room, there was an uncomfortable awkwardness. I opened the door and paused at the entrance. Reverend Pellerine snuck a glance at the ceiling. As I recalled, he'd been dismissive of the ghost stories. Telling him about the pacing seemed silly and counterproductive.

"Thank you for walking me back," I said.

"Of course." His shoulder brushed the door frame. The candle-light played off the dark fringe of hair framing his warm brown gaze.

We stayed quietly pinned in place. I played with the notion of asking if he had ever felt the difference between love and admiration. I was certain most young ladies like Hettie doused him with waves of admiration every Sunday. But had he ever been in love? Experienced heartbreak? I pictured him standing behind the pulpit, preaching about the love and admiration of God.

"Sleep well," he said, giving me a slight bow of his chin.

I started, unaware of how long I'd been staring at him. The usual chill of Faraday replaced any warmth my daydream had created. "Yes, good night."

Then I thanked him once more and closed the door, fighting the urge to watch him saunter down the hall.

Long after he left, I lay awake, agitated until I convinced myself thinking of the reverend was a necessary respite to ease my nerves in this crumbling seaside estate. Once I had accepted this reasoning, I understood part of my restlessness was due to a sense of doom that had clung to me since hearing Hettie's stories. The rain tapered off to a fine mist, coating the window. I heard the waves crashing on the rocks at the base of the cliff. I envisioned the smashed dory from Hettie's story.

And that's when I grasped what was so bothersome. The new information about Faraday's history was troubling. The curse hadn't started with Esther, as Captain Graves believed. The fatal misfortunes that befell the women of this island were part of a recurring theme that went even further back. I wasn't bothered by the folklore aspect of the rumors, but the tragic drowning of the privateer's new bride made one fact undisputable: at Faraday House, the wives always die young.

CHAPTER SIXTEEN

The following morning, I breakfasted in the dining room by myself. Captain Graves was with Georgina while Reverend Pellerine was outside with Moses.

I sprinkled salt on my hard-boiled egg and mentally prepared myself to address certain topics for my visit with Georgina. She and I had both seen the stain on the ceiling, and I reasoned she would have better insight into her condition than anyone. I had to think of a way to ask without her reacting as before. But how could I tell her I was worried about the wives of Faraday curse without letting it slip I was next in line?

When I went to the second floor, I found her bedroom door closed. I pressed my ear against the wood, but there was only silence. Terror seized my heart. I pictured her still face and unbreathing corpse.

I knocked impatiently.

Footsteps came from the other side, slow but determined. Mrs. Clayton's tired face blinked back at me. "She's had a rough night," she said. "Come back this evening instead." Her gruffness was diminished greatly.

Relief eased through my veins. "I'll return this evening, then," I said, still shaky from the scare.

Without further explanation, she closed the door.

I returned to my room with plans to get dressed for a walk

outdoors and to see if I could find Reverend Pellerine to take Frederick's letter to the mainland.

I was reaching for my red cloak when a sudden *thump* sounded from the sunroom, nearly shaking the walls. I tentatively moved closer to the tapestry. I waited as the silence stretched thin. Then came a second, louder *thump*. That time I jumped. I heard the unmistakable sound of the doorknob being rattled.

My entire body went cold.

Someone was trying to get out of the tower room. Again.

All the unexplained moments came back to me with a terrifying certainty: the pacing, the face in the window, the stain on the ceiling. Whatever had been making the noises last night, whomever I had seen in the window, were they now in the sunroom?

It's blood. Her blood.

Another loud bang jolted my bones. It sounded like wood shattering. I put a hand over my mouth to hold in the scream. Hettie believed ghosts walked around completing tasks they normally did during their lifetime, but this sounded violent.

I glanced at my bedroom door, wanting nothing more than to run down the hallway. But where would I go? Each place in this house harbored the weight of impending death; not even the grounds were an escape.

I had to face this.

I had to find out who was behind this scheme to scare me. Shaking, I edged my way toward the sunroom. My fingers gripped the edge of the tapestry, and I steeled my nerves, trying to build up my courage. With my heart pounding a panicked rhythm against my ribs, I gripped the tapestry and whipped it aside.

"Oh!" I gasped. "It's you."

Mr. Clayton regarded me with a similar surprised expression.

He was in his work clothes, but the field jacket and cap were gone. He looked younger without them.

He stared back at me, holding a hammer and chisel. "Pardon me, Miss Fitzpatrick. I was told you were at breakfast." He looked sheepish. "I can come back and finish this later, if you like." There was a pile of shavings at his feet.

My heart eased back down my throat as I took in the scene.

He motioned to the door. "Hettie said it was sticking. No wonder—the wood swells with the dampness." He shifted his weight, then gave a quick nod.

He seemed nervous. The last time we were together he had plucked me from a certain death—an accident he'd been responsible for, actually.

"I'm glad you're here," I said. "I've been hoping to see the view from the tower, and I know I would be helpless if I had to use all these tools."

A relaxed grin graced his features, and he explained how he'd had to take the hinges off and then shave the edges of the door before it would open and close easily. "Still needs a bit more trimming."

"I don't mind," I told him. "Please continue. I'm anxious to see it for myself."

A strange flash of remorse slid across his face. "Are you looking for anything in particular?"

"No."

With a tug, he managed to open the door. A waft of cold air swept over us, carrying a staleness that reminded me of unboxing summer dresses after a long winter. He took the planer and moved it up and down the long edge of the door. Curls of wood floated to the pile at his feet.

"Do you have to do this to all the doorways?" I asked, thinking they'd eventually get so small they'd have to be replaced.

He opened and closed the door again, and this time there was little resistance. "Just a few," he answered. "But this one hasn't been opened for some time." I couldn't help but notice he left it closed.

Georgina said she might have put her paintings up there. Captain Graves mentioned she added a surprise to each one.

Mr. Clayton rummaged through the toolbox and took out a small hand broom and dustbin. I got a strange sense he was delaying my access to the tower.

A few secret rooms. It's a queer place to be sure.

I thought about the pacing and the stain on the ceiling. Someone had been up there, and I was about to find the evidence.

Crouching down, Mr. Clayton began to clean up the shavings. I had never seen anyone use a hand broom so methodically. I thought of all the dusty corners in the house and how odd that he paid so much attention to this spot.

I said, "Faraday is a big house. That's a lot of doors to fix. Which rooms are yours and Mrs. Clayton's?" I asked.

He rested on one knee and looked up at me. "We live in the cottage past the pond. It used to be the original owner's when the house was being built. It's not as grand as the house, mind you, but I prefer the coziness of a smaller place."

"And you've lived on the island for how long?"

His expression grew melancholy. "Nearly twelve years. In fact, the first time I set foot on this isle was the first time Esther saw it as well."

Even though the door was closed, a sliver of cold air escaped from the tower room.

Mr. Clayton rose and emptied the dustbin into a small pail beside his toolbox. "All done," he said. "Sorry for the inconvenience."

"Not at all," I replied, already at the door. It opened easily, revealing a spiral staircase. Whatever game Hettie was playing, I was going to find out.

With anticipation growing, I held on to the handrail and climbed the dusty steps. My stomach was in a million knots. I crept higher, craning my neck as the floor came into view.

I emerged into a circular area with curved edges and bare walls. The daylight spilled through the long window, painting a pattern on the plain wooden floor. Opposite to where I stood, an extension of about eight feet wide stretched across the upper story, nearly mimicking the length of my rooms below. But for all the space, there was no furniture. There were no paintings. There was nothing.

The air was much colder. I thought I could see my breath. Tentatively, I went to the window. Dust billowed at the bottom of my skirt. All was silent, but the space had an invisible energy. A tremor started at the base of my neck and stretched down to the bottom of my spine, like a spider stringing its web.

I stood in front of the window, eager for the glimpse of a ship, but like the floor, it too was covered with a layer of dust. I reached up and wiped away a circle with the sleeve of my dress. In my mind, Mrs. Shackleton scolded me for ruining the silk.

I took in the unblocked view with a sense of accomplishing a small victory. Whitecaps dotted the harbor and outward to the unending ocean. I stared at the horizon, willing the sails of Frederick's ship to appear.

"All right up there?" Mr. Clayton's voice interrupted my stupor. There was a tinge of urgency to his query. I wasn't sure how long I'd stayed there, squinting at the cold waves of the Atlantic rising and falling. It was strange he'd waited for me instead of leaving, or even coming up himself.

Mrs. Shackleton's voice answered, *That's what a gentleman does, instead of forgetting about you.*

I pressed my palm to the window as if trying to reach out to Frederick—like I had seen Hettie do the other morning. In fact, I was standing in the same spot she would have been.

The spider crawled up and down my spine now, sending a million shivers over my skin. I turned and studied the floor more closely. The wooden boards were thick with dust and undisturbed.

The only footprints were mine.

The room had been completely neglected and undisturbed for some time, just as Hettie had said. I hugged my elbows, feeling a sudden chill.

Mr. Clayton called out again.

Suppressing a shiver, I went to the top of the stairs and saw he had come up halfway, but no farther. The concern on his face was unexpected but appreciated.

He said, "It's much too chilly up there, Miss Fitzpatrick. Come down now, and be sure to hold on to the railing." Then he held out a hand from the bottom step in case I needed it.

"Thank you," I said, my shoes tapping on each step.

When I emerged into the sunroom, he closed the door and gave it a push, making sure it was latched. "Wouldn't want you to suffer a cold breeze," he explained.

A gentleman, for certain, I thought. And someone I could trust.

I retrieved my letter for Frederick from the writing desk and held it out to him. "Can I trouble you to post this the next time you go to mainland?"

He gave me another relaxed smile as he tucked the letter into his toolbox. "Certainly. Is tomorrow fine?"

I had to accept the delayed service; still I thanked him.

He nodded to the ceiling. "Did you find what you were looking for?"

"An uninterrupted view of the ocean," I said. "Yes, I will enjoy the view." I wrung my hands.

"So you'll go up again?"

Even though I was relieved to not be in the tower room any longer, it was also the only place I could watch for Frederick's ship. I pictured myself sitting by the window for as long as it took. "Of course," I replied.

He looked rather sheepish with one hand holding the small pail and the other in his pocket. The toolbox was at his feet. I noticed the various tools all had white handles. He acknowledged my focus and chuckled. "My eyesight ain't the best. I misplace more tools in the garden and my workshop than I'd like to admit. The white makes them easy to find."

"Very practical."

Mr. Clayton rolled back on his heels. I had a notion he was lingering for a reason. He nodded to the tower door. "Esther spent a lot of time in that room. She always wanted to make sure she knew when the captain would be returning."

Outside, the spruce trees swayed back and forth with the gusts off the ocean.

At the graveyard, he'd spoken of her with a genuine adoration. Intrigue prompted me to consider questioning him about Esther. There wasn't the risk of anger I experienced with Mrs. Clayton. And Georgina was so fragile that any prompting could upset her and negatively affect her already-compromised health.

Mr. Clayton was the safer option for information. I'd be foolish to ignore his leading statement. I had a notion Esther and Georgina might be suffering from similar afflictions, and he might be able to tell me something that would help me keep Georgina alive long enough for Frederick to arrive.

I smiled encouragingly. "It sounds like you knew her well."

He nodded, then his eyes filled with tears. He mumbled an apology and took his handkerchief and dabbed his eyes. "Don't mind me, Miss Fitzpatrick. It's better to talk about her than not." He gave me a quivering smile.

"Tell me about her," I said.

"She was unique; her mind worked overtime, more than regular folk, you know? She could sit at the piano and play for ages, making up songs as she went. Just lovely, really—you'd swear Beethoven was playing." He chuckled weakly. "She loved the grounds too, always came back to the house with a bunch of wildflowers or wishing stones from the beach." He looked out the window, seemingly lost in a memory.

I was hanging on his every word. Willing him to continue. "It's such a tragedy she became sick so quickly," I added. "Captain Graves said he arrived only in time to bury her."

Mr. Clayton's expression hardened. His blue eyes darkened like a warning. "He's the one who put her in that grave. He put pressure on her to have a family. A namesake for him." Mr. Clayton said the words as if they tasted sour. "It became her entire focus. As time went by and she still wasn't with child, things became salty between them.

"His trips became longer. Esther wandered the isle for hours, except this time she never brought back flowers or beach stones. She'd go out in any kind of weather, no coat, sometimes no boots. It scared me. I told her she needed to go to the mainland, even for a change of scenery, but she refused. I couldn't understand what she was doing with all that time."

Then slowly, she began to change.

When Mr. Clayton spoke again, his voice had a heavy, regretful tone. "I was worried about her, but back in those days we had small crops on the north side. Even though we had a few men from the mainland helping, it was long work, and by the end of the day I was exhausted. Still, I should have kept a closer eye on her."

He continued, "The missus tried all her special teas, but Esther seemed to slip further into herself." There was a curious hitch to next statement. "The isolation wasn't good. She should have left the island. I should have made her go, but she was determined to stay. I prayed the captain would convince her, but she only worsened each time he returned."

Once she even had a violent fit and locked herself in her room.

He let out a heavy sigh. "The last night he left for sea, they had a terrible argument. I heard it all the way downstairs." He paused and added in a different tone, "Mrs. Clayton and I used to have a set of rooms off the kitchen then. I don't know exactly what he said, but I heard enough to know he believed God had determined she wasn't fit to be a mother and that was the reason she hadn't been able to conceive."

"How horrid." I put a hand on my stomach.

"Exactly." He nodded. "They'd had their disagreements, of course—all married couples do."

I recalled overhearing his own argument with Mrs. Clayton.

He continued, "I sincerely hoped he would apologize before he left. She didn't see him off the next morning. That was something she always did, said it was bad luck not to. I guess she was too upset." Mr. Clayton looked out the window, staring at the trees, focused on something only he could see.

I understood her reasoning. "She wanted him to regret it the entire trip," I said. "Make him miserable with grief so he'd never treat her like that again." I blushed and cleared my throat. "At least that's what I imagine."

Uncertainty settled in his gaze. "I'm not sure how Captain Graves spent his time over the following months, but she continued to go out, even at night. It made no sense. It was like she was possessed."

The silence in the small room took up all the air. The muscle in his jaw tightened. I had the impression he was holding back a fierce emotion. "It must have been all the wandering around in all kinds of weather, no coat, all that exposure."

"The fever?" I carefully prompted.

"It came on suddenly. By the time the doctor arrived, it was too late to do anything, and she was too fragile to be moved to the mainland." The explanation came out matter-of-fact and devoid of the previous sentiment. I reasoned he had said this many times to anyone who asked. I kept forgetting Faraday House was the source of much gossip.

There was an emptiness in the air now; all the pent-up anxiety and fear had been stretched out and pulled back again, exhausted and lax. He retrieved the toolbox and started to leave, but then paused before he reached the tapestry.

"It's interesting," he said, his tone surprisingly light. "I go to her grave to pay my respects, but I feel closer to her here. I wish I hadn't avoided this part of the house for so long."

"Why is that?"

His blue eyes regarded me, and I felt the cold chill again, despite the door being firmly shut.

"Didn't they tell you?" he asked. "The tower room is where Esther died."

CHAPTER SEVENTEEN

I only thought I saw Esther at the window.

I only thought I saw a stain on the ceiling.

I only thought I heard someone pacing above me last night.

Everything had a reasonable explanation.

My overactive imagination coupled with all the gossip made the situation ripe for misinterpretation.

I kept telling myself this as I prepared for dinner. Picking out a dress calmed me, and even though I had to struggle with some of the buttons on the waist, the reflection in the mirror reminded me who I was and where my strengths lay. The task helped me forget Esther died one floor above. Whenever I thought of the dark stain, I mentally covered it over with a vision of Frederick rowing to the beach, looking over his shoulder to see me waving from the rocks.

It was becoming more difficult to create those images.

Sitting at the vanity, I brushed my hair, then pinned it to the nape of my neck. I leaned forward and pinched my cheeks for color. In the mirror I saw the entryway to the sunroom behind me. The tapestry was pulled aside.

Icy fear washed over me, freezing my bones. Interwoven into the fabric was a silhouette staring out the window in the tower.

Panic fueled my movements. I made my way to the main floor, one hand lifting the hem of my skirt as I raced down the stairs, careful not to tumble. I would not be spending another night in that room. I was going to tell Captain Graves I needed to be moved. Surely he would understand, given the tragic past of this house.

The foyer was already bathed in the evening's darkness. At the base of the staircase was a small table with a selection of chamber candlesticks of various sizes, each with a fresh taper. I took one and lit it from the nearby sconce.

I went to the door of Captain Graves's study and knocked. Impatient, I opened the door and walked in. "Hello?" The oak door creaked, sounding like thunder in the empty space. He was not there. My gaze landed on the desk by the window. A curious desire to go through some of the drawers surfaced inexplicably. He felt he was cursed, not the house. Was there a past mistake or some terrible sin for which he needed to atone?

I was reminded of the locked drawer in Georgina's desk. What had Mrs. Clayton been hoping to find there?

No matter—standing in a dark room wasn't helping my situation. Fear had lodged itself under my skin, making every hair stand on end. I turned to leave when something on the wall glinted against the reflection of the candlelight. I took a closer look at Georgina's mural. How was it possible I had not seen this feature before? An invisible hand curled around my throat.

On the hill beyond Faraday House was the large oak tree and around it the gravestones. They were merely gray shapes, meant to be without detail as they were in the background, but I counted three. Why would Georgina paint her own headstone?

The piano sounded from across the foyer. It was the same tune as the first night. Chills swept over me, covering my arms in goose bumps. As I entered the foyer, the music stopped. But that door was now partially open—as if someone had left quickly. And the candelabra beside the piano was lit. I looked around. Was Hettie watching me? How many "secret rooms" did Faraday have?

Strange things were happening, but in that moment, I needed a small bit of assurance. Something to let me know I wasn't going crazy. How could I trust myself if nothing I saw or heard was true?

Shaking, I entered the ash-gray room and approached the piano. The wedding portraits of Esther and Georgina watched me with their unmoving eyes. I could swear their expressions changed from demure smiles to grimacing fear.

I reminded myself everything had a reasonable explanation.

Mrs. Shackleton kept a small music box on her dressing table. It had a tiny mechanism inside that produced music when you wound it up. There could be a similar device under the piano's lid, plucking the strings. It was highly improbable, but not impossible. I stared at the keys, now quiet and still. "Go ahead, then," I prompted. "Scare me with your sonata."

A soft *thud* sounded from behind me. I turned and saw a large book lying open on the rug. There was an empty space on the shelf where it must have tumbled from. I walked cautiously toward its open pages; there was something sinister about an object falling to the floor by itself.

I nudged the book with the toe of my shoe. It remained still and lifeless. I knew I should replace it on the shelf, but my heart started hammering at the thought of touching it.

There was a creak from the foyer. I screamed and twirled around.

Reverend Pellerine stood tall and dark, studying me with his deep-set eyes, wearing a surprised expression. "My apologies, Miss Fitzpatrick."

"You startled me," I said.

"Evidently."

"The book . . . um . . ." What explanation could I give him? Certainly not the truth. Hearing the piano play by itself was one thing, but admitting objects were moving on their own was another level of madness. He'd asked me to share any further visions, but I knew I wouldn't sound sane, and I wasn't entirely sure I could trust him. The vision of him pretending to read the Bible at Georgina's beside had left me with an uneasy feeling. The holy water in the flask hadn't been explained either. If I told him everything I had experienced, what would stop him from going to Captain Graves? I shuddered, remembering his conversation with Mrs. Clayton and her talk of restless spirits looking for souls to claim. I would be locked in the tower room, the third mad wife no one ever heard from again.

Reverend Pellerine was still staring. However, I was not so witless as to believe it was my newly styled blond curls or figure-flattering dress that had transfixed him. He was analyzing me, no doubt watching my eyebrows for any indication I was lying.

"Literature moves me so," I said, purposely frowning to appear serious. "Sometimes the passages are so passionate I drop the book in a state of appreciation." I tried not to wince at my feeble excuse.

"I see." His expression smoothed as he came into the room and crouched down for the book. He straightened up as he flipped through the first few pages. "This is a ledger for the cabbage crops."

I blinked back at him. "Cabbage," I repeated. "Yes, it's a decidedly unappreciated vegetable."

His brown eyes pinned me in place as he stayed quiet, letting the silence grow. I suspected he would be a good hypnotist.

"Someone needs to champion the poor things," I said.

Reverend Pellerine cleared his throat, then handed the book to me. "Supper is prepared," he said. "If you've had your fill of harvest information, we can walk to the dining room together."

I smiled nervously and slid the book back into its place on

the shelf, snuggled beside a field guide to mushrooms. I thought about the brightly colored ones I'd seen on my walk. I made a mental note to come back and retrieve the field guide.

As we made our way down the hallway lined with schooner paintings, I glanced back to the closed doors to the study. I knew I had left one open. I was tempted to ask the reverend if he'd closed it or if he'd seen anyone in the foyer before finding me in the music room, but I feared the unease would show in my expression.

The dining room table was set properly with a linen tablecloth and two candelabras. Covered dishes were already arranged. I noted a third place had been set at the head of the table.

Reverend Pellerine and I took the chairs opposite each other.

"Should we wait for Captain Graves?" I said, placing the napkin on my lap. Having skipped lunch, I was famished. I poured myself half a glass of spruce beer.

"If we don't start, the food will get cold." He lifted the cover of the nearest dish and ladled fish chowder into his bowl. "As well, I believe Captain Graves went to the cottage to speak with Mr. Clayton."

I pulled my shawl tighter, suddenly chilled. What would he want to talk to him about? I remember how Mr. Clayton blamed Captain Graves for Esther's death, but surely no one would know about our discussion. Then I remembered the grate in the floor. If I could hear conversations in the kitchen, maybe someone overheard us.

I looked over my shoulder to the long windows as if the answer was there, but the curtains were pulled across. The fabric reached all the way to the floor, with the moth-eaten trim grazing the faded rug.

When I turned back, Reverend Pellerine dropped his gaze, but not before I caught him staring. Perhaps he had noticed the lack of color in my cheeks or how I flinched at every small noise. Whatever the reason, it created an awkward air between us. I had unanswered questions about Georgina's treatment, but I had to choose the best way to broach the subject. And I knew I would think more clearly after eating.

I helped myself to a generous serving of chowder. The creamy broth was full of white flaky cod, boiled corn, carrots, and onions. I added a fresh roll to my side plate. When I cut it in half, a wisp of steam rose.

As we dined, the only sound was the clinking of our spoons. From the corner of my eye, I watched him dip his roll into his bowl, sopping up the last bit of broth. Mrs. Shackleton would have been mortified. I, however, was tempted to do the same. Finally, I said, "I saw Georgina yesterday."

"Yes, she mentioned your visit. She enjoyed your company and hopes you'll see her again." He finally raised his eyes to mine. The room stilled as I redecorated the walls with bright colors and pictured sun spilling through the windows. There were no cobwebs or dusty candelabras. Reverend Pellerine would be sitting beside me, leaning closer, those brown eyes, strong and unwavering, daring me to close the space between us . . .

Wind rattled the panes. The real Faraday slipped back into place with the spiders and shadows. I blinked back at the reverend, unable to remember if he'd asked me a question or not. I was alarmed at how quickly my imagination concocted a scene for the two of us. "I'm going again this evening, before I turn in," I stated.

"I'm pleased to be of use."

His spoon hovered over his bowl as if he was going through the motions without eating. I had a feeling he was stalling. "It's a unique situation you're in." There was almost an apologetic tone to his answer.

"I prefer for this situation . . . to stay as it is, if it avoids the alternative." I took a sip of beer.

He placed his spoon carefully on the edge of the dish. There was a heaviness to his actions. "My apologies, Miss Fitzpatrick. I am inept at conversation this evening." He cleared his throat and said, "I'm not used to having a dining companion."

I liked how he said "companion," as if we were a team. I abandoned my own meal. The time had come to press him. "Please, Reverend," I began. "There is an urgency on my part that prevents me from minding my table manners. It concerns Georgina's treatment, or rather, lack thereof." It may have been the spruce beer that eased my inhibitions, but any remaining hesitancy was overshadowed by my growing panic. "No one has been able to rightly say what her diagnosis is, but I am certain there are better treatments than bitter tea and Bible recitations."

He slouched and let out a tired sigh. "She cannot be cured. She is dying, and Mrs. Clayton is treating her symptoms and doing her best to keep her comfortable, physically and spiritually." He quickly wiped his mouth with his napkin and placed it beside his bowl. "It's a sorry situation, and I'm doubly upset on your behalf, but there are many factors out of our control." His air of annoyance riled my nerves.

A fire grew in my chest. "How about your flask of holy water?"

He paused, then said, "It may be unconventional, but it's how I always carry the holy water. Much safer than a glass bottle."

"I suppose you blessed it after you left breakfast yesterday morning?"

His expression froze, then smoothed to weary regret. "It's Georgina's and Mrs. Clayton's belief that matters. What is faith but the belief in something without proof?"

Insanity, I wanted to say.

"If she believes it's holy water," he continued, "it gives her the reassurance she requires."

"That's a very dishonest way to rationalize your actions," I huffed. "Especially since Mrs. Clayton is using it as part of her treatment for Georgina."

He frowned. "It's my understanding the nurse left enough medication with instructions."

"Have you checked what is actually inside the bottle she claims is medication?" I felt a vibrant flush of energy. Being this bold on behalf of someone else was a new sensation. I sat taller.

"You haven't been at Faraday for long, Miss Fitzpatrick. What gives you the authority to—"

"I cannot stay silent about what I have seen and heard since arriving. Surely we can give each other the same respect after our discussion in my room about the ceiling."

The color drained from his face. He leaned closer and whispered, "I thought we agreed it was only a dream."

"But Georgina knew exactly what I was speaking of," I replied, my own voice lowered as well. "She looked terrified, and she told me what the stain was. . . . She said it was blood."

His eyes widened in alarm. "Whose blood?"

"She never finished, as Hettie interrupted us." His new look of concern was reassuring. I began to hope I wasn't truly alone in this situation. "Then this afternoon Mr. Clayton told me Esther died in the tower room."

"Esther?" He frowned, the lines adding another layer of concern. "The first wife? That was so long ago." He spoke hesitantly, unsure. "There must be a reasonable explanation."

"That's what troubles me most." My voice shook, and whatever previous bravery I'd had dissipated under his fretful gaze. "How do you explain both Georgina and me seeing the same thing? If her fatal disease is causing hallucinations, then it would be logical that I now have the same affliction."

He shook his head. "That can't be possible." He started to reach across the table. "We'll figure this out."

Footsteps sounded in the hallway, heavy and purposeful. Reverend Pellerine nodded to me, then leaned back, hands on either side of his place setting.

Captain Graves appeared in the doorway, head down, looking at his pocket watch. "Evening," he muttered, not making eye contact with either of us. He took his place at the head of the table and pulled the largest tureen toward him. "How is the chowder, Reverend Pellerine?" he said, the ladle hitting the side of his bowl several times as he hastily served himself, leaving fat drips of fish broth on the white tablecloth. "It looks like you've already finished." There was a hint of disapproval.

"Very good, thank you." Reverend Pellerine caught my eye and gave a quick shake of his head.

Captain Graves blew on his spoon, then slurped. He looked my way, but then blinked a few times, as though slightly confused. "Pour me a glass, please . . . er, Miss Fitzpatrick." He nodded to the pitcher of spruce beer.

I poured his drink with a careful smile, certain he'd momentarily forgotten my name.

He helped himself to a roll and bit off a chunk. The ferocity of his table manners stole my appetite. "High tide will be a little after nine tomorrow morning," he said to Reverend Pellerine. "Mrs. Clayton has a few items that need to be picked up. You can manage, yes?"

"Of course," the reverend replied. "I have other parishioners I need to visit and a few errands, so—"

"Good." Captain Graves replied. His gaze fell to my neglected dinner. "No appetite?"

Several reasonable excuses were on the tip of my tongue: I wasn't used to Mrs. Clayton's rich cooking, or I had talked off Reverend Pellerine's ear about my lovely walk around the grounds, but either of those would require a further explanation or invite him into a conversation, and at that moment I only wanted to leave and see Georgina.

Without waiting for an answer, he shook his head disapprovingly and said, "You must eat." He stared pointedly at me, waiting. "Even if you have to force yourself."

So I did. The chowder had cooled by this time, but it wasn't the temperature that made it difficult to swallow. I continued to eat as a necessity instead of enjoying the meal. When I glanced across the table, Reverend Pellerine was staring at his own place setting. The fingers of each hand slowly curled into fists, the knuckles tucked under and resting on the table.

Captain Graves watched me in silence, then continued with his own meal. His spoon scraped noisily on the bottom of the dish. "Winter is coming, and you'll need to be healthy. Mrs. Clayton has some excellent teas. I'll make sure she starts you on them tomorrow." He grabbed another roll.

"That's very kind," I said. Something deep down told me to quietly accept his offer.

He murmured into his chowder, "I cannot suffer another loss."

I bit my tongue to stop from commenting on what a wonder it was that I'd survived all these years without his counsel.

"Have a good evening." Reverend Pellerine stood so quickly his chair nearly toppled backward. His movements were usually so fluid; the lack of finesse stood out. "I'm going to check on Mrs. Graves."

"That is very considerate," Captain Graves said as he gave him an appraising glance. He tucked back into the meal with a sigh. "Hopefully it won't last much longer. I hate to see her suffer so."

Reverend Pellerine gave me one last glance then took his leave. I tried to plead for him to stay in that quick moment. I wished I could have gone with him. Miserably, I finished my roll as Captain Graves served himself another helping.

I thought about Georgina's missing paintings. When she spoke about her art, it considerably brightened her complexion with rosy cheeks, and she seemed more energetic. Something that gave her pleasure would surely help her tolerate the miserable tea and might even give her a few extra days. And a few extra days meant the world to me.

I cleared my throat and put on my best smile. "You said I could redecorate Faraday?"

His face immediately lit up. "Of course."

"Is there a way we can bring more color into the house?"

He waved a hand at the wall, then around the room. "Paint, curtains, new upholstery . . . whatever you want."

"Lovely, and I was hoping we could hang more of Georgina's art?"

The lines around his mouth deepened as his expression fell. "I would love that, truly. But she only painted the schooner in the hallway and the mural in the study."

"Oh." I had the distinct notion he wasn't lying. But Georgina seemed adamant about there being more. She also mentioned she used to destroy any work she didn't like.

He pushed his bowl out of the way, causing wrinkles in the tablecloth. His unused napkin remained perfectly folded. He sat tall and stared at me.

I automatically put a hand to the back of my hair, wondering if a piece had come loose.

"And now," he started, "I have a question for you." Reaching inside his jacket pocket, he pulled out a letter and placed it on the table between us. "Who is Lieutenant Fletcher?"

CHAPTER EIGHTEEN

It was the letter I had given to Mr. Clayton earlier. Fear momentarily stole my voice. I couldn't tell if he'd broken the wax seal or not. I struggled to conceal my shock as he confronted me with his stare. I was sure he could hear my heart race.

I crinkled my nose. "No one important." I refilled my glass with spruce beer, hoping he couldn't see my hands shake. I took a sip, trying to drown the panic. "A son of a dear friend of Judge Shackleton whom I met at the house when they were there for dinner with the admiral. He's nervous about sailing to Bermuda next month, so Judge Shackleton's friend asked me to write him. Unfortunately, I completely forgot and only remembered this morning." I tried to read his face, but there was only a steadfast expression. "I felt terrible for breaking a promise to the judge."

He tapped his finger on the envelope a few times. "Trust is very important," he said. "When I married Georgina, I trusted she would be healthy enough to give me children."

My knees shook under the table.

"Can I trust that you are telling me the truth?"

He obviously hadn't read the letter, or else he would have reprimanded me for lying. Or so I hoped. Telling the truth now would guarantee my demise. I had nowhere to go and no money. What if he kicked me off the island? Frederick was supposed to come here for me. I imagined them telling him I had never arrived, and they had no idea where I was.

"Yes." I tried to say it with as much conviction as I could. "I'm going to be your wife. You can trust me."

"And you can trust me." He showed me the seal of the letter was still intact. "I would rather this incident disappear." Then he held the corner of the letter over the open flame of the candle. I had to watch with unconcern as my pleas charred and turned to smoke.

I counted a hundred heartbeats until he said, "You're not part of the household yet. You must be more careful with your requests to the staff. Mr. Clayton should have explained that to you." His words were cold and held a warning. "He knows better now."

STILL SHAKING FROM my dinner with Captain Graves, I rushed to the second floor. Along the bloodred hallway, my elongated shadow matched my hurried steps.

Exhausted, I entered my room and lit all the candles. I pulled the curtains across the windows, hoping to block the chilly drafts. The ocean continued to crash into the rocky beach below.

I pressed my thumbnail into my finger and began to pace. What was I going to do? That letter to Frederick had been my only lifeline to him. I was so preoccupied I almost didn't hear the voices coming from the sunroom grate. Dishes clattered over the words, making them hard to discern. I crouched, listening intently.

"She's talking about seeing things," Hettie said. "Same as Miss Georgina."

I was unsure if she was referring to my accusation from the other day, or if she'd been eavesdropping on the reverend and me this evening.

"If that's true, there's not much any of us can do about it," Mrs. Clayton answered grimly.

Hettie continued, undaunted, "I wonder if she's using it to get extra attention from Reverend Pellerine. Has he mentioned it to you?"

"No." There was a pause, then Mrs. Clayton said, "I wouldn't be too worried about this one, though. You can tell by the look of her she won't last. Faraday isn't for the faint of heart." A loud *clang* was followed by the splash of water. Hettie said something I couldn't make out, but her tone was undoubtedly anxious.

There was a snort. "I knew it!" Mrs. Clayton exclaimed. "You're sweet on Reverend Pellerine. Well, listen to me, deary, you'll need to do more than wear a cross and memorize a few Bible verses."

This was met with a sullen silence. I pictured Hettie pouting. Then Mrs. Clayton asked, "Any luck?" There was an unexpected teasing in her question.

"He's not exactly said no," Hettie replied. "He only said he's not the right fella for me, and that my future is not with him. But then he smiled at the end of it like he was giving me a special clue."

"Oy! You're special, all right. Too bad you don't have at least a clue."

The *clink* of silverware filled in the gap between their comments. Then Hettie sighed. "Reverend Pellerine said he has to go to the mainland tomorrow. Why can't Mr. Clayton go instead?"

A broom moved across the floor with rushed strokes. "The fool walked into the cottage door and gave himself a black eye," Mrs. Clayton said. "He can't very well go into the village looking like that. Just as well, the reverend is required to see his other parishioners. We can't keep him all to ourselves."

Black eye? Dread twisted my stomach as I remembered how Captain Graves coolly said he knows better now. A miserable weight of guilt settled over my shoulders.

Hettie offered, "The reverend's up there with her now. I listened at the door; they're having a good yarn, but I couldn't make it out exactly. She did say something about her art supplies, like she wants to paint."

The broom stopped. "She wants to paint again?" Mrs. Clayton's voice rose slightly. "I hadn't realized. She barely utters more than two or three words in a row when I'm there."

"Maybe she's getting better?" Hettie suggested carefully.

Dishes clattered again. "Here, tea's ready, take it up now. Reverend Pellerine will be needing a cup as well, and I'm sure Mrs. Graves will be noticing the pain's come back. Just a few drops in her pot, like I showed you. That's it. And for the love of God, don't mix up the pots."

Hettie replied, "I'm not sure, maybe Reverend Pellerine would be a little more receptive to my charms if he took the treatment." Then a shrill burst of laughter. "You should see your face!"

"Jesus, Mary, and Joseph," Mrs. Clayton reprimanded. "We're not playing house. You think death is a laughing matter?"

"I have medical experience, Mrs. Clayton." Hettie's tone was hot. "More than you, probably."

"Doesn't matter a lick. I don't trust to close my eyes anymore, I tell you that. One night we'll wake up and she'll either be gone into the ocean or standing over us with a knife in her hand. Accidents have a way of happening in this house when you least expect them—even to smart-mouthed maids. Now hold your tongue and do as you're told. Just because you were hired especially for the present Mrs. Graves doesn't mean you'll stay on for the next one. You can easily be let go, even before this one passes on."

Without hesitating, Hettie replied with the confidence of a hundred Mrs. Shackletons, "Captain Graves might have something to say about that." After Hettie's steps left the kitchen, Mrs. Clayton swore under her breath, then all was quiet.

I returned to my bedroom, steaming mad at how casually Mrs. Clayton spoke of Georgina dying—and my own demise as well! I took the small green bottle she'd given me my first night and emptied it into the chamber pot.

CHAPTER NINETEEN

Dearest Frederick,

I escape the unpleasantness of real life with my imagination, but this time my imagination is creating anguish. I'm unsure if what I see is real or a dream. How can my mind deteriorate so quickly?

I have lost track of the days here, but I know it has been two months since our sweet intimate encounter, and I fear I will never be in your arms again.

I don't even care if I ever see the Bermuda sun, for all I need is you. I would happily stay in the cargo hold for the entire trip, eating scraps and sleeping with the rats. That's how destitute this place is, Frederick.

You must come on racing horseback or the fastest ship. I fear my very life depends upon it.

Yours for eternity,
Emeline

I sealed the letter and tucked it into my dress pocket. The mention of the rats might have been a bit much; however, when it came to convincing a man, exaggeration was sometimes called for. My first letters to Frederick had been from the heart, but now my head had taken over, conniving to write the most desperate scene to propel him into action.

I took my candelabra and made my way to Georgina's room. Reverend Pellerine would be going to the mainland tomorrow, and I dared to hope he'd take my letter as well. Captain Graves had proven he was in charge, but Reverend Pellerine was the closest I had to an ally.

It was a great risk to try and send another letter, but it was the only way I had to contact Frederick. It would be worth it, though, for I was certain if he knew how ghastly the situation was, he would come at once. And while I still hoped he was already on his way, this letter would at least give him the conviction required to make haste.

Along the hallway, the shadows were pushed out of my way by the candlelight, only to swirl behind me as soon as I passed. I lingered long enough in front of the large round window to see my own pale and frightened face reflected.

There were so many candles burning in Georgina's room it almost appeared brighter than in the daytime.

Reverend Pellerine sat by her bed, watching her sleep. I was hit with an unexpected urge to go in and explain I didn't want to marry the captain or have him tell me what to eat.

I knocked lightly on the door frame. Georgina blinked lazily as she roused.

Reverend Pellerine rose and began to make his way toward me. I purposely waited at the threshold, wanting to speak with him privately. His expression was rigid and difficult to read. There was an unusual formality to his stance that only accented the exhaustion around his eyes. No small wonder, as he now regarded me as someone who was also having visions—like Georgina.

That issue had been pushed to the back of my mind as a more

urgent matter had surfaced. I handed him the letter. "I do not desire to put you in a position of betrayal with Captain Graves, but I am desperate for your assistance. Are you able to take this with you tomorrow?" I whispered. "It's very important."

He glanced at the front of the letter before tucking it inside his jacket pocket. There was a question in his gaze, but he remained quiet. I wished I could explain why I was writing to a lieutenant in the Royal Navy, but that story was too long and complicated for this time of evening. If only we'd had more time to talk at dinner before the captain arrived and ruined everything. "Of course," he agreed. "I am not compromised in the slightest, Miss Fitzpatrick. He has no authority over me." His words of assurance were hollow and held no comfort. I had the disconcerting notion he was upset with me.

I added, "And no one can know."

He nodded. "I understand."

We shared an uncomfortable beat of silence until I could no longer hold back from the issue of our last conversation.

"I've been thinking about what I told you earlier," I started quietly. "And I think you're correct: there is a logical explanation. The light plays tricks in that room. I'm sure it was only shadows and the lack of sleep." Then I nodded to his jacket pocket. "That letter is my biggest concern." Now that I had given him Frederick's letter, a calmness had slipped into place, and I was no longer eager to discuss the possibility of shared visions and what they might mean.

He looked over his shoulder. Georgina had fallen back to sleep. "She'll rest well tonight, hopefully." His lids were heavy.

I could tell he was exhausted, and while I hadn't had much restful sleep, the fright at the table with Captain Graves had washed away any tiredness. "I'll sit with her until Mrs. Clayton arrives," I offered.

He nodded gratefully, but stood in place, lingering without reason.

"I'm sorry I had to leave you at dinner," he said. His tone was polite, yet there was an underlying irritation. "Forgive my bluntness, but you cannot allow him to treat you that way."

I was stunned for a moment before I replied with a boldness I usually kept solely for my thoughts. "I would have gladly followed you," I said. "Eating a cold meal to avoid being chastised by a man to whom I have been promised is not my ideal dinner either, Reverend, but at least you were allowed to leave. I could not. You are the one who has more autonomy. You could have easily said something; instead you chose to leave me alone with him."

He held his palms out in a frustrated gesture. "What more could I do? Sit there and be a witness to your humiliation? I cannot interfere; it is not my place. It is not my purpose for being here."

His reasoning was sound, but interfering was exactly what I wished he'd done. When he'd left, it felt like a betrayal. "You said he has no authority over you," I reminded him.

"He doesn't, but if I overstep my boundary, he may see fit to make me leave. Georgina has made it clear she wants me to be present when she dies. How can I deny a dying woman's only request?"

I immediately felt guilty. And hurt. I wished he would see me as someone other than the third wife. I wanted to say all that, but I knew the words would come out sounding spiteful and spoiled. "I understand," I said. I crossed my arms in front of my chest, closing the topic.

He dropped his chin and let out a sigh. When he locked eyes with mine again, his expression had softened, deep and mournful. "I'm sorry," he repeated.

My mouth stayed rigid. I didn't need his apologies; I needed him to stop holding himself back from doing what he knew was the right thing.

When the grandfather clock on the landing struck the hour, we both eased away from each other, tired and frustrated.

He gave me a nod. "Your letter will make it to the mainland tomorrow." Then he added, "I promise."

I turned away so he couldn't see me roll my eyes. The promises of men were the reason I was at Faraday House. I quietly went to the railing and watched as he took the stairs to the main level, and I wondered for the first time where his room was. Reverend Pellerine was proving to be increasingly frustrating, I couldn't determine if he was to be trusted entirely or not. And what was the use of only trusting someone part of the time? Being truthful once did not guarantee they would always be truthful.

Honestly, I was more annoyed with myself for caring what he thought. I closed Georgina's door all the way to give us privacy and to remove Captain Graves's bedroom door from my view. The only small consolation that allowed me breathing room was his stalwart decision to not consummate our marriage until our wedding night. I tried to manifest an image of myself halfway to Bermuda by then.

I took my place at Georgina's bedside. She was wearing a white nightgown with a ribbon tied at the neck.

She smiled at me. "I feel spoiled with all this attention. Tell me, what do you think of Reverend Pellerine? It looked like an intense meeting between you two."

I huffed. "He reminds me of an approaching storm you cannot help but watch, even though you know you're in its path and will eventually regret not moving."

Georgina grinned.

I added, "I've never met anyone French before, so perhaps they're all as opinionated and mysterious."

"Yes, he's handsome, and the accent only adds to his allure." She waved a hand at me when I opened my mouth to protest. "He's not just French, he's Acadian. You must know the stories. Quite tragic, really. Families split apart, land taken from them . . ."

I nodded as if understanding, but all my knowledge of Acadians was through the voices of those loyal to the British king. They refused to pledge allegiance to the crown in times of war. "But that was long ago," I finally said.

She frowned. "Sixty years is not that long. And something as horrendous as the expulsion trickles down for generations. You should ask him. It will help you understand him."

I sat in the chair mulling over what she'd said. His offended expression when I handed him the envelope made sense. I pictured him burning the note, just like Captain Graves.

Georgina asked for water. I helped her sit up, and she took dainty sips from the glass. I noticed her brittle hair and how it bunched up in the back with tangles. I couldn't believe the thoughtlessness of Mrs. Clayton and Hettie.

Georgina's vanity only held the folded washcloths; there was no hairbrush or ribbons. "I'll do your hair tomorrow," I offered. "Won't that be nice?"

"I must look frightful enough to scare off a ghost." She said it as a joke. There wasn't any of the fear or panic from our earlier conversation about the sunroom. Her words were clear and caught me by surprise. She was alert as well.

I decided I should try and talk to her more about the vision. "When I asked you about the ceiling in my room, you told me it was blood. Whose blood?"

"Blood? Why would I say such a horrid thing?" She clutched the sheets in a fist and started to twist. "Why?"

"I'm sorry." I sat on the bed and put my hand over hers. "I don't mean to worry you. I wanted to let you know it was the late-afternoon shadows." It was a lie, of course. One I hoped I would accept if I repeated it enough.

"Shadows." She nodded, then her breath calmed. Her hand plucked at the sheets.

"Do you want me to fetch Mrs. Clayton?" I asked. "Are you in pain?"

"No." She shook her head. "I prefer your company, and the medicine makes my mind foggy; it only dulls the stomach pain."

"When did the pain start?"

She worked her bottom lip. "I can't remember, it was so gradual."

"Before you came to Faraday?"

"No, definitely after." She counted on her fingers. "Maybe six months." She grew melancholy. "I know because Edgar and I had been trying to start a family. Six confirmations that I had failed him. He had such hopes, and so did I. All I've ever wanted was to have a son or daughter to raise. But months went by, and I still wasn't with child. It was maddening; we didn't know what was wrong." The corners of her mouth turned down. "As women, so much happens to our bodies without us having any control . . . or in my case, nothing happens."

Nature could be so random and cruel.

She put a hand to her head and winced. "I'm sorry," she uttered. "The words come out too quickly sometimes. I go for long periods of not talking at all, then I feel well and try to say all the things I was too tired to mention earlier."

"I'm sorry you were never with child," I said. "You would be a lovely mother."

"Distract me, please. Tell me a story; your voice is soothing. Maybe something of your dear parents?" Georgina looked at me with her hopeful brown eyes, like a young deer.

I had many memories of my parents, but in that moment, I could only think of the one story that had been with me the longest. I hoped it would be enough for her.

I began, "After my mother died and I had gone to live permanently with the Shackletons, I would spend hours in my room, staring out the window, making up stories in which my parents would come and rescue me. I convinced myself they had to make everyone think they were both dead so Father wouldn't have to pay back all the bills. They were forbidden to notify anyone of this ruse, even the Shackletons. The most difficult part for them was waiting until I was old enough to keep their secret. Only then would they be able to return and rescue me.

"I pictured them living on an island somewhere warm, with colorful birds and sand as soft as Mrs. Shackleton's face powder. I would always fall asleep waiting for them. The next morning, I worried I had missed their carriage. I reasoned they must have come the night before but didn't see me watching from the window, so they drove on."

Georgina placed her hand at her throat, pinching the ribbon of her nightgown.

"I vowed the next night I would stay up. And then the next, and the next. I don't remember when I stopped; it was gradual. The judge would whisper to Mrs. Shackleton that something was wrong with me. 'Look at the dark circles under her eyes,' he'd say to her, staring at me across the dining table. 'She's falling asleep over her meal. Take her to the doctor.'

"Mrs. Shackleton's remedy was a new dress and bonnet. And tighter curls. And more hair ribbons." I sighed. "I eventually stopped, but I confess I pause by a window at night every few months and make a quick wish. I may be almost twenty-one, but I will never outgrow my parents."

Georgina was quiet. Her finger had wound around the end of the ribbon. I wondered if she thought that was incredibly infantile of me.

She released the ribbon then finally she said, "Oysters spend their entire lives at the bottom of the ocean. By all appearances they're rather unbecoming—two hard shells glued together. But sometimes the smallest bit of sand will get inside their shell. The irritation causes the oyster to secrete a substance that covers the grain of sand to ease its pain. And it keeps doing this, adding layer after smooth layer until there is a pearl." She smiled at me in a knowing way. "You're like that. You use your imagination to ease your pain, and in doing so you secretly create something beautiful."

"I've never thought about it that way." My spirit grew lighter, joyous even. I sensed this was what confession with Reverend Pellerine must feel like.

Georgina chuckled softly. "The most beautiful thing about you is the one thing no one can see."

She may have been at death's door, but she had a quiet courage I greatly admired. Mrs. Shackleton had a string of pearls from the judge. She told me you could tell if they were real by how they sounded against your teeth. She said they were so strong it was impossible to crush them.

It was a new idea to think of something as being beautiful and strong at the same time.

Georgina closed her eyes. Her grasp on my hand lessened— only slightly, though.

She gave me a groggy smile. "Please light another candle," she whispered. I was about to tell her that all the candles were burning, the room practically glowed, when she said, "It's the only thing that keeps my head clear."

I brought one of the larger candelabras that had been placed on the writing desk and positioned it on top of the vanity, close to her bed. She seemed to feel the extra illumination, and it calmed her as she eased back onto the pillows, her expression completely content.

The simple joy I received was almost enough to help me forget why I was at Faraday House and all the worry and anguish that accompanied it.

She sighed. "Night is the worst."

"I won't leave you," I said.

A chill breezed through the room, causing all the candle flames to flicker at the same time.

I went to the settee, where a blanket had been draped over the armrest. I wrapped it over my shoulders. My attention drifted to the serving tray that had been placed on the table. There was the familiar small green teapot, and then a white one with blue flowers around the trim. The prettier teapot, the one I assumed Hettie had served Reverend Pellerine from, was completely drained. A few ideas swirled around my mind and began to fit together. I picked up the small green one and lifted the lid, peeking at the dregs on the bottom. I inhaled and immediately winced, remembering the same awful scent that had been in Georgina's cup yesterday.

But this time I remembered where I had smelled something similar. The dirt on my cloak. I pictured the brightly colored mushrooms that led me to the pit. I had clawed the ground, trying to find purchase, mashing them into the fabric.

Georgina's tea smelled exactly like those mushrooms.

CHAPTER TWENTY

I gave Georgina's sleeping form a glance before I closed her door behind me. I knew I was breaking a promise, but I had to return to the music room before anyone woke. With one hand shielding the candle flame I snuck down the stairs, hating how each step sent out a creaking echo, announcing my secretiveness. Faraday itself was my enemy.

The gray walls made the music room feel like a witch's grotto. The candle only accented the cracks, giving the impression they would topple at any moment.

Carefully, I went to the piano and pressed a key. Nothing happened. It seemed the instrument only played for certain people. I gingerly lifted the lid to inspect the strings to see if Hettie had put some kind of contraption inside, but the candlelight afforded only a limited view. I would have to check again tomorrow, in the daylight. I eased the lid back in place, reminding myself I had to hurry with my task then get back to Georgina before she woke.

Halfway to the bookshelves, I froze. A coldness rained down on me, dripping all the way to my toes.

On the floor at the base of the shelves was the same book that had fallen earlier in the evening. I didn't remember hearing it hit the rug.

With shaking hands, I reached for the book and carefully

picked it up. There was nothing special about it. As Reverend Pellerine said, it was a ledger for the cabbage harvest. I leafed through the pages, sending a plume of dust into my face.

I sneezed. The sound blasted in the bleak darkness. If I wasn't more careful, I'd wake the captain. I quickly grabbed the field guide, eager to return to Georgina. I paused. There was something at the back of the shelf where the two texts had been. It was round with a tiny red flower painted on it. I leaned closer and realized it was a doorknob.

Could it be one of the secret rooms Hettie had talked about?

Dropping the books, I reached in and wrapped my fingers around the doorknob. It was cold against my palm.

A quick turn was all it took. There was a creaking noise, then the entire bookcase swung outward, revealing a doorway to a black void of mystery. I held up the candle and stepped into the shadows.

It was a small space, but instead of weapons or casks of rum, or cursed treasure for that matter, it was filled with paintings. Georgina's missing artwork! Some were framed; others were just the canvas, rolled up. I chose one from the middle.

My throat closed over in shock, stealing my scream. It was Esther, but not like she was in her wedding portrait. She was dressed in a white nightgown soaked in what I suspected was blood. With a trembling hand, I chose another painting. It was of the tower room, except the floor had a pool of blood with a thick trail leading to the staircase as if a body had been dragged away. I winced. It was incredibly disturbing. The remaining canvases were covered in frantic black scratch marks. I thought I could see letters crudely hidden among the jagged lines. When I leaned closer, it looked like dried blood was mixed in with the paint. A violent shiver rattled my bones. I dropped the canvas, not wanting to touch it any longer.

The grandfather clock announced the time, letting me know I had already been away from Georgina half an hour.

Closing the door, I tucked the mushroom book under my arm and ran back up the stairs on tiptoe. My heart raced to keep up with the jarring thoughts.

Georgina's room still glowed with all the candles. She snored quietly like a princess bound to sleep for eternity under a spell from a cruel troll. As I quietly made my way across the room, her legs became restless. She said something incoherent in her sleep as bony fists grabbed the edge of the sheet.

"Graves," she mumbled. Her voice was scared.

I took my place in the chair by her bed. "It's Emeline," I whispered. "I'm here." I touched her hand. Why had she painted such violent images? How terrified she must have been to see such things.

Her breathing eased.

I put my attention back on the book and leafed through until I found a picture of the mushrooms I'd seen beside the pit. Poisonous. An icy finger traced my spine as I read the symptoms.

She was dying, but not from a disease, and not from possession of restless spirits, and certainly not from a mysterious curse from a long-ago stolen treasure.

Someone was poisoning her on purpose. But why would anyone want to kill Georgina?

A new resolve took over me. My original task had been to keep her alive to postpone my own nuptials until Frederick arrived. As I watched her sleep, I realized Georgina was a real person, and not just the second wife I was hoping to keep alive. A connection had started in my heart with Georgina, and if there was some way to take her with me, I would do everything in my power to make that happen. Frederick would be rescuing not only me, but Georgina as well.

And to ensure that, I had to stop the poisoning and figure out who was doing this to her.

"Miss?"

I woke to Mrs. Clayton nudging my shoulder. I sat up and winced as my back muscles spasmed in protest. I'd fallen asleep in the chair.

The room was cloaked in darkness. The only lit candle was the one held by Mrs. Clayton. The light created unnatural shadows on her face, giving the impression of hollowed-out cheeks. She frowned at me. "Get yourself to bed before the captain knows you've been here all night. He'll be right upset if you don't get a proper amount of sleep. Go on now." She put a hand under my arm and hoisted me to standing before I could wave off her efforts.

The mushroom book had fallen to the rug by my feet sometime during the night. I kicked it under the bed and out of sight. "I have to stay," I said.

She shook her head. "I won't have two patients. And if you don't get back to your room this instant, I'll tell the captain, and he'll make sure you don't get to visit anymore."

I stared back at her, shocked by her force.

Mrs. Clayton leaned close to me. "It's for your own good, trust me."

I most certainly did not trust her. I glanced at the tray she'd brought. It was only a steaming washbasin. No green teapot.

She looked across the hall at the captain's bedroom door and wrung her hands on her apron. "Please," she said. "Let me get Mrs. Graves prepared for the day. He gets upset when things aren't done before breakfast."

Outside, the sky had begun to lighten from black to a dusty slate gray.

Georgina yawned then and woke. She smiled sleepily as Mrs. Clayton went to the head of her bed.

"Morning, Mrs. Graves," she said gently.

"I'm still here." Georgina sighed. "Still alive."

"It's a blessing." Mrs. Clayton smiled. "Let's get you freshened up and changed into a new nightgown. Won't that feel nice?"

"Thank you," Georgina said. "I'm so grateful you're here."

Mrs. Clayton turned to me, and we shared an understanding glance. I left, knowing I would have to return when the green teapot arrived for breakfast.

As I slipped on my own nightgown to catch a few hours of sleep, I began to make a list of suspects.

Hettie and Mrs. Clayton were the ones who brought the tea, but Mrs. Clayton was the one who added the "medicine." That blue bottle she kept in her apron.

But what would be her motive? I thought of Mr. Clayton describing the captain as someone he blamed for Esther's death. And Mrs. Clayton talked last night about him having a black eye. It was obvious they were afraid of him, even though they'd worked at Faraday for over ten years. Mr. Clayton spoke of Esther with great admiration.

I could understand their disgust with the captain, but why harm Georgina? Revenge for Esther? Neither of them struck me as the coldhearted type. And ten years was an awfully long time to hold a grudge. I yawned into the back of my hand. The lack of sleep was catching up with me. The main thing was that Georgina was safe for the moment.

I would have to make sure I was back in her room before the green teapot arrived for her breakfast with the captain. Unless . . .

I opened my eyes, urgency pushing away sleep.

Unless I found where the mushrooms were kept in the kitchen and got rid of them.

I tightened the tie of my dressing gown and made my way to the kitchen.

CHAPTER TWENTY-ONE

I took the hallway to the dining room and continued until I reached an archway. It led to a small passage lined with shallow shelves filled with jars of preserves and various crockery. I even spied several bottles of blueberry wine. I scanned all the containers, but nothing was labeled as "mushrooms" or "tea."

The aromas of yeast and spice lured me farther down the passage until I discovered the kitchen. It was a large room with two thick timbers running the length of the ceiling. Drying herbs hung from tiny hooks. Off to the side was a plain wooden table with chairs down one side and a bench on the other.

A stone fireplace dominated one wall. A cast-iron crane supported a large pot over a slow flame. A gentle bubbling played calmly with the snaps and crackles of the fire. This part of the house seemed cozy and insulated from drafts.

A wooden block had been scrubbed clean and a butcher's knife was embedded in the cutting board with its handle pointed upward.

There was another door, and a hallway that I assumed led to the outside. Quietly, I opened the door and discovered another pantry. A breeze of cold air flowed over my skin and through my dressing gown. With the candle flame reflecting off the glass jars, I moved along each tall shelf inspecting the contents. My fingers grew stiff in the coldness.

At last I found an entire row of dehydrated mushrooms, looking shriveled and unappetizing. I unscrewed the first lid and inhaled. It was earthy, but not at all like the tea from the green pot. I considered getting rid of all the mushrooms when I chose the last jar. I didn't even have to sniff the contents. As soon as I removed the lid, the pungent odor hit me.

I reached in and took out one of the mushrooms, studying it carefully. Doubt began to creep in. The book had many pages of illustrations, but they were black and white. I may have identified them incorrectly. What if these weren't poisonous? I needed more proof.

I smelled it, then gave it a quick lick. I shivered in my nightgown, waiting for the stomach pains to begin. Nothing.

"What are you doing?"

I screamed and dropped the glass jar. It shattered on the floor between my feet. Turning, I saw Reverend Pellerine standing in his nightshirt, holding a candle. Moses sat beside him with his large head tilted in confusion. They wore matching quizzical expressions.

His dark hair was mussed, and a lingering laxness still clung to his posture, but his eyes were sharp and fused me to the spot. Seeing him in this fashion and so unexpectedly sent a warm flush across my skin. I wrestled with my conscience. How could I be in love with Frederick and still be attracted to another? I wished my cheeks would stop glowing. I remembered Georgina saying we sometimes have no control over our bodies. I reasoned my physical reaction was purely involuntary. That's all the blush was, of course. A simple reaction, nothing more. Especially when I had his full attention, like at this very moment.

I couldn't hold his gaze. My focus went to his throat, where a hint of chest hair started at the cut of the neckline. I had to drop my gaze further, all the way to his feet. "I had a stomachache," I sputtered. Despite the circumstances, there was something ridiculously funny about seeing his bare toes. I bit the inside of my cheek to stop myself from giggling. "I didn't want to bother Mrs. Clayton and take her attention away from Georgina."

Moses ventured closer, pawing one of the mushrooms. Reverend Pellerine ordered him to stay. Then he commanded the same of me. "Don't move," he said as he made to leave the pantry.

That snapped me to attention. "Please don't tell the captain," I blurted out. He was already displeased about the letter.

Reverend Pellerine frowned back at me, then his features smoothed out. "Of course not. I'm going to get a broom to sweep up first. I don't want you walking over the glass."

My pulse calmed. "Thank you."

He returned with a broom and dustpan and began to carefully clean up my mess. He had also slipped on a pair of trousers and socks. When he was finished, he nodded to the back shelf and said, "Cinnamon is good for an upset stomach. I can brew you a cup of tea if you like."

I looked at the sack on the floor. "Is that the cinnamon?"

"That's a twenty-pound bag of flour. You don't bake much, do you?" Then he came closer, nearly standing toe to toe. I saw the rough beginnings of a beard he was most likely going to shave later. He reached over my shoulder and picked up a small earthen jar. I silently but begrudgingly acknowledged the tingling across my skin where his arm nearly brushed against mine.

Wordlessly, I followed him back into the kitchen, where he placed a few extra logs on the fire to increase the flame. I may not have been able to "test" the suspicious mushrooms, but I did claim a small victory, as I'd gotten rid of them. I hoped there would be an improvement in Georgina's condition as a result. I wondered how long it would take.

Soon the water was boiling for tea. I took a chair at the table while Moses sat at my feet. I stroked his head, liking the feeling of his smooth fur. He closed his eyes, leaning into my touch.

"Where is your room?" I asked, wondering how loud I must have been to rouse him from sleep.

Reverend Pellerine nodded toward the hallway. "Down the hall. It used to be the Claytons', but they prefer the cottage now."

He moved around the kitchen with ease, filling the teapot, getting out mugs, putting a bit of cinnamon in one, and leaving the other without. He then cut two slices of bread and withdrew a small pitcher from one of the cupboards.

All of this was brought to the table in an easy fashion. He was comfortable in the kitchen, and I wondered how often he spent time here.

He sat in the chair opposite me as I wrapped my fingers around the mug and inhaled the cinnamon aroma. He then took the small pitcher and tilted it over an empty plate, letting a slow river of molasses lazily pour out. There was no window in the kitchen, and he hadn't lit any of the lamps, so our two small candles were the only light. In a swift motion he righted the pitcher and used his finger to catch the drip then brought it to his lips.

I concentrated pointedly on taking a sip of my tea instead of staring at him.

He then tore a small piece of bread and dipped it into the molasses. He said, "I want to explain my reasoning behind my words the other night outside Georgina's room."

Heat rushed up my neck as I remembered how we'd ended the conversation, tense and fuming with each other. It seemed he'd spent time thinking about it and was ready to voice his apology. I took a corner of bread and mimicked his actions. Mrs. Shackleton would have fainted to see me eating with my hands.

He continued, "But if you are to marry the captain, you should be careful how you allow him to speak to you. What you permit you promote." There was no hint of an apology. He helped himself to another piece of bread, carefully dipping it first.

I swallowed my molasses-soaked bread, enjoying the sticky sweetness while I mentally composed my reply. "You have the luxury of viewing the conversation from the point of view of a man," I told him. "If I react quietly without the other person being aware, isn't that more powerful than throwing a punch or replying with an unsavory comment?" Then I added, "But more important, I've been taught that talking back is most unbecoming."

"And to be becoming is important to you?"

I casually lifted a shoulder. "One must protect and highlight one's assets."

He leaned back and took a sip of tea, regarding me over the rim. "Are you determined to not be honest with me? You may have charmed others with your defensive distractions, but I see through your guise. You use humor to avoid anything that would be uncomfortable for you."

"What's wrong with avoiding discomfort?" I took a larger bite of bread and molasses and chased it with another sip of tea.

He replenished my cup with more hot tea. "And you think you'll be comfortable at Faraday?" His question had an added serious tone.

"More comfortable than the convent," I replied without hesitating.

He nearly spit out his tea. "As a nun?" His coughing turned to laughter.

I scoffed at his reaction. "I'll have you know I'm absolutely serious."

He laughed harder, using the back of his sleeve to wipe his face.

"Are you crying?"

"Forgive me, Miss Fitzpatrick, but I'm trying to picture you in a habit, and it's not coming to me."

"I would look fantastic," I said, dipping my last piece of bread.

"I'm quite certain you would," he said. "You'd have all the priests wishing to leave the church." His laugh petered out when he saw I was not laughing along with him. "My apologies; it was impolite to assume you'd not be serious about taking vows. The church cares little for physical beauty." He picked up his mug of tea again.

His French accent was stronger this morning, and it swirled around his words, making everything he said sound lyrical. It only added to the playful quality of his teasing. I missed the natural attraction of flirting. It wasn't forced; I hadn't coerced him with my smile or whatever dress I was wearing. I was flirting with my words, and it was empowering. Imagine only being able to walk, then one day you discover you can fly. If this feeling were wine, I would have drained the whole keg. I allowed the moment to continue. "It's not like handsome reverends don't exist. How's that different from a beautiful nun?"

His mug stopped halfway. "Reverends are allowed to marry," he said. "Some would agree that's a significant difference."

Oh yes, I thought. "Different rules, but the same God?"

We stared at each other across the table. I had the sensation we were approaching a path neither of us had expected. He finally said, "We all serve the same purpose."

I found his relaxed tone interesting. I pressed him further. "Sometimes you work to hide your accent. Is that on purpose?"

"The answer to that question is complicated."

He stayed quiet, and I grew bolder. "It's easier to avoid topics that make you uncomfortable, isn't it?"

His jovial expression slipped away, and I knew I had pushed the flirting too far. "The name Pellerine is definitely French Acadian, but if I sound like most people, it calms them."

"Why would people need to be calmed around you?" I asked, thinking he'd tried to sidestep answering the question properly. "You're a man of God; that's calming for most people."

He gave me a patronizing look. "When people hear me speak or learn my name, they know my heritage. The first time we met, I saw the mistrust in your eyes. There are whispers, even in the congregation. Everyone is accepting at first, but then they start to question your loyalty, especially if there is any hint of conflict on the horizon."

He continued, "I suppose living in a city surrounded by the Royal Navy has afforded you a pleasant view of history, but I grew up listening to stories of how the British ripped apart my grandmother's family. When they refused to pledge allegiance to the king, they were forced off their land and taken away in ships. My father was just a young boy. He and my grandmother managed to escape into the woods. The only reason they survived that first winter was because of the Mi'kmaq. My father was a young man by the time they were able to return to the valley where their farm was, but all the land they'd cleared and established had been taken over by loyalists from New England.

"They dared not say who they were. Instead, they headed to the north shore and found other Acadians had made a new home there, now fishermen instead of farmers. The church was essential in helping them build a new home; the priest was very kind.

"I grew up hearing those stories. There is a great sense of Acadian pride, but that fear never goes away. I wanted to give back to the church and was going to become a priest, but my father was against it. I was the only son. He said the family had gone through too much to have our name vanish."

"You had to compromise," I said, in awe. The reasons for his being in this very spot with me seemed incredible.

"Yes. I changed denomination and became Protestant so I could be a reverend."

"I had no idea," I said. "I'm sorry."

He nodded, quietly accepting my comment. I put my attention back to finishing my bread. I had ruined the moment with my selfish request to keep him talking.

His finger tapped the handle of the mug. "When we first met, you mentioned your guardians had sent you, not your parents."

"They're dead," I replied matter-of-factly, choosing to keep the details as stark as possible out of respect to his own tragedy. It was completely different from when I shared it with Georgina. Reverend Pellerine and I were beyond any need to romanticize the truth.

"I reasoned the same." He stayed quiet. Then he said, "I'm sorry." We traded sad smiles.

"It was long ago." Then I told him about the ice from the tavern roof killing my father. "And my mother choked on a cup of tea. There was a shilling hidden inside. No one had checked before they served her." I kept my part in her death to myself.

I expected him to give me a pedestrian answer about how she was watching over me from heaven. Instead, he said, "How cruel that something of little value cost you so much."

The breath caught in my throat. No one had ever phrased the irony in such a tragically poetic way.

Moses lifted himself from the floor and gave a long stretch. He smacked his jaws a few times and waddled over to Reverend Pellerine, where he received an ear scratch. I smiled at the distraction Moses provided, helping to dissipate the grief between us.

Reverend Pellerine smiled too. "Interesting, though," he started. "If you had gone to the convent and I had stayed Catholic and become a priest, we might still be doing this very activity of having tea together."

I laughed lightly, imaging that scenario. Both of us in our black church garb, stealing away to the kitchen at dawn. Would it still feel the same? Forbidden, but with a notion something stronger was trying to bring us together?

He took a watch out of his trouser pocket and made a surprised noise. "It's later than I thought. Hettie will be down soon, and I must get to the mainland before the tide changes." There was a new urgency to his voice.

I stood. "Thank you for the tea," I said. "The cinnamon helped."

"I'll mail your letter," he said. "Don't worry."

I had completely forgotten about Frederick.

Back in my room, I settled under the quilts for a quick nap, but his voice played on repeat in my mind. I tried to mimic his accent as I whispered his name, but I couldn't make it sound the way it came from his lips. Pellerine, Pellerine. Pellerine.

I huffed and rolled over to my side. His lips were the last thing I should be concentrating on.

Before I feel asleep, I realized our names rhymed.

Emeline Pellerine.

Unable to help myself, I smiled into the pillow.

CHAPTER TWENTY-TWO

The late-afternoon sky was heavy with low-hanging clouds like a drooping bed canopy slowly descending over the island. My times were becoming mixed up, adding to the disorientation of Faraday. The hallway seemed especially narrow as I walked to Georgina's room. The more I tried to take a deep breath, the worse the stagnation seemed. Even the cold drafts weren't affording any relief.

The anticipation grew as I neared her room.

I was eager to see if there was any change since she would have missed the breakfast dose of mushroom tea. I had to ask her about the paintings I found. As disturbing as they were, I sensed she would remember if I mentioned them. I even considered sneaking one up to her room.

When I knocked on the door, Mrs. Clayton shooed me away, saying Georgina was too tired and that I should come again after supper. I tried to peek around her hulking form, but she closed the door in my face.

Mrs. Clayton remained at the top of my suspect list. I thought again about the treasure rumor. Although from the conversation I overheard, it seemed Mrs. Clayton thought only fools would go looking for the cursed gold.

I had to be careful and make sure there was proof. For now, I had to wait until after supper. Hopefully Georgina had improved and was eager to talk.

Hettie stood at the large round window. She was staring forlornly at the scenery. When I came near, she lifted her nose. "Bad weather is coming," she said. "If Reverend Pellerine isn't back in an hour, he'll have to wait until low tide tomorrow."

I tried to hide the disappointment in my expression. "Where's Moses?" I asked, worried about the coming weather.

She smirked. "They're together. I walked them to the land bridge this morning while you were still asleep."

I smiled to myself, thinking of the secret tea we'd shared before dawn. My happiness quickly deflated, though—as Captain Graves's fiancée, I had no place in any competition for Reverend Pellerine's affections. A vague glumness settled over me.

Then she added, "Captain Graves is looking for you."

I instinctively cowered, remembering what he'd said the other night. His calm demeanor as he burned my letter was more terrifying than if he'd raged and stomped his feet. Wanting to avoid the captain, I put on my cloak and bonnet and snuck out the back of the house, taking a shortcut through the kitchen.

The sharp air jolted me awake. With my hands tucked inside the cloak, I made my way down the path alongside the carriage house. I found the familiar brightly colored mushrooms and wished I had taken the book with me to confirm these were indeed toxic. I wasn't far from the site of my accident the other day.

With my boots softly crunching on the forest floor, I hesitantly neared the hole in the ground. Mr. Clayton had said he would mark the area to prevent someone else falling in, but nothing had been done. I regarded the area more closely knowing it could very well have been my grave that first day. My claw marks were visible in the dirt among the trampled mushrooms. A shiver that had nothing to do with the temperature rolled over me. I found a rock and tossed it into the black mouth. I counted to four before I heard the echo of it hitting the bottom.

I backed away, fighting images of my body sprawled at the bottom, my unblinking gaze forever staring upward into the sky. Dead.

I couldn't shake the feeling I was a ghost, walking among the other spirits of Faraday, unaware of my own death.

Ghosts don't even know they're dead. They wander around, completing their daily tasks same as when they were alive.

Returning to the path, I saw movement through the trees up ahead. Mr. Clayton was digging up something. He had his back to me.

I hid behind a tree trunk and watched. Grunting, he crouched down and plunged his hands into the soil, working the dirt. Then he made an exclamatory sound and tossed something into a small basket. After a few more handfuls he stood and turned.

I gasped.

His right eye was swollen shut. And across his cheekbone was an angry gash. He froze when he saw me. Then, with a quick hand, he adjusted his cap, but the damage was still visible. Guilt pressed into me, heavy and unrelenting. I came out sheepishly from behind the tree.

"I don't begrudge your reaction at all, Miss Fitzpatrick. I'm uglier than my name today."

"I didn't mean to spy, Bagnall," I said, hoping he would take me using his first name as a peace offering. "I heard a noise and thought you were a bear." That was only a partial lie since the forest held all kinds of dangers in my mind.

He started to walk toward me, and I to him, being careful not to trip on the roots zigzagging across the forest floor. We met on the path. The basket hung over the crook of his arm. He carried a small shovel in his other hand.

I tried to look only at the unmarred eye.

"Maybe this would be a good time for me to give you a tour of the grounds?" He saw my hesitation and put a hand tenderly to the right side of his face. "Please don't let this distract you. It looks much worse than it feels. The missus is always telling me to pay better attention. I'm terribly clumsy."

I sensed he wasn't going to mention Captain Graves, or the letter, and I was happy to play along.

"I'll make sure you see my handsome side," he joked, turning his face to hide the bruised part. He was an attractive man, and I could see how he would have turned many heads in his day.

I happened to look inside his basket. A chill ran through me. "What are those?" I asked, my voice shaking.

"Agaricus campestris." He held up a pale mushroom with a wide base. Dirt still clung to the top. "The missus gave me a list." He tilted the basket to show the assortment he'd collected. However, there were not any brightly colored ones. "You have to be careful, though," he warned. "Some of them are quite harmful."

"What does Mrs. Clayton use them for?"

"A variety of uses: mostly stews and gravy, and frying up with butter, but some she dries for tea." Then he looked a bit impish. "And some are best enjoyed on their own in small amounts because they can make you feel like you've had an entire cask of rum. They'll even make you see things that aren't there." His laughter petered out and he became more serious. "I think she even puts a tad in Mrs. Graves's tea. Anything to help with the pain."

Had my visions been the result of Mrs. Clayton's mushrooms? I didn't remember seeing any of them in my meals, but the teas were another matter. The bitterness could be masked with herbs or even honey.

A small alarm started at the back of my mind.

Mr. Clayton took me along the path that wound around the island. He pointed out different kinds of vegetation and the various berries Mrs. Clayton made into wine. His voice droned on as I reconsidered my earlier suspicions.

We ended up leaving the woods as the path opened to a clearing. A large pond was surrounded by spruce trees on one side, protecting it from the ocean breeze. There was a fragile layer of ice on the surface.

Everything was brown and lifeless, but there was a sense of hidden danger. As if something was waiting under all the decay to grab my ankles and drag me into the pond, never to be seen again.

Faraday House stood on top of the slope, ever looming. There was a flicker of movement at the study window. I suspected Captain Graves was watching us.

Mr. Clayton said, "The path continues around the pond and eventually leads to our cottage."

The wind picked up. He tipped his cap back and looked at the sky. "It looks like we're in for a rough night," he said.

"I'm sorry Reverend Pellerine won't make it back today."

His expression became guarded. "We'll be just fine without him."

"You don't sound like an admirer." His attitude was the very opposite of his wife's.

"No other Frenchmen are around this part of the coast. Makes me wonder why he chose to come to Shoreham." He narrowed his eyes, then leaned closer. "Some people might question where his loyalties lie. We just got out of a war; who's to say it won't start up again in a few years? Faraday is a strategic spot. A solid house built like a fortress with cannons on the roof could be a valuable place indeed."

My jaw dropped at his blatant declaration. However, the fact he'd shared this allowed me to consider he might be willing to speak more. "You don't trust him?" I asked.

He tightened the grip on his shovel then shrugged. "The missus knows the Bible inside and out and could recite any passage. Not him, though. I find that worrisome."

"That he doesn't have the Bible memorized? It's more about the lessons, isn't it?"

He studied me for a moment, and his expression changed, became closed, as if he sensed I was not going to join his bullying. Then he chuckled lightly in an attempt to erase all that he'd just said. "Don't listen to me. I'm rambling. Spending the better part of my life on this island has altered my way of looking at things."

It seemed Mr. Clayton didn't trust or like either Captain Graves or Reverend Pellerine. I began to wonder what he secretly thought of me.

He looked through the trees at the bay. "It's awfully pretty in the summer, though." He smiled, but it made his swollen eye seem more disfiguring. "I hope you'll be happy here."

CHAPTER TWENTY-THREE

After supper I was allowed to see Georgina. She was as frail as the last time I saw her, but there was a difference in her expression; it was more relaxed and at ease. There was even a spot of color to her complexion, though it may have been a reflection off the pink walls, made vibrant by the number of candles burning. Her bedroom was an oasis of light within the melancholy house. The pearl within the oyster.

She smiled and took my hand as I sat by her bed. "Your cheeks are red," she said. "Into the wine already?"

"I was going to ask the same of you."

Mrs. Clayton grumbled under her breath as she stayed within earshot, folding cloths that were already folded.

Ignoring Mrs. Clayton, I replied to Georgina, "Would you like some? I could run to the kitchen." I remembered the bottles of blueberry wine in the pantry.

Mrs. Clayton answered for her. "How can you even offer something like that to Mrs. Graves? Her stomach can't handle wine." Her accusatory tone cut deep. "I know you have no brain, but do you lack compassion as well?"

My heart dropped. An apology for my lack of sense was on my lips, but Georgina spoke first.

"More candles, please, Mrs. Clayton," she requested.

Mrs. Clayton stopped folding. A look of adoration replaced her typical scowl, making her appear younger. She smiled at Georgina.

"Of course, Mrs. Graves." She made a quick departure but fired a hard glance my way before she left. Her dislike of me seemed more out of proportion than usual. Why the sudden hate?

Georgina gave my fingers a playful swat. "Why do you let her speak to you that way?" she asked. "You're going to be mistress of Faraday; act the part."

Surprise and shame stole my voice for a moment. "I'm so sorry," I finally said. "I wanted to be honest from the beginning, but I was worried it would upset you."

"No need to be apologetic, Emeline," she said. "I may be dying, but I'm not deaf, nor am I stupid." She squeezed my hand. "I know this will sound strange, but I have enjoyed your company."

"I have too. I wish you to stay alive. I would be more than happy to be your maid instead."

"It gives me comfort to know you'll be taking my place. Edgar can seem harsh, but he's used to ordering a crew around. And his first wife died so tragically, leaving a void in his heart." She paused a moment as if struck by something she hadn't thought of.

"Esther," I prompted her.

She put a hand to her temple and started again. "Yes." Her brow crinkled. Apprehension clouded her eyes. "It's so confusing . . . not knowing who or what is real or just a dream."

Even though we were alone, I leaned closer. "I found your paintings," I told her. "They were hidden off the music room. There's one of Esther." I tried to gauge her reaction. "She's wearing a red dress." I wasn't sure if I should fully describe the scene, as troubling as it was.

"Red." She said that one word in a trembling whisper.

I nodded. "And there's one of the room in the tower."

She chewed her lower lip. "I don't remember." Her thin fingers started gripping the sheets, and her breathing sped up. "Perhaps Edgar knows. Can you ask him?"

My hands rested gently over hers. "That's a good idea." I smiled, hoping the panic didn't show on my face. "I will."

The worried frown lines melted from her thin face as she sighed and leaned back onto her pillow. Georgina blinked lazily at me a few times, and I suspected she would soon fall asleep. Instead, she snickered and said, "Your cheeks are red. Have you been into the wine?"

The smile froze on my face. Her memory had worsened. Taking away the mushrooms hadn't made any difference. She really was dying.

"Tell me a story," she prompted, unaware of my agony. "Your voice is so soothing."

With my heart silently breaking, I told her how I had wandered the island today with Mr. Clayton. She fell asleep while I described the ice over the pond.

I let go of her hand and leaned back in the chair. My earlier optimism had completely eroded, leaving me bone weary. I ducked my head low and checked under the bed, but the field book was gone.

I reasoned Mrs. Clayton had found it and returned it to the music room bookcase. Regardless, there was nothing else I could do about the mushrooms. I had to admit they were just a coincidence.

As I sat in the softly lit pink room, listening to Georgina breathe, I reviewed everything I knew was true about Faraday House, including everything I'd seen and heard.

I knew the ceiling stain was true. I knew the sound of pacing in the tower room was true. I knew Esther had died in that room.

Being open to any possibility meant there was only one answer.

The reason was Esther. Or rather, Esther's ghost.

After all, people have souls—what happens to that soul after they die? If people believe in heaven and hell, is it such a stretch to believe a soul would stay on Earth?

Esther's ghost was real and trying to communicate with us.

Once I allowed myself to accept this theory, my heart clutched it viciously. And while I was only beginning to wonder what she was trying to tell us with the dreams and visions, I was left with one very important question: Why were Georgina and I the only ones at Faraday affected?

Esther had known the Claytons and Captain Graves, of course. But she hadn't met Hettie or the reverend while she was alive. So why only try to communicate with Georgina and, now, me?

Then it came to me. We were the only ones she trusted.

CHAPTER TWENTY-FOUR

S hh," someone whispered. A light touch nudged my shoulder. I blinked drowsily in the chair. Sunlight poured through the window. I stretched my arms, feeling my stiff back protest. Slowly the room came into focus.

A vase of bright wildflowers sat on the windowsill, giving the room a fresh scent. Birdsong trilled sweetly outside.

I gazed around in confusion.

On Georgina's vanity were tiny bottles of perfume, a glass bowl of face powder, and a silver-handled hairbrush. A pair of ornate hair combs with inlaid pearls were placed delicately on a lace handkerchief. They looked familiar.

But where were the washcloths and the basin? And the bottles of medicine and Mrs. Clayton's holy water? And Martha, the doll?

An uncertain nervousness began to grow in me. I turned to Georgina and my heart stopped. The bed was empty, but the pillow still had the indentation of her head, and the covers were flung back as if someone had gotten up quickly.

I jumped up and looked around wildly. The serving tray with the teapots was gone as well. With my pulse racing, I clambered from the room. Where could Georgina have gone?

Across the hallway, Captain Graves's bedroom door was open. I hesitated, unsure. I tried to ignore the gnawing panic as I waited and listened for any familiar voices, but only the clock on the landing answered my silent plea. At least it was familiar, though, and it gave me enough of a push to look tentatively beyond the captain's door.

It was a masculine room with a large four-poster bed in dark wood with a matching armoire and small table and chair by the window. There were no soft edges or floral patterns. In fact, all the material, from the bed coverings to the drapes, was dark blue patterned with only a thin strip of silver trim.

The bed was neatly made. There were no personal effects on either of the bedside tables or in the sitting area by the window. Long drapes had been drawn closed, blocking any daylight and giving the room an abandoned feel.

It was clear Georgina was not in that room either. A horrible realization hit me. Had she wandered off and fallen down the stairs? I ran to the railing and looked down at the foyer, fearing the absolute worst. Relief coursed through my veins when I saw the area was clear.

But where was she? She seemed so fragile I hardly imagined she'd have the energy to even make it down the hall. I had to consider she may have gone to my room. Had she tried to return to the tower? Light spilled through the large round window, filling the second floor with a golden warmth.

I turned on the spot, disoriented by the subtle changes in the house. It was too bright for November. Too warm.

Faint sobbing came from below. I descended to the main level, jumping the last few stairs. Any leftover grogginess of sleep was completely gone. I stood in the foyer, trying to see and hear any kind of clue.

The crying came again, followed by hushed pleas.

What was happening? I ran past the schooner paintings but stopped abruptly at the last one. Georgina's picture wasn't there. I pressed my palm to the empty space on the wall. It was cold and hard.

It was like she'd been erased. Had she died in the night while I slept in the chair beside her? Nothing made sense. Before I could try and reason it out, the crying sounded again.

The familiar shelves of blueberry wine and various crockery greeted me as I sped to the main kitchen area.

Out of breath, I skidded to a stop.

Hettie sat at the kitchen table with her head in her hands, weeping. Her dark brown hair was untied and cascading down her back. "Shh . . . there now." Mrs. Clayton stood over her, patting her shoulder. "It's going to be all right. We'll figure something out."

Despite the questions going through my mind, Hettie's desperate tears pulled on my heart. She was truly terrified. A gasp followed by more sobs. I stayed still. Neither one of them noticed me, watching from the shadows.

"Shh," Mrs. Clayton continued.

Her voice went through me like an arrow. The familiarity of the word was chilling.

Hettie stayed bent over, face still covered with her hands. "I feel so guilty," she said, her voice thick with despair. "He'll find out what I did. He'll never forgive me." Her shoulders shook as she let out another series of ragged sobs.

I went completely numb with shock. Hettie had killed Georgina! She'd finally given her enough poison, and now Captain Graves will discover her murderous scheme.

Mrs. Clayton grimaced in similar desperation. Then her expression rallied. "He won't return for a bit, so we've got time to prepare."

What? Where did Captain Graves go? A coldness wrapped around me. Unless they're talking about Reverend Pellerine.

"I'm so scared of what will happen." Hettie sobbed.

Mrs. Clayton then said, "I've got all kinds of teas we can try. Don't you worry." Her tone was firm, supportive, encouraging.

I could stay quiet no longer. Anger propelled me to come out of the shadows. Poor, sweet Georgina. They had already gotten rid of her painting as if she never existed. Taking in a deep breath, I marched into the kitchen. "How dare you!" I hollered.

Mrs. Clayton continued to pat Hettie's bowed head, unaffected by my sudden appearance. My voice was swallowed up in the quiet space. Neither woman looked my way.

"I'm going straight to the magistrate," I said.

Again, I was ignored.

"Come now," Mrs. Clayton soothed. "The kitchen floor will be covered in more salt water than the ocean. There's no wishing your cake was dough. You're not the first woman to find herself in this situation. Trust me, my mother sold more of these remedies than her chest cold poultices."

Hettie's breathing seemed to calm.

Mrs. Clayton said, "We can start tomorrow. For now, get yourself to bed—you'll need to be rested up."

A sniff, then Hettie finally raised her head. I saw her tear-streaked face. "I don't know what I'd do without you," she said to Mrs. Clayton. "Thank you." Except it wasn't Hettie.

It was Esther.

I WOKE TO someone touching my shoulder and whispering my name.

I started with a jolt.

Captain Graves leaned over me, his thick brows drawn together in concern. "Did you stay all night?" There was an edge to his question, like an accusation.

With the dream still fresh in my mind, I looked at the bed. Georgina was there, and still alive.

I checked the vanity: the pearl hair combs were gone, now replaced with the neatly folded washcloths. Martha sat in her little chair with her crumpled parasol over one shoulder.

Hettie placed a serving tray noisily on the table in front of the settee and started to set up breakfast for the captain and Georgina. "I suppose I'll be having to make another trip to the kitchen for an extra breakfast," she said. She was overly confident to the point of being haughty. Almost as if she knew she was impervious to consequences from her employer.

"No need," Captain Graves told her. "Leave the tray for me when I return." Then he helped me to stand. His hair was combed back, and his shirt was white and crisp. "Come, Emeline," he said, putting a hand under my arm and helping me stand. "Your devotion does me proud, but I can't have you getting sick too."

Without looking at Georgina, he put his arm around my waist and escorted me to the hallway. Even through his jacket and waistcoat, I could feel the firmness of his grip on me. I was in no doubt he would have carried me in his arms if I was too groggy.

I could still feel the lines of the quilt on my face, and my mouth was full of cotton. Mrs. Shackleton would be murderous if she knew I'd allowed my fiancé to see me this way.

Captain Graves said, "I may not be able to be there all day long, but I make sure we share the first meal of the day together. I prefer to be with her alone. Many things can be said."

I nodded, dumbfounded as the dream replayed through my mind. Had I seen a vision from the past? That would explain Georgina's missing painting and why the room was different. Esther was showing me the scene for a reason, and only Mrs. Clayton would be able to confirm. I wasn't sure if I could trust her, let alone approach her without fear of being reprimanded or betrayed to the captain. I still remember how she spoke about me not lasting long as if I were a delicate flower trying to bloom in the winter frost.

Captain Graves continued, "I used to pretend she was going to improve, but now we use that time to just be with each other; sometimes words aren't necessary."

I was torn. I didn't know who to trust, but I needed help. I decided I would wait for Reverend Pellerine to return this afternoon. Even though Mr. Clayton had made his reservations clear, I couldn't care less about the reverend being French.

Being haunted put things into a new perspective.

Captain Graves opened my bedroom door and ushered me inside. "Please rest in," he said. "I'll have Mrs. Clayton send up a tray. I don't want you to ever want for anything."

The thought of seeing Mrs. Clayton in person set my nerves to jittering.

He looked at me questioningly, then his eyes became soft, apologetic. "I confess, I was hasty in chastising you the other evening about not being part of the household." He took my hand and held it between both of his. "I can only pray God will see fit to absolve me of any further tragedies and finally bestow happiness on me." He bowed over my hand, pressing his dry lips to it.

It was impressive how the captain continued to see himself as the victim.

After he left, I slipped under the quilts and tried to organize my thoughts.

It's blood. Her blood.

Esther died in the room above me. What did she feel so guilty about? And how was Mrs. Clayton going to help her? Whatever their plan, obviously something horrible had happened.

A distressing thought occurred to me. Captain Graves wanted an heir more than anything. Being married to someone who couldn't give him one would be disastrous in his mind. Was that what had happened with Esther? And was it happening to Georgina?

If he was as ill as Mrs. Clayton believed, his time was running out quickly.

Mushrooms may not be the poison, but Captain Graves certainly had reason to make sure he didn't have to wait long before marrying his next wife.

Me.

THE SUN WAS already past the midday arc in the pale sky when I woke. I grew anxious to see the horizon. There were tendrils left over from a dream of Frederick on a ship, but I was uneasy with the image of him smiling at the turquoise ocean instead of the dark waves of the North Atlantic.

Wrapping myself in my dressing gown, I went to the tower, shivering in the cold as I climbed the spiral steps.

The only signs of life were my footprints from the other day. I went to the window and squinted through the film on the outside of the glass. It made the view permanently foggy. I had to find a way to the beach. I needed to stand watch so I wouldn't miss his ship.

I returned to my bedroom, pulling the tapestry back into place. There was a knock at the door, followed by Hettie's impatient voice. "Breakfast." I was relieved it wasn't Mrs. Clayton.

She brought in a tray. The smell made my mouth water. I perched on the bed, eager to tuck into the meal of toast and hard-boiled egg.

Hettie frowned as she looked around my room, silently critiquing how I'd left my clothes in a heap at the foot of the bed.

"Thank you, Hettie. That will be all." The order sounded strange coming from my mouth.

She started to leave as she grumbled under her breath, "Must be nice to sleep in so late."

"Wait, do you know how to get to the beach?" I asked her.

Pausing at the door, she answered over her shoulder. "There's a path that goes through the woods. Just follow it until there's a split. Upward takes you to cemetery hill, the other down to the beach."

I thought of the hole. "I will definitely stick to the path," I said.

Hettie yawned behind her hand. "Why do you want to go to the beach?"

"I was going to bring back something pretty for Georgina to paint. She misses the outdoors. Maybe a bouquet?"

"A bouquet of what, eelgrass and seaweed?" She rolled her eyes then closed the door behind her.

I finished the breakfast quickly, then dressed for the day and put on my red cloak and bonnet. The face in the mirror had grown pale and sickly looking. I looked into Georgina's room. She was asleep. It may have been my imagination, but her cheeks appeared rosier. The anxious grip around my heart eased.

Captain Graves sat at the foot of the bed. I noticed he'd moved the chair from its usual spot to farther away. He looked pained as he watched her breathe. But as much as I prayed for her breaths to continue, I wasn't certain his hope was the same.

CHAPTER TWENTY-FIVE

Following Hettie's instructions, I found the path that led to the shore and finally emerged onto a rocky beach. To the left was the mainland with its hills dotted with houses and the road along the water. It was another world altogether, one where curses didn't exist. Even though I could easily cross the land bridge on foot at low tide, the fear of missing Frederick's ship kept me anchored to this island.

Straight ahead was the North Atlantic, the unobstructed view I'd been obsessing about. Finally seeing it felt like an accomplishment. I squinted at the horizon, imagining the whitecap of each wave to be the sails of a schooner.

Moving closer to the water, my feet worked to find purchase on the sun-bleached stones. A smooth one fit perfectly in my palm. My thumb rubbed over it, polishing the powdery salt off its surface. There was an unbroken stripe all the way around its circumference.

A gull was nearby, busy with something in a large mass of seaweed. I made my way carefully over the slippery and uneven terrain to see what had interested the bird so much. I could bring something interesting back for Georgina.

I screamed as a face stared up at me. My stomach lurched, and I fought to keep my breakfast down. There wasn't much left of the poor creature, only the flippers and tail. The insides had been picked over, exposing the skeleton.

A seal.

I stumbled away, heavy with the realization I could not escape death no matter where I ventured on this island.

A dog barked in the distance. I shielded my face with my hand and squinted as a silhouette came into view. The broad hat and easy gait were recognizable at once. A large package was under one arm.

My melancholy was replaced with anticipation.

Moses padded over on his massive paws. Strings of drool hung from either side of his jaws, swaying back and forth.

"Miss Fitzpatrick," Reverend Pellerine called out. "Are you all right?"

I felt a needle of insult to my pride. Did I look that helpless? I was about to retort with a sarcastic remark when I remembered I'd nearly fallen down an abandoned pit the first day, so I supposed it was a fair question after all. "Just taking in the view," I finally replied.

He put down the package and made his way closer. The irregular terrain of the beach rocks didn't seem to hamper his travels, and he easily navigated to where I stood. Moses barked and waited beside me, but his tail continued to swish through the air.

It was comforting to have the dog between us. I tried to phrase how I would bring up the vision of Esther and Mrs. Clayton.

"How is Georgina?" he asked carefully. I suspected he reasoned if her health had taken a bad turn, it would have shown on my face.

"This morning she was comfortable," I said. "And last night we had a long chat."

"Glad to hear it." Reverend Pellerine picked up a piece of driftwood and gave it an impressive throw into the waves.

I gasped as Moses launched into the water, ignoring the waves crashing around him as he battled against the tide. "He'll drown," I cried out.

The reverend laughed. "Moses is a Newfoundland dog. He was bred to live by the ocean. You should see him cross the ice flats when the harbor freezes—he's like a frog on a lily pad. He's as agile as any sailor or fisherman." The jovial expression was so foreign to see on his face. Hettie would have fainted from the rush of desire.

Soon I was smiling back—a genuine one. It felt effortless. Moses continued to lumber into the waves each time Reverend Pellerine tossed another piece of wood.

It was comforting to watch.

The wind changed, and Moses put his snout in the air. He started toward the dead seal. Reverend Pellerine whistled, calling him back.

Moses returned immediately and shook his great mane like a lion, spraying everything close by with seawater and sand. I squealed wholeheartedly, trying to shield myself from the flying mess. "No wonder I thought he was a bear."

Reverend Pellerine nodded with a smile. "He could survive the worst storm. That's how I found him, actually. Ships wreck along the coast all the time. A few years ago I was searching the shore after high gales sent a clipper onto the rocks. We were looking for survivors and whatever else had washed up."

I cringed, picturing the corpses of sailors. "Sounds gruesome."

His expression was neutral, but he shrugged in reply, making me think he was used to such things. "I heard noises by the edge of the water, then this black nose pops up through the seaweed."

"Ah, that's why you call him Moses. Has he parted the ocean for you yet?"

He laughed again. It was a soothing sound. "Only when the tide goes down and the road emerges to the mainland."

Moses shambled over and dropped the wet stick at my feet. He looked expectantly up at me with large eyes. "And he's been with you ever since?" I asked. I wondered if the reverend was in a hurry to return to Faraday House. Selfishly, I wanted to keep us both on that beach with Moses a little while longer.

Reverend Pellerine let out a poorly disguised laugh as I attempted to toss the driftwood into the waves. It barely made it to the edge of the water. "A dog's loyalty is unsurpassed," he said. "Moses loves unconditionally. Much like a parent."

I could not remember my parents' love, only a terrible hollowness where something used to exist. The words came out before I had a chance to check myself. "You're lucky to have him," I said.

The wind played with the edge of his cloak, sending it backward. He hit me with those eyes. "Accepting that unconditional love is as important, though."

His words carried an unspoken weight, and I had to look away for fear he could read my heart and see my torment. But most worryingly, I feared he would see my secret. A sin in God's eyes if ever there was one.

The waves continued to wash over the shoreline close to our feet. Neither of us attempted to move back as the tide crept in. He looked at my hand. "You've found a wishing stone."

I was still holding the rock with the perfect white band. "Do they really work?" My voice sounded hopeful, and it must have been painfully obvious, because the look he gave me bordered on pity. I sounded like a child, thinking a wish could fix my worries.

His voice softened. "The important thing is that you have something to wish for. To be hopeful."

I wasn't hopeful for Frederick to rescue me, I was desperate. "Hope is not the same thing as a wish." My words were clipped, curt. I was more upset with myself than with him. He looked at me quizzically. I offered, "I'm hoping to see a ship from Halifax, a bit of home." I turned back to the ocean.

"I see." He took off his hat and ran a hand through his dark hair, staring at the ocean. "I mailed your letter," he said. "First time I've ever sent something to the Royal Navy, I can assure you." Sternness hardened his words.

A gamut of emotions swirled in my soul, but I kept my expression neutral. "Thank you." I waited for the relief. My goal had been to send that letter, but the confirmation brought no sense of accomplishment or victory.

His fringe of dark hair blew back. He put his hat back in place, pulling down the front with an extra tug against the wind. He pointed in the direction he'd come. "We're close to the main path to Faraday. Can I walk you back?"

I nodded, putting the stone in my pocket, my wish on silent repeat in my mind. Reverend Pellerine retrieved the large package as Moses trotted ahead, loping over the uneven beach.

"This is for you," he said. "Arrived at the post office today by carriage. It's from Halifax."

I took a close look at the written address. My heart jumped madly as I recognized Ada's script.

"I'll carry it," he said, tucking it back under his arm. "It's a bit cumbersome."

"Yes, thank you." I had no idea what would be in such a large package, but anything from home was welcome. It had to be a positive development. A series of lovely possibilities crowded my mind.

Frederick must have explained everything. The relief sent rivers of happiness through me. I imagined taking Georgina with me, and nursing her myself, back in Halifax. Then we would both leave for Bermuda together. I gave the wishing stone in my pocket an extra rub with my thumb.

Moses led us to a path different from the one I had used earlier.

I was beginning to appreciate that the island was full of opportunities to get lost . . . or killed. "He seems eager to return to the house," I said.

"Moses hates the house." He chuckled. "I can only get him as far as the kitchen. He prefers the cottage. Mrs. Clayton spoils him with table scraps."

A gentle comfort slipped around us as the tension from the beach dissipated. We walked along a pathway through the tress until we emerged on the main road to the house. I was all exuberance and smiles, picturing my exciting future. "How did you find me?" I asked, realizing the beach wasn't viewable from the road.

"Moses ran off. I simply followed him."

"You didn't whistle for him?"

He shrugged. "He seemed to know where he was going—thought I'd tag along."

I gave Moses a pat on his massive head as he walked alongside me. "I'm glad you did."

The tree-lined road was more pleasant in the daytime and provided shelter from the ocean breeze. The only sound was our boots crunching on the small stones. A lovely calm settled over our trio.

Moses let out a fierce bark and loped into the forest, quickly disappearing.

We both stopped. Reverend Pellerine sighed heavily and put down my package. He looked at me. "Squirrel," he said apologetically.

I squinted into the woods, thinking of the deep holes around the island. "Should we go after him?"

Reverend Pellerine cupped his hands around his mouth. "Moses!"

We waited. No rustling through the bushes, no barking.

Then Reverend Pellerine whistled. It was an impressive pitch, and it echoed through the forest.

"I would suggest caution," I told him. "You'll summon an army of forest creatures."

"It's all in the frequency, Miss Fitzpatrick." He whistled again. Moses's bulky form emerged from the trees up ahead. He sat in the middle of the road, waiting for us. Reverend Pellerine wore a satisfied smile. "We all respond to our own special frequency."

"Are you saying we all have our own whistle? How mortifying."

"Not to be heard but felt." He put his hand over his heart. "A certain tone of voice, for instance, or a note on a piano, can resonate deeply with one person and not another." He tilted his chin down, staring at me from under the band of his hat. I suspected he knew how intense it made his eyes appear. "It's not what the whisperer says but how the vibration feels against the ear. The vibrations call to us, especially."

I felt scarlet heat fill my cheeks, impossible to hide under my bonnet. "Does that mean Moses will only answer to your whistle?" I challenged.

He touched the tip of his hat and stepped aside. Then he picked up a stick and effortlessly sent it sailing far ahead of us. Moses went after it, his black body bounding happily.

"Go ahead," Reverend Pellerine said. "Whistle him back."

I had no idea how to whistle. I puckered my mouth and blew. It sounded like a wounded bird.

His faced scrunched up in exaggerated discomfort. "That vibration will resonate with no one."

Moses had the stick in his mouth. He flung it in the air, then pounced on it and started to chew the end.

"You have to curl your tongue and wet your lips," Reverend Pellerine said. We exchanged a glance that lasted a heartbeat too long. His face began to redden. He cleared his throat, then picked up the package and started up the road.

Lesson over.

I stood my ground. I hated not being able to do this one simple thing. I wet my lips and tried again. The result was slightly better, but far from a whistle.

Reverend Pellerine turned around, his eyebrows raised in surprise.

"Oh?" I replied. "Was that your frequency? My apologies. I was trying for the dog."

He gaped at me, clearly shocked by my obvious flirting. I had finally crossed the overstretched boundary of appropriateness with him. Silently chastising myself, I readied an apology in my head, but then, slowly, a corner of his mouth lifted. He gave me a crooked smile as he touched the brim of his hat. In his usual graceful style, he turned and strolled after Moses. His pace was much slower, and I caught up to him easily.

The rest of the walk back gave me enough time to produce an actual whistle. I shyly felt very proud of myself. Moses came to me each time, and I rewarded him with an ear scratch. I was thinking I should ask Frederick to get a dog for us. Surely a big dog would be an asset on the ship.

"If you continue to practice, you'll have him at your service no matter what." Reverend Pellerine switched the package from under one arm to the other.

"My service? I thought he was loyal to you."

"He can be loyal to more than one. Moses is a good judge of character. I trust him."

"Why didn't you take a carriage back?" I asked, seeing how arduous traveling by foot was with such a heavy load. I tried to look concerned for his strength but was secretly preoccupied by what the surprise could be. The heavier the better when it came to presents.

"I did. The driver dropped me off at the beginning of the island."

"That's rude of him," I said, noting the large package.

"It's superstitious nonsense." He nodded to the north. "That part of the island had a run of successful crops, but each year fewer workers returned until there was no one to work the land." He shrugged. "It's a shame—think of all that lost cabbage potential."

I turned away so he couldn't see me smile behind the brim of my bonnet.

Soon the road curved, and gradually the first corner of Faraday came into view. Moses held back, whining.

The door opened and Hettie came running out. "Welcome home," she said. Neither Reverend Pellerine nor I replied. I was inclined to believe he didn't consider Faraday his home either.

She focused on the large package in his arms. "What have you brought us?" she asked, eyes dancing.

We exchanged a quick look. He passed the package to her. "Please take this to Miss Fitzpatrick's room."

She smiled tersely, most likely fighting the sneer that was just below the surface.

"I'll join you partway," he said, using a consolatory tone. "I'd like to check on Mrs. Graves."

That gave her grin a lift. I followed behind as they made their way into the foyer. I checked over my shoulder, expecting to see Moses ramble off. Instead, he waited until I was inside, then eased himself down in the middle of the drive. His massive head dropped to his paws. I liked the idea of having him close. I felt special, chosen.

"You're back. Finally." Captain Graves stood in the doorway to his study. He stared at the reverend and me with dark eyes, severe and challenging. He must have found out about the second letter. Foreboding encircled me in a suffocating grip.

"As the tide dictates," Reverend Pellerine answered, standing tall. I admired the steady tone.

"I need a word, Reverend." Then Captain Graves turned briskly and disappeared back into his study. I feared I had gotten Reverend Pellerine in trouble. I hated to picture him with a black eye. Although part of me suspected he would be able to handle a punch, and maybe throw one or two of his own for good measure.

I considered trying to whistle Moses into the house as a backup fighter.

The door to the study shut loudly, making me flinch. "I hope nothing is wrong." I turned to Hettie, my stomach in knots at the image of a fight breaking out in the study.

"Nothing I have to worry about," Hettie replied. She made no attempt to hide her expression of devilish anticipation as she sauntered casually to the staircase.

CHAPTER TWENTY-SIX

After gathering a few items from my vanity, I made my way to the other end of the hall, to Georgina's room. I knocked on the closed door and announced myself.

Mrs. Clayton's voice came from the other side, gruff and clipped. "Just a moment."

I could hear Georgina's softer reply. I put my ear to the door. ". . . what's real and what's a dream?"

She sounded scared. Had our conversation about her paintings brought more nightmares, or was it Esther reaching out? I wished I could take all the visions so Georgina could rest easier.

Mrs. Clayton opened the door and ushered me inside.

She busied herself tidying up the washing things and tucking them into the basin. This was the first time I'd been with her since my dream about Esther in the kitchen. From the corner of my eye, I saw her give the writing desk a quick glance. She said, "I'll be in the kitchen if you need anything." Her usual ornery attitude was more docile.

I made my way to Georgina's bedside. She looked pale, but she was in a clean nightgown, and her face, although thin, had a slight pinkish hue.

"I brought you something," I said, slipping the wishing stone into her palm.

Georgina lifted it to her nose and closed her eyes. "I can smell the ocean." She kept it in her hand, letting her thumb smooth over the surface. I had only one wish: for Georgina to stay alive. I had moved Frederick below her.

Then I showed her my brush and ribbons. With only gentle coaxing, I soon had her sitting forward as I stood beside her bed, brushing her hair.

"That feels so nice," she said.

"I may not have many talents, but hair is something I have confidence in. Back home, Ada would do this particular style . . ." A large clump of hair came away from her head. My hands shook.

"Is something wrong?" Georgina asked.

"I want to be mindful of the tangles," I said. I started to use the brush again, but more carefully, taking care not to pull at all. Only then was I able to see that the back of her head was mostly bald. I supposed that was the reason they never brushed her hair. I wondered when it had started falling out.

Tears threatened to come. How cruel death was to rob her of her beauty before it took her life.

The small bit of care with the brush made a difference. I divided what little hair she had into thirds and started a braid. When I finished, I let it trail over her shoulder and halfway down her chest. Georgina pinched the end of it, her fingers feeling the ribbons I had used.

"You are too sweet," she said. "I feel like a person again. Thank you."

I bit the inside of my cheek to keep myself from crying. "Should I give Martha a brush as well?" I tried to joke, reaching for the doll nestled beside Georgina. I frowned at the dress. There were black stains all along the hem. "What happened to her outfit?"

Georgina put a hand over the doll, blocking my reach. "She's showing her age; she hates getting old." Letting out a heavy sigh, she stared at the window. "This bed is like a raft in the middle of the ocean: I can't leave it or I'll die." She smelled the rock again. "I wish I could breathe fresh air one more time."

I had the bizarre suspicion she was trying to distract me.

"At least Hettie is bringing your tea this evening. It will be less bitter."

Georgina frowned at me. "Not always."

I WALKED BACK to my room in a fog, troubled by Georgina's behavior. When I opened the door, I had to blink a few times to confirm what I was seeing.

Hettie was standing in front of the mirror, holding up a white dress. Her face blanched completely. "Sorry, miss," she said, with no hint of her usual confidence. "It's just so beautiful. I was only unfolding it before I put it in the wardrobe so it wouldn't be wrinkled."

My focus left Hettie's harried explaining as I looked at the dress. Despite the gorgeous satin trim and intricate beadwork on the veil, dread squeezed my heart.

"You'll look mighty pretty in it," she said, now laying it carefully across the bed. The lace brocade bodice matched the trim on the cuffs. Each pleat at the waist was pressed to perfection. I imagined Ada carefully packing the dress. Did she cry, knowing she'd never see me wear it? Did she miss me? The setting sun caught the white fabric, giving it a rosy glow.

My wedding dress.

That was the package from home.

"This must have been placed inside." Hettie crouched down and picked up an envelope from the floor. "It has your name on it."

The script was only my first name. But it wasn't Ada's writing— it was Judge Shackleton's. I took it from Hettie, hoping she couldn't see my fingers tremble. "I'd like some privacy, please," I said.

She nodded, keeping her eye on the letter, then turned and let herself out. I could see the gears moving inside her head, wondering what news could possibly be important to me.

I pressed the envelope to my chest. A thousand whispered hopes and wishes burst from my soul. Judge Shackleton had never written to me, so I knew the letter would be of great importance. Please let it contain the truth about Frederick and me, and that he and Mrs. Shackleton have blessed our engagement. The wedding dress could very well be meant for my marriage to Frederick. His ship must be arriving soon. We'll be married on board! All thoughts of graves and ghosts disappeared. I would be leaving Faraday! I carefully unfolded the note, wanting to preserve it like the most delicate flower.

Dear Emeline,

Forgive my shaking hand. The news I am to relay is most shocking.

As soon as you left, I knew I had made a hasty decision. However, when you read the rest of this letter you will appreciate, as Mrs. Shackleton and I do, that we have avoided a great disaster by removing you from Halifax.

I have been making inquiries about your Lieutenant Fletcher. I confess, I am partially to blame for your attraction to him, as we hosted many dinners with the admiral and I may have voiced such fondness for the Royal Navy's service and bravery that it influenced your perception of any young man in a uniform.

It was confirmed by the harbor master that shortly after your departure, Lieutenant Fletcher was on the

first vessel that left that morning bound for Bermuda.
The admiral himself confided the trip had been arranged
weeks ago.

I looked up from the page, confused. That would mean Frederick had been at sea for several days. He should have been here yesterday. Dumbfounded, I continued to read.

It has been discovered that he had promised an
engagement to another young lady one county over—
whom he has also left behind.
    Do not waste your tears of jealousy, for the girl and
her family deserve our pity. He had taken a considerable
amount of money from the young girl's father in the
guise of investments. And now that family has been left
in considerable debt with no hope of recouping the lost
income.
    Mrs. Shackleton and I take it as God's providence we
have been spared that burden. Your marriage to Captain
Graves will sever any further connection to Lieutenant
Fletcher in the eyes of society and, more important, his
disreputable loaners.
    The admiral warned that more financial issues may
come to light as debt collectors are tracking down all
his acquaintances. Some are ruthless. Mrs. Shackleton
insisted we hire several men to guard the premises. It
seems like an exaggeration, but I would be remiss if I
did not also share this concern.
    All things considered, it gives us tremendous comfort
knowing you are taken care of and no longer associated
with that man. We are unsure when the danger will pass.

As such, it is imperative that you do not return to Halifax until you are married. I make this decision based on my own logic and care not only for you, but for what your parents would have wanted. To see their only child be ridiculed in society would be a failure on my part of the most disastrous kind.

I deeply regret not being able to attend your wedding, but we know you'll be the most beautiful bride.

It is fortunate indeed that you are safe with Captain Graves at Faraday House.

The note ended with his usual swirling signature.

The letter dropped from my hands as I went completely numb.

CHAPTER TWENTY-SEVEN

N o," I whispered. *It's lies. It's all lies.* Something the judge and Mrs. Shackleton had conjured up to convince themselves sending me away was the right choice. He was doing this to absolve himself of the guilt he felt for not having seen me off. They were trying to convince me it was in my best interest to stay at Faraday. They must have found out Georgina was still alive and feared I would return to them. Feared I would bring my disgrace back to them.

A darkness crept into the room from the edges. *I'm dying,* I thought. And I welcomed it. Frederick would arrive in time for them to put me in Georgina's grave. Maybe that's what the first dream was about.

I read the letter again. No, it wasn't true. It couldn't be true. I wouldn't let it be true.

I closed my eyes and heard Frederick whisper how much he loved me, how I was the most beautiful creature he'd ever seen. Whispers against my ear.

It's not the words, but the vibration.

I sat on the bed, unmoving. It was already darkening outside. I lit a candle and stared at the flame.

Hettie came to the door and told me supper was ready and that Captain Graves had requested my presence.

I couldn't even stand. I put a hand on my stomach. "No. I . . . I'm not feeling well. I think I caught a cold on my walk today."

"Captain Graves said . . ."

"Send up a tray instead," I choked out, close to tears. My thumbnail pressed deeply into the crook of my finger. There would be a permanent crescent shape soon. I couldn't let Hettie hear me cry.

Silence, then she said, "I'll return with a tray." Her voice was unusually kind. I was immediately suspicious.

"Leave it at the door, please."

The darker it became outside, the more my soul absorbed the misery. I continued to stare at the tiny candle flame, fighting the sighs of truth that began to creep into the room. I could hear them sliding under the door, breezing around the tapestry, coming up through the cracks in the floor. Reminding me of what I had been ignoring these last two months.

I mentally pushed them away.

Every time the tears threatened, I forced myself to picture Frederick on a ship off the coast. I pictured him looking through a spyglass, trying to find Faraday House. I should put a candle in the window of tower room.

There was a light knock on the door, then Hettie said, "Tray's here, miss."

"Fine," I answered curtly.

When her footsteps faded, I opened the door a crack, making sure the hall was empty. The tray was laden with several dishes. I carried it to the sunroom and decided to have my supper on the settee. I lifted each cover, feeling an odd mix of gratitude and reluctance. There was pork with a dark, thick lumpy gravy, boiled squash and carrots, and a side of pickled cucumbers. Dessert was applesauce and cream.

In a trance, I started to eat, taking small bites of the meat first, then moving to the vegetables. I tasted nothing. And only when I swallowed the last spoonful of applesauce and cream did I realize

I had neglected the wine. I finished it in one gulp, ignoring how it trickled out of the corner of my mouth and down onto the front of my dress.

A sudden weight of fatigue pulled me to the bed.

I woke to the candle nearly burnt to a nub. The quilts were pulled up to my chin and the wind screamed under the eaves. Outside was black as coal.

There was a creak from above. Pacing started back and forth in the tower room—not a house settling, but a real person walking with weight and shoes. But *was* it real? My mind was clouded with theories of mushrooms, Georgina's confused mumblings, and Mrs. Clayton's vague warnings. My soul was raw and exposed. I gritted my teeth, tired of ghost stories and all the deception. All the betrayal.

I sat up in bed, then swung my feet to the floor. I was still in my dress from earlier. Then I heard the deliberate footfalls of someone coming down the spiral stairs.

I took the candle and moved in front of the tapestry, reaching for its edge. My hand froze. The silhouette had returned to the fabric, but it was no longer in the tower room window. It was in mine.

My mouth went dry, staring at the newly appearing figure. The candle shook in my grip.

The heavy steps continued down the stairs, then the doorknob rattled. I stared at the tapestry, not wanting to know what was on the other side. The hinges moaned as I imagined the door opening. The footsteps began again, dull and lifeless. Deadweight. They stopped.

Whatever had been in the tower room was on the other side of the tapestry.

I held my breath. This was different from the visions during sleep. This was real, and I couldn't escape by waking up. It was so quiet I heard the clock on the landing.

Tick. Tick. Tick.

My pulse raced three times as fast. The tapestry swayed gently as if pushed by an invisible hand. Soft footsteps padded on the rug, coming closer. My gaze went to the vanity, and I wished I had kept the small bottle of holy water from Mrs. Clayton. Terror was making me lose all reason, but I would gladly hold up a Bible like a talisman.

With my teeth chattering, I waited for the ceiling to rain blood or someone to scream murder. But the touch I eventually felt was a hand resting on my shoulder, light as a bird. "Shh," they said. An icy breath gave a quick puff, and my only light blew out, plunging me and my ghostly guest into complete darkness.

I was grabbed by the sternum and pulled forward. Like a weightless shadow I slipped out of the window, over the treetops, past the beach, and across the waves. Salt water rushed into my mouth as I screamed.

WHEN I OPENED my eyes, I was on the deck of a schooner. Only the mainsail was up; the rest were furled tightly. The sky was black with a million pinpoints of stars. Ropes glistened with ice as giant swells moved the boat up and down.

A quiet laugh echoed. I trembled. Reverend Pellerine was correct about frequency. I knew the vibration of Frederick's voice by heart.

Then I saw him.

Frederick stood at the side of the ship, staring into the night. Tears trailed down my cheeks. I ran up to him, but he looked through me as if I were made of the wind.

I said his name, but nothing came out of my mouth.

He continued to scan the sea. I studied his eyes, trying to see inside his soul. Was he thinking of me?

Another officer came over and shared a bottle with him. They spoke fondly of what waited for them in Bermuda. Sun, warm sand, rum—and women.

Like a starving stray cat, I stayed by his side. I followed him everywhere, saw where he slept and where he ate. I heard him speak with the other crew. He was content, excited to be on this adventure. But most cruelly, I discovered he was unrepentant. When he returned to his cabin and closed his eyes for sleep, I could finally see into his heart.

And I was nowhere to be found.

I WOKE IN my bed, my body aching and my head throbbing. My stomach lurched. Dropping to the floor, I pulled out the chamber pot just in time. The dark, lumpy gravy from supper was sour and rancid. I spat twice, trying to rid my mouth of the taste.

Although I didn't remember doing it, Judge Shackleton's letter had been ripped into pieces and scattered over the rug. Wiping my chin, I leaned against the bed and stared out the window.

The darkness outside started to lighten. Dazed, I watched the sky change colors. First a deep pink, then lighter, until it hit a vibrant orange. The exact shade of Frederick's hair.

I remembered combing my fingers through it as he promised me how our life would be in Bermuda.

"Take care of me," I'd said to him. "Promise."

"I promise." Then he kissed me, his hands all the while searching for the ties to my bodice.

I thought of the letters I'd written with so much desperate passion. Mr. Clayton had even received a black eye for trying to get word to him. All this time, he had sailed by, never looking back, only straight ahead to his limitless, unrestrained, unfettered future. He was free.

A surge of fury erupted. I could feel nothing but boiling rage as I tore down the stairs and out of the front door. Like a possessed woman, I thumped along the forest path until I reached the beach.

I grabbed a rock the size of my fist and stumbled to the water's edge. I let the freezing tide grab my ankles. And then my knees. I walked deeper into the water until my dress pooled around my thighs, pulling me back and forth with the waves.

I threw the rock as hard as I could. "Why wasn't I enough?" I screamed at the orange sky. "Why wasn't I beautiful enough for you? Why? Why did you leave me?" I continued to scream as the sky changed to a light blue.

I saw my mother's eyes, wide and unblinking, looking up from the parlor floor. The teacup in broken pieces beside her.

"Why wasn't I beautiful enough for you? Why did you leave me?" The tears came, mixing with the ocean.

Someone called my name urgently.

I reached into the freezing water. Knives stabbed my arms, but I didn't care about the cold. I grabbed another handful of rocks. One of them was a wishing stone. I wanted to gnash it with my teeth. I wanted to swallow all the rocks to weigh myself down so I could walk along the bottom of the ocean.

I'd creep among the seaweed until I reached Bermuda. With putrefied skin covered in barnacles and starfish clinging to my hair, I'd emerge from the turquoise waters to claim a terrified Frederick. His screams would be my lullaby as I dragged him back to the ocean, keeping him tightly in my arms as he drowned. Both of us resting at the bottom in an eternal watery embrace.

There would be sea shanties about us that would rival any ghost story about Faraday House.

A massive splash broke the water beside me. Jaws clamped on my sleeve, pulling me back to the beach. "No," I screamed, tugging free. Barking mixed with the wind.

An arm reached around my waist, lifting me up. "Leave me!" I punched and kicked uselessly.

When we reached the beach and I gained footing, I whipped around and pummeled Frederick's chest. His navy-blue uniform and brass buttons mocked me. "Why?" I screamed at him. "Why?"

He pulled me close. "Stop it!"

I continued to protest, but then my muscles melted, played out, exhausted. His fingers dug into my shoulders. I leaned my cheek against his chest and took a few breaths.

"It's all right," he said, more calmly. "I'm here."

The wind picked up, slicing through my wet dress, clinging to my legs. The sky was completely blue. The orange hues were erased. Gone.

"I'm here," he repeated.

His arms slowly released me, testing if I could stand on my own or at least would not run back into the ocean. I looked up at Reverend Pellerine. Water dripped from the black waves framing his face. He took off his cloak and laid it over my shoulders. He said, "Steady now, I've got you."

I shook my head. "No." Hot tears streamed down my frozen cheeks. "No one has me."

"Whatever the crisis, I can help—you're only in socks?" His voice was stunned. As if my being without shoes was the last thing to remove any semblance of normalcy from this situation.

I let the icy wind turn my hair to icicles. The temperature matched my dying heart. "You can't help," I told him darkly. "No one can."

The last few weeks I had been ignoring all the signs, stupidly hoping I was wrong. Even though I dared not acknowledge it, even to myself, I could no longer deny the truth. I had a secret sin to confess to Reverend Pellerine, but it wasn't the shilling that had caused my mother's death.

I paused, wanting to memorize his face because I knew he would never look at me the same way again. Then I told him the truth, the reason I was so desperate for Frederick to rescue me and make everything right. The one thing I refused to even allow myself to consider because saying it out loud would cause my world to crumble. "I'm with child."

CHAPTER TWENTY-EIGHT

H is lips parted, but he made no reply.

"Frederick's not coming for me," I sobbed. "I saw the truth. I saw him." I collapsed in his arms, spent and destitute.

The wind lashed our red cheeks. "I have to get you back before you catch your death," he said.

I leaned into him as he led me back to the house, his arm around my waist as Moses trotted ahead. A loyal dog, he would stop and check we were still following, then turn and lead again.

My tears continued, uninhibited. I was morbidly numb. Everything had crashed down and trapped me in its rubble. So dreadful and appalling was my situation, so immense and horrendously incomprehensible, it was too massive to absorb.

Instead of the main door, Reverend Pellerine took me around to the side, and we entered Faraday through the back entrance and into the kitchen.

The early hour meant the space was empty, the large grate only a pile of cooled gray ash. Nothing seemed real. I was a ghost in the corner watching as Reverend Pellerine sat me down in the nearest chair, and then tended to the fire. He lit several candles and filled the kettle from the hand pump at the large sink. I stared at the flickering flames, seeing only the orange hue of Frederick's hair.

A tightness squeezed my chest, making it hard to breathe.

The cloak was removed from my shoulders and replaced with a soft quilt. A footstool had been placed under my feet, and my sodden and muddy socks were hanging off the back of another chair, drying. My bare feet stretched to the flames, eager for the drying warmth.

Reverend Pellerine moved about the kitchen in a determined but calm manner. Moses sat on his haunches. His eyes slid between me and his master.

Soon a steamy mug was offered. "Drink this," he said, sitting in the chair beside me. I noticed his wet things were still on. "It will warm you from the inside." He took a drink from his own mug.

I wrapped both hands around the drink and took a sip. I coughed immediately. "Rum and tea," I said. "All out of holy water?"

A faint smile graced his lips. "There's the wit." There was a noticeable relief to his tone. "I'm glad. I thought I'd lost you for certain."

Only then did it occur to me that he'd been out at sunrise as well. "How did you find me?" I asked.

He ran a hand down his face, looking defeated. "Moses was pawing at the door to be let out. It's uncommon for him to wake so early. As soon as I opened the door he rushed off. I followed him to the beach. Then I saw you standing in the waves." He dropped his chin and left the rest of the scene unfinished. Maybe he was trying to give me some semblance of respect.

Upon hearing his name, Moses waddled over and gently placed his chin on my lap. I began to stroke his head. He closed his eyes and gave a lazy sigh.

I finished my tea in silence, trying to organize my thoughts. Reverend Pellerine watched me. The panic of the moment had eased, but as my body thawed, the terrible reality started to grip me in its talons, unwilling to let go.

"I never meant to marry Captain Graves," I said.

Reverend Pellerine met my gaze. Those brown eyes stared back from behind the dark fringe of hair, calm and unprejudiced. Perhaps he had been expecting my confession since we'd met.

And maybe I had been waiting for someone to hear my story this whole time. The words flowed easily. I told him everything leading up to the ball at the admiral's and how I had been hoping for Frederick to come for me. He listened quietly, never interrupting.

Then I told him about the letter from Judge Shackleton. "I was convinced he and Mrs. Shackleton were lying to ensure I stayed here," I said. "I reasoned they had heard Georgina was still alive and worried I would return to them, bringing my soiled reputation and ruining their social standing among the city's upper crust."

His stare was unwavering. "You were so violent on the beach, though. What changed?"

I paused, unsure whether I should share Esther's connection. How could I explain the trip I had taken to his ship? Reverend Pellerine had made it clear how he felt about ghosts, and I was already sharing my deepest confession. Esther would only cloud this tangled situation. And in that moment, I couldn't explain why, but I knew I wanted to keep her a secret.

I answered, "It was so heartbreaking and shocking, it took all night for me to accept the truth." I sniffed and wiped my eyes, fighting a fresh round of tears.

He leaned forward, elbows on his knees. "You may not believe it, but you will be much happier without Lieutenant Fletcher." He looked pained as he said the next part. "And the captain will be overjoyed to be a father, finally."

I shook my head. The situation was more dire than he realized. "But I'm already two months," I said. "Captain Graves might be able to accept a child with red hair and blue eyes if I tell him my own people have that coloring, but he will know by the early birth the baby is not his."

"I suggest he'll be so concerned for the well-being of you and the child he won't be bothered by it. That's what he said to me yesterday. He's worried about your health, particularly your lack of appetite. Also, he wanted to make sure I brought back the marriage license."

I looked at him incredulously. When we returned from the beach, the captain had seemed angry. "Truly?" The smallest amount of relief eased into my bones.

Reverend Pellerine nodded. "It's in his study, already signed . . . by him. I told him I cannot sign it until the time comes."

I did not share the reverend's confidence. The memory of our dining experience was fresh in my mind. "That doesn't change the fact he'll find out what I did. A marriage license cannot guarantee my safety."

He'll find out what I did. Esther echoed those very same words in this room. *He'll never forgive me.*

A ringing started in my head, like a warning. I stood, feeling the walls start to close in. The quilt fell to the floor.

He stood with me. "I promise it will be all right."

I wanted to believe him, but I could no longer slip into fanciful daydreams to escape reality. Ada's words echoed back to me. I had to grow up and face the consequences of my actions.

My silence was mistaken for agreement. "For now, let me take you back to your room," he offered, already looking like he'd been up all night. His hand reached out to touch my arm, then stopped. We shared a glance, knowing nothing would be the same between us.

"No," I said. "We can't be seen together this early; it will create too many questions." I dragged myself past the shelves of blueberry wine, toward the hallway to the dining room.

"Miss Fitzpatrick."

I turned and saw him and Moses side by side. I said, "After everything we've shared, you can call me Emeline."

He put a hand to his chest. "Please call me René." Then he took a step forward. "I will keep this a secret; however, I feel you haven't told me everything."

I shook my head, unable to utter any more excuses.

He pressed his lips together and came closer. The floor creaked under his boot. "At the beach you told me you saw the truth, that you *saw* him." His gaze was intense.

I rubbed my forehead, trying to hide my lying eyebrows. "As shocking as it was to confront, I finally saw him for what he was."

He let his control slip, and an expression of hate darkened his features. "A British soldier being immoral is hardly shocking."

I knew from where he was basing this opinion, and although Frederick couldn't be blamed for what Reverend Pellerine's family had gone through, I said nothing to contradict him. He was asking too many questions, and exhaustion was making my thoughts blurry.

I nodded a goodbye. "And thank you," I said. "For saving me."

"You're welcome."

"I was talking to Moses."

Reverend Pellerine dropped his chin, accepting the rebuff.

I'd made it to the hallway with the schooners when I heard him run up behind me. His partially dry clothes were encrusted with salt. "If I hadn't been there this morning, can you for certain say if you'd still be breathing at this moment?" He wrung his hands. "I'm anxious to let you go by yourself. Your expression in the waves was determined, and it's my greatest fear that you will succumb to that hopelessness again."

"I still feel that hopelessness," I told him truthfully. "But I won't act on it."

His shoulders eased. "There's always another solution," he said. "I don't know what it is yet, but there's one—let me help you with this . . . Emeline."

When he spoke my name, it sounded like a prayer. There was a profound sense of hope in his tone, but maybe that was something he preached so much it was an automatic expression, similar to my years of pretend smiling. And yet he wasn't a fanciful sort of person who had a rose-colored view of the world. If anything, he was bitter in certain respects, hardened by his family's history.

I reached the staircase and ascended, the creaks and moans of wood marking each step, another moment in time.

At Faraday House, the wives always die young.

The pale sunlight entered the round window. When I reached the top of the stairs I was paralyzed with the most horrible truth. Something neither the reverend nor I had considered. I reasoned this lapse was the result of a deep connection and not the casual dismissal of her.

Because regardless of my needing to be married as soon as possible, there was one event that had to occur before I could wed Captain Graves. And it was ironically the one thing I had been trying to prevent since coming to Faraday.

Georgina would have to die.

CHAPTER TWENTY-NINE

My body shook with nervous energy as I waited for the rest of the house to wake. I had already washed and changed into a new dress and combed and pinned back my hair. Doing those familiar tasks usually cleared my head and made me confident, but not this time.

I was truly at a loss. The kitchen memory Esther had shown me proved she feared the captain—a warning from beyond the grave.

Time was running out. I had to marry him soon if Captain Graves was to believe my baby was also his. I could not risk finding out what his reaction would be otherwise. Reverend Pellerine suggested he might be so thrilled to have an heir he would accept the lie.

Love has little to do with the success of a marriage.

It didn't matter how far away I was from her, Mrs. Shackleton's words would always find me.

The image of Mrs. Clayton trying to soothe a destitute Esther was etched into my brain. But was there a way to save myself *and* Georgina?

My footfalls padded softly on the rug. I glanced at the ceiling, thinking of all the ghostly pacing I'd heard since coming here. Was it a premonition of my own future?

There was a knock at the door, followed by Hettie's voice announcing she had a breakfast tray for me.

As soon as I opened the door, she brushed past me, cheeks red and mouth in a firm line. "Captain Graves's orders," she said briskly. "He wants to make sure you don't skip any more meals." She set the tray on my bed.

"I'll take this to Georgina's room and have breakfast with her." I reached for the tray.

The hardness of Hettie's expression melted as her eyes gazed at me with pity.

I felt all the blood rush to my feet. "No," I whispered.

Realizing my misinterpretation, Hettie replied quickly, "It's not what you think—she's still with us. Although she had another terrible night. Mrs. Clayton was up with her the whole time. She's in such a miserable state without the mushroom tea. Captain Graves was furious. I'm surprised you didn't hear the argument this morning. He demanded to know why she was in such pain. Apparently, Mrs. Clayton has been rationing the medication Nurse Gibson left because she's not sure how long Georgina will go on. She'd been supplementing with her mushroom tea, but since that's gone, she's only had the dropper dose."

I closed my eyes, silently cursing my own stupidity. I thought I was saving her, but I was only making her condition worse. "I thought she seemed better," I offered timidly.

Hettie uncovered the plate, letting the steam rise from the porridge and brown bread. She poured a cup of tea and said, "It's not uncommon for terminal patients to have a surge of energy right before the end."

I sat on the bed in a daze. I had done this to her. I was the cause of her extra pain.

Hettie's voice took on a lively tempo as she replayed the details of the argument for me. I found her excitement hard to reconcile with the fear I experienced when Captain Graves burned my letter. And there was Mr. Clayton's black eye. But most telling was Esther's memory.

How was it so different with Hettie? She was brave, but she struck me as someone who didn't take unnecessary risks either. I said to her, "Were you not afraid to be there when he was so angry?"

She lifted her chin. "Captain Graves doesn't talk down to me the way he does with the Claytons."

I questioned her superior tone. "But they've been loyal employees for so long."

"Exactly. That's all he sees when he looks at them: employees."

"And he sees you differently?" I prompted.

"I'm mature for my years. He appreciates my potential."

Confidence by the bucketload, this one. "How is Mrs. Graves this morning, though?" I asked, moving the focus back to Georgina.

Hettie shrugged. "It's a queer ailment; she's competent in the daytime but at night . . . It's almost like she's possessed. Mrs. Clayton thinks she's good for another week, but I see her wasting away much quicker than that."

Everything stilled. Mrs. Shackleton's voice echoed in my mind. *It's just what you need, dear. And why let the poor pet suffer? This is the best option for both of you.*

No great shock that Mrs. Shackleton would be pushing for the quick marriage. And hadn't I always done what she'd asked? Hadn't I always made choices based on what she told me was the proper thing to do? Except for Frederick. I owned that disaster entirely. Mrs. Shackleton was right: I couldn't take care of myself.

I had to marry the captain, but I refused to give up on Georgina. It was unacceptable for her to die, especially in pain. A pain that I'd caused. I would have to somehow keep her alive and comfortable.

"I have to see her," I said.

"You have to eat." Hettie pointed to my tray. "Captain Graves's orders." Her face was like stone. She was doing his bidding. "He wants to see you after you finish." It even sounded like an order coming from her. They made an impressive team. I thought again about the grate in the sunroom. If someone had been listening while Reverend Pellerine and I were in the kitchen this morning, they would know everything.

A tremor rippled through me. I tried to hide my shaking as I quickly ate all the porridge and finished the tea. I coughed and put a hand to my chest, feeling an ache.

Hettie gave me a look. "Are you all right?"

"Just a sniffle," I said, keeping quiet about my icy sunrise plunge in the ocean.

"You're flushed too." Hettie touched my forehead. "Sakes, you're burning up." A look of panic crossed her face. "The captain will be right furious if he finds out you're sick. Get into bed." She started to pull back the covers.

"I have to see Georgina," I pleaded.

"And expose her to your germs? I think not!" she reprimanded. "She'd be in the grave by lunchtime for certain."

I let out a cry of protest. I needed to see her. I needed to talk with Mrs. Clayton and tell her I'd ruined the mushrooms. I'd get more—I'd scour the island all night with a candle if I had to.

"I'll bring you a special tea." Hettie helped me into bed. I was hardly able to put up a fight. My limbs betrayed me, wanting nothing more than to settle for a long nap. Why was I so tired suddenly?

She took the tray and closed the door behind her.

My eyes closed. There was a whisper against my cheek as sleep pulled me under.

I SAT UP, gasping. My throat burned as if I'd been screaming. I pulled back the covers and swung my legs to the side. My dress was stuck to my skin with sweat.

Outside, the late-afternoon sun had already begun its descent in the western sky. I had slept the entire morning.

I stopped. On the rug was a splotch of blood. The trickling trailed under the tapestry and into the sunroom. Terror pressed down on me.

A scream came from above. Then Mrs. Clayton's voice answered, "One more push."

Another round of screams shook the walls. There was a moment of silence so heavy and thick it nearly choked me.

Shaking, I went into the sunroom. The door to the tower was open. There were bloody footprints going all the way up the spiral stairs. Numb with fear, I began to climb, careful to avoid the blood.

Halfway up I heard a baby cry.

Relieved sobs replaced the earlier urgency in the air. I continued upward until I could peer over the edge of the floor.

Esther was on a bed of quilts, her dark hair plastered to her forehead. "What is it?" she asked breathily.

"A little girl." Mrs. Clayton examined the baby, who was slick and squirming. She bundled it up and handed the child to Esther. She looked down at them both with a motherly affection. There was a pull behind my ribs.

On shaking legs, I walked toward them as an invisible witness.

Esther was pale but radiant. Mrs. Clayton kissed the top of her head. "See? Told you there was nothing to fear. I knew you could do it."

"She's beautiful, isn't she?" She licked her dry lips. "And he won't be upset once he sees her. He'll forgive me." Esther looked at Mrs. Clayton hopefully. "Yes?"

"Oh . . . that's hardly a concern now. You must rest; we'll discuss it later."

Esther's expression intensified. "Something's wrong." She gritted her teeth and groaned in pain. A bloom of red grew on the quilts between her legs. So much that it trickled onto the floorboards.

Mrs. Clayton took the bundle from Esther's arms. The baby started to cry, then the cry intensified to a scream. I squeezed my eyes shut and clamped my hands over my ears.

The sound dissolved around me until there was only the wind in the trees that lined the cliff's edge. I cracked my eyes open one at a time.

The air was so cold I could see my breath. But that was all. The tower room was as dusty and empty as it had been the first time I saw it.

Esther had had a baby in secret! But something had gone wrong, horribly wrong. Something so wretched it had tethered her spirit to this island.

As troubling as the scene was, it gave me the smallest spark of hope. I was now certain Mrs. Clayton had been working with Esther to hide her pregnancy from the captain. Would she do the same for me?

All this time I thought Esther was showing Georgina and me the past as a warning to prevent our making the same mistake. I began to consider she was showing me those visions to help me.

There was one critical element missing: the truth of what happened next. And there was only one person I could go to.

CHAPTER THIRTY

With my heaviest shawl wrapped over my shoulders, I made my way to Georgina's room. Esther had secretly had a baby, and Mrs. Clayton knew! But why was it a secret, even after her death?

There was only one reasonable explanation, and it was chillingly close to my own situation.

The father of Esther's baby was not Captain Graves.

I recalled Georgina whispering, "Graves," in her sleep. I wondered if she had different visions. It was possible Esther was showing each of us different parts and we would have to piece them together to understand what she was hoping to convey.

And what exactly had Mrs. Clayton done?

I thought back to what Hettie had said that night in the kitchen when she was telling me the history of Faraday: she'd said ghosts don't even know they're dead, they just keep going about the motions of their daily lives, unaware.

But Esther was aware. She was showing me things, specific things about her past, just as she had tried with Georgina. What if Georgina's poor health had been the reason she couldn't absorb the visions without them draining her? Or was the haunting the cause of her illness all this time?

I remained unsure about Mrs. Clayton's motives, but I had no other option.

I hurried past the round window not even bothering to glance at the gray sky. I reached Georgina's room out of breath, distracted, with a mind full of anxious speculation and a heart beating with impatient hope. I entered the room without knocking.

Despite the time of day, every candle was lit. Georgina was dozing, her face relaxed and chest rising and falling with each easy breath.

"What's going on?" Mrs. Clayton snorted from under a quilt on the settee. She sat up and rubbed her pale face. Wiry hair poked out from under her white cap. She looked more like the patient than Georgina.

I thought of her working in the kitchen, making the meals and then coming up here to be with Georgina. When she told me about Nurse Gibson leaving, she said it matter-of-factly without begrudging the extra work it meant for her.

Once when I was sick, Ada stayed in my room all night, putting a cold cloth to my head to help with the fever. The memory was bittersweet; it unlocked a longing for a mother whose touch I had long forgotten—it reminded me of how Mrs. Clayton had looked at Esther. I hoped that maternal urge would translate to me as well.

I closed the door and rushed to the settee.

Mrs. Clayton's expression was rigid. "Hettie said you had a fever. Best be staying away if you care anything for Mrs. Graves."

"I need to speak with you about Esther." I had to be direct; time and options were dwindling steadily. "And why she came to you about her pregnancy."

She sputtered. "Pregnancy?" Her face turned crimson as her hands worked to tuck her hair back under the cap. "Of all the fanciful notions and cruel gossip . . . Why are you determined to turn a tragic death into your own entertainment?" Her entire face pinched into a sneer. "I bet you're hoping to catch me in a lie so that you can go to the captain and have me fired. Is that it? You want Mr. Clayton and me to be thrown off the island with no place to live?" Her voice was laced with hatred . . . and fear.

My knees trembled. I could ruin everything with one wrong word. But if I didn't act quickly, I could end up dying in the tower room too.

I glanced at Georgina in her safe slumber. I didn't have to lower my voice; she already knew the same thing. She'd been getting the same visions.

I leaned closer to Mrs. Clayton with wildfire in my eyes. "I saw the blood," I said. "There was so much it leaked through the floors and stained the ceiling, didn't it?"

"Your morbid fascination with Esther must stop. I've already told you everything." She shook her head. "I don't know what you're talking about. She had a virus; it attacked her heart."

"A virus did not make her so fearful that she kept her pregnancy a secret, Mrs. Clayton. A virus did not scare her so much that she gave birth in the only room in the house from which she could see her husband's approaching ship."

"Stop being so vicious," she tried to reprimand. The mad blush had weakened to an ashen paleness. She sought to compose herself, but I saw her chin quiver. "Why are you insistent on disgracing the image of the poor woman?"

"I need to know why she was so afraid of Captain Graves." I put my hand on my stomach. "Because my very life depends on you telling me the truth."

She looked at my waist, understanding beginning to dawn on her features. She asked, "How far along are you?"

"Two months," I replied quietly.

Her eyes softened at the edges. She pressed her lips together as if weighing a decision.

I could no longer afford to be demure. I said, "My only choice is to tell the captain I am already carrying another man's child. You know his temperament far better than I. If you think he'll be so overjoyed with the idea of finally getting an heir, then we have nothing further to discuss. I can go sit by Georgina and hold her hand and enjoy every second with her and not worry if she continues to fight her illness and delay my nuptials."

Mrs. Clayton started to wring her hands. "You can't tell him. Not unless you want to end up in that damn graveyard."

I was incredibly tired yet an excited urgency stirred deep within my bones. I would finally get the truth.

She glanced at Georgina's bed, then back to me. She spoke in a hushed manner. "Wood holds on to memories," she said. "I must have scrubbed the floor of that room a thousand times, but the bloodstain kept resurfacing." She sniffed. "Mr. Clayton can't stand the sight of the room, even after all these years."

Mrs. Clayton hesitated, as if the words were too painful to say.

"Please," I begged.

Letting out a heavy sigh she began. "While Captain Graves was away, Esther had an affair with one of the seasonal workers and became pregnant. I tried to give her tonics my mother had used for the woman in her own village, but they didn't work. She was terrified because even if you're a dunce at math you know full well that if you return after being away for nearly a year to a wife with a newborn that looks four months old, it ain't yours. He would be furious! You've seen his temper. You never know when he's going to explode, but it's there all the time—any kind of match can set him off.

"Esther paced in front of that widow's walk as her belly got bigger and bigger, worried she'd see his ship on the horizon. She made up her mind: she'd have the baby and then leave before he got home. She told me her lover had promised to take care of her and the baby. They were going to leave this part of the country for good. She wanted me to tell the captain she'd drowned."

She grimaced and took out a handkerchief from her sleeve. "It was such a hard labor, and she was only a slip of a thing." Mrs. Clayton dabbed her cheeks. "In the end, I didn't have to lie. She bled so much." Her shoulders rocked up and down as she continued to cry. "She died the next morning, right at sunrise."

"And the baby?"

"Passed away in her arms a few hours after she gave birth. It broke her heart." Mrs. Clayton blew her nose. "That's what truly killed her: losing that baby."

She motioned to the window that faced the cemetery. "They're buried together. We bundled the wee thing up and placed it beside her."

I tried to gather my thoughts. "But Captain Graves said he made them open the coffin before they buried her."

She rolled her eyes. "He's one for creating a romantic image of himself, isn't he? He barely blinked at her. Although, if I'm being fair, he put her pearl hair combs in place. His wedding present to her."

We sat in silence, listening to Georgina snore. I remembered how she'd mumbled, "Graves," in her sleep. I thought she was speaking of the captain, but she meant Esther's grave and her baby's.

"Thank you for telling me," I said. "It's obvious you cared a great deal for her."

She blew her nose again, then said, "Mr. Clayton mentioned you had a long talk the other day in the forest."

"He's very kind. I enjoy his company."

She smiled oddly. "You remind him of Esther."

I stayed quiet, sensing we had created a delicate truce.

Tilting up her chin, she said, "We're raised to believe men are strong and will take care of us, but it's the women of this world who bear the burdens. Who takes care of the sick and the young? Who creates the home and keeps it clean and makes the meals?" She gave me a satisfied nod. "And the captain? He doesn't shy away from talking about his adventures at sea or how much money he makes. The man can't even spend more than a quick breakfast in this room." She huffed. "He's a grand one for spouting the Bible and such, but he listens to the devil on his shoulder more often than not."

It was clear she didn't like or trust the captain. I had to pull her onto my side. "If you could have done anything differently for Esther," I asked, "what would it have been?"

"I would have told her not to be afraid. That we were smarter than him, and braver. I was young then too, only ten years older than Esther, but I had no confidence in my own thoughts."

"And now?" I prompted hopefully. She had the look of some-one who was on the edge of figuring out a complicated puzzle, eyebrows together but with a glimmer in her eye.

She put a finger to her chin. "If you conceive tonight, it's still believable that the baby could be his. It will be your first, and it's perfectly reasonable to be a few weeks early."

Although I cowered at the thought of conceiving with the cap-tain, I said, "He told me he will not take me to bed until we're married."

"You don't have to seduce him, only make him think you were in his bed." Then she fished in her apron pocket and pulled out the tiny blue bottle.

"No," I said. "I can't take the last of Georgina's pain medicine. Hettie said she was getting low. Captain Graves was furious. I cannot allow you to face his ire."

"I let him blow off steam regularly, it gets it out of his system." Mrs. Clayton looked mischievous. "I have a secret stash of mushrooms at the cottage. Made a fresh pot of tea earlier." She motioned to Georgina, who had been snoring the entire time. "Does she look uncomfortable to you?"

"No," I answered truthfully. In fact, her complexion was pink.

Mrs. Clayton pressed the bottle into my palm. "One drop will put him out for the night. He'll be snoring away, unaware. Tuck clothing of yours between the sheets, maybe a hair ribbon, or even better, a shift. And make sure you leave evidence that proves he was your first lover." She raised her eyebrows, and I nodded my understanding.

She tapped her chin again and stared across the room as if speaking to herself. "Yes, this will work. I'll make sure you're served moose steak for supper. It's his favorite. I'll put out extra beer as well. Just add a drop to his drink when he's not looking."

I stared at her with wide eyes. "Why can't you add it to his supper?"

"I'll be up here with Mrs. Graves. Hettie's in charge of the kitchen tonight. She'd manage to mix it up and you'd be the one on the floor, out cold for the night."

I was hesitant. "What if he doesn't believe me, though?"

She made a sound at the back of her throat. "If you act like it's the truth, he'll accept it. But you must confront him in the morning, face-to-face. He may not want to believe you, but a man rarely refutes evidence when it's staring him in the face. Even if he calls your bluff at first, you must be steadfast; your conviction will tip the scales and convince him otherwise."

I let her solution settle on my brain. It was a good idea. I said to her, "I never thought of this island as home, but you and Mr. Clayton have been so kind. I want to make sure you stay on after Georgina . . ." The word stuck in my throat. I couldn't say it out loud. "After I marry the captain," I finally said.

She squeezed my hand. "I wouldn't dare think of leaving you now."

From my very first night at Faraday, Mrs. Clayton and I had had a complicated relationship, but since she'd relayed the secret truth to me about Esther's baby, I sensed we had taken a turn for the better. She would be a valuable ally.

I returned to my room seeing Faraday with new eyes. I needed someone to take care of me, and with this plan, I could have that. Mrs. Clayton was more in charge of Faraday than anyone. She would be with me while I had the baby. She would keep me safe from the captain's temper. I even wondered if I could convince him to return to sailing the trade routes again.

Not to mention, his own health wasn't the best. I wondered how long until he was in his own sickbed. Five years at the most?

Then Faraday would be all mine.

When I entered my room, I was surprised to see an envelope on the floor. It had my name written on it.

Emeline

I didn't recognize the penmanship.

I opened the note.

Dear Emeline,

I did not want to interrupt your visit with Mrs. Graves. I have something important to discuss with you in private.

I'll be waiting by the pond.

René

I read it over several times, liking the sound of his voice in my mind. I could even hear his accent. *I'll be waiting by the pond.*

I had a vision of myself, back at Halifax, anxious for the post to arrive, and the continuous disappointment of not hearing from Frederick.

I slipped the letter under my pillow.

CHAPTER THIRTY-ONE

My hands shook as I tied the knot of my cloak. It was curious how a short note had completely lifted my mood. It was only a few lines from him, but I couldn't deny how precious it felt to receive it.

I was in too much of a rush to bother with my bonnet and instead pulled the red hood of my cloak up over my hair.

I carefully made my way down the stairs and out the main door, making sure I wasn't seen. Tension was building for tonight, and sneaking out to see the reverend to have a private discussion only heightened my already taut nerves. I took the heavily flattened footpath that rounded the corner of the house, making sure to hug the rocky foundation and stay in the shadows.

The trail led to an opening between two oak trees where it diverted from the house and skirted the edge of the forest. There was a downward slope that afforded a stunning view of the bay. Below, the path ended at the pond. I began my descent, eager to hear what he wanted to discuss.

Among the muted brown and gray tones of early winter, Reverend Pellerine's black cloak stood out, taking all my attention. He tipped his head back and looked at me from under the brim of his hat. There was no wave or smile of acknowledgment, but his eyes pulled at me with an urgency. The red cloak billowed behind me as I hastened, my pulse matching my quickening footsteps.

Once the path flattened out, he closed the distance between us with a few long strides. I noticed he was freshly shaved, and his hair was held back at the nape of his neck. "Thank you for coming," he said. He had a look of unexpected relief. "You look well."

"I'm glad to see you," I said, partly out of breath. There was a strange mix of emotions pulling on my heart. Our last conversation was vivid and raw, but now that I was with him again, an unexpected calm had descended. "Where is Moses?" I asked.

The corner of his mouth curled up slightly. "He'll be thrilled you asked. He's at the Claytons' cottage being spoiled with steak scraps. I thought it best to come alone, since whenever he's around I have to compete for your attention."

"You have it now. Fully."

He led me to the edge of the pond. The water was still as glass. Steam rose from the surface like smoke, lifting into the cooler air. It was vastly different from the energy of the beach, with the salty breeze and waves crashing into the rocks over and over.

He took in a quick breath and met my gaze as if steeling himself. However serene our surroundings, Reverend Pellerine's expression was one of intense caution. He said, "I've been going over in my mind all day what we were discussing this morning, and I have an option you may want to consider."

"Truly?" I asked hopefully. If there was an alternative to drugging my fiancé, I would certainly be interested in hearing more. I couldn't imagine what he had conjured up.

He concentrated on the ground for a moment, shifting his weight from one foot to the other. "If I understand correctly, you must marry someone soon, but do you have to marry Captain Graves? Is he your only choice?"

"According to Judge Shackleton, yes. Faraday is isolated enough to assure my safety."

His brown eyes focused on me again. "Surely changing your

last name and moving to another location would afford you the same protection. I cannot imagine it would be worth the trouble for Lieutenant Fletcher's loaners to track you down."

My heart raced. "Who else are you suggesting?"

He removed his hat and held it in front of him, fingers edging along the brim in a nervous fashion. "Myself, actually."

Everything stilled. I studied his expression, trying to gauge if he was serious. "You're proposing?" I whispered.

"I know I'm not your first choice, or even your second, and I don't have a private island, but I should be able to get us a home with enough space for a cabbage garden. I'm afraid there won't be many occasions for fancy dresses or dances. And I don't have a cook." He winced, as if picturing how his proposal made our future sound as lackluster as a piece of driftwood. "There'll be no maid either. Nothing you're used to."

His words were rushed and unsure. It was strange to see him struggle to express himself. "*Mon dieu*," he sighed. Then he laughed nervously. "And, granted, French and English is an uncommon match, but I can teach you a few phrases. I won't give up my heritage, and I won't be loyal to the king. I can't."

My mouth was dry. "I wouldn't expect you to." A heaviness settled around my heart, making it hard to breathe. I hoped he would add more, but he only stood there, waiting for my reply. Was it so difficult for him to give me a notion that his offer was rooted in something more powerful than obligation? Was there an inkling of love? And if not love, could he sense we would be a good match and make each other happy?

But he remained quiet. He'd made his offer in full, apparently. All that remained was my answer. "I . . . I can't leave Georgina," I said.

He stepped closer. "You won't have to. Both of us will stay at Faraday; nothing will change. Once she passes, you can leave with me, and we can marry. I'll be able to secure a parish on the North Shore—it's fishing villages mostly, but you'll be safe." There was an expression of triumph in his gaze. He was enjoying the thrill of rescuing me, and perhaps he was imagining the look on Captain Graves's face as he stole his fiancée. I knew both men disliked each other.

Again, I waited for him to give me another reason. Even Captain Graves, who had only known me for a few hours, had managed to spout a pleasant proposition. He had our future mapped out in his mind with children, promising me a life of comfort.

But Reverend Pellerine didn't speak of how it would be a happy life. He only listed reasons why it wouldn't be. Logically, I knew his offer was the safer alternative, but my heart cried out in despair. How was it possible we'd spent all those moments together, eyes locked and cheeks blushing, only for them to have meant nothing to him? After everything I'd shared with him—all my secrets, all my sins. I'd bared my soul to him. I felt stupid for having allowed myself to imagine his attention was more than friendly concern.

Finally, I asked, "Are you certain? I don't want you to regret your decision. What if you lose all the buttons from your vest because I sewed them on so poorly?"

"Buttons?" He let out a confused chuckle.

"I appreciate your frankness," I said. "But can you think of one reason why you want to marry me?"

He looked taken aback. "I cannot let you marry that man. Any decent person would offer you the same; it's the responsible thing to do."

The pressure around my heart squeezed harder, crushing it. Any glimmer of hope was stamped out. "Of course," I replied. Reverend Pellerine was responsible. And good. And kind. And handsome. And he knew I was utterly helpless.

Mrs. Shackleton was right. I was lovely, but that quality was useful only for securing a husband, not keeping one happy. And I dearly wanted Reverend Pellerine to be happy.

His proposal was inspired by pity, and nothing else. The complications he'd listed earlier would haunt our marriage with a spiteful irony. We would be miserable. Reverend Pellerine needed a wife that was more than lovely to look at. I was saving him years of regret.

When I spoke next, my words sounded dead. "While your intentions are admirable, this feeling of gallantry will fall short after reality sets in. You deserve someone you see as an equal, or at least someone you can imagine a content and fulfilling life with."

His eyebrows came together. "No," he said, shaking his head. "You're twisting my words."

He stared at me with confusion. I kept hoping to see the same look in his eyes as when he was teaching me to whistle. I wanted him to tell me what he'd really thought when he caught me in the pantry wearing only my dressing gown. I wanted the connection we had over simple bread and molasses. I wanted him to confess his proposal came from more than a desire to keep me safe.

"You are enamored with the idea of rescuing me," I said. "You would never be proposing if our circumstances were different."

His bewildered expression was slowly replaced by a sharper focus as it dawned on him I hadn't said yes. There was a new edge to his voice. "But you were more than willing to be rescued by your British naval officer. Are you saying I'm not good enough to take his place? If he is the ruler you measure your spousal compatibility with, then our marriage will be a sorrowful disappointment for you. I have nothing in common with that louse."

I put a hand on my stomach. "That louse is the father of my child. I cannot let you be a parent to this baby when it's so obvious your hatred of the British will always influence your ability to love them." I knew the emptiness and unfulfilled existence of growing up with guardians who were distant and cool. It didn't matter how many hot meals I was served or how many nice dresses were in my closet—the heart knows when it's starving.

His lips parted with a stunned expression of hurt. "That's a rather crude assumption based on our previous conversations. You know my history, but you also know me as a person." He looked at me suspiciously. "Is that what you truly expect my reaction will be to your child?"

I shook my head. We were saying all the wrong things to each other. How could I make him understand I wanted a family that gave me strength, not reminded me how helpless I was? Captain Graves would provide the baby and me with comforts, and see us with appreciative eyes, making us feel treasured. He'd die peacefully, knowing his legacy was secure. I could be the head of Faraday within only a few years. But if I accepted the reverend's offer, a few years would be all the time it took for his sense of obligation to turn to tired regret, stuck with a wife he didn't love, and a baby that wasn't his—I would quickly become an unwelcome presence. A burden. Just like at the Shackletons'.

I wanted freedom, but I also wanted to be loved—or at least regarded with a semblance of being valued. The emotion of the moment was growing too big. I was bursting mad and desperate for him all at once. My heart was galloping. I could feel an oncoming wave of sorrow about to crash over me, and I was helpless to stop it. I gazed at him with a painful longing.

"Emeline," he pleaded. "Your child is the reason we're having this conversation. I know Captain Graves has promised you the position of being the mistress of Faraday, but Georgina has not left the island since she married him. Ask yourself why I come once a week to do private sermons."

I fought the tears. "I don't know."

"He likes control. He'll keep you and your child prisoner on this island. The only way you'll ever see the Shackletons again is if he allows them to visit. If, not when."

A fist lodged itself in my throat.

He put both hands on my shoulders. "Please accept my help. I will take care of you. I will take care of your child as if they were my own."

My own.

His words were chillingly similar to Mrs. Shackleton's promise to my mother.

I would never be able to make him understand why I couldn't accept his offer. Being taken care of was not what I wanted. That was not love. That was not freedom. That was ownership.

I said, "Captain Graves has promised to marry me, and I know he will love and cherish this child. Mrs. Clayton said he's not well. I may have to tolerate his controlling tendencies for a few years, but I'll eventually have Faraday. I'll never have to worry about providing my child a safe and comfortable home."

He took a step back and wiped a hand down his face, erasing all emotion. "I see. And all I can offer you is a modest life as a reverend's wife."

My lips trembled. All he had to do was offer his heart, but I wasn't enough to stir that kind of pledge from him.

He put his hat back on, pulling the brim down. "It appears you have arranged a solution to your situation that guarantees your comfort and safety. I'm pleased for you, honestly. This way you can wear your gowns and as many hair ribbons as you like." His words were cool, well rehearsed, and even tinged with relief.

I sniffed and meanly replied, "If you are eager to start a family, Hettie will not hesitate to accept your offer, no matter how poorly you pose the question. I daresay you'd only have to grunt in her direction." I hated the pleasure I received from being so spiteful.

Without hesitating, he said, "Hettie doesn't need my help."

The words lingered in the air between us as if written with an invisible hand. A fiery rage boiled in my veins at the insult. Of course Hettie didn't need his help! She was brave and smart and capable, and far superior to me in every way. But I didn't need to hear him say it out loud. My fists curled under the cloak.

I wanted to grab him by the collar . . . I wanted to grab him by the collar and bring my face close to his. I wanted him to see the real me.

I wanted to spend nights by the fire with him, playfully arguing and challenging each other. I wanted to tell him all the stories I used to make up. I wanted to tell him about the island I'd imagined for my parents so he could be in that dream with me.

I wanted him.

I wanted his arms around me as he whispered in my ear. I wanted the vibration of his voice against my earlobe. I wanted to wake up with those brown eyes staring back at me as he reached over for a kiss.

But the man who stood in front of me wanted none of those things. He continued to stare at me darkly with a brow furrowed in confusion and wounded pride. At last, he told me, "There's nothing more for either of us to say."

Heat burning behind my eyes, I turned on my heel before he could see me cry. I made my way back up the slope toward Faraday House, with its hard stone walls and empty black windows.

CHAPTER THIRTY-TWO

I shivered as I changed for the evening. The wind battered Faraday, icy and raw. I suspected my earlier fever was creeping back. I sniffed, unable to erase the expression on Reverend Pellerine's face when I turned down his proposal. Would he ever smile at me again? I selfishly wanted that, just one more time. As something to tuck away, a secret I could revisit whenever I needed an escape. It was a futile wish, though, and I had to concentrate on more pressing matters.

From every blond curl I pinned back to the drops of perfume I placed behind my ears, Mrs. Shackleton praised my attention to detail.

I stepped into the pink dress I'd worn the night of the admiral's dance. I chose it for two reasons: it was my loveliest gown, which showcased my assets best, and it had a pocket. My heart kept up a solid pounding inside my chest as I considered all the things that could go wrong tonight. When I faced the mirror and fanned out the gown's pleats, I saw the glowing result of my efforts.

A beauty, to be sure. However, I knew my most important accessory was determination. I had finally accepted Frederick was not going to save me, and Reverend Pellerine had practically admitted our marriage would be built on a foundation of his charitable nature. I would be another Moses to him, some poor creature he'd found in a dire situation.

I had to do this on my own. There were numerous ways the

plan could fail miserably, but the risk was worth the reward. Not only would it erase any suspicion on Captain Graves's part regarding paternity, but it also meant I could concentrate on keeping Georgina alive. A new idea began to bloom.

If Captain Graves was concerned about the legitimacy of the baby, I could suggest he claim the baby was his and Georgina's. No one on the mainland would be the wiser. Then I could stay at Faraday as her personal companion. We would raise the baby together.

Hettie wouldn't be needed anymore.

I imagined spending time in the kitchen with Mrs. Clayton learning how to cook and bake—and maybe to sew too. Captain Graves's health would decline, but he would have the comfort of knowing he had a legacy, an heir. He would be content. And a content man who had all his aspirations and comforts met would be pleasant to be around—or at least less demanding and brutish.

I envisioned Georgina painting by the pond this summer. And for many summers after. Lovely vignettes developed as my imagination added wildflowers to the hillside by the second. Then I mentally added trips to the mainland every Sunday for Reverend Pellerine's sermon. Perhaps if he saw me in a new light, one where I didn't need rescuing . . .

A knocking pulled me back to reality.

I was embraced by the dark and cold surroundings of my room. Nervous trembles shook my fingers as I opened the door to see Hettie standing there. Her bored expression instantly changed as she looked me up and down. "You're an absolute vision," she said. There was none of her usual snark. I wondered if she'd been watching my argument with Reverend Pellerine and was thrilled to not have any competition.

"I'm almost ready," I said. "Let the captain know I'll be down shortly."

"Of course." Then she added, "Mrs. Graves wants to see you as soon as you're able."

I frowned at her. "Is she all right?"

"All right as she can be."

I went to Georgina's room with a growing sense of unease burrowing under my skin. Any prior optimism vanished. When I arrived at her room, she was sitting up in bed and holding her own cup of tea. My heart sang. The lace gauze of my skirt swished as I quickly made my way to her bedside. "You look so well," I exclaimed.

Every candelabra and chamber candle was burning, banishing any darkness. The glow reflected off her cheeks. Her brown hair was no longer in the braid but instead tucked under a nightcap.

Her eyes grew in surprise as she took in my appearance. "You are very elegant tonight." There was a question in her tone. A note of suspicion.

I was dressed for seduction, and there was only one man whom I would be dressed like this for. No wonder she was confused. Or maybe even jealous, I hated to admit. And I realized my terrible fault. Her own hair was falling out, she was thin and pale, and she hadn't even worn anything but a nightgown in months. I'd waltzed in with my hair shiny and full of ribbons, smelling of a summer garden and wearing a figure-showing dress.

The heat of shame worked its way up my neck. She continued to look at me expectantly, waiting for an answer. I stammered a few words about having wanted to wear something colorful.

Mrs. Clayton tidied in the background, giving us privacy.

I perched on the end of her bed and reached out, putting my hand over hers. I considered telling her my plan, but it seemed cruel to put that burden of anxiety on her. I would relay the event when it was over.

Georgina leaned forward with a determined stare. "You must leave Faraday," she whispered. "I see you in a grave. Esther showed me. You need to leave at the next low tide."

A tremor reached all the way to my toes. I shook my head. "I refuse to leave you."

Georgina's eyes welled with tears. "You're in a deep hole in the ground. Dead."

"It's a warning, not a certainty." I licked my lips and bent close to her ear. "Trust me, everything will be fine by tomorrow morning."

Mrs. Clayton cleared her throat and made her way to the door. The chimes of the clock sounded the hour. She said, "You don't want to be late, Miss Fitzpatrick."

Georgina's gaze slid to the doorway, fearful. She gripped my puffed sleeve, nearly ripping the cuff. "My pictures don't lie," she said.

Her fingertips were stained. "What have you been doing?" I asked.

"Leave," she repeated, more harshly. "I'm dying anyway; don't let the curse take you too." Georgina's fingers let go as she eased back into the pillow and put an arm around Martha. I noticed the doll's dress was smudged even more. And now the parasol was missing. Everything she held dear was falling apart, just like her.

I didn't have time to explain the plan to Georgina or why Mrs. Clayton was the only person I could trust to help me with this. I kissed the top of her head. "I will not leave you," I said.

When I entered the hallway, Mrs. Clayton pulled me close. Her face was lined with worry. She pressed the bottle into the palm of my hand. "A drop is all you'll need. There's plenty of spruce beer on the table, so keep filling up his glass. It'll make the medicine act faster." The darkness under her eyes hinted at how exhausted she was. However, in that moment I felt all her energy and focus.

She whispered, "You're stronger than you think."

I steeled my nerves as I walked down the gray hallway to the dining room. I paused by the last picture for only a moment, wishing I could jump into the painting and sail away. My imagination couldn't save me now. I had no choice: I must do this.

I would give the captain one drop of the medicine to make him sleepy enough so all he'd remember was me escorting him to his bedroom. Tomorrow morning the proof would be in bed with him, and next month I would tell him I was carrying his heir.

Mrs. Clayton and I could worry about the other details later of letting out my dresses so I wouldn't show as much to make him think I was newly with child. The confidence Mrs. Clayton had professed was gaining momentum in me with each step. By tomorrow morning everything would be fixed.

I entered the dining room and took one look at the scene. My heart dropped.

CHAPTER THIRTY-THREE

Reverend Pellerine stood by the fireplace. His wounded gaze never wavered from my face. "Good evening," he said. "You look well."

My mouth was unable to form any words, for what could I say to him that wouldn't sound insulting? There was a powerful urge to take his arm and lead him back to the pond so we could retry the proposal. I had to remind myself those moments would only be happening in my imagination. I had to be comforted with the knowledge that one day he would understand I had saved him from a miserable marriage. One day he would not think so ill of me. I clung to that notion.

Captain Graves rose from his chair with a grunt. His white shirt and cravat were clean, but his evening jacket was wrinkled and unbuttoned. "Evening," he muttered, smoothing a hand over the back of his head, trying to tame a wayward piece of hair. I would swear he'd just woken from a nap. Then he took in my dress. I wasn't prepared for his reaction. He grimaced with such a look of disgust.

Shame rolled over me in waves. My instincts had led to disaster. Mrs. Clayton had told me to add the medication when he wasn't looking. Immediately I'd thought of distracting him with my appearance, my only asset. But from his reaction, it was clear I had displeased him.

The swollen face of Mr. Clayton came back to me. A new fear settled uneasily over me.

Nodding a greeting, I moved my attention to anywhere else in the room other than him.

The table was set with a freshly laundered white cloth. The wineglasses sparkled in the candlelight. A bouquet of pine boughs and red berries had been added between the candelabras, giving off a fresh scent. The romantic intention of the scene was obvious. I supposed I had Hettie to thank.

Standing quietly in my best dress, I was as useless as the polished silverware. Reverend Pellerine probably thought I was torturing him on purpose. My face burned with regret and guilt.

"Sit," Captain Graves said. The impatience was hard to miss.

I sniffed, then coughed into my hand.

Captain Graves frowned at me. "Are you ill?" There was no concern in his voice, only accusation.

"Not at all. It's the fresh air I've been enjoying while exploring the island," I offered meekly. "My cloak and bonnet are warm enough, I assure you. I'm sure I'll feel perfectly fine by tomorrow." I coughed again.

He looked at me accusingly. "Hettie saw you walking on the grounds without proper attire." There was a patronizing growl to his tone. "How could you be so inept? Any germ coming into this house, no matter how mild, is lethal to Mrs. Graves."

A coldness crept over my shoulders. I practically fell to my knees with remorse. "Georgina is dear to me; I would never do anything to harm her." I sneezed.

"That's enough," Captain Graves ordered, putting his hand up. "I forbid you to visit her anymore. Say your goodbyes via letter."

"No." That one word came out garbled, mixed with new tears and desperation.

Reverend Pellerine handed me his handkerchief. I noticed how quickly he let go, as soon as I touched it, careful our fingers didn't meet.

"Please reconsider this demand," I begged the captain.

But he remained stoic, arms crossed in front of his chest as if he were at the head of a ship, ordering the crew to change direction.

Reverend Pellerine offered the following solution: "Mrs. Graves would be devastated by the stoppage of visits as well. Surely precautions can be put in place so that Emeline can visit."

Captain Graves's expression hardened into an unmistakable warning. His next words were sharp enough to cut the air. He replied, "How dare you address this lady by any other name than Miss Fitzpatrick." He tilted up his chin the smallest amount, but it spoke volumes. "I can appreciate someone of your customs and upbringing may not be concerned with civility of the Commonwealth, but manners still count in this house, Reverend." The ugly prejudice dripped from his words.

Reverend Pellerine stood like a statue, unblinking at the captain. I folded the handkerchief in my hand. "It's my own doing," I stated.

"No, the fault is mine," Reverend Pellerine interrupted, suddenly back to life. When he looked at me, there was a veil in front of his eyes. "I used a familiar term out of turn. My apologies if it made you uncomfortable."

Captain Graves interjected, "Her comfort is no concern of yours." Then he motioned to the doorway, dismissing him. "This matter is closed."

"Enjoy your meal, then." Reverend Pellerine turned to go.

I dared not look his way. I knew he wasn't prepared to challenge the captain and risk being dismissed before Georgina's death. Especially not after I'd turned down what he believed was the best option for me. He was content to leave me this time with a clear conscience. His footsteps disappeared down the hall.

"Come." The captain's fingers snapped, then pointed to my chair.

I smiled to hide a wince as I took the seat closest to his.

Hettie brought in the meal. She snuck glances between Captain Graves and me, then she gave me a wink. It was all so miserable. She uncovered each dish with an exaggerated flair: moose steak, mushroom sauce, pickled cucumbers, roasted parsnips, and steaming biscuits. She finished by pouring each of us a glass of beer.

"I'll be returning with dessert," she said. "Spiced pumpkin tart."

"You've outdone yourself," Captain Graves said, all compliments and gaiety. "Make sure to do up a plate for the reverend as well."

I was dumbfounded at how quickly his moods rose and lowered like the tides. He carried the temperament of the ocean in his veins.

"Thank you, sir," Hettie replied, nearly giving him a curtsy. "Reverend Pellerine and I will be enjoying our own small supper in the kitchen."

Captain Graves chuckled at his own private joke as he reached for his spruce beer. He slurped it down quickly and tore into his steak like he hadn't eaten in weeks. Between mouthfuls, he said, "I hope Hettie stays on after."

After. He didn't even bother mentioning Georgina's name.

"Shame to lose such a good cook."

"What about Mrs. Clayton?" I asked.

He stabbed a chunk of parsnip and gulped it in one bite. "She and Mr. Clayton have been with me for a long time, that's certain, but sometimes it's good to have a rotation of staff. I don't want them thinking of Faraday as their own. And you shouldn't bother yourself with such matters. I run the household; you know that." He returned to his meal, making sure to add extra mushrooms to a piece of steak.

There was a wet gnashing sound as he chewed. I imagined the meat being torn up inside his mouth. My throat closed up, thinking of the fist-size portions he swallowed.

Mr. and Mrs. Clayton had worked for him for over ten years. They'd looked after Faraday while he spent all those years trading along the coast. It made no sense. Had he no regard for their loyalty? I was about to ask him this but decided to bite my tongue. My focus should be on creating a distraction.

I ate the roasted parsnips, but they tasted like sawdust.

He sniffed and drained another glass. I watched the level of the pitcher of beer go down. My hands shook as I added a bit of butter to my biscuit. Watching it melt, I imagined the cozy scene in the kitchen. Interesting how the same food would taste much better with different company.

"You need to eat more," he said, plopping a slab of moose meat on my plate. "I'll not have another sickly wife to take care of." His words were slightly slurred.

The beer was revealing his truths.

My reply was automatic. "I'm grateful for your attention to such matters," I said, cutting off the smallest piece of meat. He watched while I chewed, then took another piece. I noted the knife with the serrated edges could fit in my pocket.

He gave me a satisfied smile. His chin was shiny with grease from the meal.

"I love the warmth of a fire," I said, taking my glass and going to the fireplace. I placed it on the mantel as I reached my palms closer to the flames.

"Mmm." He nodded distractedly. He scraped the plate, pushing more food onto his fork.

With my back to him, I took the bottle out of my pocket. I tipped it on its side and started to add a few drops to the glass.

"Come finish your meal." He pounded his fist on the table, making me jump. The bottle fell from my hand, smashing on the stone hearth. I stared at the tiny shards of glass and few spots of liquid.

"What's that?" he grunted. He stared at me, full of accusation.

"Nothing at all." I swept the mess into the fire with the side of my shoe. I quickly returned to the table with my glass. I stood by his side and put a hand on his shoulder, making sure to lean over enough. His gaze dropped to the front of my dress—as I'd reasoned it would. Despite his lack of attention to me physically or any sign of anticipation for our wedding night, he was still a man.

I gave him my best smile. "I'm truly grateful for your company this evening."

His fist was still curled on the table.

"A proper wife should make sure her husband's glass is never empty." I poured half of my beer into his. "A toast," I said. I clinked my glass to his. "To our future," I said, my voice shaking.

He gave me a hesitant smile and drained his glass, letting it smack down on the table.

I pretended to take a sip, then raised my drink again. "And to the future of Faraday House."

Staring at his plate, he only gave a tired sigh.

"And to your future heir," I said.

His head bobbed in a lazy nod as he held out his glass for another refill and we repeated the toast together.

The tension in his shoulders eased under my touch. He said, "Reverend Pellerine has already signed the marriage certificate. We won't have to wait long."

I kept the smile frozen on my face as I slid back to my chair. "Is that why he was here earlier?" My pulse was suddenly in my throat.

"Partly. He also told me he'll be leaving Shoreham as soon as he marries us."

I FELT AN unexpected torrent of anger toward Reverend Pellerine. I knew it was unfounded, but I wanted to scream and pound the floor with my fists. The betrayal stung, brutal and undeserved. I had no claim on him. What did it matter to me if he left? I told myself this as Captain Graves became sleepier during dessert, spilling the pumpkin puree on his wrinkled jacket.

We took the staircase together, mostly because he needed me to help him. I wasn't sure if it was the effects of the beer or the medicine. He mumbled incoherently to himself. I had no idea how much of a dose I'd delivered. The broken vial on the hearth had had hardly any liquid left. Georgina's door was slightly open. In the soft candlelight, I saw Mrs. Clayton resting on the settee, the Bible in her lap.

Quietly, I opened the door to the captain's bedroom. I had been here before in Esther's vision of the past. Instead of a tidy room with no personal effects, there were clothes strewn about the floor and the pungent odor of a full chamber pot. A large trunk was positioned at the foot of the bed. It was covered in dark leather and outfitted with leather straps and a large brass buckle. A thick layer of dust covered the lid.

Captain Graves mumbled then flopped onto the mattress, practically a rag doll. He snored away, unaware. He was a large man, and by the time I had him undressed and under the covers I was slick with sweat. I watched him breathe, waiting until I knew he was in a deep enough sleep that nothing would wake him, then I took out the steak knife from my pocket and slowly approached the bed.

CHAPTER THIRTY-FOUR

The next morning, I eased out of my own bed from under the layer of quilts, taking care not to put much weight on my left leg. I checked the bandages I'd fashioned last night. I had ripped one of my pillowcases into strips. The wound was sore to the touch, but I'd been careful to only cut my calf superficially. It rendered enough blood to leave splotches on the sheets.

After dressing in my most modest frock, I put the shawl around my shoulders and went directly to Georgina's room. I gave Captain Graves's door a wary glance. I had to be prepared for all his questions. I would let him know what had happened, and how I was reluctant at first, but then he convinced me we were already practically married in the eyes of God. The marriage certificate had already been signed by both himself and Reverend Pellerine.

Regardless, he wouldn't be able to ignore the evidence I'd left in his bed. As Mrs. Clayton had said, I must act like it's the truth and be steadfast in my conviction.

Hettie sat in the chair at the foot of Georgina's bed, busy darning a sock. No question whose it was. The dull ache of jealousy pulsed under my skin, making me forget about the small cut to my leg.

There was a tray with a steaming pot of tea and even a small bowl with a used spoon and the scraped remains of a few dollops of porridge. Georgina was back on solid food!

As I approached the bed, Hettie looked up. "How is Mrs. Graves this morning?" I asked.

"Same," she sighed. "But still alive—the poor thing is a fighter."

Yes, she is, I thought.

I crept to her bedside and placed my hand over her clasped ones. Her fingers were so frail and thin, it was like holding a bird. There was movement behind her eyelids.

Hettie gave me a curious look. "Sleep well?" There was the lift of an eyebrow.

"Thank you for the meal last night. Everything was delicious." She waited, but I gave her no details. I did not share her enthusiasm, nor did I have the strength to play along.

Georgina was groggy, unable to rouse herself awake.

Hettie whispered, "Mrs. Clayton said she didn't sleep much last night, kept having bad dreams and such."

I noticed the flask was on the bedside table. Hettie saw where my attention was. "He was here earlier, reading from the Bible," she said in a self-satisfied way. "He knows it comforts her."

I knew for a fact that neither one of them found it comforting. I wondered what they were really discussing. "Where is he now?"

"Captain Graves? I haven't seen him yet. Must be sleeping in."

I knew she was purposely being coy. "Not the captain. Reverend Pellerine."

"Had an early breakfast. Now he's walking with the dog, I suppose."

Georgina squeezed my hand. "Graves," she mumbled.

"I'm here," I told her. "The captain is still asleep." I supposed she was used to him joining her by now.

She blinked a few times, then a look of recognition graced her features. "You're safe?" Her eyes grew wide. "I had terrible nightmares."

"I'm fine," I assured her.

She furrowed her brow at me, looking unconvinced.

Behind us, Hettie lingered, leaning closer while still sewing. "You can leave now," I told her. "I'll stay with Mrs. Graves."

After she tucked away her mending, Hettie left promising to bring up a breakfast tray for me. Captain's orders, she added. I rolled my eyes after she departed.

With the room to ourselves, I confessed to Georgina what I had done to secure my safety and how I thought it might be possible for her to recover. The more I spoke, the more awake she became. She even pushed herself up in bed with one hand to hear me better. She was getting stronger.

I shared my hope of Faraday being her canvas, with murals for each room. Captain Graves would fade into the background. I could start making him dishes with lots of mushrooms, the kind that made you feel like you'd had a keg of wine. Keep him happily drunk until death claimed him.

A shocked smile of disbelief graced her thin face. "Are you sure?"

I nodded. "It worked. I was a little worried, thinking I might have given him too much. But it worked."

She fell back into the pillow. "I'm glad." But there was no conviction to match the statement.

Hettie dropped off the tray, then muttered something under her breath about the captain's chamber pot and went across the hall. I began to eat the porridge and cream, pushing the edge of the spoon, making tracks in the oats.

I should have felt relief. Even though I didn't have Frederick, and Faraday was a far cry from Bermuda, I had everything I wanted: a husband to take care of me, a home of my own, and a comfortable life provided to me. So why did it feel like something was missing?

Georgina started snoring daintily. As her hand relaxed, a key fell from her fingers. It was the one from the missing parasol.

Images linked together as I thought of the stains on her fingers and the doll's dress, and how I'd seen Mrs. Clayton trying to open the locked drawer of the writing desk. The stains were ink!

I went over to the writing desk. Shaking, I slid the key into the lock. It fit perfectly. With a quick glance to the bed to make sure Georgina was still asleep, I turned the key, hearing a satisfying *click*.

I grabbed the drawer pull just as Hettie screamed.

"He's dead!" she cried out.

CHAPTER THIRTY-FIVE

Hettie's voice reverberated through the air, filling the hallway with her terrified shrieks.

I raced out of Georgina's room and found Hettie staring at Captain Graves's bed. She was hugging her stomach. I stepped around her and gasped. I had left Captain Graves sleeping soundly, but something dreadful had happened to him. Something macabre.

His eyes were open and staring at the ceiling, but most disturbing was his open mouth, frozen in a silent scream. This was not a natural death.

I was flooded with panic.

"There's blood on the sheets," Hettie whimpered, tears streaming down her face. It was like she was nailed to the spot, unable to look away or close her eyes. "What happened to him?"

I swallowed a whimper. It was my blood on the sheets from the cut on my leg. The "proof" Mrs. Clayton had told me to leave behind.

Voices echoed from the foyer, overlapping and urgent. They were the concerned tones of Mr. and Mrs. Clayton.

Hettie was crying uncontrollably. I took her by the shoulders and gave her a gentle shake. "We'll wait outside," I said.

The others rounded the top of the stairs as we came into the hallway.

"Oh, my dear." Mr. Clayton reached for Hettie. She pressed her face into his shoulder as she pointed to Captain Graves's bedroom.

Mrs. Clayton's gaze settled on me, strange and unexpectedly frightened. Over her shoulder I saw Reverend Pellerine approach in long strides.

"What's happened? Who's hurt?" Reverend Pellerine's questions rose above Hettie's sobs. He had ruddy cheeks and windblown hair from his morning walk. His eyes locked onto mine. There was an immediate smoothness to his features, easing the worry in his brow.

He'd thought I had been the one hurt. I selfishly allowed myself to memorize the contours of his face.

"The captain is dead," I told him. "Hettie found him this morning."

Mrs. Clayton gave me a concerned side glance.

Reverend Pellerine waited for me to elaborate.

"I . . . I don't know what happened," I said. "It's unexplainable."

Mrs. Clayton went to the bedroom door. "Jesus, Mary, and Joseph," she whispered, crossing herself. She turned back to us, drained of color and trembling.

Reverend Pellerine asked her to step aside, then he walked into the room. All was quiet except for Hettie's sobs, muffled by Mr. Clayton's jacket lapel. He had a protective arm around her shaking shoulders.

Finally, the reverend emerged from the room, closing the door behind him. He cleared his throat. "Mr. Clayton, I think the magistrate will need to be summoned. We'll keep the door closed to ensure nothing is disturbed."

"I can go," Mr. Clayton offered. "But the tide's turnin'. I'll need to leave soon."

"We all need to leave, Reverend!" Mrs. Clayton exclaimed. "His death proves evil walks these halls." Her gaze slid to Georgina's room.

I knew Georgina wasn't responsible, but the image of Captain Graves's fatal scream reminded me of what Hettie had said about ghosts being harmless. I wasn't sure any longer. Had Captain Graves been involved with Esther's death?

Hettie pushed away from Mr. Clayton and pointed at me. "It was her! She did it." Her breathing picked up as her chest rose and fell excitedly. "She took him to bed last night. I saw her. I was watching from my bedroom doorway in the dark."

The floor seemed to drop from under me as if I'd stepped back into the abandoned pit. I turned to Mrs. Clayton for help, but she appeared as shocked as her husband.

A spasm of panic began to churn in my stomach. I trembled under their accusing stares. Reverend Pellerine's, however, had an added layer of confusion and hurt. I addressed him directly. "No," I said. "It's not what you assume."

"Then how do you explain this?" Hettie held up my shift. "It was in his dead fist."

Without thinking, I made a grab for the garment, but Hettie pulled it out of reach, moving toward the stairs. "You were with him last night," she accused. Fat tears flowed down her face.

"You don't know what you're talking about." I lunged forward, hand outstretched, but she backed up quickly. Her attention was focused on Reverend Pellerine and not on what was behind her. She took one more step backward and disappeared, tumbling down the staircase.

I bolted to the top of the steps. Pressing against the railing, I saw her lying in an awkward heap on the landing at the foot of the clock. She let out an earsplitting scream.

Mrs. Clayton shoved me aside and rushed to her. She tried to soothe Hettie as she untied her shoe and peeled back the stocking. A jagged tip of bone poked through her shin. Blood gushed down her leg.

Mrs. Clayton took in a quick breath through her nose. She looked at Reverend Pellerine. "She needs to get to the mainland at once. I can bandage this, but she's losing blood and I'm worried about shock."

Reverend Pellerine rushed out the main door, heading to the carriage house.

Hettie's shrieks made the air vibrate.

Mrs. Clayton's voice faltered for a moment, then she cleared her throat. "You're strong, my dear. Don't worry. We'll get some good whiskey in you."

"I'll fetch it." Mr. Clayton had turned a shade of green. He awkwardly moved around them on the landing, trying not to look at Hettie's leg.

"Aye," she said. "And get bandages and quilts, and a good cold pail of seawater. Now, Bagnall!"

He jumped the last few steps and ran toward the kitchen.

"I can help," I offered meekly.

"Hold her leg so it doesn't move," Mrs. Clayton ordered. "I'll go to Mrs. Graves's room for the mushroom tea. It'll take the edge off." Dumbfounded, I took her place, gingerly supporting Hettie's foot while Mrs. Clayton lumbered back up the stairs.

Hettie started to shiver. This was my fault. "I'm so sorry," I whispered.

Her stare was razor-sharp. "Why didn't you leave the first night, when Mrs. Clayton warned you?" she hissed.

"What?"

She spoke through gritted teeth. "You've ruined everything. All he wanted was an heir, but you've destroyed his chance at a legacy. I swear on my dying breath you will never get Faraday."

I was speechless. Everything slowed down as if in a dream. I had assumed this whole time Hettie had her sights fixed on the reverend. However, I was beginning to understand she'd had loftier ambitions. Had she been hoping to become the next Mrs. Graves after Georgina?

Coincidences spun in my mind and started to fit together logically. Hettie's room was next to Georgina's, and she had full access to the kitchen. She'd even boasted of having medical knowledge, and had taken a keen interest in the history of Faraday itself. She knew she could use the curse to create a narrative around Georgina's illness.

Most telling, though, was the fact Georgina's symptoms had started shortly after Hettie had arrived. Nurse Gibson had been hired, but she only lasted a few weeks before her "accident." What if she had begun to suspect poisoning—just like I had?

I'd never accepted Georgina having the strength to push the nurse down the stairs. Hettie must have dressed in one of Georgina's nightgowns. With her hair down and covering her face, she would have easily been mistaken for the captain's wife. It played convincingly into Mrs. Clayton's belief that Georgina was bothered by restless spirits. The scheme got rid of Nurse Gibson, leaving Hettie to continue poisoning Georgina unencumbered.

But then I came along and ruined her plans.

And now she was making me pay for taking away her future life as mistress of Faraday.

Hettie still had a death grip on my shift. "I'll make sure you hang for this."

CHAPTER THIRTY-SIX

Mrs. Clayton arrived with a quilt under one arm and a teapot in the other hand. She pushed me to the side and fitted the thick blanket under the broken limb to prop it up and keep it from moving.

Hettie cried out again, matching the wind howling outside. The pain was taking over. She grew more ashen by the moment. Mr. Clayton's rushed footfalls returned. He came up the stairs while looking anywhere but at Hettie's wound. He dropped a pile of kitchen cloths.

"Here's the whiskey," he said, thrusting the bottle at me. Mrs. Clayton grabbed it and poured a small amount in Hettie's mouth. "Give me room, Bagnall," she ordered as she started to make temporary bandages.

He pressed his lips into a hard line. "You said no one else would get hurt." His words sounded like gravel.

Mrs. Clayton turned to me with a fierce defiance in her eyes, but oddly in control. "Let's get more whiskey in her, all right, Miss Fitzpatrick?"

Hettie gladly took another sip. Her anger had melted into pain-induced delirium. My attention flitted between the Claytons. Nothing made sense. Who was Mr. Clayton talking about? Esther and her baby? Captain Graves?

"That'll have to do," Mrs. Clayton said, finishing her first aid. The leg was covered in strips of cloth with two ties at the top and bottom, creating a makeshift splint. "She'll need to move soon." Then she took the whiskey from me and gave Hettie another sip herself. She put a hand to her cheek. "Don't worry, my girl. It'll be all right."

Mr. Clayton's face was the color of chalk.

Reverend Pellerine returned through the main door. Moses paced back and forth in the foyer, not wanting to come any farther into the house. "The horse and carriage are ready," Reverend Pellerine said, casting a worried gaze at Hettie.

I stared directly his way, silently begging him to look at me.

Mrs. Clayton said, "You'll have to take her, Reverend. Bagnall's useless around an open wound. We're lucky it's low tide, but you'll need to leave now." There was a crack of thunder in the distance. Things happened quickly. Hettie was wrapped in more quilts and carried out by Reverend Pellerine to the carriage. Moses ambled after them.

"Thank you, René," she sighed. The whiskey bottle was in her fierce grip. I'd lost track of my garment and could only assume she still had it clutched in her other fist. Surely that wouldn't be enough to send me to prison—or the noose. Georgina's foreboding prophecy came back to me: *I see you in a grave.*

Mr. Clayton held the horse by the reins as the wind lashed his coat open.

Reverend Pellerine said to him, "I'll return with the magistrate. Don't let anyone in the captain's room."

Mr. Clayton nodded gravely. "I'll take care of things here. Hurry or you'll miss low tide."

Reverend Pellerine mounted the horse and turned to me. I felt it was my last chance to speak to him. "Please," I said. "It's not what you think."

His expression collapsed into one of uncertainty. "I don't know what to think, Miss Fitzpatrick." The use of my formal name cut through me. "Take care of Georgina. I'll be back as soon as I can." He then whistled for Moses, but the dog had run off into the forest. He whistled again, squinting through the trees.

"You need to go." Mr. Clayton's voice rose to near panic.

Reverend Pellerine snapped the reins. Mr. Clayton and I watched as the carriage made its way toward the mainland, the heavy fog swallowing it up.

Mr. Clayton curled his hand around the crook of my arm. He led me back to the house, both of us quiet. The heavy door closed behind us, filling the foyer with a dull echo. The bloodstain on the stairs greeted us gruesomely. Mrs. Clayton was nowhere to be seen.

"I should go to Georgina," I said, thinking she must be worried, hearing all the frantic noises.

Mr. Clayton's grip tightened on my arm. "She's not a concern," he said, his voice eerily calm. "But you need to be dealt with."

CHAPTER THIRTY-SEVEN

B ut Georgina!" I sputtered as he dragged me to my room. I tried to pull away, but he was strong. It was like being tied to a horse. The cut on my leg burned. "Please," I pleaded. "I didn't hurt the captain. Please, talk to me. We're friends."

He opened my door and pushed me inside. I stumbled forward, catching the edge of my bed to keep from falling.

"I hate to admit it, miss, but it appears the evidence points to you as having had something to do with the captain's death. I can't have you wandering the house. Mrs. Clayton said someone stole the pain medication." He said it matter-of-factly, like we were discussing the different kinds of mushrooms. "And guess what I found in the dining room fireplace this morning?"

I didn't need to hear him say it—I knew it was the shattered remnants of the blue vial.

Then he closed the door. With horror I heard the key fit into place and turn.

"No!" I rushed forward and tried the knob, but it was locked fast. I pounded my palms on the wood. "Don't leave me in here. Please! I didn't do anything. Please, let me be with Georgina."

"It's for your own good." His voice came from farther down the hall. He was already leaving me. "Not until the magistrate arrives tomorrow."

Tomorrow.

I pressed my back against the door and slid to the floor. I stared at the ceiling, barely breathing. How had it gone so badly so quickly?

There was no scenario I could muster in my imagination that would allow me to conjure a way to fix any of this. I was only good at escaping in my mind, not in real life. Useless.

I pictured the magistrate arriving on the scene fully aware my shift had been found in Captain Graves's death grip. Mr. Clayton was correct: all the evidence pointed to me. And even though it looked like he'd died of fright, I'd probably very well poisoned him last night. I had no idea what was in that vial. I only assumed it was Georgina's pain medication because that's what I believed— because that's what Mrs. Clayton told me. She was following her own rules of manipulation.

If you act like it's the truth, he'll accept it . . . Even if he calls your bluff at first, you must be steadfast; your conviction will tip the scales and convince him otherwise.

I hadn't even questioned her. I was being lied to by everyone, it seemed. Were the Claytons working with Hettie? Why would they all hate Georgina enough to kill her?

You can't take care of yourself, Mrs. Shackleton piped up as if she were sitting in the room with me. *How could you listen to that woman? I told you all you had to do was wait! Now look at what you've done.*

Her lecture continued as she presented an image of me in prison. They would postpone my hanging until the baby was born. The waterfront would be packed with people eager to watch the once-legendary beauty of Halifax hang for murder.

I put a hand on my stomach. The room blurred, and I thought Esther was going to show me another vision, but it was only my tears. She had abandoned me as well.

Muffled voices broke through my gloom. The Claytons were arguing.

I pushed back the tapestry and crouched down by the grate in the sunroom.

". . . no other option," Mrs. Clayton said. "You know I'm right, Bagnall. She knows too much."

"Let the magistrate take care of it," he said. A chair scraped on the floor.

"You're just going to drink spruce beer until then? That's your plan?"

He growled something in reply, but his words were muffled. I pictured him taking a long drink.

"You'd rather see her hang?" Mrs. Clayton continued. "At least we can give her a quick and painless ending. When the magistrate arrives, we can say she escaped and took the dory. In a few days, one of her shoes will conveniently wash up on the shore." Her voice grew excited. "People will blame her death on the curse. Please, Bagnall, we're so close. After all these years, we can finally be free."

There was a *thud*. "I'm sick of this," Mr. Clayton answered. His tone was hard, unrepentant. I imagined his bloodshot eyes staring her down. "I did everything you said, and we're still paying for our past sins."

She gasped. "You're as much to blame."

Silence.

When she spoke again, her words were softer. "We just need to keep our heads a few more days and everything will be ours."

"Ours?" There was a crack in his voice, a small splinter of surrender. "It doesn't matter how many damn holes I dig—we'll never find it. That's the real curse." His earlier fortitude began to crumble.

Mrs. Clayton must have sensed it too. "Lost your nerve?" she needled. Spite sharpened her tongue. "Like that day when she fell through the pit cover? All you had to do was let her drop. We wouldn't be in this mess if you'd had the stomach to walk away and let gravity work."

"Shut up, woman! I had no idea you wanted her dead."

"I wanted her off the island, you damn fool, but lying at the bottom of that thing would have been just as good. We could've blamed the reverend since he's the one who suggested the walk."

There was the sound of water sloshing in a basin. Then the clank of a spoon tapping the edge of a pot. Mrs. Clayton moved about the kitchen, sounding as if she was carrying on with her chores. "You know I'm right, Bagnall. It's either her or us. There's no other option."

There was a soft curse, followed by the slamming of the back kitchen door.

I pushed myself away from the grate, shaking. I could hardly comprehend my situation. Mr. Clayton was going to arrive at my door any moment to kill me. And what about poor Georgina? What horrible plans did they have for her?

My heart thumped painfully. Rushing to the window, I pushed up the sash, feeling a blast of wind. I considered climbing down the ivy, but as the ground swirled below, I knew I'd grow dizzy and fall to my death for certain.

I turned on the spot, seeing every item in my room as a potential weapon. I wondered if any of my perfumes could blind him. Then I saw the steak knife was still on my bedside table. I remembered how Mrs. Clayton had tried to open the writing desk with a knife.

She wasn't successful, but I was fighting for my life and wouldn't give up. I slipped the tip of the blade into the keyhole. I twisted it and cursed enough times that it eventually clicked open.

The distance to Georgina's room never seemed so long. The faster I ran, the more the hallway stretched. Gasping, I raced into her room. Terror gripped my throat, stealing my breath.

Her bed was empty.

CHAPTER THIRTY-EIGHT

The top drawer of the writing desk was open. Sheets of paper were strewn on the rug, trailing to the bed. I crouched down and saw the same image had been done in ink over and over. The paper was almost completely black except for a few straight lines. I thought I saw the letter *L*.

A hand reached out from under the bed and grabbed my ankle. I nearly burst out of my skin as I screamed. A weak voice called out my name.

I dropped to my knees and saw Georgina hiding under the bed. Her face matched her white nightgown. "I know who's responsible for Esther's death," she said.

I gently eased her out of hiding.

Her fingers were stained with the ink as she clutched another bundle of drawings. "Look," she said, laying them out on the bed. By themselves they were meaningless, but put together each of them was revealed to be a piece of a whole. Against the black background, the letters were scratched out to spell one word. *CLAYTON*

"We have to get off this island."

She grabbed my hand, her eyes welling up. "I'm too weak to run, but I can stay under the bed; they might not find me."

I hugged her. "I'm not leaving without you. Can you make it down the stairs? We can go to the secret place off the music room." I put her arm over my shoulder. She weighed hardly more than a feather. Together, we crept to the hallway.

She said, "The Claytons know every inch of this house and the grounds by heart. There's no place we can hide together they won't find." Her thin fingers gripped my waist as she leaned into me. We couldn't go far. Even the stairs were out of the question.

I chewed my lower lip as I stared at the captain's bedroom door. "Then we'll have to go to the one place they won't think of looking."

Anticipating Mr. Clayton rushing up the steps any moment, I opened Captain Graves's door without hesitating. Georgina moaned at the sight of the corpse. "Never mind him," I said, and I pulled the sheet over his face.

"I had no idea you were so brave," she panted. The trip across the hall had clearly exhausted her.

I settled her on the trunk at the foot of the bed. "Reverend Pellerine will be back," I said. "All we have to do is keep hidden until then. It will be all right. We can stay here and let the Claytons kill each other."

"No." Georgina pulled on my wrist. "There really is a curse."

"What are you talking about?"

The main door slammed several times in quick succession. No person would be strong enough to move such a heavy door so quickly and with such force. We jumped at the sound.

With tears in her eyes, Georgina explained, "It's the only way the haunting will end. Esther's soul is stuck here, and if we don't find out the truth, I'll be doomed to the same fate."

"How do you know this?"

The piano sounded loudly, echoing up from the music room, as if someone was pounding it with their fists.

Georgina's lips were blue-tinged. "You must return to the blood; that's where the answer is."

"Tower room?"

She nodded. "I'm so weak. We don't have much time left. You must uncover the truth, or I'll be tethered to Faraday like Esther."

I imagined Georgina doomed to haunt this drafty gray house forever, weak and helpless. "I can't leave you alone in here."

"The trunk," she sighed. "It's our only option." She stood shakily and lifted the lid. A waft of mothballs rose. I recognized the sword and the long coat with the shiny buttons Captain Graves wore in each wedding portrait. She began to remove the items one at a time. The sword thudded softly to the rug followed by the jacket, the boots, and then a leather strap and pistol. "Help me," she said, dropping a pair of breeches on the floor.

I balked at the thought of closing her inside that trunk. "Never!"

Shaking her head, she said, "I must hide here, and you must go to the tower. Please, Emeline. You're the only one who can do this for me."

From down the hall, another door slammed several times, making the entire house quake. Was Mr. Clayton searching the rooms or was Esther's ghost tired of waiting and was now ready for revenge?

Georgina removed the last few items and stepped into the large trunk. The weight of the chore was not the reason I hesitated. The stakes were too high if I failed. I could never put her life . . . or her soul at risk. "But I'm so inept I'll make everything worse."

Her bony fingers dug into my wrist. "You have the pearl inside you, Emeline," she said. "I know you can do this." Her confidence sparked a new energy in me. She was the last one to believe in me. I nodded, filled with a newfound sense of nobleness.

A tear rolled down my cheek, but I wiped it away with the back of my hand. I gathered the overflow from the trunk and began to shove it into the wardrobe. My hand hesitated over the pistol and leather strap. It was only a matter of time before Mr. Clayton came for me. I had to be prepared.

The holster belt was too big for my waist, so I wore it over my shoulder and across my chest. The weight of the pistol felt foreign.

Georgina regarded me with equal parts awe and trepidation.

I caught sight of my reflection in the long mirror. My hair had fallen out of its bun while the holster wrinkled my dress. Mrs. Shackleton would have fainted.

"Do you know how to load it?" she asked. "Or even fire it?"

"No," I said, pointing the gun at the mirror. "But I can act like I do."

Even if he calls your bluff at first, you must be steadfast; your conviction will tip the scales and convince him otherwise.

Mr. Clayton may not truly believe I can fire a gun, but if he's facing the barrel of the pistol, he might pause long enough to give me a fighting chance.

The grandfather clock on the landing announced the time, unbothered by the turmoil of the house. Georgina sat on the bottom of the trunk, hugging her knees. I gave her the steak knife and kissed the top of her head. "I'll be back."

"I know you will."

I scuttled down the hall and along the walkway. Thunder crashed outside as heavy rain beat against the round window. Eerily, the doors had stopped slamming and the piano was silent.

I was unsure how long I'd been gone from my room, and hoped Mr. Clayton was still grappling with my murder assignment. Gripping the doorknob, I tentatively opened it a fraction, aware he could be on the other side, waiting for me. Even though I heard their conversation and saw their name spelled out with Georgina's sketches, I had the most difficult time understanding how either of them could be cold-blooded killers. What had happened in this house ten years ago?

Whatever truth Esther needed us to uncover, it was tremendous enough to influence the rest of the Claytons' lives. If one thing had been different, Georgina and I may never have had to set foot on this island.

With one hand on the pistol, I quickly opened the door all the way.

An icy plume enveloped me, erasing my surroundings. Someone had been waiting for me, but it wasn't Mr. Clayton.

CHAPTER THIRTY-NINE

S hh . . ." she whispered in my ear.

When I opened my eyes, I was standing in the tower room again, a silent witness to the past.

Esther was ashen and lying on the bloody sheets. Mrs. Clayton was crouched beside her and holding the wee bundle in her arms. "Tell him I'm sorry," Esther said. "And that I love him."

Tears rolled down Mrs. Clayton's cheeks. "Aye."

"Promise me." Her voice was hardly a whisper.

Mrs. Clayton nodded. Then she bent down, letting Esther see the child. There was a faint gurgle.

"I love you, my little angel." She looked at Mrs. Clayton. Her breaths were ragged and shallow. "She's so small. Protect her."

Mrs. Clayton watched the baby sleep in her arms. "I promise," she said. "Mr. Clayton has already gone to fetch the doctor from the mainland."

Esther nodded, then one last breath eased from her chest. Her eyes became stone still.

Darkness crept in from the edges, keeping the light only on Esther. In that moment she stood and walked toward me. Her nightgown was red from the waist down.

"She lied," Esther said directly to me. "Mr. Clayton never went for the doctor, and my baby girl stopped breathing. When Edgar returned from the sea, they never mentioned the pregnancy. They were worried he would blame them for not fetching the doctor sooner." She said all of this with an air of indifference, as if the emotion had become diluted with time. "I am partly to blame. I was upset he sailed so often, and we argued his last night. I knew I was pregnant and purposely kept that news from him, reasoning I was delaying his joy as a way of punishing him. How differently things would have turned out if I'd told him."

I replayed the vision from the kitchen with new understanding. I stayed quiet, unsure if I was allowed to ask questions. Mrs. Clayton had fabricated the entire story of the affair. Most likely to shift suspicion from herself.

"Mrs. Clayton told her husband to take my child and bury her somewhere on this island in an unmarked grave." She tilted her head as she looked out the tower window. There was nothing to see but darkness. We were suspended in between real time.

Graves. This was the truth. She wanted to be reunited with her child, to have their remains claimed and given a respectful burial beside her.

She turned back to me, and her bones seemed more prominent. "But instead, he did the unforgivable. And it is his secret that chains me to this place. I cannot rest until the truth is revealed. Wood remembers . . ."

As she took a step closer, her flesh thinned, becoming translucent. Her skeleton underneath rose to the surface, stealing her soft beauty.

Esther said, "I secretly feared Edgar was away so much at sea because he didn't love me. Only with time have I realized this misbelief was my downfall. I was too afraid to see he was working hard for our future." Her lips rolled up and disappeared, revealing her teeth and bone. Her skeletal face said to me, "We're all prisoners of our fears."

The light dimmed, taking Esther with it.

The present room revealed itself, dusty and cold. Rain hit the window, running down in rivulets to the sill. I was stunned by the revelation. It dawned on me I was no closer to helping ease Esther's soul as I had no idea how to get Mr. Clayton to confess to where he'd buried the child. Georgina was adamant the truth would be found in this room. It couldn't be the vision I'd witnessed, as Esther would have shown her the same thing.

"The truth is hidden," I repeated.

Wood remembers.

Mrs. Clayton said the same thing about the stain on the floor.

I went to the area where Esther's birthing bed had been. I crouched down and brushed away the dust. The faint outline of old blood was still there. I shifted my weight and the boards creaked as one of the edges lifted. The pacing!

What if the noises hadn't been Esther's restless spirit but instead her prying open this board? With a little experimenting I was able to pull up the small section and see the cubby space below. A blank envelope was tucked inside. Was it something Esther had written? And who was the intended recipient?

I eagerly started to break the wax seal when the sound of footsteps started up the spiral stairs.

CHAPTER FORTY

I tucked the letter into my dress pocket and put a hand on the pistol.

"You should have left when you had the chance," Mr. Clayton said, with a slur to his words. "The missus even tried to warn you the first night, gave you a vial of holy water and tried to scare you with the threat of evil spirits." He shuffled a few steps closer. "Then she put mushrooms in your supper to make you hallucinate and hopefully fall down the stairs or into another pit, but you threw it up in the chamber pot. So now . . . here we are."

Struggling to stop my hand from shaking, I raised the pistol, pointing it at him.

He only hesitated for a moment, then tilted his head, giving me a patronizing glance of pity. "Pretty girl like you shouldn't play with guns."

If you act like it's the truth, he'll accept it . . . a man rarely refutes evidence when it's staring him in the face . . . be steadfast; your conviction will tip the scales and convince him otherwise.

I squared my stance. "I'm from Halifax," I declared. "In a city full of soldiers, a girl learns a thing or two about combat."

"Fair enough." He lifted his hands in surrender. "I came here to save you. The missus, she's all confused and upset. She's wanted the island forever. That's why we kept rumors going all these years. We knew the captain was going to leave us the land, but then he went and married another wife."

I gritted my teeth, staring at him down the barrel of the gun. "You poisoned Georgina for a supposed treasure. And now you're trying to frame me for the captain's death."

He shook his head and took another step closer. "I know you didn't kill the captain. There was only water in the blue vial; she told me herself."

"You're lying," I said. I had to use both hands to keep the gun steady. He was no more than another arm's length away.

"I'll take you down to the dory. You can make the mainland under dark." There was a tremor tying his sentences together like he was running on a shaking bridge. "But we have to leave. She'll be coming up here soon. Quick, now, please." He held out one of his hands, nearly touching the gun. His teary eyes were filled with a watery plea.

I had to consider his offer as there was no way I was leaving this room without his permission. He readily accepted I could handle a firearm, but he was strong enough to physically overpower me. One pretend attempt at firing the gun wouldn't give me enough time to rush past him. Agreeing to leave with him was the only way out of the room. I already had the letter Esther had wanted me to find.

Mr. Clayton was offering me an escape. I could reach the mainland, get help, and return for Georgina. I lowered the gun. His shoulders relaxed as he dropped his hand.

Thunder boomed outside, nearly shaking the panes. I saw a flash of white in the reflection of the window. A white handle stuck out of his back pocket.

A white handle.

Ice water poured over me as the horrific realization of his intent became clear.

He reached around and withdrew a hammer. I made a fist

around the gun and stabbed it into his bruised right eye. He let out a garbled cry as he dropped the hammer and covered his face. I pushed past him, rushing to the stairs. His kick swiped me from behind.

My back smashed into the wooden floor, knocking the air from my lungs. At once his weight was upon me, crushing my chest.

"I'm sorry, miss." He loomed over me, his right eye bulging and angry looking. His rough hands gripped my throat. "It's better this way, though—less mess. Don't fight me. It'll be over soon."

A tremendous pressure built behind my eyelids as he squeezed tighter. I scratched at his chapped knuckles uselessly.

"I'm sorry," he repeated, sobbing. "You should've left."

Stars burst across my vision as my lungs burned. I kicked my legs and batted at his hands. He was so strong, impossible to fight. From the corner of my eye, I saw the floorboards stained with old blood, still a rust color.

Blood.

I reached my left arm down as I bent my leg. Blindly, I torn away the bandages and dug my fingers into the shallow wound. The pain was nothing compared to the steel grip on my throat.

Slick with my own blood, I brought my hand up and pushed it into his face.

He grunted out a cry of disgust. His fingers eased enough for me to wiggle out from under his grip. Coughing, I half dragged myself to the stairs.

"Why didn't you leave?!" he screamed, holding the hammer over his head.

The wind shrieked outside, then grew louder and turned into Esther's scream. I covered my ears, but it continued inside my head. Mr. Clayton winced as well, his posture crumpling.

The one note continued at a frantic volume, getting higher. It was her agony. Her pain. Her tremendous fury. I thought my head would split open.

The window shattered into a thousand pieces, covering the floor in shards of glass. A gust of wind blew inside, nearly pushing me to my feet. Lunging to the window's ledge, I looked down at the ground far below. My stomach lurched.

Mr. Clayton spit out a battle cry as he ran at me, holding the hammer above his head. My bloody handprint stained his face. I crawled over the ledge and dropped.

CHAPTER FORTY-ONE

With a white-knuckled grip, I hung from a thick rope of ivy. The rain beat down on me, cold and slick.

I had no natural skill in climbing, but the desire to stay alive propelled me to put one hand under the other as my shoes found toeholds on the lower vines, using it as a precarious ladder to the ground.

Knowing I would become dizzy the first moment I looked down, I concentrated on my hand placements. Mr. Clayton yelled out.

Looking up, I saw his face explode into a wide-eyed panic as his entire body fell forward as if launched from the tower.

I clung to the vine. Our eyes met for a split second as he dropped to the earth. I continued my descent until my foot slipped and I tumbled the rest of the way. A hot fist of pain smashed into my left foot.

With my wet hair covering my face like curtains, I limped over to Mr. Clayton. He was on his back and unmoving. The hammer was nowhere in sight. "Where did you bury the baby?" I demanded.

His eyes pleaded with me. "No," he said.

I leaned over him, expecting him to beg for mercy. Instead, he gave me a confession.

The rain washed over his lopsided face. His right eye was engorged and distended, the bruise bleeding under the skin, across his jaw and down into his neck.

Even though he must have been in incredible pain, he was focused entirely on me. "I had the wee bundle in my arms and was going to the shed when it started to squirm. It was my fault Esther died. I hadn't gone soon enough for the doctor, and the missus said Captain Graves would be wanting me dead if he discovered there'd been not one but two deaths. There couldn't be any evidence she was ever with child." His breathing grew labored. "I took the babe to the mainland and left her at the church."

"Esther's daughter is alive?"

He nodded. A sickening gurgle came from deep inside his chest. Then his entire body stilled, the grimace easing into an expression of peace.

A gutted scream split the air above me. Mrs. Clayton leaned out the tower room window, crying at the sight of her husband's body. She aimed her gaze on me with murder in her eyes. She disappeared, and I imagined her picking up the hammer on her way to bludgeon me. If she had any reservations about killing me before, thinking I was the reason for her husband's death would be more than enough to overcome them now.

Frantically I limped toward the carriage house. A crack of thunder shook the ground as cold rain pelted down. The mud grabbed at my shoes. I escaped into the edge of the forest and leaned against the first large tree, gasping for breath. Weakness was setting in. The main door of Faraday slammed open.

Through the sheets of rain, Mrs. Clayton's silhouette came into view, charging from the house. There was something in her grip.

Terror propelled me forward as I half crawled and clawed my way deeper into the woods. I stumbled, slamming my knees into the ground. Spruce needles poked into my palms. The dirt clung to my hair and the hem of my dress as if the ground were claiming me.

I see you in a grave.

Mrs. Clayton called out, "This will end one way or the other, but it will end."

She was much closer than I'd thought. My leaden feet scuffed along. I tripped over a tree root, sprawling onto the earth. I breathed in the familiar scent of pungent mushrooms. Pushing myself up, I saw the bright red and yellow colors just ahead, and beyond, the hole I'd nearly fallen into. A frenzied energy surged through me. I snapped off a few branches and laid them across the opening, then I crawled through the dirt and spruce needles and situated myself on the opposite side of the pit.

Mrs. Clayton cursed under her breath as she swiped away a low-hanging branch. She stepped into the area and saw me huddled and shivering. Revenge and ire had twisted her face menacingly.

She had the pistol.

She pointed it at me and said, "Living under the threat of privateers means knowing how to load this properly. You should have left that first night, but you're too stupid." Her usually wiry hair was plastered against her face, making her appear even more unrecognizable. "And now that you've killed Bagnall, you're going to pay."

CHAPTER FORTY-TWO

He fell from the window after trying to kill me on your orders!" I yelled.

Ignoring my explanation, she replied, "I didn't mean for anyone to get hurt. I loved Esther, truly I did. But when she died, I knew Captain Graves would blame us. I had to make up the story about the fever." She sniffed, and her eyes hardened. "I was never sadder in my whole life." She adjusted her weight, one step closer to the pit. I forced myself to not look down, to keep my gaze focused on her. I had to keep her talking.

"And what of Esther's daughter?" I pleaded. "You allowed her to become an orphan when the whole time she had a father and a home. How could you keep that a secret, especially when the captain was so adamant about an heir?"

"The babe was so small, so wee. It probably didn't survive long at the church. We did the captain a blessing by sparing him that pain." Then a strange pride slipped across her face. "While he escaped to the sea, cowering in grief, we took care of Faraday for him, year after year. The house would be in ruins if it weren't for me and Bagnall." At the mention of his name, her tears started.

Her logic was warped. I had to distract her, lure her closer before she could fire a shot. "You're not the hero, Mrs. Clayton. Captain Graves paid you to take care of Faraday. You never had to worry about food or shelter. It was a good life. You could even search for lost treasure without anyone being the wiser. But then he brought home a new wife . . . Georgina."

Her expression grew dark. "She went into trances, painting awful pictures as if she was possessed, creating images that were too close to the truth. She had to go. A little bit of the right mushroom each day in her tea was doing the trick. I had to get rid of the nurse, though—she was starting to catch on."

"You pushed Nurse Gibson down the stairs?" It dawned on me that Hettie was completely innocent.

Mrs. Clayton waved the gun through the air dispelling the notion. "She fell on her own after I put brandy in her tea. I told the captain I'd seen Georgina push her." She looked at me queerly. "Speaking of the captain, I never pegged you for a killer. I was planning on him being so upset by your attempt to seduce him, he'd kick you out of the house. Then you'd finally be gone, and I could slowly start to weaken his already poor health. But he wasn't supposed to die before Mrs. Graves, you stupid girl!"

So Mr. Clayton had told the truth about the blue vial. Then who or what had killed Captain Graves? I needed to play along—anything to get her closer to the pit. "You're right," I said. "The captain became angry last night in the bedroom and threatened to send me away, so I took matters into my own hands." I swallowed my growing panic. "And now, we can help each other. When the magistrate arrives, I won't mention your involvement in Esther's death or Georgina's poisoning, and you can convince them I'm innocent. The mainlanders won't question the tragedy; they'll blame the curse. We can have Faraday all to ourselves. Please, I'll need you when the baby arrives." I smiled with quivering lips and stretched out a hand. "Come closer, help me back to the house."

She laughed and the sound sent a chill to my bones. "I know every inch of this island," she said. Then she picked up the branches I had used to cover the pit and tossed them aside. The hole in the rotten planks looked like a mouth opening wide. Mrs. Clayton stood close to the edge, a mere five feet from where I cowered. She only had one bullet, but she wouldn't miss.

I pushed backward, feeling the prickly evergreen shrub.

She pointed the gun at my chest. "The magistrate can bring an army of mainlanders, but no one will ever find your body." Her tone was calm and more terrifying than any growl.

There was an unexpected surge of rage in my heart. It was her cowardice and selfishness that caused all the pain at Faraday. I knew I was about to die. Esther's truth would never be told. Her spirit would continue to haunt the island. If her daughter was still alive, she'd be ten years old. I pictured her sitting by the orphanage window, wishing for her parents to rescue her—just like I had.

Every muscle in my body coiled tightly.

Mrs. Clayton said, "This tragedy will play into the folktale nicely. Everyone knows: at Faraday House, the wives always die young."

I licked my lips. "That's true," I said quickly. "But you're forgetting the most important thing. Captain Graves and I never married. I'm not a wife of Faraday House—but you are."

She frowned for a moment in confusion, lowering the gun slightly. In that second, I sprang forward, launching myself over the pit. I collided into her skirts as we thudded into the ground. We rolled in a scuffle. Grunting, I made a grab for the pistol.

"Argh." She pulled back.

The shot blasted between us, and we both froze, staring at each other. A warm stickiness oozed between my fingers. Mrs. Clayton let out a shuddering sigh. Pushing myself away, I slowly stood, watching the red stain grow from the hole in her chest. She simply looked at me with unfeeling eyes. Her breathing eased, then finally stopped.

There was a moan followed by a loud *crack*. I glanced down too late before I realized I was standing on the moss-covered boards at the edge of the pit. I screamed as the earth dropped away, taking me and Mrs. Clayton into the darkness.

CHAPTER FORTY-THREE

My scream ended with a jolt as my body stopped midair, then bobbed in place. The leather gun strap around my chest dug into my ribs, the other end miraculously snagged on the tip of a broken board. Far below my swaying feet, Mrs. Clayton's body hit the bottom with a sickening *thud*.

Beads of sweat coated my upper lip. Tentatively, I reached up, feeling the splintered board. I wrapped both hands around the mossy plank, but I was not strong enough to pull myself up. I dangled hopelessly above my doom.

"Help," I cried, but my chest was so constricted my plea was barely above a pitiful whisper. Seconds felt like hours. How long would the board hold me?

My entire body was one panicked heartbeat. The sensation started to disappear from my fingers, replaced with pins and needles. Tears welled, blurring my vision. How long would it take them to find me at the bottom of the pit with Mrs. Clayton? What would they think had happened?

I imagined my parents' graves and was sorry to not be buried with them.

A strange calmness took over. I envisioned my parents' tropical island. Perhaps death was my final escape to be with them. A place where I would be loved. A place where I mattered to someone.

When death wraps its arms around you for the fatal embrace, you think the purest thoughts. I'd believed I was incapable of anything other than looking pretty and that I was meant to be admired but not loved, for who could love anything so useless?

We're all prisoners of our fears.

What are you most afraid of, Miss Fitzpatrick? I imagined Reverend Pellerine asking me.

"Being alone," I whispered. "And not mattering to anyone." Hearing myself say the words sparked a buried truth. "I want to matter." A teardrop rolled down my cheek and dropped off my chin, disappearing into the dark void.

I thought of Georgina, hidden in the house, waiting for me. I thought of Esther, waiting for the truth to be revealed, and her daughter, somewhere this very moment dreaming of parents to rescue her one day. I thought of Reverend Pellerine and his promise of a cozy house with a cabbage garden and sunny morning walks with Moses.

I would never be able to explain why I turned down his proposal, how I was convinced I was unlovable and would make him miserable with regret.

Now I realized I mattered to them. And not because of how I looked, but because of who I was and how I had tried to help. And there was Moses, who loved me unconditionally.

Moses . . .

Mrs. Shackleton's voice pierced the darkness like a flash of lightning. *You only have one ability, Emeline. Use it! Haven't you been practicing? That's just like you to give up and not try.*

I worked to build up enough of a breath, then I licked my lips and blew.

CHAPTER FORTY-FOUR

The tone rang clear. I took a few careful small breaths, then repeated the whistle.

I counted ten seconds then blew again.

I had been so afraid of being alone, I'd convinced myself what I felt for Lieutenant Fletcher was love. But I discovered the truest love is the unconditional kind, self-love. Moses had taught me I was worthy. Georgina had shown me I was brave and smart. And Reverend Pellerine had helped me recognize I deserved real love.

I was only concerned about my appearance because I thought I had no other attributes.

But surviving Faraday had shown me I was more.

I could depend on myself. And my baby could depend on me. And I would get both of us out of this godforsaken pit. After all, Esther had proven a mother's love was capable of the impossible.

I whistled again, using every ounce of air I had.

A bark sounded through the dark.

"Moses!" I screamed. I whistled again. The barking drew nearer. Darkness started to creep in from the edges of my sight. My hands were losing feeling. Helpless, I watched as each finger started to peel away from the board. My breath hitched, giving one last whistle.

Paws appeared at the edge of the pit. He gave an urgent bark then dipped his large head closer, jaws opened wide to grasp the leather strap. He started to pull back, but the strap slipped from his mouth.

I screamed as I felt the board begin to let go. An arm reached around Moses and grabbed my wrist with a steel grip. In one swift motion, I was lifted out of the pit and pulled back on solid ground.

Reverend Pellerine had a look of sheer terror on his face. *"Mon dieu."*

I sucked in mouthfuls of air as strong arms fitted around me. I clung to him. *"Je suis désolé,"* he said, his voice quivering. "I'm so sorry. I knew I should have made Mr. Clayton take Hettie instead. I shouldn't have left you."

"You returned—that's all that matters." After a few moments, my head cleared enough that I realized there was seaweed in the top of his boot.

Still catching his breath, he said, "I rushed back once I delivered Hettie to the doctor on the mainland. The tide caught me. I had to swim the rest of the way."

There was so much to be said, but it would have to wait until later. With my arm draped over his shoulder, we made our way back to the house to rescue Georgina. Moses ambled alongside us, trotting eagerly. The rain had died to a drizzle.

"Thank you for saving me," I said.

"Bien sûr." He turned his faced to me and smiled. "Of course."

"I was talking to Moses."

CHAPTER FORTY-FIVE

I reached on tiptoes to adjust the chain of berries Georgina had helped me string the night before.

"Mind the sap, dear," Mrs. Shackleton warned from her spot on the settee. Despite the robust heat from the fireplace, she had a quilt on her lap. She took a sip of her Christmas punch. "You'll get it in your hair, and Ada will have to use the goose grease to get it out."

"I prefer my goose grease on potatoes," I answered. I stepped back with my hands on my hips and regarded the tree. Georgina wanted it to have a natural look, so Ada and I had walked the property gathering pinecones and wild rose hips. The heady scent of the fir tree mixed with the bowl of oranges evoked a calmness that spread through my entire soul.

The study had undergone a few small but determined updates. The drapes were always drawn back to let in the most sunlight. More seating had been added, along with a row of bookshelves. There was still room for dancing, though. Georgina thought hosting a ball every month for the mainlanders would go a long way toward gaining trust and redressing Faraday's reputation.

She knew she needed staff to properly turn Faraday into the kind of house where she wanted to live. The Shackletons were shocked when she told them she would continue to run the house with me by my side, then she said they were welcome to visit us anytime.

Now, a month after that tragic day, I was decorating my own Christmas tree with all the important people in my life looking on. I placed a hand over my stomach, feeling the small cabbage-size bump. The pregnancy was still a secret. Luckily, Nurse Gibson was also handy with a needle and thread and had let out a few of my dresses. The high-waistline style gave me another month or so before I really started to show.

Georgina told me Faraday was as much my house as hers and there was nothing to stop us from raising the baby together. For the moment, I let that be my option. The panic was no longer there. Any decision I made regarding my future would be guided by love, not fear.

"It's quite convenient to have a tree lot on your property." Judge Shackleton peeked over the cover of his book. He sat in a wingback chair with his feet resting on the footstool by the fire. A stein of spruce beer was on the small table beside him. "I know people in the city who would pay handsomely for such a fresh Christmas tree."

I shared a glance with Georgina, who sat on the settee beside Mrs. Shackleton. I had assured him Georgina was well off financially since inheriting all of Captain Graves's fortune. But it was difficult for him to accept a young woman being independent.

Her complexion was rosy, and she was gaining weight. The doctor wanted her to stay in the hospital another few weeks, but she was tired of being a patient and said she didn't survive the Faraday curse to spend the holiday in the hospital. We hired Nurse Gibson back, and she was now staying in Hettie's old room.

Georgina offered the position of head housekeeper to Hettie, but since her stint in the hospital, Hettie had decided to pursue a nursing career instead. We heard the surgeon who'd operated on her was handsome and single.

The Faraday curse was the commanding gossip of Shoreham and nearly the entire province, Mrs. Shackleton told me. Both she and the judge arrived at the hospital breathless and panic-stricken as soon as they found out what had happened, or at least that was what we told everyone.

The official story written in all the papers was that Mrs. Clayton had been slowly poisoning Georgina to make it look like a natural fatal disease. She knew Captain Graves was unwell and was hoping he'd die soon after his second wife, leaving the property to her and Mr. Clayton.

But when I arrived, she realized she would have to somehow get rid of me as well. The magistrate didn't need much convincing after hearing Reverend Pellerine's testimony. Hettie even vouched for me once I privately explained the true circumstances of the shift being in the captain's bed. Her fascination with Faraday made her fiercely loyal to him.

Reverend Pellerine told me he'd been coming down the main road, still soaked and freezing from crossing back from the mainland, when Moses greeted him. Then at once the dog tore off into the woods, barking wildly. Reverend Pellerine recognized the urgency of the bark and followed him to where I was.

I wrote to the premier to ask for a medal for Moses. Judge Shackleton told me I needed to go higher and suggested I write the king of England.

Reverend Pellerine was the first person I saw at my bedside when I woke the next day. He told me Georgina was doing well and undergoing tests for her liver. She would be in the hospital's care for some time, but she should make a full recovery.

His expression crumpled. "This is all my fault," he'd said. "I never should have left you."

My twisted ankle was sore, and I was still trying to process all the recent events. However, I was alert enough to know what I wanted from him wasn't another apology.

"You look worse than I feel," I'd teased tiredly. His clothes were wrinkled, and his eyes were weary.

"Last night I kept having nightmares I didn't find you in time," he'd told me. "I reach the pit just as you lose your grip and start to fall. For a few seconds all I see is your upturned face before you drop, disappearing into the blackness." The lines deepened on his face, aging him considerably. "I would have entirely lost my faith if you'd died."

I remembered how he stopped reading the Bible to Georgina as soon as Mrs. Clayton had left them alone. I sensed there was more he wanted to say, but I needed to confess something. "One of my biggest regrets is not telling you why I turned down your proposal."

His eyebrow quirked, the sleepiness gone as he became more alert.

"I believed certain things were essential for happiness." I relayed a bit of growing up with Mrs. Shackleton, and her reinforcing of the importance of wealth and beauty. "It was easy to convince myself I was in love with Frederick because I was in love with the idea of escaping her and having my own home. I was using him, just as I was using the captain. But I couldn't treat you with the same disservice. A marriage started on lies would make us both miserable. I wanted you to be happy. I still do."

He placed a hand over mine. The warmth of his touch flowed outward from my chest, all the way to my sprained ankle. His eyes sent a message of such intensity I prepared myself for his confession of love. "I understand," he'd said. "And now I can finally be at peace with your refusal. I wish you all the happiness you deserve."

It left a hole in my heart the size of the pit, but I gave him a fake smile and told him I was lucky to have such a good and loyal friend as him.

Our conversations since then had all been conciliatory and formal. It ached deeply, more than it ever hurt with Frederick. Real love came with real heartache. When Mrs. Shackleton saw my swollen foot and scratched face from the tussle with Mrs. Clayton, she started to cry. She was more worried about the assault to my skin than my having narrowly escaped death . . . twice.

I allowed her to fuss over me. She may not have changed, but I had. I recognized her attention for what it had been all along, well-intentioned but misguided. The judge was a different matter altogether. Crying, he broke down at the hospital, saying he'd thought he was keeping me safe by ensuring I stayed at Faraday. He also told me Frederick's loaners had been arrested recently for an unrelated matter involving rum-running.

It was safe for me to return to Halifax. My scandal, in their eyes at least, was now viewed through the lens of my trials at Faraday and was deemed minute in comparison. They wanted Georgina to live there as well. Mrs. Shackleton had taken a real shine to her and was determined to make sure her hair grew back lustrous and thick and kept bringing in various shampoos and oils for her to use.

Ada came into the study singing "God Rest Ye Merry Gentlemen" with a tray of raisin tarts, molasses cookies, and slices of rum-soaked cake. Nurse Gibson went around the room and refilled everyone's glass. The fire crackled, sending flickering waves of light over our red cheeks and smiling lips.

"Who's going to start with the ghost stories?" Ada asked. "Christmas Eve is the perfect time. Nothing gruesome, though," she said, making a face. "I only want a fun shivery tale, something to match the chills from outside."

Georgina and I shared a quick glance. We never spoke of Esther's ghost. It was something we both decided to keep secret. And oddly, neither of us could sense her spirit anymore. It seemed Esther was no longer chained to the island. Her spirit was free.

The truth had been uncovered. The only chill I felt now was from sitting too close to the drafts.

The letter I found in the floorboards of the tower had been written by Esther. It was a love letter to her child in case she didn't survive the birth. Apparently, Esther's mother had also died in childbirth, and she was afraid (with good reason) the same would happen to her. That's why she went to Mrs. Clayton asking for assistance: it was to ensure she stayed healthy for the pregnancy.

In her letter, Esther alluded to growing mistrust of the Claytons since she suspected they were secretly digging on the island for the lost treasure. She left the note in the floorboards thinking her child would use the tower as a playroom and come by the hiding spot naturally.

Reverend Pellerine was diligent in scouring the church records on the mainland. However, as of yet, there had been no mention of the child. Sadly, Georgina and I had to accept that the small babe had not survived after going to the mainland.

Georgina sipped her punch and said, "I've always enjoyed charades more, but let's save that until after supper."

I took my own glass of punch and two raisin tarts. Mrs. Shackleton started to comment on the number of sweets I'd already eaten, but then paused and helped herself to one as well.

There were piles of presents under the tree. The Shackletons had arrived by carriage, loaded down with packages, bundles of food, and another carriage of servants.

In no time, Faraday was dusted and full of light sparkling off the polished brass and crystal. Georgina was already making plans to paint more murals to put her own stamp on the house, to reinvent it. Material would be ordered for new curtains and brightly patterned rugs. In the spring she wanted to plant fruit trees around the cemetery so that it blended in the with the forest.

We buried Captain Graves in Georgina's plot. He'd died of natural causes, after all. His heart was poor, apparently. I liked to imagine that he was reunited with Esther, and that they were enjoying a private paradise together somewhere. Mr. and Mrs. Clayton's corpses were sent to the mainland and buried in the village churchyard. Faraday had enough bones in the ground, thank you very much, and Georgina saw no need to have her would-be murderer's headstone on her property.

Sleigh bells jingled outside. "Who is arriving this time of the evening?" Judge Shackleton sat up in the chair, groggy from the beer and the warm fire. "Bit early for Saint Nicholas." He chuckled.

One of the Shackletons' staff opened the main door. Barking sounded, making my heart speed up. A jovial exchange was heard in the foyer, and soon Reverend Pellerine was standing at the entrance to the study with several packages under his arm. A red scarf was wound around his neck. He took off his hat. "Merry Christmas," he said. His gaze moved to everyone in the room, then last, to me.

"You're looking well," he said with an open expression of friendship.

I managed to smile while my heart raced. "It's a new dress," I said, smoothing out the dark green velvet. Mrs. Shackleton had insisted I open it early to wear especially for tonight. There was also a matching cape with fur trim.

Moses padded in behind him and waited at his heel. A string of drool hung from the corner of his mouth.

"You're letting that beast in the house?" Mrs. Shackleton said with obvious disdain.

"That beast saved my life," I said. I went over to Moses and gave him a scratch behind the ear.

"The dog helped too," Reverend Pellerine replied. I allowed

myself to share a grin with him as I took his packages and slipped them under the tree. Heat traveled up my neck as I reminded myself we could be cordial to each other as friends. It would take practice to not blush in his presence.

"Please come in." Georgina chuckled. "I'm so glad you received my invitation."

Ada gave him a glass of cheer. "Thank you," he replied with a broad grin. "I would have arrived earlier, but I received a letter as I was on my way out. It's for the mistress of Faraday House." He pulled an envelope out of his jacket pocket, then handed it to Georgina.

Frowning, Georgina put down her punch and started to open the letter.

Reverend Pellerine spoke quickly, his words dancing around us, spinning the air into excitement. He said, "I heard from a retired priest who used to preach one county over. He saw the newspaper article about Faraday and was reminded of the baby girl that had been abandoned at his church around the time of Esther's death. He said they never expected the child to survive because she was so small. The nuns took her to a convent in New Brunswick."

"Catholics." Mrs. Shackleton *tsk*ed.

His eyes were shining. "I wrote to see if they could confirm what happened to her."

I grabbed his arm. "Is she alive? Was she adopted?"

Georgina put a hand to her mouth as she read the letter. "She's there! She's alive and well!"

The room erupted into cheers. Georgina spoke quickly, reading parts of the letter out loud while adding her own excited commentary. "Her name is Sara. The nuns require us to visit in person before we can adopt her. Of course, we must go without delay, Emeline."

I nodded, blinking away tears. Sara. I repeated it in my mind.

She continued, "Good reader. Smart at math . . . The poor thing has been alone in the world. All this time . . . She's the heir to Faraday, of course . . . but she's still a child. A child who needs a mother." She put the letter to her chest. "I'll paint a portrait of Esther holding her as a baby as a gift."

"She must have a closet full of dresses waiting for her when she arrives," Mrs. Shackleton said. "I can't imagine what the nuns have forced the little flea to wear."

"We can turn the captain's room into a nursery," Ada said.

"We'll need to build stairs to the beach," Georgina added. "The rocks are too much for a child."

Judge Shackleton added, "And those trees should be cut down. You can't even see the ocean from the front of the house."

Everyone continued talking at once, creating a loud din. Ada cheered as she poured more punch into everyone's glasses. "A child is exactly what this house needs." She looked at me. "I remember how you brought sunshine when you came to us."

I was too stunned to reply. I'd never thought of myself as having brought anything but woe and bad luck.

"A toast," Reverend Pellerine said, raising his glass. "To the heir of Faraday."

Ada was in the process of offering him one of the sweets from the tray when she motioned to the window and exclaimed, "Oh, look! It's started to snow. Christmas snow is magical."

Mrs. Shackleton grunted as she reached for a molasses cookie.

Georgina's cheeks glistened with tears. "I would love to see the house from the pond with the snow falling. I would love to paint it for her. For Sara. She'll be scared to come to a new place."

I said, "We can get the wheelchair and take you down." Nurse Gibson nodded in agreement.

Georgina shook her head and tightened the shawl around her shoulders. "I wouldn't dare catch a cold now, not with such an important trip coming up. Maybe you can go for me? You're so descriptive, I'd be able to re-create whatever you describe to me."

"Alone?" Mrs. Shackleton put down her glass. "I think not. You'll slip on the ice and ruin your new dress."

Reverend Pellerine wrapped his scarf around his neck again. "It would be a sin to mar such a lovely frock. Let me accompany you."

I put on my new green cape and pulled up the hood. One of the staff handed him a lantern even though it was barely dusk.

Ada started another round of carol singing. Georgina and Mr. Shackleton began to plan the trip to New Brunswick.

CHAPTER FORTY-SIX

Reverend Pellerine and I took the path around the house and down the familiar trail to the pond, my hand linked through the crook of his arm. There was no wind, and lazy snowflakes spiraled between us, sticking to whatever they landed on, outlining even the spindliest blade of tall dry grass by the water's edge, the fur trim of my hood . . . the knot of his scarf.

He stopped us close to the location of our disastrous conversation about marriage. I wondered if he even realized.

"She's right," he said, stepping away from me and turning to look up the slope. "It would be a nice picture."

I took in Faraday with its bright windows and sounds of Christmas carols drifting through the frosty air. When I first arrived, I thought it looked like a prison. But it had only been lonely. And now that someone loved it, it literally glowed.

We stood there, quietly staring at the house. Puffs of air filled the space where there should be words. He turned back to me. A snowflake clung to his long eyelashes. "You did that," he said. "You brought it back to life."

"It's a fair exchange," I answered, knowing my trials at Faraday had made me stronger.

"No," he said, shaking his head. "You discredit the reach of your achievements. You're the reason Sara will finally have a home."

"You have every right to claim that as well."

"But it only came about because of your bravery. No, it's true, don't shake your head. You have no idea how much influence you have on the world . . . myself included. I have to confess . . ." He shifted his weight, looking unsure. "I used to grapple with the cruelty of man, and how the church sometimes all too easily forgave those sins. The truth is, I secretly feared the indifference of God, and that prayer was useless." He took in a breath and smiled at me. "But you have shown me that when there is indifference, we must be the light. My faith was lacking in myself, not in God. You have given my life new meaning, Emeline. And I will be forever grateful."

Tears of gratitude stung my eyes as I laughed nervously. Enjoying his company would always be an exercise in torturous willpower until I accepted our fate of friendship. He had a way of touching my heart and breaking it all at once. I sniffed then said, "And I will be forever grateful to you as well. You taught me I deserve to make decisions based on love instead of fear."

He reached into his coat pocket and took out a piece of paper folded many times over. "I have an early present for you," he said.

I took it from him and unfolded the document. "It's the marriage certificate for Captain Graves and myself." I gave him a quizzical look.

"Ashes are a powerful symbol in the church; they represent sacrifice and rebirth. I thought you might want to burn this as a way of setting your own intention for the new year." He took the top off the lantern, exposing the candle's flame.

Holding a corner over the flame, I watched the paper catch a bright orange.

Bright orange. Like the sunrise, like red hair . . .

It slowly turned to a blackened ash. Feathery and fragile, it swirled and joined the snowflakes, spreading over the pond.

A lightness filled my chest. I smiled at him fully. "That is the best present. Thank you." I wanted to throw my arms around him.

However, this reunion was delicate, and I didn't want to spoil his gallant gesture. I must be more determined to see him only as a friend.

He reached into his pocket again and handed me another piece of paper. I started to unfold that one, but he put a hand over mine.

"Before you open that," he said, "allow me to explain." His expression became anguished as his voice took on a serious tone. "I have replayed my proposal to you many times since that night, and I am ashamed of my lack of insight in regard to both your situation and my own shortcomings. I saw myself as your rescuer, and I thought that would be enough. You needed a man to be your husband, to keep you safe, to take care of you, but I also had feelings for you then, deeper feelings I wouldn't allow to surface because you were another man's fiancée."

I stayed quiet, desperate to know if his feelings had changed.

He continued, "The past few weeks I've gotten to know the Shackletons, and I'm only beginning to understand the span of your experiences. I was so wrong to assume I knew what you needed. I know you don't need me," he said. "But I need you. I cannot think of spending another day without your voice, your touch, your wonderful wit—though you don't even realize how clever you are." He gently pushed back my hood, letting the snow land on my hair as he turned my face up to his. "And I love you. Please," he quietly begged, "at least consider this proposal as the authentic one, for I would never forgive myself if I left without offering you all my heart."

I was quiet, unable to speak at first. I put my hand on my stomach. "I am not the only one you will be making a life with," I reminded him. That had not changed.

He put his hand over mine, cupping the small bump there. "If you deem me worthy enough to share both of your lives, I will love *le petit chou* as much as I love you."

It wasn't a lover's whisper against the earlobe, but I felt the vibration of his declaration from my snowflake-covered head to the toes of my boots. I couldn't deny the thrill of making a decision based on love instead of fear. "You're right," I said. "I don't need you. But I love you, and I want you too." I reached up and took hold of his red scarf, tugging him closer. "Yes, I'll marry you," I said. I stared at his lips as he leaned down and kissed me.

His hand moved from my stomach to my lower back, pressing me closer. The kiss was slow and warm, like rich molasses drizzling on my tongue. I breathed in the scent of him, soft and fresh. I felt his other hand cup the back of my head, gentle, supportive. There was a sweet pleasure in the movement of his lips with mine, the taste of him, the sighs between breaths.

Frederick had always rushed his kisses, urgent and impatient, never lingering.

This kiss was nothing like I'd experienced before. It was a kiss that promised a lifetime of love, so there was no rush. There was only this moment of us in each other's arms with the snow falling. Freedom.

I leaned back and stared at those brown eyes, crinkling my forehead. "'*Petit chou*'?"

He smiled. "Little cabbage."

EPILOGUE

Dear *Frederick,*

Lily is very much like you in appearance: flaming red hair and blue eyes.

We named her after the orange flowers that grow along the lane that leads to our farm. She has four younger brothers, speaks French and English, and has the heart of a poet and the mind of a scientist.

My husband and I bought what was once his family's land. The ground is welcoming under our feet and the sky is full of promise, but Lily has a calling to academics and will be leaving the farm for Halifax soon to attend university.

She knows who you are and will be the one to deliver this letter to your grave. She will say her piece to you in private. They buried you in the military cemetery last week. There's a nice view of Halifax Harbour from there.

I haven't thought of you for decades, but this letter is an opportunity to thank you for not rescuing me all those years ago, for I would have been denied the life I have now. My true happiness wasn't having someone take care of me. It was the freedom to matter to someone else.

I hope you mattered to someone, eventually.

With gratitude,
Emeline Pellerine

ACKNOWLEDGMENTS

First, I want to thank you, reader. If you made it this far, I safely assume you read the entire novel. I hope you enjoyed the journey. The only reason I continue to write is because of you. A story unread or unshared is a dying thing, so thank you for keeping this writer's dream alive. The world is a better place with readers like you in it.

Next, I must give a large paragraph of gratitude to my editors, Julia Elliott (William Morrow), and Iris Tupholme and Julia McDowell (HarperCollins Canada). This novel was a buried treasure, nearly impossible to find under the weight of thousands of pages and mountains of words. It needed to be excavated sentence by sentence. They had to read so many versions! And yet they were nothing but positive and kind, confident the book was there, hidden among all the flotsam and jetsam. Simply put, *The Third Wife of Faraday House* would not exist without them.

My agent, Jill Marr, is many wonderful things. She is marvelously intelligent, helpful, supportive, the best cheerleader, and is always available—which is amazing since she lives on the opposite side of the continent.

Thank you to Kate Forrester for creating the gorgeous cover you're all admiring. I'm very much aware how lucky I am to have this story dressed up in Kate's original artwork. I love her whimsical style.

As well, thank you to Janet Rosenberg for the unglamorous task of copy editing. Her keen eye and thoughtful comments were the final bit of polish that made this book shine.

I continue to be ever grateful to my parents, Eric and Ethel Bishop, without whom I would not exist. They're also really lovely people so I'm doubly thankful. Their near embarrassing praise has stayed constant since my first publication ten years ago, never wavering or tiring.

And lastly, thank you to Ken, and Ruth and Adam. Writing is great, but real life with you is better. And let's not forget Oscar, the best dog in the world.

ABOUT THE AUTHOR

B.R. MYERS is the Edgar Award–winning and internationally bestselling author of *A Dreadful Splendor* and nine YA books, including *Rogue Princess* and *Girl on the Run*. Always in the mood for a good scare, she spent most of her teen years behind the covers of Lois Duncan, Ray Bradbury, and Stephen King. When not putting her characters in precarious situations, B. R. Myers works as a registered nurse. A member of the Writers' Federation of Nova Scotia, she lives in Halifax with her family—and there is still a stack of books on her bedside table.

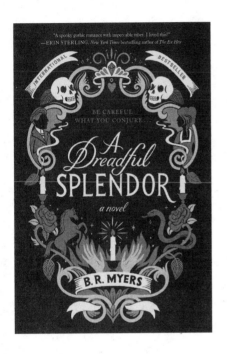